THREADS
AND
FLAMES

THREADS AND FLAMES

ESTHER FRIESNER

VIKING

An Imprint of Penguin Group (USA) Inc.

VIKING
Published by Penguin Group
Penguin Group (USA) Inc., 345 Hudson Street, New York, New York 10014, U.S.A.
Penguin Group (Canada), 90 Eglinton Avenue East, Suite 700, Toronto, Ontario,
Canada M4P 2Y3 (a division of Pearson Penguin Canada Inc.)
Penguin Books Ltd, 80 Strand, London WC2R 0RL, England
Penguin Ireland, 25 St Stephen's Green, Dublin 2, Ireland (a division of Penguin Books Ltd)
Penguin Group (Australia), 250 Camberwell Road, Camberwell, Victoria 3124, Australia
(a division of Pearson Australia Group Pty Ltd)
Penguin Books India Pvt Ltd, 11 Community Centre, Panchsheel Park,
New Delhi – 110 017, India
Penguin Group (NZ), 67 Apollo Drive, Rosedale, North Shore 0632, New Zealand
(a division of Pearson New Zealand Ltd.)
Penguin Books (South Africa) (Pty) Ltd, 24 Sturdee Avenue,
Rosebank, Johannesburg 2196, South Africa

Penguin Books Ltd, Registered Offices: 80 Strand, London WC2R 0RL, England

First published in 2010 by Viking, a member of Penguin Group (USA) Inc.

1 3 5 7 9 10 8 6 4 2

LIBRARY OF CONGRESS CATALOGING-IN-PUBLICATION DATA
Friesner, Esther M.
Threads and flames / by Esther Friesner.
p. cm.
Summary: After recovering from typhus, thirteen-year-old Raisa leaves her Polish shtetl for
America to join her older sister, and goes to work at the Triangle Shirtwaist factory.
ISBN 978-0-670-01245-9 (hardcover)
[1. Immigrants—Fiction. 2. Jews—United States—Fiction. 3. Triangle Shirtwaist
Company—Fire, 1911—Fiction. 4. New York (N.Y.)—History—1898–1951—Fiction.] I. Title.
PZ7.F91662Th 2010
[Fic]—dc22
2009050306

Printed in U.S.A.
Set in Palatino
Book design by Sam Kim

Dedicated to the memory of Rebecca Eiber Tessler

Her spirit will always warm us
Her light will always shine

THREADS
AND
FLAMES

Chapter One

TO TRICK AN ANGEL

Raisa's world was fire. The blaze was everywhere. She was lost in the heart of the flames. Wherever she turned, walls of heat beat against her like hammers. The air throbbed and rang, filling her head with merciless thunder. Sometimes she thought she heard other sounds, urgent voices calling to her, trying to help her find a path out of the fire, but then she realized that they weren't calling her name but *Alteh! Alteh! Come back to me, Altehleh!*

Who is Alteh? she wondered, her head spinning. *Such a strange name . . . not really a name at all.* She'd heard the word for *old woman* many times in her thirteen years. The little Polish shtetl where she lived had many old people—men and women, scholarly and ignorant, a scattering of rich, a swarm of poor—but not one of the *altehs*, the old women, had Alteh for a name. She had a faint memory of a sickly little boy named

Alter, from one of the village families, but he was only eight, far from being an old man.

She tried to hold on to her thoughts, but they trickled away like water. Water! She was so thirsty. She couldn't feel her lips, only harsh, scaly skin, her tongue like a rasp, her mouth a desert. When she tried to ask for a drink, all she could do was whimper. And the fire burned on until the whole world was filled with it. It devoured everything until the only thing left for it to consume was itself. The scorching light flared wildly, casting up soaring plumes of dancing flame, then all at once it dove into an abyss of starless midnight, absolute and all encompassing. Raisa sighed with relief and tumbled into the cooling darkness.

When the light came back, she fought against it, twisting her head away, throwing one arm across her eyes. "No, please, leave me alone!" Fresh light meant fresh fire. She had to get away.

"Shhh, shhh, lie still, little one. It's all right, you're safe now. Lie still." Soft hands touched her face with tenderness. Raisa smelled bread, and a sudden pang of hunger creased her belly. The hands withdrew, and a damp cloth stroked her cheeks and forehead. She'd never felt anything so good in her life. When it pulled away, she made a little cry of protest and was shocked by how pitiful her own voice sounded, weak as the chirping of a baby bird.

"Yes, yes, hush, I'll do it again. Let me soak the cloth in fresh water for you. Don't worry, you'll feel much better soon.

Ah, thank God, thank God!" The cooling cloth bathed Raisa's face once more. Water trickled past the corners of her mouth. She tried to lick it up, but there was far too little to quench her thirst.

Then something smooth touched her mouth. Someone was holding a cup to her lips. Water spilled over the brim. She gulped it greedily and protested when it was taken away. Who was tormenting her so cruelly? She sobbed without tears.

"My sweet one, shhh, you'll have more water, but slowly, slowly, I beg of you. Too much won't be good for you. You don't want to be sick again."

The voice was soothing, familiar. Raisa tried to focus, to see the face behind the voice, but when she opened her eyes the world was still a blur. The light dazzled her. If she lifted her eyelids too much, it felt like someone was jamming a wreath of needles onto her head. She wanted to speak, to thank whoever it was that had brought her comfort and relief. She wanted to say, *You saved me from the fire. I owe you my life. How can I ever repay you?* But the words would not come. Instead, her eyes closed and she returned to the darkness.

When she opened her eyes once more, the blinding light had faded to a single flame, glowing inside the milky white glass of a flower-painted lamp. Raisa turned her face toward the light. The lamp sat on a small table by her bedside, a table that also held a thick-sided green drinking glass, a battered book covered in brown leather, and the dull glint of a circular gold brooch set with seed pearls. One pearl was missing, and for a moment the tiny cavity drew Raisa's gaze until she imagined it was opening up, blossoming before her eyes. Soon it filled her sight, a bottomless abyss gaping at her feet, hungry for her to tumble in. She gasped and snapped her eyes shut. When she opened them, the dizzying illusion was gone and the brooch was just a bit of broken jewelry again.

Her eyes drifted to the drinking glass. Was there water in it? Raisa's tongue scraped over her parched lips. She tried to reach for the glass, but her arm refused to obey her. It was as if someone had boiled her bones until they were as limp as overcooked noodles. How she hated that helpless feeling!

With a mighty effort, she forced power back into her arm and made a grab for the water glass, but only succeeded in knocking it off the table. It hit the floor with a dull crash, though not before taking the book and the gold brooch with it. The lamp rocked back and forth, perilously close to the table's edge.

"Ah! What are you trying to do? Burn down the house?" Strong hands darted out to steady the teetering lamp. A woman's face ducked low, into the mellow lamplight, and Raisa heard the scraping sound of chair legs being dragged over wooden planks just before the woman sat down at her bedside. She looked closely at Raisa, stroking her forehead with one hand, clasping her fingers with the other. "This is all my fault. I never should have left you alone. What do you need? More water? I'll get it for you right away." She patted Raisa's hand and got up again.

"Glukel, wait, don't leave me!" The words flew out of

Raisa's mouth much louder than she had expected. Her voice was coming back. It sounded healthier than she felt.

The woman turned sharply, a look of delight on her weary face. "You know me," she said, as if that were a great miracle. "You remember my name."

"How could I forget . . . ?" Raisa began, but the dryness in her mouth and throat forced her back into silence.

"Hush, not another word!" The older woman raced off into the shadows, returning swiftly with a new glass—fresh water. She sat on the bed, one arm supporting Raisa's back, the other holding the glass to her lips. "Drink it slowly."

Raisa did her best to obey, but the water tasted so good that soon she was gulping it down. When Glukel tried to pull the glass away from her lips, Raisa clutched the older woman's wrist with both hands and held on stubbornly. Still, Raisa wasn't strong enough to win that tug-of-war. She made a weak protest as she was forced to let the glass go.

"Shhh, shhh." Glukel stroked Raisa's cheek with her free hand. "You can have more soon. I don't want you to make yourself sick again, that's all. Your stomach's not used to having so much in it all of a sudden. Patience, and I promise that soon you'll have more water and maybe a little soup and even a nice egg! And tea! Tea with honey—it's good for you, my darling Alteh. You'll see."

"Alteh? Glukel, why do you call me that? I'm *Raisa*." She pronounced her given name fiercely, defending something precious.

"Not anymore, dear one. When you were so sick that I

thought I was going to lose you, too, I changed your name. The Angel of Death"—Glukel spat three times to cast away any bad luck that might be attracted by mentioning the name of such a dreadful being—"was looking for a girl named Raisa. A *young* girl. What young girl would be called Alteh?" Glukel appeared doubtful, as if she didn't believe her own words of explanation, but she spoke as if she did.

Raisa shook her head. "I don't like that name. It's—it's not who I am."

"It's who you are now. What does it matter? It's such a little thing, and it saved your life!"

"You believe that?" Raisa gave the older woman an incredulous look. "You think it's so easy to trick an angel?"

Glukel looked uneasy, as if she sensed an invisible, dangerous presence in her own home. "Don't talk like that. Don't mock what you can't understand! You should be thankful that we could fool the Angel of—that we could fool him."

"I *am* thankful," Raisa maintained. "Glukel, you took care of Henda and me like your own daughters since Mama died and I'm grateful—I'll never be able to repay you for it—but how grateful would I be to Mama if I abandoned the name she gave me?"

"May she rest in peace," Glukel said automatically. She sighed. "She was my closest friend. I can hardly believe she's been gone for so many years. *She* would understand what I've done to save you, but you? Who can argue with you girls these days? So headstrong! Fine, have it your way; I'm too exhausted to fight you. I've had to have one new grave dug already. I'm just thankful there won't be a second one now, *k'n ein' horeh.*" As she spoke the words to avert the evil eye, she began to weep.

"Glukel, whose grave? Who died?" Raisa used what little strength she had to sit upright and throw her arms around the older woman's shoulders. Her embrace accidentally pulled off the faded blue kerchief covering Glukel's hair. Raisa was shocked to see that it was all an icy white instead of the brown streaked with gray that she remembered. "Don't cry. Oh, please, don't cry!"

Glukel drew back, the tears still wet on her deeply lined face. "It's Nathan, my sweet one. Nathan is gone."

Raisa gritted her teeth in spite of herself and Glukel noticed. "Is this how you act when you hear my nephew is dead? Such a look, so full of hate! He wasn't the easiest man to get along with, may he rest in peace, but I don't remember him ever treating you that badly."

It wasn't me *he treated badly.* Bitterness flooded Raisa's thoughts. *It was Henda. Your nephew made my sister's life a torment. He's the reason she ran off to America four years ago, when she was only sixteen. America! Henda used to tell me stories she'd heard about that rich, rich land, wonderful stories! We talked about going there together—crossing the ocean, making an easy living, sending money back to you, and one day even bringing you over to live with us there, in comfort. Then Nathan ruined all our plans. He wouldn't leave her alone. Henda had to escape him, and she couldn't take me with her because I was too young to travel as fast as she needed to go. Do you know how much I miss her? But he left her no choice. He was going to force her to marry him, and he would have succeeded. Who was going to stop him? You, Glukel?* Unbidden tears slid down her cheeks.

He called himself the man of this house, the "scholar," hiding behind his books, while every bite of food we ate came from your hard work. You were always bent over your dressmaker's needle, ruining your eyesight so we could survive. I fetched and carried the orders from the time I was three. Henda and I both worked hard mending and making clothes, and what did Nathan do? Nothing. And you never said a word.

"Altehleh, what's the matter?" Glukel's voice was low and soothing. "Are you angry with me? All right, maybe you and Nathan didn't get along—what do I know? I can't be everywhere—but he's gone now. If you have any hard feelings against him, let them be buried, too."

Raisa shook her head emphatically and regretted it at once; the action set the room whirling around her. She collapsed back against her pillows and groaned. Glukel gave a little cry of alarm and dabbed at Raisa's brow with the damp cloth, her words of concern turning into unintelligible noises that faded away in a rising pool of darkness.

When Raisa awoke again, she felt much better. Daylight was streaming into the room through a half-shaded window. *I must have slept through another night*, she thought. And then she wondered, *How many nights have I lain here, so sick?* Even with the window shade lowered, she could still glimpse the young oak outside her bedroom window. Its branches were thick with summer greenery. The last time she'd seen that tree, those leaves had been nothing more than fat springtime buds. The idea of so much time lost forever saddened her. The bedside lamp was out, and the sound of many voices wafted up through the floorboards from the kitchen below. She took a deep breath and smelled fresh cake. Her mouth watered.

She sat up in bed and was happy to discover that her dizziness was gone. Casting a glance around the room, she saw Glukel's green shawl with the red flowers draped over the back of a chair. Carefully she swung her feet out of bed and stood up, leaning on the bedside table until she was sure that she could master the shakiness in her legs.

"Come on, I can do this," she muttered. She took a few tentative steps to the chair, picked up the big shawl, and draped it around her. Feeling light-headed, she reached up to cradle the side of her face.

"Ah!" A gasp of shock escaped her lips. Instead of the long braids she always wore crisscrossed, encircling her head like a crown, Raisa's fingers brushed against the bristly remnants of her dark copper-colored hair. "What did she do to me?" she whispered. "Why?" Slowly she made her way out the bedroom door, seeking Glukel.

She heard the voices more distinctly when she was halfway down the stairs. Yossel's deep, gravelly tones, so surprising coming from a man only in his twenties, set him apart from the other villagers. So did his hulking body, the muscles hardened by his labor as a blacksmith. His new wife Sarah's piping voice played over, under, and through his words, like a sparrow hopping everywhere, pecking at whatever it found. When Yossel was away from the forge, the two of them were almost never apart, and as a result he never got to finish a sentence without his adored little wife interrupting him. When a third voice said, "Sarahleh, let the man speak," Raisa knew Reb Avner had come to call, as well. There was no mistaking the calm, fatherly way the shtetl rabbi spoke. Even when he scolded, it sounded comforting.

"Let him speak? Who's not letting him speak?" Sarah's voice skirled high as a tin-whistle tune. "I let him talk as long as he likes, Reb Avner. Are you saying I'm a bad wife? Yossel, have you been complaining about me behind my back? For you to run and tell the rabbi that I don't let you—"

"Sarah, Sarahleh, sweetheart, I never—" Yossel began.

"—get a single word in . . . ?" Sarah concluded just as Raisa entered the kitchen.

Her appearance made Sarah go suddenly silent, her dark eyes as wide as if she'd seen a monster or a marvel. Glukel's three guests were seated at the kitchen table, thick-sided glasses of hot tea before them, a plate of sliced poppy seed cake within easy reach. Yossel's huge hand was just reaching for a piece, but the instant that his eyes met Raisa's, he froze. Reb Avner sucked his breath in sharply and released it in a softly murmured prayer. At least, Raisa presumed it was a prayer: it was in Hebrew, the language of the synagogue and the scholarly men and boys who studied Torah there; she couldn't imagine anyone using it for something besides worship, pleas, or blessing.

"Sweetheart, what are you doing up?" Glukel was out of her chair and across the room in a heartbeat, her arms enfolding Raisa tenderly.

"Glukel, why—why?" Raisa pushed the older woman away and gestured helplessly at her shorn head.

"Oh, my dear, I'm so sorry. I had to cut off all your beautiful hair. Too much hair drains away a sick person's strength and sometimes you thrashed your head so much when the fever was on you, your hair fell out of its braids and got all tangled. Don't worry, it will grow back."

"I know, but—"

"Never mind, never mind. Come, sit. Are you hungry? Thirsty? Let me give you some tea. Sarah brought you her special vegetable soup with barley and mushrooms. No one makes it better." The blacksmith's wife giggled at the compliment. "I'll fill you a bowl. Here, rest."

Glukel steered Raisa across the floor as if it were a wolf-haunted forest path fraught with perils, and settled her into her own just-abandoned chair. Raisa blinked in amazement at how quickly the promised tea and soup appeared in front of her, along with a small piece of dark rye bread. She was used to taking care of herself, not being treated like a pampered child, and it made her feel uneasy.

"Soak that in the soup before you try to eat it," Glukel

counseled. "It will be easier to digest." The steam rising from the heavy blue bowl smelled wonderful. Raisa picked up her spoon and began to eat, but after the first few mouthfuls she found herself gobbling it down like one of the local peasants' pigs at a trough.

"Alteh, slow down a little." Yossel's powerful hand closed gently on her wrist. "You'll hurt your stomach. It's not used to so much after so long going without. Put down the spoon, have a nice sip of tea, rest. No one will take the food away from you."

Raisa smiled at the big man, with his thick, badly groomed black beard. "Maybe not the food," she said. A mischievous spark kindled in her eyes as she turned bold and added, "But my hair, yes. And worse, my name."

Yossel looked bewildered. Glukel spread her hands in a helpless gesture. "She refuses to be called Alteh, even though that's what saved her life," she explained to the company. "What can I do?"

"But no, that's a terrible thing!" Sarah cried. "The Angel of—the angel came looking for Raisa and left empty-handed, thank God, but if you keep that name, you think he won't remember? You think he won't return to collect what he first came looking for? Where's your common sense? Burned up with the fever? If you haven't got the brains to save your own life, I'll do it for you. Your sister Henda was my dearest friend. What kind of a person would I be if I didn't look out for you when she's not here to do it herself? Not one soul in this village will call you any name but Alteh; I'll see to that, believe me! It's for your own good."

The rabbi laughed. "Ah, Sarah, what shall we do with you? Less than a year ago you and Raisa were like sisters, but now you're married, you're trying to be her mother? Better have children of your own, my dear." Sarah blushed and fell silent. Reb Avner then turned his mild gaze on Raisa.

"So, you don't want your new name?" he said. "I don't blame you. We live in a new world now, a new century, even if it is less than ten years old. Moving pictures, flying machines—so many marvels, so many changes! But changing your name to change your fortune? That is one marvel I find hard to believe. Live and be well and keep your name, Raisaleh. You were named after your father's grandmother, a wonderful woman, strong and brave. She simply showed up here one day and said that she'd come from a Russian shtetl no one ever heard of. There was a pogrom, a dreadful massacre—half the village destroyed by fire, all of her family slaughtered. God alone knows why she didn't settle in any of the other villages she passed through on her way here. She wouldn't say, and no one could ever get it out of her, not even your great-grandfather. She wasn't much older than you are now, and she was just as strong willed. I think that was what preserved her."

"Henda and Glukel told me how much Mama used to talk about her," Raisa said very softly. "I wish I could have known her."

"If you'd known her, you couldn't have been named for her," the rabbi replied. "You'll just have to take my word for it when I tell you that she, too, faced down the Angel of Death in her life. I was only a child, still clinging to my mother's apron, but I still see her, so young, coming to our shtetl with little more than the clothes on her back and the one family treasure she saved from the pogrom, a pair of candlesticks."

Glukel smiled fondly over the memory. "Silver ones! They were so beautiful. Mine are only brass. When Henda turned twelve, I remember how we used to welcome Shabbos together, and how lovely it was to have two pairs of flames light our home." She sighed. "Now there's only one."

"Those candlesticks travel more than some people," Sarah remarked a little enviously. "From here to Warsaw, from Warsaw back to here, and then back to Warsaw again!"

"Back to *here*?" Raisa looked up sharply.

"Isn't it strange how such things happen?" Sarah chattered on. "You know that merchant who used to live down by the cattle market, the one nobody here can stop talking about because he did so well that he moved to Warsaw, what, twenty years ago?"

"Pan Menachem Laski," the rabbi said.

"Pan?" Glukel echoed. "Don't you mean *Reb* Laski? Pan's what you call a Pole, not a Jew."

"And yet, that's what the Poles call that Jew," the rabbi replied. "The ones who want to do business with him. It's a mark of respect."

"I trust their 'respect' like I'd trust a cat with a pitcher of cream," Yossel grumbled.

"Who cares about cats?" Raisa piped up. "I know Reb Laski. He's the one who helped Henda get to America. She sent us a letter telling how she gave him those candlesticks and Mama's jewelry for ship passage and travel money. How did they get back here?"

Sarah sniffed. "How do you think? They walked? Reb High-and-Mighty Laski sent a messenger with them."

"But *why*?" Raisa felt her heart begin to beat faster.

"Maybe Reb Laski realized you're all grown up now, a young woman," Yossel said a little too quickly. "He's rich; maybe he felt he could afford to give the candlesticks back to you without waiting for Henda to redeem them."

"Why didn't the messenger leave them here, then?" Raisa cried, drowning in unanswered questions. "Why did he just turn around and go back to Warsaw? Why?"

Glukel grasped Raisa's wildly gesturing hands. "Yossel, she's not a little girl anymore. Don't try to shield her from everything. Tell her the truth."

Raisa looked from her guardian to the blacksmith. Yossel only shook his head. It was Reb Avner who responded. "The messenger came with the candlesticks while you were still so sick. It was just a little while after Nathan died." A murmured "May he rest in peace" went up from Glukel, Sarah, and Yossel. Even Raisa joined in, reluctantly. "I think Reb Laski never wanted to hold on to them or your mother's jewelry in the first place. He was a good friend of your father's family. If I know him, he probably tried to give Henda the money for her passage, and if I know Henda, she refused to take charity. In any case, the man he sent here was born and raised in Warsaw. He didn't know our shtetl. He had no notion of where to find Glukel's house, so he stopped by the inn to ask. The only one around at the time was the innkeeper's son, Lemel." Reb Avner took a deep breath. "He's a good boy, but . . . not quickwitted. His mind is a jumble. He forgets, confuses things. He confused you and Nathan—both living under the same roof, both stricken with typhus, and so"—he paused and looked at her, his eyes sorrowful—"he told the messenger you were dead—"

"God forbid it!" Glukel cried out.

"—and the messenger left with the candlesticks before anyone could tell him the truth," the rabbi finished.

"But if that's so . . ." Suddenly, Raisa gasped. The full meaning of what had happened hit her like a blow. "If the messenger believed I was dead, he told Reb Laski, and then *he* would have sent a letter to Henda saying—" She leaped up from her chair and stood there, swaying dizzily. "Henda! *Henda!* Oh my God, my sister thinks I'm dead!" The room spun around her, and she fell into Glukel's waiting arms.

Chapter Two

LETTING GO

Yossel carried Raisa back upstairs, where Glukel tucked her into bed and Sarah fluttered around, fussing. Last of all, Reb Avner came in to speak with her. The others left the two of them alone.

The rabbi sat by Raisa's bedside. "A terrible thing," he said. "A terrible, terrible thing, to think about what a shock your sister must have suffered. But let us thank God that at least we have the power to set this right."

Raisa sat up in bed and gazed steadily at the rabbi. "Today," she said. "Promise me that you'll send a message to Warsaw *today,* so that as soon as possible Reb Laski will let Henda know I'm alive. Please."

"I'll do that and more," the rabbi reassured her. "But you must promise *me* you won't fret about this. An unquiet mind doesn't let a sick body heal properly. Put aside your worries and your anger. Concentrate on regaining your strength."

"Anger?" Raisa repeated. "I'm not angry at anyone."

The rabbi raised one silvery eyebrow. "Not even at the inn-keeper's son for what he told Reb Laski's messenger?"

Raisa shook her head. "How could I be mad at him for that? Lemel's almost thirty, but he acts like a boy of nine. He tries so hard to help his parents, to do the right thing, and he takes it to heart badly when he fails." She touched the rabbi's hand. "Does he know what he did? Please tell him not to be upset. He couldn't help what happened."

"True, true." Reb Avner nodded. "You were so sick, that— let me be frank, Raisa—Lemel wasn't the only person in this town who was sure we'd lost you, God forbid. But sometimes the same hammer that breaks a chair to pieces builds a bet-ter one in its place. As soon as Glukel knew you would live, she told Sarah. No better way to make sure the whole village found out in a hurry, eh?" He chuckled.

"Of course Sarah ran to tell her husband. Yossel was at the inn, checking their horses for loose shoes and sore feet, Lemel helping him out by making the beasts stand still. Yossel told me that the poor lad heard your name from Sarah's lips and thought she'd seen a ghost! He was terrified, until his father calmed him down and explained you were as alive as he was. That was when a light kindled in his eyes and he blurted everything he recalled about Reb Laski's messenger. So you see, none of us might have heard one word about the man from Warsaw if not for Lemel!"

He stood up slowly, groaning a little. "Ah, old bones, old

bones . . . I could never make the journey that's waiting for you. Lie down, now, and rest well. If you don't get your strength back, how can you travel to Warsaw, let alone America?"

"America?" Instead of lying down, Raisa sat up even straighter in bed.

"My dear, do you think I don't know?" He gave her a gentle, kindly look. "These past four years, your sister has been sending Reb Laski money to keep until there'd be enough to bring you to her."

"How did you find out?" she asked, thunderstruck. The arrangement had been a secret between the sisters. Raisa still remembered how Henda had held her close the night she stole out of the house and took the road to Warsaw. *"Once I reach America, I'll get work, Raisaleh,"* she'd whispered in the dark of their shared bed. *"I'll work hard, and I'll send back everything I can so you can join me. But remember, you mustn't tell anyone about this until there's enough money for your ticket."*

"Not even Glukel?" Raisa had whispered back.

"If you tell Glukel, you might as well tell Nathan, and if you tell Nathan . . . I'm not going to America just for a visit, Raisaleh; I'm going to stay, to make a new life for both of us. If Nathan finds out, he'll try to make you stay here, to keep us apart, maybe even to force me to come back."

Raisa remembered being puzzled by her sister's vehemence. *"Do you really think he'd do something like that, Henda?"*

Her sister's face had hardened. *"You don't know what he's already tried to do to me. Do you think I'd leave you like this, go so*

*far away over nothing? I love you, Raisaleh, and if you love me, you
can't tell anyone about the ticket money—no one at all!"*

The memory faded, but Raisa's question remained. "Who told you, Reb Avner?"

The rabbi rubbed the small of his back. "My good friend Menachem—Reb Laski—is not a young man. He wanted to make sure that someone else knew about the money from America so that you would get it if, God forbid, anything happened to him. As soon as he received his first letter from Henda, saying she'd arrived safely in New York City, he wrote to me, insisting that I was the only man he could trust with something so important."

"And you, Rabbi . . . you've told no one else?"

Reb Avner gave her a sad smile. "Why don't you ask me what you really want to know, Raisaleh?"

Raisa looked down at her hands, folded atop the feather-stuffed quilt. "Does Glukel know?" she asked softly.

"Not yet." He stood up. "And from my mouth, never. Reb Laski explained to me about your sister's fears. Poor Nathan."

"Poor *Nathan*?"

"He's dead, may he rest in peace, and while he lived, he lived unwisely. All the days of our lives, we are given the choice to do good or to do wrong. How can I help but feel pity for a soul that made so many bad choices? He could never see anything beyond the immediate satisfaction of his own desires. He never spared a moment to imagine how other people might feel, how his actions might hurt them."

"I hope . . ." Raisa began, her voice very low. "I hope I can remember that when I tell Glukel I'm going away." She looked up into Reb Avner's sympathetic eyes. "Can you help me? Can you tell me what to say?"

He shook his head. "There are some things you will have to do for yourself. More, now that you're going into the world on your own. Be careful of how you choose to do them. I'm going to write to Menachem. He didn't send a man all this way just to return a pair of candlesticks. Unless I miss my guess, that messenger's true purpose was to let you know that Henda's finally sent him enough money to pay for your passage. If it was just to return the candlesticks, he'd have done so long ago. He wanted to give your sister the money for her passage without taking anything as a pledge except her promise to repay him. The only reason he accepted the candlesticks and your mother's jewelry was because Henda insisted—*ach*, Henda!" He clapped a hand to his cheek. "Menachem must send her word at once, letting her know you're well!"

"I wish you could write to her yourself," Raisa said. "It would be faster."

"You know as well as I do why I can't. I don't know where to address the letter. We've done much in these past four years to make sure Nathan never learned where your sister was living."

"Do you think he would have followed her to America?" Raisa couldn't believe it, though she was ready to believe almost anything else of him.

"He was a very . . . *determined* young man. Do you remember when Henda's first letter arrived?"

"Of course. You brought it to our house. I wondered why she sent it to you and not to us."

"She didn't send it to me, but to Menachem, who put it into a different envelope," Reb Avner said. "He wrote to me separately, saying he thought that the whole complicated hide-and-seek business was silly, but he soon learned better. The moment I finished reading you all Henda's letter, Nathan snatched it out of my hands."

"Ah! I remember that," Raisa said.

"And do you also remember how he vanished for at least a week afterward? The letter didn't give him any hint of where Henda was living in New York City, but the envelope had Menachem's address in Warsaw."

"He went there?"

"Like a wild man. He arrived uninvited, barged into the house, and demanded to know where Henda was. *Demanded!* Menachem stood firm against all of Nathan's bluster and bullying, until the servants threw him out the door."

Raisa grinned. "I wish I could've seen that."

"The only reason Menachem didn't have him arrested was to spare Glukel the shame," Reb Avner went on. "After that, there was no question about the wisdom of hiding Henda's address." He clicked his tongue. "And now, when it would make things so much simpler to write to her directly, we can't do it. Well, with luck, she may get the good news about you before the bad. When a letter has so far to go, who can say when it's going to arrive? We can only do so much. Be well, dear Raisa." He left the room and after a little while, she slept.

When Raisa woke up, the sunlight had faded from the sky and the flowered lamp was lit. She turned her head and saw Glukel sitting in the chair beside the bed. Raisa reached out and gently laid one hand over the older woman's work-worn fingers.

"I have something to tell you."

Glukel never once interrupted while the girl spoke about Henda, Reb Laski, and the plans for her own journey to America. Even after the whole story had come out, she remained silent for such a long time that Raisa's heart began to beat fast with alarm. "Are you mad at me? I don't want to leave you, but I need—"

"You need to be with your sister," Glukel concluded. She nodded slowly. "And you're right; you should be with Henda. How can I be mad at you for something so natural? You need your family."

"You're my family, too, Glukel!" Raisa exclaimed. "If not for you . . ." She couldn't finish the sentence. Memories of her mother's death choked her. "I won't go! You're our second mother. I can't leave you behind."

The older woman freed her hands from Raisa's grasp and stroked the girl's closely shorn hair. "I'm not asking you to stay. Haven't we all heard the stories about America? So many opportunities! What would become of the little birds if their mama didn't push them out of the nest? They'd never learn how high they could fly." She forced a smile. "A good mother wants her child to have a better life than hers. If that means saying good-bye . . ." She took a deep breath and let it out slowly.

"Not forever," Raisa said, throwing herself into Glukel's arms. "When I join Henda, we'll both work hard and we'll save every coin we can so that the three of us can be together again. We'll bring you to America. We'll take care of you the way you always took care of us, and you'll never have to work another day in your life. It will happen before you know it; wait and see. I'll *make* it happen; I swear it!"

"Of course you will, my darling," Glukel murmured, but her voice was sad.

By the time Raisa was well enough to travel, it seemed as if the whole village, Jews and gentiles alike, had come to see her. Having one of their own on the brink of making the journey to the Golden Land was a great event. The parade of visitors became such a daily occurrence that Glukel finally had Raisa come downstairs every morning and spend the day in an arm-chair, cradled in a nest of pillows with her feet up on a cushioned stool.

"Forgive me, dear one, but some of these people are like family to us and others are my best customers," Glukel explained while she fluffed Raisa's pillows after the fifth day of visitors. "I can't turn them away."

"Even if you tried, they wouldn't listen," Raisa said, smiling.

"Well, may God bless them, no one's come empty-handed. A coin here, a coin there; it adds up! I can rest easy knowing you won't be traveling in poverty. Plus there's the money that Reb Laski sent to the rabbi, to pay your way to Warsaw. He insisted on adding some of his own funds to what Henda sent."

It was a special joy for Raisa the first time her friends came to see her. She'd grown up with Yitta and Avigal. They overwhelmed her with armloads of wildflowers gathered from the fields and baskets full of sweet treats they'd baked themselves. Yitta also brought her little sister Dina. As soon as the toddler saw Raisa, she let out a squeal of joy and clambered onto her lap.

"Dina, no!" Yitta exclaimed. "Get down. Raisa is too tired to play with you now."

"Too tired for my special girl?" Raisa hugged the child close. "Never! Did you miss me, my sweet one? Did you miss our games? Do you still have the rag doll I made for you?"

"She won't go to sleep without it." Yitta lowered her voice and added, "She loves you, Raisa. Even our mama calls you Dina's little mother. What's she going to do when you go?"

"What are *we* going to do?" Avigal put in. "Oh, Raisa, isn't it odd to remember how we all used to talk about how exciting it was, imagining Henda's new life in America? And now you're going there, too! Do you know when you're supposed to leave?"

"Not yet," Raisa replied. "When the doctor says I can, I guess."

"Will you send us letters?"

"If I can find someone to write them for me."

Yitta clicked her tongue. "It will be enough if she sends letters to Glukel and puts in a word or two for us. It costs money to send mail from America."

"So what?" Avigal countered, flashing her dimples. "There's lots of money in America! She'll be able to send as many letters as she likes."

Yitta, Avigal, and Dina visited Raisa many times after that, but it was Yossel and Sarah who came every day, always bringing a basket filled with treats. One morning they arrived with a bigger gift than usual.

Glukel raised one eyebrow as she took the heavy basket from the blacksmith's hands. Besides the freight of baked goods, two bottles of dark red cherry cordial clinked together. "All right, what's the special occasion?"

"She leaves in three days," Yossel replied. "Is that special enough?"

"How did you know?" Raisa asked from her pillow-laden armchair. She no longer needed to sit all propped up and tucked in, but Glukel still insisted on fussing over her. As much as she hated being treated like an ailing infant, Raisa let the older woman have her way. She didn't want to argue with Glukel when she didn't know when or if they would ever see one another again. "The doctor was just here to say I can go, but we haven't told anyone about it."

"Since when does my Sarah need to be *told* anything?" Yossel spread his hands in a gesture of complete helplessness.

"Ignore him," Sarah said briskly, unpacking the basket. "He spends so much time with horses that he's got the manners of one. Here." She thrust a fat bun, sticky with honey and fragrant with cinnamon, into Raisa's hands. "Eat while you can. Who knows what kind of pig slop you'll have on that ship? And America! You'll be lucky if you can find a decent loaf of bread, never mind a piece of cake that doesn't taste like brick dust!"

Yossel laughed. "Sarah, you sound like an old housewife. Why wouldn't she find good bread in America? It's the *goldineh medina,* the country where the streets are paved with gold!"

Sarah folded her arms and stared at her husband. "You *believe* that?"

"Well, not *all* of that, but—"

"So tell me, Mr. Know-it-all, if the streets in America are paved with gold, why did it take Henda *four years* to save enough money for her sister's ticket? What, maybe she walked down the wrong streets?"

Sarah was still pecking at Yossel when another knock sounded at the door. Glukel went to answer it and came back into the room followed by the innkeeper's son. Lemel was a big man but he walked with small steps, shuffling his feet over the plank floors. His head was bent, his eyes downcast, and he held his hands cupped together in front of him, as if he held a firefly.

"Hello, Lemel." Raisa took care to keep her voice friendly and calm. Lemel was shy and well known for dashing away without warning if he feared he was about to be scolded or punished. "I'm glad you came to see me. Sarah brought me lots of good things to eat. Would you like some?"

Lemel shook his head emphatically. "Don't deserve it," he muttered. "I . . . told the man the wrong thing. About you."

Raisa stood up with her quilt wrapped around her and fetched another sticky bun from the basket on the table. Lemel still refused to raise his head, so she held the treat where he couldn't help but see it.

"It's all right," she told him. "You made a mistake, just like all of us do. Come on, eat. Please."

Lemel slowly raised his head and gave her a shy look. "You're not mad at me?"

She smiled at him. "No, but if you don't have some of Sarah's baking, she will be."

It was wonderful to see how the big man's eyes lit up with pure joy, but before he accepted the bun, he looked back down. "Oh! I forgot. I made you a present." He opened his cupped hands, revealing a tiny wooden horse, perfect in every detail. Astride the animal was a regal woman dressed in flowing robes, crowned with a wreath of flowers. "It's you," Lemel said, blushing. "How you will look when you come back from America—a rich lady, a queen."

Raisa accepted the gift, marveling at the skillful carving, the delicate way every tiny flower had been painted. "She's much too beautiful to be me, Lemel," she said while Glukel steered her back into the big chair and tucked the quilt snugly around her once more.

"All right, so she's Henda," Lemel replied cheerfully. He gobbled up the bun and licked his fingers.

Lemel didn't stay long. Everyone in town knew that he was ill at ease at even the smallest gatherings, more content when there was only one other person talking to him, happiest in the silent company of the inn's horses. Glukel used a napkin to wrap up a big slice of her honey cake for him to take home. He held it close to his chest and headed for the door, but before he left, he turned back for a moment and blurted out, "Henda is the queen, Raisa, but you are the princess!" His face flushed a deep red, and he ran out of the house as if his feet had caught fire.

Sarah laughed. "Well! Maybe you shouldn't go to America after all, Raisa. It looks like you've made a conquest here. A man who's his father's only son, heir to an inn that always does good business, *and* he thinks you're a princess? You could do worse."

"Stop it, Sarah!" Glukel snapped. "A nice match you want to make for my Raisaleh! Poor Lemel has the mind of a child."

Sarah couldn't resist teasing Glukel just a little longer. "So how different is that from plenty of other men?"

Before Glukel could respond or Yossel could intervene, Raisa broke in. "How could I marry Lemel? A princess has to marry a prince." She ran her hand over her shorn head and laughed. "A fine princess I make now! But Lemel's right about my sister; Henda *is* beautiful enough to be a queen, even if they don't have queens in America."

"No queens, maybe, but rich people?" Sarah said. "Plenty, believe me! Yasha the butcher's cousin went to America and keeps sending him pictures from the newspapers about all those millionaires with their fancy clothes, their big mansions, their wives covered in diamonds. And it's not just the gentiles with all that money. There are Jews like us living over there who have houses bigger than this whole shtetl, armies of servants, dinners served on silver platters!" She grew breathless describing the imagined splendor of such a life.

"You believe that, but not what Yossel said about the streets being paved with gold?" Raisa asked.

Sarah lifted her chin. "The difference is, *I* know what I'm talking about."

On the morning of her departure for America, Raisa woke up before dawn and stole out of the house without waking Glukel. The sky was just beginning to turn light when she returned.

"Where have you been?" Glukel demanded, coming out of the kitchen just as Raisa was trying to go back upstairs as quietly as possible. "And without your coat! What were you thinking?"

"I just wanted to walk through the shtetl," Raisa replied, turning around and coming back downstairs slowly. "And it's not that cold out, really."

"Hmph!" Glukel grabbed Raisa's wrist, studied the girl's arm, and ran her fingers over the thick cluster of goose bumps. "This says otherwise. Never mind. Come into the kitchen and have some breakfast."

Raisa drank a tall glass of hot rose-hip tea, holding a sugar cube between her teeth to sweeten it while she sipped. Glukel set down a plate piled high with fresh bread, poppy seed cake, and rolls just out of the oven and watched approvingly as Raisa spread thick layers of butter and raspberry preserves on the bread. "At least your walk around the village gave you a good appetite," she remarked. "So, where did you go?"

"Nowhere," Raisa replied. "Anywhere. I walked to the marketplace, past the inn, the synagogue, the dry-goods store, Yossel's forge . . . you know. The birds were singing. I passed Meyer's daughter, Liba, taking some goats down to the river, and Danek bringing in a horse cart full of beets and cabbages. And, oh, Glukel, there were such good smells coming from the bakeshop!"

"Better than these?" Glukel smiled gently as she gestured at the slowly vanishing heap of bread and cake on the table.

Raisa's answering smile was a little sad. "I can't believe I'm really going. I wish you were coming with me."

"So do I." Glukel drew up a chair and sat beside Raisa. "Now that Nathan is gone, there's nothing tying me here. Oh, I have my friends, but if you and Henda can make new lives in a new land, I can make new friends." Glukel shook her head and smiled. "But today it's your turn; mine will come, I know. After all"—she embraced Raisa warmly—"what can I trust if I can't trust my daughter's promise?"

Raisa sat on the seat board next to the peddler who would take her to the train station. He wasn't from her shtetl, but he was well known to Reb Avner as a trustworthy family man with a good reputation. In spite of this, Glukel kept glaring at him as if he were a villain with a record of crimes as long as the road to Warsaw. She stopped scowling only long enough to speak to Raisa.

"Write to me, my dear one. Don't forget to write to me."

Raisa's face reddened. "Glukel, you know I'm not very good at—"

"Then find someone to write for you! Surely in America *someone* knows how to write a letter. And while you're at it, have them teach you. I blame myself; I should have seen to it that you had more time to practice reading and writing instead of always sewing, sewing, sewing like a slave!"

"I didn't mind."

"That's not the point!" Glukel held up one finger. "If we don't see to it that our children turn out better than we did, what will become of the world? Promise me, Raisa; promise me that you'll learn."

Raisa's promise was lost in a fresh outburst of tears and hugs. She leaned over so far that she almost toppled out of her seat and onto Glukel. Luckily Yossel was standing nearby and stepped in just in time to help Raisa settle back safely.

"Be careful, Raisaleh," the big man said, giving her his own pocket kerchief to dry her eyes. "You want to reach America in one piece." He could manage only half a smile.

"Thank you, Yossel," Raisa said, wiping the tears away. "Where's Sarah? Isn't she coming to see me off?"

"She'll be here."

As if to prove Yossel right, his wife's unmistakable voice rang out through the morning air. "Wait! Stop! Don't go yet! Here I am!" She rushed up to the cart like a miniature whirlwind and pressed a large covered basket into Raisa's lap. "For the journey," she said.

"All the way to America?" Yossel couldn't resist the urge to tease.

Sarah was in no mood for that. Her angry stare blazed hot enough to singe the beard right off her husband's face. "Maybe *you* should go to America, too," she said. "Alone."

Yossel was still trying to make peace with his wife when Reb Avner approached the wagon. The rabbi recited the prayer for a safe journey, and everyone who had come to bid Raisa farewell raised a thunderous "amen" at the end. Then Reb Avner reached up and took Raisa's hand.

"My dear, you have Henda's address safe?" Raisa nodded.

The precious piece of paper had come from Warsaw shortly after Reb Avner wrote to his friend about Raisa's recovery. "I've heard from Reb Laski again. He's written to your sister, letting her know you're alive and well, but hasn't heard back from her yet."

"The important thing is that his letter reaches her and that she knows I'm all right," Raisa replied.

"Yes, yes, I'm sure it did." Reb Avner nodded. "Perhaps she was too overwhelmed by the happy news to think of writing back to him."

"Not as happy as I'll be to see her again," Raisa said, smiling in spite of her tears.

The peddler announced it was time to leave.

"So soon?" Glukel clutched the horse's bridle, her face the color of frost.

The peddler looked at her with heartfelt regret. "I'm sorry, but if I'm going to get this girl to the station in time to board the train for Warsaw—"

"Yes, fine, all right, go!" Glukel released her grip on the bridle and turned away abruptly, hugging herself and shaking.

"You heard her," Yossel said. "Go *now*." He gave the horse a strong slap on the rump. It whinnied and set off at a brisk trot, leaving the peddler to try and regain control of his animal.

As they traveled through the streets of the shtetl and out onto the open road, Raisa heard her name called out from many lips, together with a flurry of farewell wishes for a safe journey. She set Sarah's basket down on the floor of the cart and twisted around in her seat, waving to the people and straining to keep the village in sight as long as possible. She cupped one hand over the brooch she'd pinned so carefully to her shawl. It was the same circle of pearls with one missing that Raisa had always kept close, the sole remaining piece of Mama's jewelry, the one Henda had insisted she keep, "so you won't ever forget Mama . . . or me." *As if I ever could do that!* Raisa thought, and clasped the brooch even more tightly as fresh tears stung her eyes.

Far too soon, the road took the peddler's cart into an alleyway of linden trees. When they emerged on the other side, the shtetl was gone.

Chapter Three

BETWEEN TWO WORLDS

After a long and arduous journey by cart and train and finally on foot, from the shtetl through the countryside to the great city of Warsaw and beyond, Raisa reached the docks in the bustling port of Bremerhaven, Germany, her gateway to the *goldineh medina*. She trudged from the train station to the docks in the midst of a crowd of travelers like herself, all speaking Yiddish, all talking about the impending voyage, yet she felt utterly alone. No one spared her a single word. It was as if she'd become invisible. No sooner were the great steamships in sight than everyone scattered, blending in with all the other people swarming along the waterfront.

Raisa took out her ticket and looked from the printed words on the paper to the painted words on the various ships and buildings. It was very frustrating. *If I knew how to read better, I could take care of myself, and I wouldn't have to do it this way!* she thought. When she found a match on a sign labeling the side of a long dockside structure, she joined the mass of people jostling one another outside the doors. Inside, a man in a steamship company uniform snapped foreign words at her, but at least she could guess what he wanted when he stuck out his hand for her ticket. She breathed a sigh of relief when he read it, nodded, and pointed her to a line of people moving slowly through yet another door.

By the time Raisa was allowed to climb the gangplank of the waiting ship, she felt as though she'd walked halfway to America, carrying her heavy bag all the way. At every step of the preboarding process she'd been besieged by short-spoken, short-tempered officials with flurries of documents, barrages of questions, and the occasional shove sending her to the next station. A doctor made her take off her kerchief, then interrogated her about the reason for her short hair. He had worked with enough Jewish emigrants to have picked up some practical Yiddish, but he seemed almost disappointed when his thorough, painful examination didn't turn up head lice. While his fine-toothed iron comb bit into her scalp, Raisa clenched her teeth. *My sister went through this,* she told herself. *She could bear it; so can I.*

At last she stood on the deck of the great ship, looking down at the docks of Bremerhaven. She crossed to the other side and gazed at the rippling water. It was the first time she'd seen the sea or heard the screams of the swooping gulls. The harbor smelled of salt and oil and garbage in the sun. Shadows cast by clouds streaming from the ship's three black smoke-stacks chased each other across the planking while passengers, porters, and members of the crew hustled by. Raisa set down her bags, leaned her arms on the rail, and murmured as much as she could remember of the blessing for a good journey. Reb Avner had recited it for her not just on the day of her departure, but from the first day of preparations for her leave-taking. After so many repetitions, she'd learned it almost perfectly, and reciting it now was both a prayer and a comfort in her solitude.

Someone tapped Raisa on the shoulder and spoke to her in German, jolting her out of her reverie. She turned to face a crewman with a harried expression on his young face. When she shook her head to let him know she didn't understand, he frowned and started yelling the unknown words at her, pronouncing each one slowly and meticulously.

Raisa's scalp still stung from the medical inspection, and her feet hurt from spending so much time moving through lines that crawled along. She had no patience left for any more nonsense. "*Stop* that!" she shouted back. "I told you, I don't recognize a word you're saying! It doesn't make any difference how loudly or slowly you talk, I . . . don't . . . *understand*!"

Her outburst took the crewman by surprise. He stopped yelling and peered at her as if she'd sprouted a second head. Then his frown deepened and he went right back to shouting at her, underscoring his incomprehensible words with emphatic gestures. He pointed at her, then her bags, then a nearby doorway. She paid him back frown for frown, but before she could say another word, he snatched up her luggage and carried it off through the doorway at a dead run.

"Wait! Come back with that! What do you think you're doing?"

Raisa ran after the young man, calling out first in Polish, then in Yiddish. It made no difference. None of the passengers or crew made any attempt to stop him. As for the young crewman, he ignored Raisa's protests, plunging down one stairway after another until he reached a large, windowless compartment deep in the belly of the ship. The air was warm and stagnant, smelling of sweat and boiled cabbage. Rows of bunks lined the walls. Countless people milled around, talking, laughing, arguing, weeping. Children squealed and shrieked. The whole space throbbed and echoed with voices.

The crewman dropped Raisa's bags on the floor in the middle of this tumult, then began shouting at her in German again. He extended one hand, palm upward, and slapped it briskly with the other. No matter how many ways Raisa tried to tell him that she didn't know what he wanted, he kept on barking at her until she felt ready to howl with frustration.

"He wants to see your papers." A pretty brown-haired girl seemed to pop up out of nowhere between Raisa and the young crewman. She spoke Yiddish with a slightly different accent than Raisa was used to. "The papers they gave you before you came on board. He wants to see them so he can tell you which bunk you've been assigned." Her dark eyes shone brilliantly when she smiled.

"Oh! Oh, of course." While Raisa dug into her bag, the girl

spoke rapid-fire German to the crewman, who nodded briefly and marched off. Raisa was confused. "Didn't he want to see these?" she asked, holding out the papers.

"I told him I'd take care of you," the girl replied breezily. She glanced at the papers. "Raisa, huh?" She shook hands with comic formality. "An honor to meet you, Miss Raisa. I'm Zusa Reshevsky. I hope your bunk's near mine. Hmm. You know what? If it isn't, I'll move. Come on, then." She picked up the almost-empty food basket and walked away, swinging it.

With Zusa's help, Raisa soon found herself settled in the top berth of one of the double-stacked bunks. The lower bunk was occupied by a skinny, middle-aged woman who gave her a dirty look and declared, "You'd better watch where you put your nasty feet when you go climbing up there, you little brat! I've got my eye on you, and if you so much as touch me, I'll complain to the captain!"

"As if she could ever get within shouting distance of the captain," Zusa whispered. Raisa giggled.

"*What* is so funny?" the woman demanded.

Raisa stifled her laughter and put on a serious face. "I was just wondering if you might prefer the top bed, ma'am," she said.

"Don't you *dare* 'ma'am' me! I'm not that old, thank you very much! If your eyes are that bad, you'll be shipped straight back here the moment the American doctors get a look at you, believe me. And I wouldn't have the top bunk if Emperor Franz Joseph himself gave it to me. One wrong turn in the night and I'd tumble out and break my neck. You'd like *that*, I'm sure!"

"Pardon me, *miss*," Zusa said smoothly. "You'll have to forgive my cousin. She hasn't got any manners, but what can you do? We can't pick our relatives. I'm stuck with her, but I wish there were some way that you wouldn't have to endure her company. Is there any chance you'd trade beds with me? I have a lower berth, too, on the other side of the ship."

The woman wrinkled her nose. "Why should I go to the trouble of moving my belongings to suit *you*? This bed's no prize, but for all I know, yours is worse."

Zusa placed one hand on the burlap-covered mattress in Raisa's bunk and pushed down. It crackled loudly and gave off a faint briny smell. "Hmm. Is yours stuffed with seaweed, too, miss, like this one?" she asked. "In that case, never mind trading. I've got one of the few mattresses on board that's stuffed with nice, fresh hay. I'd rather have my dreams haunted by meadows than mackerel!" She gave Raisa a kiss on the cheek and said, "Sorry, cousin, but you're on your own," before sauntering away.

The woman was out of her berth and had caught Zusa by the arm before she'd taken ten steps. Raisa listened, awestruck, as her new friend not only negotiated an exchange of beds, but got the woman to sweeten the deal with a handful of dried fruit from the supplies she'd brought aboard. It didn't take long to move the woman's luggage to Zusa's old place and bring Zusa's bags back. Soon the two girls were sitting on the lower berth, sharing the dried fruit and laughing together as if they'd been friends for years.

"How did you *do* that?" Raisa asked.

Zusa shrugged. "When my father was still alive—may he rest in peace—he was a horse trader, one of the best. I used to love watching him make deals on market days! What about your family? What was their business?"

Raisa shook her head. "I never knew my father, and I was very young when Mama died. Her friend Glukel took care of my sister Henda and me and taught us how to make clothes, but she never told us how our father made a living. Henda must have known, but I—I never thought to ask her."

"I wish I had a sister," Zusa said with a sigh. "It's just Mama and me, and her cousin Selig, the one who brought her over to America. Now it's finally my turn!" She popped a pinch of raisins into her mouth and chewed happily, then jumped up. "Say, now that you know where you're sleeping, we'd better get the rest of your things."

"What things?" Raisa asked. "I only have one bag and a basket."

"Well, do you see that grumpy-looking man down at that end of the hold? He's got to give you a meal pail and some utensils or you'll be drinking soup out of your bare hands! Oh, and he'll give you a life preserver, too."

"A life preserver?" Raisa echoed, eyes wide. "Do you think this ship will sink?"

Again Zusa shrugged. "I hope not, but who knows? Like Mama says, all we can do is pray and prepare. Meanwhile, do what everyone else does with it and use it for a pillow. It's the only one you'll have."

Raisa nibbled a prune, savoring the sweet taste. "Thank you for everything you did for me, Zusa," she said. "I'm sorry you had to give up your good mattress for one that smells like seaweed."

"Seaweed smells like the sea, and I like that," Zusa replied cheerfully. "Besides, it's just as comfortable as the ones stuffed with hay. In other words, not very. At least now when I turn over in my sleep and all that crackling wakes me up, I'll have someone to talk to!"

The great ship left Bremerhaven and began the westward voyage to America. Raisa and Zusa went up on deck to watch the departure together.

"How long before we arrive?" Raisa asked.

Zusa made a *who knows?* gesture. "Depends on the ship and the weather. It could take as long as twelve days, though I've heard some people make the crossing in only six. Rough seas can add days."

"Twelve days sounds like forever," Raisa said glumly.

"Why expect the worst? For us, probably about nine or ten days, God willing. I'm just glad we're living now, and not back when all they had were sailing ships. We'd be at sea for more than nine or ten *weeks!*"

"You know a lot, Zusa." Raisa spoke with honest admiration.

"It's nothing." Her new friend smiled. "I like to listen to

people and people like to talk. You learn plenty of interesting stories that way."

"I'd like to hear them. Nothing interesting ever happens to me."

Zusa chuckled. "If that's true, be thankful. I don't want an 'interesting' life. It's one thing to hear about narrow escapes and another to live through them."

"I think you're right."

The voyage went on, and soon the great ship was well on its way across the Atlantic, with nothing to be seen on the horizon but water and sky. For the first time in her life, Raisa had no real work to fill her hours. She was used to having tasks to do. Aside from time spent waiting on lines—when she wanted to wash up, to eat, to use the toilet—the routine of life aboard a ship did little to occupy her.

Thanks heaven for Zusa! she thought. Her new friend had a knack for finding ways to enjoy their time at sea. When the sea was calm, she made sure they spent every moment possible out on the deck. It got crowded when everyone else from steerage had the same idea, but early on the third day of the voyage, Zusa decreed they'd try to sneak into those parts of the ship reserved for the second-class passengers.

"What's the worst that can happen?" Zusa asked, grabbing Raisa's hand as they crept up a gangway.

"You always say that," Raisa said with a smile.

"Well, it's never a bad question. What *is* the worst that can happen, I mean *really* happen? Can they whip us? Can they drop us overboard? Can they send us back? Ha! Not likely. It costs the steamship company a *lot* of money for every person who's not allowed to land when we get there."

"I didn't know that," Raisa said.

Zusa bobbed her head vigorously. "Oh, it's true! That's why they take such pains to make sure everyone's in good health before they let us on the ship. And it's also why some people who aren't in the best of health try anything to fool the doctors. We don't want to go back and the company doesn't want to take us back, so we're all on the same side."

Zusa's bold venture didn't get far. She and Raisa were stopped by a member of the crew before they could set one foot onto the second-class deck.

"So, we're all on the same side, are we?" Raisa whispered mischievously as the two of them were herded back down the gangway. Zusa only pursed her lips and frowned.

The long, empty hours gave the girls plenty of time to talk about the lives they were leaving behind and the unknown prospects waiting for them in America. At first, Raisa kept the conversation light, telling Zusa amusing stories from the shtetl. She spoke about Henda only in passing, never mentioning her concerns about her older sister.

Zusa and I have only just met, she thought. *We're little more than strangers. How can I bother her with my worries?*

But by the fourth morning, Raisa suddenly found herself opening up to Zusa, pouring out the whole story of Henda's escape to America and all that had come after. She didn't know why she did it, only that it somehow felt right. *You're not a stranger,* Raisa thought, looking into Zusa's eyes. *You're my friend.*

"It's been four years that Henda and I have been apart," she said while Zusa listened attentively. "Even when she wrote to say she was sick, it wasn't so bad because we could pray that she'd get better, and be happy when her next letter told us she was healthy again. The only thing I regret is . . ." She folded her hands over the gold brooch with its missing pearl, pinned carefully to the bosom of her dress. "Don't laugh at me, Zusa, but I wish—I wish Henda could have written to *me,* sometimes. Just to me. It was hard, having to get all our news about her from Reb Avner for four whole years."

Zusa gave Raisa a hug. "Who's laughing? *I* wish the two of us had come from the same shtetl. Then I could've fixed that stupid Nathan so he wouldn't *dare* grab someone else's mail!"

"Well, even if I had gotten letters straight from my sister, I still couldn't have read them on my own." Confessing that made Raisa's cheeks turn pink.

"You didn't learn how to read?" Zusa tilted her head to one side and gave Raisa a curious look. It made her blush even more.

"A little. Not very well. Not like you. When we first met and you read my papers so easily *and* you could speak German to that crewman, that was wonderful!"

"Oh, that." Zusa waved away all of Raisa's admiration. "My father learned German in the horse-trading business. He taught it to me so we could pretend we had secrets we were keeping from Mama." Her smile faded. "I miss him."

"Was it hard, learning another language?" Raisa asked.

"I don't know how hard it was," Zusa answered. "I was so young when he started talking to me in German, I just picked it up, the same way I learned to speak Yiddish and Polish."

"I hope it won't be too hard for me."

"You want me to teach you German?" Zusa seemed surprised.

Raisa shook her head. "English."

"That I can't do," Zusa said. "But I wouldn't worry about it. It's not as if we'll *really* need it. Where you'll be living, you won't hear a single word of English for weeks at a time! It'll be like you never left the shtetl."

"But what if Henda's living somewhere else?"

Zusa snorted. "*No one* lives anywhere else. None of our people, anyway. Trust me, Mama told me exactly how it is over there. We live in one part of the city, the Italians in another, and it's the same for everyone else—the Irish, the Germans, even the Chinese. Just think of it, Raisa—we'll get to see real Chinese people! Isn't that exciting?"

"I suppose so." Raisa wasn't convinced, but she couldn't argue with Zusa's enthusiasm. "But—but won't *anyone* speak English?"

"Don't be silly, of course they will! And before too long,

you'll pick up enough words to get by. But it's nothing you need to worry about learning *now*."

Raisa had her doubts about that. She thought about Zusa and her father using German as their "secret" language. *I do need to learn English,* she thought. *I need to be able to get along wherever I go in this new land. If I can't understand the language, it's like being trapped behind a locked door.*

"*Now* what's bothering you?" Zusa's question broke into Raisa's thoughts. "You've got such a serious look on your face, you must be solving the whole world's problems!"

"Nothing that big," Raisa said. "Just mine. Zusa, I wonder . . . could you help me learn to read?"

"Read? Of course! Yiddish? German? Polish? You pick one, and I'll see what I can do for you before we make port. We don't have that much time."

"Just Yiddish." Raisa squeezed her friend's hand. "For now."

Raisa's reading lessons kept her occupied, though she was often frustrated. Because reading came easily to Zusa, she couldn't seem to grasp that it was a struggle for Raisa to remember the letters and turn them into words, sentences, and thoughts. Most of the time, Zusa lost her patience and read the lessons out loud for her, leaving Raisa to repeat things she didn't fully understand. After three days of this, she wasn't becoming a reader, just a very well-trained parrot.

The only bright spot in the midst of so much discouragement was the fact that Zusa had two different books to bring to the lessons. One was a women's prayer book, the other a novel called *The Wishing-Ring,* written by a man who went by the name of Mendele Mokher Sefarim, which meant *Mendel the little bookseller.* Raisa did her best to appreciate the lessons taken from the women's siddur, but she couldn't help sharing Zusa's contempt when she explained why it was written in Yiddish rather than Hebrew: "They don't think we're scholarly enough to master Hebrew, like the boys. Ha! I remember some of the yeshiva students back home. They didn't have the brains to know which end of the goat gives milk! But *we're* the ones who aren't smart enough to learn Hebrew?" She made a disgusted sound.

It was hard enough reading the prayers without carrying so much resentment as well. Whenever her lessons came from the women's siddur, they ended in failure. It was a different story when Zusa tried to help her get through *The Wishing-Ring.* Though the words still came to her with difficulty, Raisa was eager to do better. There were even times when she stopped Zusa from taking over and doing the reading for her.

"But you're struggling!" Zusa objected. "Why can't I tell you what it says? You never mind that when we're using the prayer book."

"I—I don't know why this is different, exactly," Raisa admitted. "I just know I'm enjoying the story, and you say he's written other books. Maybe one day I'll be able to find one, and when that happens, I'll need to be able to read it on my own."

"Suit yourself," Zusa said. "Keep trying. But remember, it's only a nine-day voyage."

On the seventh day of the crossing, the sea grew rough and any hope of completing the journey in nine days sank under the wild waves. Raisa woke up to the violent pitch and roll of the ship and sounds of loud moaning from her fellow passengers. A strong, sour stink was in the air, almost overwhelming the usual smell of haphazardly washed bodies and breakfast oatmeal. Raisa hooked her hands on the edge of her bunk and leaned over to see if Zusa was awake, too.

Zusa was lying on her side, reading the Sefarim novel. *She makes it look so easy!* Raisa thought with a twinge of envy. *Will it ever be that easy for me?*

Zusa put down the book and greeted her friend happily. "Well, good morning! How are you? Not seasick?"

"No. And you?"

"Not a bit." She sat up and swung her feet to the floor. "I didn't know I had such a strong stomach."

"I wish mine were stronger," Raisa said, pulling back from the edge of the bunk and resting her chin on her hands. "I don't mind the way the ship's moving, but this stench!"

"They can't help throwing up."

"I know, and I'm sorry they're suffering. I wish there was

something I could do for them. Do you think the ship's doctor has anything to cure seasickness?"

"If he does, he's saving it for the rich folk. Have you *seen* the look on his face when he handles our examinations? I heard he's supposed to look us over daily, but he can't stand the sight of us. No wonder he skips days, or sends an underling and hopes he'll get away with it! No, we'll be lucky if the crew comes down here to clean up the mess more than once."

"Do you think it's safe to go up onto the open deck?" Raisa asked, climbing down from her berth. "I want some fresh air."

"No harm in trying," Zusa replied, standing up and starting to dress. "It might be raining, but a little water won't hurt us. What's the worst that can happen?"

The line for the toilets that morning was longer than usual, but the line for breakfast was radically shorter. The crewman dishing out ladlefuls of gluey oatmeal encouraged them to come back for seconds. "Maybe third helpings, too," he said. "Don't hesitate; there'll be plenty."

The girls ate in the company of those few people who weren't suffering from the bad weather. Everyone spoke in hushed voices, not wanting to disturb the sick. Raisa couldn't help feeling guilty for being well in the midst of so much suffering. She and Zusa gobbled breakfast and quickly scrubbed and stowed their mess kits, eager to escape.

They were heading for the gangway to the upper decks when the ship gave a crazy lurch, sending them staggering sideways. Raisa was fighting for her balance when something small and solid rammed her hip, knocking her off her feet and into Zusa. They fell together, and in the next breath so did the little girl who'd caused the collision. She sprawled across Raisa's lap, hands splayed, arms outstretched helplessly, as two meal buckets filled with oatmeal flew from her grasp. They hit the floor with a dull crash and rolled away, splattering globs of cereal everywhere. The little girl gaped, then screwed up her face and let out a wail of total misery.

"Oh, you poor thing!" Raisa exclaimed, sitting up and brushing long strands of tangled honey-blonde hair out of the child's face. "Don't cry; there's plenty of cereal today. We'll help you get some more." She stood and offered her hand. "I'm Raisa. Who are you?"

The little girl let herself be helped up, her small, dirty fingers tightening on Raisa's hand like the claws of a tiny bird. "Brina," she said in a whisper.

Zusa got up and shook out her skirt, chuckling. "And how old are you, little kitten?" Instead of answering the question, Brina grabbed Raisa's dress with both hands and buried her face in the cloth. This made Zusa laugh louder. "Well, I can see who *her* favorite is!"

Together the girls took care of cleaning and refilling Brina's meal pails. With some gentle coaxing, Raisa got the shy child to lead them back to her bunk, while Zusa followed them, carrying breakfast. It took Brina several false starts before she found the right path. "No wonder," Raisa murmured in her friend's ear. "Can you imagine how confusing this place must be for such a little one?"

"*I* can't imagine the sort of parent who'd send a child this young to fetch breakfast," Zusa hissed back. "Mothers are supposed to take care of children, not the other way around!"

"Maybe she had a good reason," Raisa said. "Maybe she's taking care of her other children. Maybe she's got a baby to nurse."

"Maybe she's just lazy," Zusa concluded.

Brina stopped beside a bunk that was tucked away in one of the darkest corners of the hold. The upper berth was unoccupied, as were the bunks nearby. The little girl crouched down and reached one hand into the shadows. "Mama? Breakfast, Mama."

Someone groaned in the darkness. Raisa bent down to peer at the woman, who turned over slowly on the crackling burlap mattress, her body huddled under an oversize black wool coat even though the ship's steerage section was so warm. The woman's thin lips parted with a sigh.

"Brina?" she said, her voice trembling. "Come to Mama, my darling." The little girl obeyed, creeping into the bunk and her mother's outstretched arms. Only then did the woman speak to Raisa and Zusa. "Thank you for bringing her back. She was gone so long, I was afraid that . . ." She bit her lip. "I'm sorry. I know she shouldn't be left to run around the ship on her own—she's not even five years old yet. But I'm—I'm so tired. That's all. I'm in good health, but the trip to Bremerhaven, and no one willing to help me with all of our things, and so many stairs to climb once we were on board!"

"And then this bad weather," Raisa added, patting the woman's shoulder. "You're not the only person who can't be up and about today."

"I hope you'll be able to eat a little something," Zusa put in, setting down the pails. "It might settle your stomach."

"I'll try," the woman said, but she made no move to let go of her child or to reach for the pail full of oatmeal.

"It'll be easier if we look after Brina for you," Raisa volunteered. "We can give her her breakfast over by our bunks and take care of her for the rest of the day."

The woman's arms closed more tightly around her daughter. "Oh, I couldn't! She'd be too much trouble for you, Miss—Miss—"

"I'm Raisa and this is Zusa. She won't be any trouble at all. In fact"—she offered the weary mother a reassuring smile—"taking care of her will keep *us* out of trouble. Honestly, you'd be doing us a favor."

"This is so kind of you." Brina's mother held her child close and spoke to her. "Will you go with them, sweetheart? You'll have fun." Brina looked from her mother's pale face to Raisa and Zusa, then gave the slightest nod. "That's my good angel." Her mother urged her gently out of the bunk. "Now, you behave nicely while you're with them and do as they say. I love you."

"I love you, too, Mama," Brina said, giving her mother one more hug before offering her tiny hand to Raisa.

The girls took Brina's meal pail with them and went back to their bunks. Brina had a healthy appetite and made short work of the oatmeal. The rest of the day was spent playing games, singing songs, and sharing stories. Brina's eyes sparkled with joy, though Raisa couldn't help but notice the faint shadow of fear lingering on the child's face.

She's in a strange place, going somewhere she can't even imagine, and her mother's not well. She must be scared half to death, she thought. *Poor little one; I have to make it better for her.* Aloud, Raisa asked, "Would you like to go look at the ocean, Brina? Maybe we'll see fish or birds."

"Are you sure we should take her out on deck?" Zusa asked. "It's still pretty rough."

"We'll put on her life preserver, and we'll both hold her hands the whole time."

"If she'll let me," Zusa said. "You're the one she likes. She must be able to tell you're the one who knows how to be a good sister."

"Don't tell me you're jealous," Raisa teased.

"Not at all. Here." Zusa thrust the empty meal pail into Raisa's hands. "Big sisters get to do the washing."

Raisa left Brina in Zusa's care while she went to clean the pail. On her way back from the washing facilities, she decided it might be a good idea to pick up the child's life preserver and take care of her mother's meal pail at the same time. She threaded her way back to Brina's berth and found the mother sleeping, her breakfast untouched. Raisa cast her eyes around until she found Brina's life preserver on the upper bunk, then hesitated a while, debating if she should trouble the sleeping woman with questions about whether she wanted the cold oatmeal left for her or cleared away. In the end she decided that the woman needed sleep and left her.

As soon as Brina saw Raisa coming back, she broke away from Zusa and ran to hug her. In spite of her protests about not caring if the child played favorites, Zusa sounded a little cranky when she remarked, "She'll need a coat, too, if we're going outside."

"I don't know where to look for that, and her mother's asleep. I don't want to disturb her. Brina can wear my coat."

"So you'll get sick and be sent back when we land? *Not* a good plan." Zusa dug into her own bags and handed Raisa a thick sweater. "She can wear this, though I'm sure she won't let *me* put it on her."

Brina loved the sea. It was all that Raisa and Zusa could do to hold on to the child's hands. Once up on deck, she squirmed out of their grasp and ran to the ship's rail, where she clung like a monkey, gazing out over the choppy water. The girls raced after her, grabbed her arms, and gave her a scolding, but she didn't seem to hear it. Her face was covered with spray and radiantly happy.

They walked the deck together, holding hands. Sometimes

Raisa and Zusa lifted Brina high between them and swung her, making the child squeal with delight. The crewmen who watched them stroll past smiled, and one of them gave the girls some raspberry hard candy. By the time they returned to the steerage compartment, Brina was red cheeked and ready for a nap. She fell asleep sitting up on the edge of Zusa's bunk while Raisa was unfastening her life preserver.

"Would you look at that?" Zusa said, shaking her head. She knelt beside Raisa and helped place the sleeping child comfortably in her bed. "Do you think she'll wake up in time for lunch?"

"Lunch?" Raisa echoed, only half hearing her friend. She was too preoccupied with trying to remove Brina's shoes and get the child tucked in.

"Never mind. I'll go bring back something for all of us." Zusa picked up the two meal pails and headed off.

Brina slept through lunch but woke up hungry when it was almost the dinner hour. The sea had grown calmer, and many of the ailing passengers had recovered their appetites. The line for food distribution was long and tempers were short. Zusa stared at the bickering crowd and sighed as she reached for the meal pails.

"No, let me do it this time," Raisa said, grabbing the pails before Zusa could get them. "I'll go see if Brina's mother wants something, too." She gave Brina some dried apples she'd saved from lunch, then headed for the child's berth.

She found Brina's mother sitting up in bed, picking at the

cold oatmeal in her meal pail. "Oh, please don't eat that!" Raisa cried. "It must be awful. Let me bring you something fresh."

The woman looked pleased. "My dear, it's good of you to offer, but I'm feeling better now. I'll be able to get dinner for Brina and me. How is she? I hope she hasn't been too much bother." Raisa told her all about Brina's morning adventures, which made the child's mother even happier. "My little one is very lucky to have met you, Raisa," the woman said. "But I can't take advantage of your good nature. I can look after my own child."

"Why don't you let us keep her until it's her bedtime?" Raisa suggested. "You'll be able to eat your dinner in peace, and I'll make sure she eats well before I bring her back to you tonight."

The woman raised one milky hand. "No need, really. I've been alone too much as it is, ever since my husband died, may he rest in peace. I want to look after my own child."

Reluctantly, Raisa did as Brina's mother asked. The woman was just getting out of her bunk when the little girl ran back into her arms. The most Raisa could do was clean the congealed oatmeal out of the mother's meal pail before bidding both of them good-bye and going to collect dinner for herself and Zusa.

"Why the long face?" Zusa asked as the two of them ate their dinner. "We won't land for at least three more days, thanks to the bad weather. You'll see lots more of your little friend before that. We can even ask her mother where they're going to stay after they get off the boat, and I'll write it down for you. It's not as if they're going to drop off the face of the earth."

"You don't have to do that," Raisa said. "I did like taking care of Brina, but once we're in New York City, we'll all have other things to keep us busy. Of course, there's no reason I can't spend more time with her *before* the ship docks."

"No reason at all," Zusa agreed. "In fact, I'll bet that little pest will come looking for you tomorrow, and the next day, and the next, until you can't wait to see the last of her!" They both laughed.

But the eighth day of the voyage passed without any sighting of the little girl or her mother. Their bunks were too far away from Raisa's to allow an accidental meeting, and though she searched the crowds while waiting for meals or toilets or the washing facilities, they were never there at the same time she was. She and Zusa filled the time with more reading lessons and walks in the sunshine on deck. It was the same story on the ninth day. Raisa grew uneasy. She couldn't seem to give her full attention to Zusa's lessons.

"Is there a *reason* your head's in the clouds?" Zusa finally asked, exasperated.

"You'll think I'm silly, but I'm . . . I'm worried about Brina," Raisa admitted. "I haven't seen her or her mother for two days, not even when we're served our meals."

"It's a big ship with lots of people aboard," Zusa said,

dismissing Raisa's concerns. "They probably get their food at different times than we do."

"I suppose you're right," Raisa said reluctantly.

"Of course I am! Now, do you want to go back to *The Wishing-Ring* again or would you rather take another walk?"

That night, Raisa slept badly. Her dreams were filled with swirling images of ordinary people and places that melted into monstrous creatures. There was no up, no down, and the nightmare skies went from sun to storm to dazzling starlight before drowning her in total darkness. She woke up gasping.

Then she realized she was not alone in her bunk. A small, warm body was clinging to her side. By the dim light of the steerage lamps she saw Brina, her eyes brimming with tears, her tiny fist pressed hard against her mouth.

"Brina?" Raisa whispered, gently taking the little girl into her arms. "What are you doing here? Is something wrong?"

The child opened her mouth to speak, but all that came out was a wild, heartbroken wail.

"Heaven have mercy, what's all the racket?" Zusa moaned from the lower berth. Other people occupying neighboring bunks added their grumbles and curses to the noise Brina was making. Raisa did her best to hush the child, holding her on her lap and rocking back and forth. She'd just gotten Brina's howling muted down to soft sobs when Zusa's sleepy face appeared over the edge of the bed. "What's she doing here? Got lost trying to find the toilet on her own?"

"I don't know," Raisa said. "But I'm going to find out." She climbed out of her berth, put on her shoes, and offered her arms to Brina. The child wrapped her thin arms around Raisa's neck and held her so tightly it felt as if she'd never let go.

Zusa trailed after the two of them as Raisa carried Brina back to her own bunk. There wasn't much light in that part of steerage. When Raisa bent down to peer into the lower berth where Brina's mother slept, she could see only shadows. "Excuse me, ma'am," she said. "I'm sorry to bother you, but—" She stopped. The lower berth was very, very quiet.

Wordlessly Raisa stood up and handed Brina to Zusa. The child didn't want the change, but Raisa was firm. Zusa's face creased with anxiety. She began to ask a question that faded from her lips as Raisa bent down again and leaned into the darkened bunk.

The woman's hands lay cold on top of the overcoat that was her blanket. Her face was so white that Raisa could see it even in the shadows. There was no sound of breathing. Raisa closed her eyes and murmured a prayer before turning back to Zusa and Brina.

"I think—I think you should go get one of the crew," Raisa told her friend. "You can speak German." She took Brina back and hugged the little girl fiercely. "I'll take her to our berths."

"All right," Zusa said. "But I don't think the doctor will come down to steerage."

"He won't have to," Raisa said. She carried Brina away.

Chapter Four

THE GOLDEN LAND

Raisa took Brina to the shelter of Zusa's lower berth and huddled there while steerage erupted into an uproar as word of the woman's death spread. She saw several crewmen briskly going about the necessary business of restoring order, heard hysterical shrieking as people demanded to know whether the cause of death was anything contagious, and tried to give the child in her arms a little comfort by singing all the lullabies she could remember. When she ran out of songs, she turned to storytelling, but her attempts to distract Brina were interrupted when a young crewman stopped beside the bunk, squatted, and asked her to come with him. He spoke good Polish, so there was no problem understanding him.

"This is the child, yes?" he asked, his eyes filled with pity as he looked at Brina. She responded by burying her head against Raisa's neck.

"Her name is Brina," Raisa said. "Can you tell me what—why her mother—you know?"

"The ship's doctor said it must have been her heart. He claims she was fine whenever he examined her."

If he examined her at all, Raisa thought bitterly.

"I'm surprised the company doctors didn't find a problem before she boarded," the young man went on. "But these things happen. How well did you know her? Did she mention any family besides this little one? Did she say anything about her plans once they got to New York City?"

Raisa shook her head. "We didn't speak much. All I know is that she was a widow. Maybe she was carrying something that said—"

"Nothing." The crewman sighed. "This is very bad. Poor angel." He patted Brina's hair.

"What's going to happen to her?" Raisa asked. "Will they send her back?"

"Back to where? Back to whom?" The young man raised his hands, helpless. "There's been some sort of irregularity with the records concerning this child and her mother, places where the information is incomplete. How could such a thing have escaped notice? It's terrible. We don't know how to find the child's relatives on either side of the ocean, or even if she has any family at all. With no one to take responsibility for her, she'll be sent back by the United States immigration authorities and that will cost the shipping company a lot of money. They have to pay a big fine for every immigrant who's rejected at Ellis Island, you know, and that's besides the expense of her passage back. And for what? So they can put her in a German orphanage? I'm betting that our captain pulls some strings and calls in some favors once we land so that he can stow her in an orphanage in New York. If he can do that, at least the shipping company won't have to foot the bill for her return."

An uneasy look came into his eyes. "I wish there were another choice for her. I once shipped with a sailor from New York. He, too, was orphaned young and packed off to one of those places. The stories he told!" A small but noticeable shiver shook the young man's body. "Whatever the captain decides, it will be a dreadful fate for the child either way."

"No," Raisa said, gripping Brina. "He can't do that to her. I won't let him!"

"Ah, that's easy to say," the crewman replied. "But to do—"

"I *won't* let him!" Raisa repeated even more forcefully, though she had no idea how she was going to stop the captain. All she knew was that this was something she could not allow to happen.

"You're a good, brave girl," the young man said, admiration in his eyes. "If it all depended on courage alone, I'd feel sorry for our captain, going up against you."

"Is that where you're taking us?" Raisa asked, her heart beating faster. "To see the captain?"

The young man gave a short, sharp laugh. "He has better things to do. One of the ship's junior officers will question you and report his recommendations about the child to our captain. That friend of yours is already there, the one who noti-fied us about the dead—about this child's mama." He patted Brina's golden curls again and clicked his tongue. "So young, and alone. Such a great misfortune."

The ship's officer was waiting in a small, unoccupied second-class cabin. He sat stiffly in a wooden chair with Zusa standing nearby, fidgeting. His eyes glittered coldly when he saw Raisa and Brina; his mouth became small and hard as a chip of flint. The young sailor who had brought Raisa and Brina into his presence snapped to attention and gave the man a smart salute that was returned brusquely, followed by a long, intense burst of German. While Raisa's escort was responding to this, she moved next to Zusa. The two girls exchanged wary looks.

"What's he been saying to you?" Raisa whispered, nodding at the officer, who was still involved in conversation with the crewman.

"He wants to know about Brina's family," Zusa hissed back. "Whatever happened—if it was just a terrible slipup or if maybe her mother had a reason to bribe someone to let her and Brina aboard with irregular documents—this man isn't going to let his ship or his company take the blame. They've gone through her mother's things. They found no mention of any relatives or family friends and they're mad as wet cats about that."

"Well, that's because if they can't turn her over to someone in New York City, they'd have to pay to—"

Abruptly, the ship's officer snapped his head in Raisa's direction and bellowed at her. The crewman translated: "He says you are to keep quiet unless you have something you want to say to him."

"I was only telling—" Raisa began.

Again the officer shouted at her and the translation came: "He says that if he wanted to listen to a lot of dirty Jew-chatter, he would filthy his boots on the doorstep of one of your damned synagogues." The young crewman spoke as if his words were saying something as simple and self-evident as *The grass is green* or *The sky is blue*. There was no hint of shame or apology in his voice or his expression.

Raisa's face burned. She took a long, deep breath and wished she could let it out as a stream of fire. *What did we ever do to them?* Brina whimpered and squirmed in her arms.

All at once, Zusa spoke up, addressing the ship's officer directly in German. He looked dubious, but with a lift of his eyebrows and a faint nod, he beckoned his translator to bend close. The two men conferred in inaudible murmurs until at last the young sailor turned to relay the essence of their conversation.

"He begs your pardon, miss," the translator told Raisa with a broad grin. "He was unaware that you and your friend here are not Jewish. He thought he heard you speaking in that tongue, but clearly he was mistaken. He asks your patience while he examines the few documents the dead woman brought on board with her. With luck, we will be able to settle the child's fate soon enough and take her off your hands."

Raisa gave Zusa a hard stare. In the softest of whispers she demanded, "Is that what you just told him? That we're not Jews?"

"You see how he is," Zusa whispered back. "He'll be nicer to Brina if he thinks she's not Jewish, either."

"Unless there's something in her mother's belongings to tell him otherwise."

"Don't worry about that, Raisa. I've been standing here longer than you. That poor woman had nothing but some clothing and a few household goods. Her only papers came from the steamship company, and from what I've overheard, they've got more holes than a beggar's coat. Her name isn't going to give her away, either. We're lucky that our official friend has cheese for brains. As far as he's concerned, good Polish Christian peasants are all naming their daughters Brina, Raisa, and Zusa."

"So you lied for Brina's sake?" Raisa said. Zusa nodded. "Good. Then you're used to it." Raising her voice, she called out to the young crewman, "Sir, please tell the good officer that we're sorry to have put him to such trouble. All we want to do is care for our little cousin, and make sure there will be no problems when we're the ones to take her off the boat instead of her mother."

The sailor gawked at her. "Your . . . cousin?" Raisa nodded briskly. She didn't dare look at Zusa. If there was the smallest sign of misgiving in her friend's expression, she was afraid she would lose control of her own face and betray her daring lie.

There was more quick conferral between the translator and the officer, followed by the inevitable question: "Why did neither of you say anything about this earlier?"

Zusa leaped at the question, babbling in German. When she was done, the ship's officer stood up, gave her the scant handful of documents, and flung a last burst of harsh words in her face before marching out of the room. The next instant, the young crewman who had fetched Raisa and Brina was shepherding all three girls back down to steerage.

"May all be well with you," he said kindly before leaving them.

Holding Brina tight, Raisa sat down carefully on the edge of Zusa's bunk and let out a loud "Whew!"

"The next time you decide to pull something like that, give me some warning," Zusa said, leaning against the wall. "I had to think *too* fast there."

"I knew you could do it," Raisa told her. "So, how *did* you explain it?"

"I said that I was too scared to mention it because I thought he was the ship's captain and I would never dare speak up to such an exalted person." Zusa lifted her chin high and pushed up the tip of her nose with one finger. "He yelled at me for wasting his time." She glanced at the papers. "So we've got a cousin. What do we do with her now? More important, what will we do after we land?"

"What do you think we do? We keep her safe." Raisa stroked Brina's back. The child had fallen asleep in her arms despite all the commotion of the meeting with the ship's officer. "We'll have plenty of help once we reach New York City."

"I hope so." Zusa didn't sound convinced. "Mama and cousin Selig wrote that we haven't got a lot of room."

"She's going to stay with Henda and me," Raisa maintained. "All that you and your family will need to do is help me find her address. I have it written down, but I won't know my way around the city."

"You're sure your sister won't mind?"

Raisa shook her head emphatically. "When our mama died, Henda and I were welcomed to a new family. We'll do the same for Brina with all our hearts."

The ship and her passengers enjoyed fair weather for the remaining three days of the voyage. Raisa's reading lessons were set aside as she and Zusa dealt with their new responsibility. Zusa secured the child's meager belongings, including her mother's few articles of clothing, and Raisa took care of the girl herself. It wasn't easy. Brina's every waking moment seemed to be filled with storms of tears and howls for her mother. She refused to eat, she wouldn't sleep anywhere except in Raisa's arms, and her rest was broken by recurring nightmares.

"My God, can't you give that child something to keep her quiet?" someone yelled from a nearby berth when Brina's terrified shrieks shattered the night.

"If I could, I'd give you a double dose!" Raisa shouted back. Her nerves were frayed from lack of sleep, but when the anger in her voice made Brina cry even louder, she was ashamed. "Hush, hush my precious," she murmured, rocking the sobbing child. "Everything's going to be all right."

Brina refused to be comforted. "Mama!" she wailed. "I want Mama! Where's Mama? Why did she go away?" All Raisa could do was repeat her empty words of comfort and try to hold back her own tears.

On the eleventh morning, she woke up to find three women and a girl standing patiently beside her berth, watching her. Raisa freed her arm from under the sleeping child's back, sat up, and returned their gazes with a puzzled look and a hesitant "Good morning?"

The three women smiled, and all of them began talking at once. Raisa couldn't understand a word they said, though from their gestures she guessed they were talking about Brina. Only the girl stayed silent. She looked a little older than Raisa and Zusa, with a single braid of shining black hair trailing over one shoulder and down the front of her dress, past her waist. While the women chattered away, the girl's luminous dark eyes were fixed on Brina's drowsing face.

The clamor woke Brina, who went from deep sleep to wide-awake fright in a second. She began to whimper, grabbing Raisa, while the women swarmed closer, still chattering, all of them vying to take the child into their arms. Their faces were kind and compassionate, but Brina was having none of it. Her whimpers turned to high-pitched cries of distress, and she dug her fingers so deeply into the flesh of Raisa's upper arms that it felt as if she was gripping the bones.

"Signore, per l'amor di Dio, lasciate fare a me!"

The raven-haired girl shoved her way between the women and the upper berth and pushed aside their outstretched hands. They glowered at her, but she held her ground, pointing at Brina's fear-stunned face and rattling off fiery words whose meaning flew straight over Raisa's head. Little by little, the girl's voice softened, and her expression went from stern to charming. The women muttered among themselves, then one of them said a few words in a grudging tone and they walked away.

"What was *that* all about?" Zusa asked testily from the lower berth.

"I have no idea," Raisa said. She looked to the black-haired girl and even though she doubted she would be understood, she told her, "Thank you very much. I'm sure they were trying to help, but she"—she hugged Brina—"she's too little and too upset to know that. This is Brina. That's Zusa. I'm Raisa." She clarified her introductions by indicating each of them in turn and hoping for the best.

"Luciana," the girl responded, touching her fingertips lightly to her chest. *"Luciana Delvecchio. Vengo da Livorno."*

Communicating with Luciana was like being caught in a strange but fascinating dream. At first it seemed that her only language was Italian, though when Zusa impulsively tested speaking a bit of German to her, Luciana stumbled through a confusing answer combining both tongues. Zusa puzzled long and hard over her reply before declaring, "I told her that I hoped her relatives—you know, those three women who scared poor Brina to pieces—weren't mad at her for chasing them away. She said they're Italian, like she is, but not family. She's traveling alone. I *think* she said that her father had relatives in Germany. I can't figure out much more. At least it explains why she can speak a little of the language and why she sailed from a German port."

Luciana plainly disliked the effort it cost her to use her scanty German, because her conversation with Zusa was the last time she uttered a word in that language. When she spoke Italian, Raisa and Zusa couldn't understand one word, and their Yiddish was just as alien to her, yet the three girls somehow managed to harness gestures, facial expressions, and sheer persistence to communicate. It turned out that Luciana had another means of communication at hand. She carried a little book of blank pages, many already filled with drawings from her travels, and used a pencil to sketch what she couldn't say. Soon she was entertaining Brina with pictures of Raisa, Zusa, the other passengers, and the child herself.

"Luciana, this is wonderful!" Raisa exclaimed over the girl's most recent sketch. "You've drawn more than Zusa's face; you've captured her spirit."

"A fine capture!" Zusa grumbled, looking at the drawing over Raisa's shoulder. "She's made me look like a fox who's just stolen every chicken in the henhouse."

"But a happy fox," Raisa pointed out, giggling. "I thought you were proud to be so clever." Zusa only snorted.

Luciana also helped calm Brina. The women she'd herded

away came back later that day, bringing small treats and comforts for the child. A warm blanket, a bit of rock candy, and a faceless rag doll sewn together out of scraps all worked their small magic. Luciana acted as the go-between, since Brina was still easily overwhelmed by strange faces. The women stood at a little distance and let the Italian girl give the child their offerings while Raisa and Zusa told her to thank the good ladies. Brina never thanked them with words, but she actually smiled at them, then let go of Raisa's hand, ran across the gently rolling floor, and gave each of them a lightning-fast hug before dashing back to safety. Their delighted laughter made her jump into Zusa's berth and hide her head under the life preserver, which only made everyone laugh more.

That evening, a uniformed man came down to the steerage section when everyone was lined up to get dinner. He blew three short blasts on a brass whistle, shouted something in German into the silence that followed, and left. Little pockets of animated talk opened up throughout the crowd as those who understood his words translated for those who did not. The news spread like ripples on a pond until steerage rocked with the din of enthusiastic chatter.

Raisa was among the first to know what was going on. As soon as the uniformed man finished speaking, Zusa grabbed her arm and gleefully cried, "Tomorrow, Raisa! We land tomorrow! We'll never have to spend another night aboard this ship; we're almost *there*!"

The girls ate in a hurry and began searching around their

berths for any possessions they'd taken out of their baggage in the course of the voyage. Everything had to be retrieved and secured for the next day's debarkation. Brina made it clear that she wanted to help. The little girl became so excited that Raisa wondered if she'd be able to get her to go to bed at all. *Never mind that,* she thought. *I wonder if I'll be able to sleep tonight!*

As it turned out, she didn't have to worry about Brina. She fell asleep almost as soon as Raisa lifted her into the upper berth. Raisa lay cradling the child in one arm and staring at the ceiling, thoughts racing. *Tomorrow . . . America! Just one more day and I'll be with Henda again! Dear Lord, how will I be able to find her house? Wait, I don't have to worry about that. Zusa's mother and cousin have been living in New York City for a long time. They must know all the streets. I hope Henda doesn't live too far away. I don't know if Brina can walk that much, and I don't know how else we're supposed to get around. Maybe Zusa's family has a horse cart. Oh! Where did I hide my money?*

She crawled out of bed and fumbled for the hem of the dress she would wear the next day. She'd sewn most of her remaining money inside. It was a precaution prompted by the memory of the shtetl innkeeper's wife coming home in hysterics from a grand trip to her sister's home, in Lublin, where the city pickpockets had stolen every coin to her name. *Why didn't I listen to my sister?* the poor woman had sobbed. *She told me to sew the money into my dress, but I didn't. Now this!*

Raisa's own coins clinked softly, reassuring her. *I'll have to exchange this for American money. And I'll have to get a job. And*

I'll have to learn English, a whole new language, but . . . not too soon, I hope. I have too much trouble learning anything. Zusa is so impatient, trying to teach me how to read, that I must be very stupid. She sighed, climbed back in beside Brina, and with a last faint thought—*maybe learning English won't be as hard as learning how to read*—she fell asleep.

She woke up with Zusa shaking her by the shoulder. "Get up! Get up! They're letting us off the ship by groups, and they've just called our numbers. Come on."

"What?" Raisa asked, still half asleep. She patted the empty space next to her in the bunk. "Where—"

"She's right here, dressed and ready to go. Now, hurry!"

Raisa rolled out of her bed and got dressed as fast as she could, with Zusa hurrying her every step of the way. They grabbed their traveling bags, Raisa took Brina's hand, and they joined the flow of passengers climbing the stairs to the open deck and the new land. Raisa's stomach grumbled. There was no breakfast being served this morning. As the passengers filed out of steerage, members of the ship's crew made sure to collect their empty meal pails and utensils.

Out on deck, it was still dark. *Did we land in the middle of the night?* Raisa wondered, until she became aware of a faint glow on the far side of the ship. Dawn was coming. In the dim light she thought she caught sight of her friend Luciana, her black braid like a streak of ink down the back of her bright green flowered shawl, but the shadows shifted and she was gone.

"A fine thing!" said a grouchy voice behind Raisa. "To come

all this way, and not to see it!" It was an old Jewish man, being helped along by his family. He pounded his walking stick on the deck and refused to stop protesting. "It's a shame, that's what it is! When my cousin Tsvi came here, it was all he could write home about in that first letter. How tall! How beautiful! How majestic! And now that God has seen fit to let me live long enough to come to the Golden Land, how do I arrive? In the night, like a thief! In an hour as black as a Cossack's heart!"

"Papa, Papa, please, you'll upset yourself," a middle-aged woman beside him crooned. "You'll see it, I promise you."

"When?" he countered. "We sailed right past the island in the dark! That's what one of the sailors told me when I asked him about seeing it."

"What's the matter with him?" Raisa asked Zusa. "What did we sail past?"

"I don't know," Zusa replied. "But I'll bet it was something good."

The girls moved along in the crowd as it carried them across the deck, down the gangplank, and along the pier. Raisa's legs felt wobbly walking on solid planks instead of a swaying deck. Several times she nearly lost her hold on Brina's hand. The going was not easy, since she was not only minding the child but also carrying Brina's belongings in a bag that had belonged to her dead mother. The poor woman hadn't owned much, so Raisa was able to tote it under one arm, her hand clutching the handle of her own satchel.

The people were steered like cattle, herded in the shadow of the great steamship. Self-important men in crisp, dark uniforms seemed to be everywhere at once, asking questions in many languages, consulting lists, taking names, pinning cards to everyone's coats, and handing out other cards accompanied by instructions that sounded like threats: "Hold on to that if you don't want to be sent back!" And at the end of all that, Raisa found herself, Brina, and Zusa pressed beside the cranky old man and his daughter on the wide-open deck of a small, foul-smelling boat. A horn tooted and the vessel began moving away from the dock almost as soon as the last passenger was aboard.

"Wait!" Raisa cried, dropping the bags and waving the cards she'd been given for herself and Brina. "There's been a mistake. They're sending us back, but we've still got our cards! Zusa, for heaven's sake, we have to *tell* them we're going to New York City and not—"

"Stop fussing, girl," a bony, black-clad woman cut in. "We're being taken to New York City right now. Nothing's wrong. The ship docked in Hoboken, just the way it was supposed to."

"Hoboken?" Raisa had a bit of trouble pronouncing it.

"It's in New Jersey, just across the river from New York. My son told me all about what to expect when he sent for me." She puffed herself up proudly. "We're on the ferry for Ellis Island, and from there we'll be taken to New York City. All provided that we pass inspection, naturally. You *are* in good health?" Raisa nodded, speechless. "Then you have nothing to fear." The woman's smile was as thin as she was, but it was warm.

She produced three pieces of dry bread from her bag as if by magic. "My son also warned me that sometimes the ships dock before breakfast. The company doesn't mind saving a little money on feeding us, and what do they care if we're hungry? So I put aside something extra at dinner last night. I'm sorry, this is all I have left."

The girls thanked her and devoured the bread. All at once, Raisa heard a growing clamor from the far side of the ferry. She turned at the sound. By now, the sky was a pearly blue banded with pink and violet on the horizon. A sliver of rising sun sent a path of gold rippling over the water. Something the fresh color of springtime grass towered in the distance. The closer the ferry sailed toward that green beacon, the louder the passengers' voices grew. Raisa and Zusa leaned against one another, straining to see.

"Papa! Papa, look! See? You didn't miss it after all!" the old man's daughter cried. "There! Do you see her?"

"I see," the old man replied. Tears were streaming down his cheeks. "I see. Blessed art Thou, O Lord our God, King of the universe, who has granted us life and sustenance and permitted us to reach this season."

Raisa stared at the ever-growing image of a magnificently robed and crowned woman, her right hand holding a torch to the sky. As the ferry sailed closer, Raisa picked up Brina so the child could share the wonder of such a sight. "Look, darling!" she exclaimed. "She's wearing the sun!" Brina crowed with joy and stretched out her arms to the woman.

"We're here, Raisa." Zusa's normal tone—playful, joking, mischievous—was gone. The woman's upraised torch cast an enchantment that transformed her voice, filling it with the soft breath of wonder and awe. "We're *here*. It isn't a dream anymore. We've truly reached the Golden Land!"

Chapter Five

"HAVE YOU SEEN MY SISTER?"

"I don't believe it," Zusa said as the girls got their first look inside the big brick buildings of Ellis Island. "It's as if there's no one left anywhere else in the world. They've all come here!"

Raisa had to agree. Although she couldn't truthfully say she'd recognize every single person from steerage, she had a rough idea of how many passengers had shared her voyage from Bremerhaven. Once the Hoboken ferry had docked at Ellis Island, everyone aboard was urged from the landing, up some stairs, and into a great hall mobbed with so many people it was impossible to think they'd all come from just one ship. The confusion, the noise, and the smell were overpowering. Worst of all was the waiting, watching groups being separated from the crowd and led away to who knew where and who knew what fate.

Officials stepped in and out of the swarm of waiting immigrants, making order. Raisa heard her name called as part of one group, gathered up her bags, instructed Brina to hold tight to her skirt, and stepped forward. Zusa followed, only to be told in crisp, definite terms that her name was *not* part of this group and that she would have to wait like everyone else.

"Oh well, I'll see you later, then," she said to Raisa. "I probably won't be too long catching up to you. We'll meet later."

"Of course," Raisa replied, smiling at her friend. But she was only half listening, too distracted to add, *But* where *will we meet, Zusa?* That question didn't seem to be so important to her just then. Her first priority was the little girl in her keeping. The official hadn't called Brina's name, either, and she had to give her full attention to making sure that she and the child weren't separated. Fortunately, Ellis Island teemed with staff who spoke more than one language. It wasn't hard for the peevish official to locate someone fluent in Yiddish, though before that person spoke a word to Raisa, he examined the list of names from which the first man was working. Raisa had no idea why the first official scowled and grumbled, until the second man smirked and told her, "The little girl's name is there, all right, written in next to yours. If that stupid jackass knew how to read better, he wouldn't have had to drag me over here for nothing."

Raisa and Brina fell into line with the other members of their group. They passed from the great hall into a smaller space, where interpreters told them to turn over the cards they'd been given aboard the ship. Raisa had jammed Brina's card and her own deep into the pocket of her coat. Even though it was warm in the building and growing warmer by the minute, she didn't dare remove the coat. She saw how easy it would be for things to go astray in the throng. Now she dug out the cards and waited.

Brina began to moan, "I'm hungry!" Raisa shushed her with promises that they would have something good to eat soon, though she didn't believe it. And yet there was food somewhere. She caught the occasional whiff of cooking, mixed with the smells of sweat, disinfectant, and the sea.

She thanked God when it came time for her to turn in the two cards and the officials allowed her to take Brina with her. For all she knew they might have insisted that she and Brina go through the process separately. Together they filed along with the other passengers down a row of men in white coats all carrying stethoscopes, just like the one the ship's doctor had used.

The medical examination was short but dreadful. Raisa tried to stay calm for Brina's sake. She had no idea what each doctor was looking for, or if having the approval of steamship company doctors to leave Bremerhaven would be good enough to let her arrive in New York City. The overall noise of the hall was sometimes spiked by the sound of a woman's cry of distress, a man's raw howl of grief, a child's shriek of terror. Raisa could only imagine what was causing so much suffering.

Something's wrong and they're being sent back, she thought while the doctor made her remove her kerchief and a nearby translator had her explain once again the reason for her shorn head. The bite of the steel delousing comb was nothing compared with the pain of apprehension. *What if he finds something wrong with me? I can't go back, not now! Especially not now. What will happen to Brina if they send me away?* She mumbled a prayer she remembered from Zusa's book and added her own words, begging God for help.

She was so wrapped up in her fearful thoughts that she was not paying attention to what was happening to the passengers ahead of her. Their sharp gasps and startled exclamations were nowhere near as loud as the more violent, terrifying cries from elsewhere in the processing area and failed to distract her from her worries. It was only the sound of the interpreter's voice that finally had the power to jerk her attention back to the moment. "Very good," he said, a tight smile on his lips. "Now, there is one last thing. You'll have to hold your sister very still for this, you know. Can you do it?"

"She's my cousin," Raisa said mechanically. "I can do whatever you need me to do for her."

The interpreter's smile warmed slightly. "That's what we like to hear." He turned to the next doctor in line and said something that got a satisfied nod in response. As the two girls approached the waiting doctor, Raisa saw that he was holding a coldly glittering instrument in his hand. It was a metal buttonhook, a device that looked much like the hooked needle Raisa used when she set aside her sewing in order to crochet shawls and stockings for the winter—although a buttonhook wasn't used for crochet work, but to make it easier to fasten shoes and boots that closed with a long row of tiny buttons up the side instead of laces.

The doctor's buttonhook wasn't used for that purpose at all.

Raisa gasped when the doctor rested the buttonhook against her left brow bone and skillfully turned her upper eyelid inside out over the rounded metal tip. Before she could react to the pain, the doctor had done the same to her lower left eyelid; then he gave her right eye the identical treatment. His deft, swift touch left her blinking and stunned while the translator told her, "That was excellent, miss. No trachoma. Now, hold the child, please."

Raisa thought her heart would break when the doctor used that horrible buttonhook to check Brina's eyes. The little girl tried to squirm free, but Raisa used her left arm to keep Brina's body immobilized while her right held the back of the child's head steady. The doctor did his work with the same speed and expertise as before, though it took the translator several tries to make his verdict heard over Brina's outraged squalling.

"No trachoma, either. You can go ahead to the Registry Hall."

That was easier said than done. Now Raisa had to carry two bags while at the same time holding on to a child who wanted nothing more than to run away from her. She didn't know what this "trachoma" thing might be, only that it was to blame for Brina's hysterical attempts to fight free of her grasp, all the while screaming for her mother.

In the Registry Hall, on the second floor of the main building, Raisa recognized some of her fellow passengers, although Zusa was not among them. They were sitting or standing in groups of about thirty, across the hall from a row of desks. Each desk was staffed by two or three men, only one of whom enjoyed the luxury of being seated. Individual immigrants stood attentively before the desks, with the occasional exception of a mother carrying her infant or toddler. As Raisa staggered along, struggling with Brina and the bags, the black-clad woman from the ferry came striding up to give her a hand.

"Poor girl, you look ready to drop," she said, scooping up Brina in a competent, no-nonsense-now manner. "Show that man your papers. I'm certain you must belong with our group, but you'd better have him tell you where to go so it's done properly. You don't want to step on anyone's toes here. They don't have any qualms about rejecting troublemakers." With that, she carried Brina back to the small mass of passengers waiting against one of the walls.

The woman in black was correct: Raisa and Brina did belong with her group. The old man and his middle-aged daughter were there, as well. By the time Raisa joined them, Brina was no longer crying or thrashing around. Raisa guessed that the bulge in her cheek must be a piece of hard candy that someone had produced to quiet her down. When she saw Raisa, she smiled and cuddled up to her willingly.

"Thank heaven," Raisa said, dropping her bags so she could sit on a bench and hold Brina in her lap. "I thought she'd never want to have anything to do with me again."

"Children forget," the bony woman in black said. "Sometimes. It was the eye examination that upset her, wasn't it?"

"I can't blame her," Raisa replied. "It upset *me*."

"You'd have been a lot more upset if the doctor found any hint of trachoma. That disease can leave you blind, and it's awfully contagious. It's a guaranteed ticket back to Europe, not just a matter for quarantine." She looked Raisa and Brina over. "Be glad you've got no worries about deportation or quarantine, my dears."

"How do you know that?" Raisa asked.

"You'd be marked if you did. Haven't you noticed some people going into the private medical examination rooms with letters chalked on their clothing? If the doctors spot any abnormality—if they even suspect it—they use a code to mark you and who knows whether or not you'll be let in or sent packing!"

"That's what happened to my sister-in-law," the old man's daughter put in. "She came over about five years ago with her family, but the doctor didn't like how her heart sounded, so he put a letter on her and they sent her back, all alone. Her husband and children stayed, and it didn't take that no-good five months before he sent word he was divorcing her to marry someone else, just because he couldn't manage the little ones! If you ask me, he's the one who had a bad heart."

"At least we know we're not going to be sent back now," Raisa said, playing with Brina's golden curls.

"Mmmm." The black-clad woman pursed her lips. "*Probably* not."

"What do you mean, '*probably* not'?" Raisa's fleeting feeling of hopefulness vanished.

"Well, you've still got to be interviewed by one of the registry clerks," the woman said. "That's what we're waiting for now. My son told me all about it. They'll want to make sure that you have some money and a way to make a living. They don't want to admit people who've come to this country just to become a financial burden on society."

"Money and . . ." Raisa felt panic rising in her chest. "But I don't have a job! What am I going to do?"

"Now, now, don't carry on like that," the woman said. "I think that question is one that's aimed mostly at the men. Girls like you only have to be able to assure the clerk that you know someone already living here who'll look out for you. There are too many vultures waiting to pounce on unaccompanied young women. I even heard that not too long ago, those creatures had agents working right here, in this very building, finding single girls to kidnap and sell as—never mind. It's sordid, and nothing a decent girl should hear about. All you need to know is that everything is much better now. The authorities here will take proper care of you, and whatever they decide will be in your best interest."

"I hope so," Raisa said, though she didn't put a lot of faith in that.

She kept Brina happy by telling her every fairy tale she could remember; she was starting all over again, hoping the child wouldn't notice, when her name was called from one of the desks. *They mustn't see that I'm afraid,* she thought as she picked up her bags once more. *They might think I'm hiding something. That won't do.* "Come with me, Brina," she said, straightening her shoulders and walking across the room.

The man seated at the desk stuck out his hand for her documents. While he reviewed them, the other Ellis Island employee began speaking to her in German. She shook her head and let him know she spoke Yiddish. He frowned, but the man who held her documents smiled.

"This will make my job much simpler, miss," he said. "We can speak directly to one another. I see that you're in good health, as is your"—he glanced at Brina, who had a hard grip on Raisa's skirt—"little sister?"

"Cousin, sir," Raisa said.

"Ah! I see. What a pretty child. She looks hungry."

"She—we're all right."

"But you could be better." The clerk spoke a few unintelligible words to his assistant, who left the desk at a speedy pace. "Now, just a few questions and we can get you on your way."

The clerk had spoken the truth. He asked his questions, listened to Raisa's answers with a sympathetic ear, and ended the interview by wishing her a happy reunion with her older sister. "You'll want to go to the currency exchange counter next, over that way." He pointed with his pen. "You'll need nothing but dollars from here on. Once you're done there, be sure to take the stairs to the left since you're headed for New York City. They'll take you to the correct ferry. The ones to the right are for the people bound for railway stations, and the center stairs, you don't want them. They're for detainees."

Raisa thanked the clerk profusely. She grabbed her luggage, told Brina to take hold of her skirt again, and was about to rush on when the assistant came back with a brown paper bag in his hand. "A little something to welcome you," the clerk said, then returned his attention to the papers on the desk.

It was impossible for Raisa to carry the paper sack in addition to the traveling bags, but Brina was eager to help. She held the brown bag proudly with both hands and still managed to stay close to Raisa. The small remainder of their time on Ellis Island went as the friendly clerk had said: Raisa got the coins out of her hem and exchanged them for American money. While the transaction was being processed she overheard another Jewish immigrant muttering about being shortchanged.

Even if it's true and the exchange clerk is cheating us, what can we do about it? she thought, gathering up the new, foreign currency. There wasn't a lot, but she still took a little extra time to get out needle and thread in order to sew all but a little of her money back into the bottom of her skirt. While she stitched, Brina peeked into the brown paper bag. Her ecstatic cry took Raisa by surprise, though not half as much as when she held open the bag to show the sandwiches, crackers, and prunes piled inside. The ferry to New York City could wait; the girls gobbled their first decent meal of the day, but not before Raisa said a blessing for the food and also for the good heart of the immigration clerk who had provided it.

The ferry ride from Ellis Island to one of the piers at the foot of Manhattan was much more pleasant on a full stomach. Raisa took Brina as far forward as they could go so that the little girl could have a good view of the approaching shore. The trip also gave them both a fresh look at the great statue in the harbor. Sunlight played over the sculpted folds of the majestic woman's gown. Shading her eyes, Raisa saw that the great lady carried what looked like a book in the hand that wasn't holding the torch, and she wondered what marvelous secrets such a book might hold if it were real.

Seagulls swooped and screeched as the ferry docked. Raisa and Brina stepped off the gangplank into the rush and clatter of the seaport. The stench of dead fish, jostling people, burning fuel, and rotting garbage was unbelievable. Raisa shifted her hold on the bags in order to grab Brina's hand and hold it with grim, unrelenting determination. One look at the crowded docks and the bustling streets beyond and she knew she couldn't feel safe allowing the child to cling to her skirt. The danger of Brina losing her grip and being swept away was too real.

There seemed to be a bizarre magic in the air of the city. As soon as the passengers disembarked from the ferry and set foot on land they became charged with an uncanny energy, a force that sharpened their senses and added sudden speed to their feet. They began to walk faster and faster with every step, until some of them were surging forward at a rate just short of an outright run. Some of them rushed from the ferry into the arms of people who had been waiting on the dock-side for uncounted hours. Others barreled right past the happily reunited couples, families, and friends and plunged into the streets as if they were taking a well-known road home. Only a few, including Raisa and Brina, stepped away from the ferry as cautiously as if walking over thin ice, then stopped in the nebulous territory that lay between the waterfront and the heart of the city.

There were plenty of people and not one friendly face. A few passersby elbowed her aside, in too much of a hurry to care about anything except their own business. They snarled as they bumped into her, foreign words that could have been either a grudging apology or a command for her to get out of the way.

Raisa did her best to hold her ground. *We shouldn't go too far from the ferry,* she thought. *Zusa will be on the next one, I know it! Or maybe the one after that. This is the best place to meet her again, except . . . except . . .* Her assurance began to dwindle, beaten back by the noise and commotion around her. *Except what if she* doesn't *come? What if she hasn't passed the medical examination? What if there was something wrong with the answers she gave the officials? What if they simply* forgot *to call her name today and no one takes care of her until tomorrow?*

As she stood there, her fears and doubts multiplying wildly, a small, timorous sound from Brina snapped her out of her worried thoughts. The child's eyes were filled with fear, and her tiny body shivered as she pressed herself against Raisa's side.

Raisa forced herself to smile. "What's the matter, Brina?" she said cheerfully. "Still hungry? Don't fret; there'll be plenty to eat once we get to my sister's house. You're going to love Henda, and I know she'll love you. We'll go soon, I promise." She took a deep, steadying breath. "*Soon,* but first—first we're going to wait for the next ferry. We have to see if Zusa's on it, all right?" The child nodded. "That's a good girl. We can't just give up on our friend. Don't worry, we won't wait forever. You need to eat. If Zusa's not on the next ferry, we'll go straight to Henda's." *God willing, I'll find our way there without Zusa's help,* she thought uneasily. "Hold on to the big bag for me and don't let go. I need to get out her address." She squatted beside the larger traveling bag, opened it, and began rummaging through her clothes. "Here it is!" She waved the paper victoriously. "Now all we need to do is—"

She stopped speaking. Something had caught her eye, the

sight of a girl with a long braid of shining black hair. Raisa thought she recognized the girl's flowered shawl, as well. She'd last seen it in the early hours of that very morning. "Luciana?" she called out hopefully. *Maybe she's seen Zusa, or knows what's happened to her,* she thought. The girl was standing on a corner just a block off, talking with an old woman and two men, but if she was Luciana, she was too far away to hear her name over the tumult of the streets.

"I *think* that's her," Raisa said, tucking Henda's address safely away once more before picking up the bags. "Come on, Brina!" She grabbed the child's hand and walked as fast as she could, crying, "Luciana! Luciana! It's me!"

They were halfway down the block when the black-haired girl heard them and turned her head. "Raisa?" Luciana's beautiful face lit up with the joy of recognition.

The face of the old woman and the two rough-looking men with her were not so pleased to see Raisa and Brina come running up to greet the Italian girl. She spoke a few tense words to the men, who hustled Luciana off the street, deep into a narrow space between two buildings.

Vultures! The black-clad woman's words of warning struck Raisa like a lightning bolt. She almost tripped over her friend's abandoned valise as she plunged after the old woman, the men, and Luciana without a second thought. Partway into the alley, the old woman turned to face her, blocking her way, shouting, waving her hands, making it clear that Raisa wasn't welcome and should leave. In the dark, stinking space, the men flanking Luciana glared threats at Raisa. Brina yelped and cowered. She began to tug at Raisa's skirt, trying to make her come away from the scary men.

Raisa didn't move. She felt the blood leaving her face, but she stood her ground in spite of the fear freezing her bones. She had no idea what these people must have said or done to have gotten their hands on Luciana, no idea how to stop them now. She knew only that she had to do something, or her friend would be lost.

"Leave her alone!" she yelled as loudly as she could. "Get away from her! Help! Help! Someone help us! Someone—"

The woman slapped Raisa's face so hard she saw dazzling bursts of light. One of the men made a grab for Brina. He was short but powerfully built, his arms bulging with muscles under a thin stained shirt. He had no trouble tearing the child away from Raisa. Brina shrieked and kicked, batting at his face. Another man might have laughed at the little girl's ridiculous attempt to defend herself, but he held her with one arm and raised the other, ready to hit her with a scarred fist the size of a grapefruit.

Raisa threw herself at him and clung to his arm, weighing it down so that he couldn't strike Brina. His companion roared with coarse laughter while he cursed and tried to shake her off. Meanwhile, the old woman seized Luciana's arm and began dragging her away. The Italian girl fought back, broke the woman's grip, and staggered to the mouth of the alleyway, shouting for aid. The old woman ran after her.

Still laughing, the second man pulled Raisa off his partner as casually as if he were plucking petals off a daisy. He must have been over six feet tall, and when he took hold of her right arm at the wrist and elbow she found herself dangling on tiptoes in his grasp. Raisa didn't understand the Italian words he bellowed, but the grinding pressure on her bones made it plain that he would break her arm if she didn't cooperate. The threat was effective. He gave a satisfied grunt as she stopped fighting.

The shorter man managed to get a tighter hold on Brina and said something to his partner. The big man had an ugly gift for being able to communicate what would happen to the child if Raisa made any sort of fuss when the four of them stepped out of the alley and back into the streets. The gesture he used was the same action Raisa had seen back home in the shtetl when she'd come across the innkeeper's wife slaughtering chickens with a twist of the poor birds' necks. Then the big man jabbed a finger at the two pieces of luggage Raisa had dropped when she went to Luciana's aid. She picked them up docilely, her thoughts paralyzed, and began to follow him out of the alley. She moved as if caught in a horrible dream.

And then, just as the man stepped into the light, Raisa saw a thick dark rectangular shape come flying through the air, hitting him right in the side of the head and sending him crashing to the cobbles. His partner shouted what must have been a curse and dropped Brina. She scrambled to rejoin Raisa just as three young men came racing past, slammed the thug against the wall, and began giving him the beating of his life. Raisa was too shocked to look away, until the young men dropped their fists and allowed the man to slump unconscious in the filth of the alley.

"Raisa! Raisa!" Luciana's voice broke the spell. The Italian girl threw her arms around her and babbled excitedly while she led Raisa and Brina into the sunlight. Raisa was astonished at how deserted that small stretch of pavement had become. The fight in the alley had the magic power to make everyone in the vicinity disappear.

Grinning, the three young men emerged from the alley and joined the girls. One of them picked up Luciana's valise; the others relieved Raisa of her bags.

"*Buon giorno, signorina,*" said the young man carrying the valises. He tipped his cap to Raisa. "*Mi chiamo Paolo, e questi sono i miei amici.*" When Raisa didn't reply, he repeated, "Paolo, Paolo," until she understood that was his name and introduced herself and Brina. There was no need to ask how he knew Luciana; the family resemblance between them was unmistakable. It was also entirely missing between Luciana and the other two men, so Raisa supposed they were Paolo's friends, keeping him company when he'd come down to the docks to wait for his sister's arrival.

The six of them walked through the streets of lower Manhattan. Luciana chatted gaily with Paolo and his friends, leaving Raisa alone with her thoughts. With no knowledge of Italian, Raisa couldn't know if Luciana was telling her brother about how she'd come to miss her meeting with him and had fallen afoul of the vultures who'd nearly trapped her. Her lighthearted demeanor made that seem unlikely, but perhaps the girl was the type of person who preferred not to dwell on past perils, as long as they were safely over and done with. Raisa didn't mind being left out of the conversation. Now that she and Brina were out of danger, she was enjoying herself, gawking freely at all the sights.

Cities! she thought, awestruck by her new surroundings. *All my life, I lived in our shtetl, where* city *was only a word. I never truly got to see such places from the train or when I was in the middle of that crowd of travelers in the streets of Bremerhaven. This is different. This is wonderful! Look at these buildings, so tall! And so many people, all in such a hurry. Where are they all going so fast? Not one tiny spot of earth underfoot—everything's paved over, and not with gold! Look at all the carts, with a whole herd of horses to pull each one, and men everywhere, pushing smaller ones. Good smells, plenty of good things to eat. Now that, at least, is something that reminds me of home, but*—she cupped one hand over her nose as they went past an especially reeking alleyway—*ugh, some of the other smells are worse than anything back home, even the peasants' pigs! So much, so much—it's overwhelming. Oh, Henda, and to imagine you came here all by yourself, with no one to help you. I wonder what you thought when you first saw all this? I wish I could remember everything you told us in your letters home. But this is your home now, Henda, yours and mine. A new home, a new life . . .* She murmured a prayer of thanks to God.

One of Paolo's friends fell into step beside her. "A Jewish prayer, yes? You are Jewish girl?" Raisa's jaw dropped. His accent was outlandish, his grammar was shaky, yet there was no denying that he was speaking to her in Yiddish.

"Uh, y—yes, I am. But you . . . you're not a J . . . ?"

He flashed her a brilliant smile. "No, no, not me. But I know some. My name is Renzo. My sister Angelina has many friends, Jewish girls, from work, making clothing in the factory. Sometimes she visits them, they visit her. Mama makes me walk with them when they go out of our neighborhood. For safety, you know? That's when they teach me. They think it is very funny. Then I teach them Italian and it is my turn to laugh."

"Do you know English, too?" Raisa asked. Brina began to fall behind, so she picked up the little girl and carried her as they walked on.

"Some. Mama says I should learn more, but why bother? Most days I help Papa in the store. All our customers speak Italian. Do *you* speak English?"

"No," Raisa said. "But I will."

That made Renzo laugh again. "When? You have a job here where you can learn English?"

"I don't have a job at all," Raisa confessed. "Not yet. I'm hoping I can find one at the same place where my sister works."

"Ah, so you do have family here? Luciana thinks you are alone. She wants her parents to let you stay with them. Of course they will agree, especially once they learn how you saved her from those—those—"

"Vultures?" Raisa volunteered.

"Worse. The people who linger by the ferry terminal, looking for innocent, unknowing girls—new to this land, alone, eager to find a friend—they are monsters. If they cannot lure the girls away, they use force. The end is the same, a shameful life in houses where men pay to—" He stopped, blushing. "Your pardon. I say too much, and nothing fit for your ears."

Raisa spoke quickly, to spare him further embarrassment. "Luciana is a good friend, but there's no need for her parents to take Brina and me in." She pointed at the bag Renzo was carrying. "I have my sister's address in there."

"Then you should get it out so we can take you to her. If she lives far from Paolo's family, you walk a long way for nothing." Renzo put down the bag and called out to the rest of the group. They gathered around Raisa while she produced the paper with Henda's address. There was a brief conference among Paolo and his friends as they wrestled with the handwriting, but at last Renzo turned to Raisa and told her, "It's good. We know this street you want. Come."

Raisa didn't know exactly when the city streets transformed around her. The waterfront was crowded enough, but as they headed north and east the human traffic grew denser and denser until there were times Raisa felt she couldn't move ahead even half a step. Little by little she became aware of other changes, as well. The streets were packed with people;

pushcarts; displays of fruit, vegetables, cloth, and other merchandise—that didn't change—but at some point she noticed that the store signs were printed in the Hebrew characters used to write Yiddish words. There were other words, too—English, no doubt—that were dwarfed by the size of the Yiddish letters and altogether absent on some signs. Raisa was pleasantly surprised when she was able to read a few of the Yiddish words. Zusa's lessons had made a difference after all!

And almost everyone here is speaking Yiddish, too! she thought. *It's just like Zusa said it would be. Zusa . . . I hope you weren't kept behind by the inspectors. Maybe you're home already, reunited with your family. Please, God, let it be so!*

On a teeming street like so many others in the neighborhood, Paolo stopped at a tall brownstone building with a soot-smirched facade and gestured at the steep flight of steps leading up to the battered black wooden door. Renzo didn't have to translate; Raisa knew she had arrived.

Looking up at the front of the building, Raisa wondered why some of the windows were blocked with what looked like railed-in iron platforms and ladders. All of these were draped with rainbows of drying laundry, and one held a trio of scraggly potted plants. The smell of boiling vegetables spilled into the street, along with a weird symphony of thumps, clangs, and hisses from within. Somewhere an infant wailed. Raisa winced as Brina renewed her frightened, ferocious grip on her hand.

"Don't be scared, sweetheart; we're all right now," she said, putting on a show of confidence for the child's sake. "This is where Henda lives. We're home." She took back the bags from Paolo's friends, kissed Luciana, and thanked everyone as best she could before starting up the stairs.

"You want us to wait?" Renzo called after her.

"We'll be fine," she replied lightly. *We will be fine*, she told herself. *This isn't the shtetl, but the people, the language, they're the same. Henda came here alone and she was able to make her way. I can, too.* "Luciana's parents must be dying to see her again. Don't keep them waiting any more."

Renzo translated this for the others. Paolo nodded, then said something to him in Italian, which Renzo passed back to Raisa. "He says to tell you, all right, we go now, but you remember this: if you ever need help, you come to Delvecchio's grocery on Mulberry!"

Raisa thanked them again and climbed the stairs to the black door. It led into an unlit foyer, the walls and pressed-tin ceiling visible only by whatever daylight came through the open door. A steep, narrow flight of stairs hugged one wall; a pair of apartment doors occupied the other. At the far end of the entry hall, she saw a third door, its small glass panel smeared over with grime so that it let in only a negligible amount of extra light. Something scuttled along the baseboards, and the stink of a badly cleaned toilet hit Raisa right between the eyes. And yet even in such a dingy, squalid setting, some long-forgotten artist had decorated the wall with painted wreaths of ivy framing fat blue urns filled with roses.

"Hey! Who's down there?" Raisa raised her eyes to see

a woman in a gray kerchief leaning over the stair rail from the second floor. "Who are you? You don't live here! Get out before I call the police!"

"Please, we don't mean any harm," Raisa called back. "We've only just arrived this morning. My sister Henda lives here and—"

"Henda?" the woman snapped. "I don't know any Henda."

"She wrote that she rooms with a family in this building, up on—on the third floor, I think. The Levis? He works as—"

At that moment, Brina pulled at Raisa's hand, beckoned her to bend down, and whispered urgently in her ear. Raisa looked back up at the surly woman. "I'm sorry to bother you, but is there someplace the little girl can pee?"

"In the gutter," the woman shot back. "But you'd probably have her do her business right in front of this building. There's a hall toilet on this floor. Come up."

Raisa had a hard time persuading Brina to venture into the dark, smelly little room with the badly cracked and yellowed toilet. In the end, she had to go with her, leaving their bags on the landing. When she came out, she found the woman crouched over Brina's open bag. She sprang to her feet at once and gave them a black look. "Are you done? Then go!"

"Ma'am, I told you, my sister Henda lives here," Raisa replied, fighting back a rising anger. "She's a boarder with the Levi family. If you don't know her, you must know them. Please tell me, where can I find them?"

"*They* live on the fifth floor, but they haven't got any boarders except a couple of greenhorns the husband hired to do piecework for him. Big man!" she said sarcastically. "Just because he's got his family *and* those two newcomers working for him, he thinks he's better than the rest of us! What next, he rents space in a *real* shop?" Her laugh was dry and brittle.

"I see." Raisa didn't believe the sour-tempered woman for an instant. *She's choking on her own envy,* she thought. *Why would she tell me the truth about Henda when she can hurt me with a lie and watch me suffer? That's probably the only amusement she's got. Well, she'll have to look for her entertainment elsewhere.* "Thank you very much," she said. She started up the stairs with Brina tagging along after.

"And where do you think you're going?" the woman demanded. "You heard what I told you! The Levis don't have any female boarders."

"Well, maybe I got the name wrong," Raisa replied. "If you don't remember my sister, they might."

"Who says I don't remember your sister?" A nasty cackle echoed up the stairwell, stopping Raisa in her tracks on the third-floor landing. "It took me a while, but I remember her now. She was the one everyone always said was so *pretty.*" The woman sniffed. "*I* never thought so. If you ask me, a girl's got to have a little *modesty* before you can call her pretty, not carry herself like she's too good for the rest of us! Oh, she talked to people, she smiled enough, but *I* could tell what she was thinking. Just because that fancy young fellow kept coming around here to see her all the time, she got big ideas.

I suppose she thought he was going to be her ticket uptown, and I'm sure he let her think that, too. That's how those men operate, waving all kinds of promises in front of a factory girl's nose until they get what they want."

Raisa's cheeks grew warm. She put down the bags and took hold of the banister. "What are you talking about? My sister didn't have any suitors. She would have written to us about them if she had."

"Oh, so you think that fancy man was her 'suitor,' eh?" The woman sneered over the old-fashioned word. "That's not what I'd call him."

"I don't care what you'd call *anything*," Raisa retorted. She was shouting mad. Doors on the floors above and below her began to open as neighbors were drawn by the noise. "And as soon as we can, Henda and Brina and I are going to move out of this place and so far away we won't have to listen to one *word* of your spiteful nonsense again!"

"How *dare* you talk to me like that, you piece of horse dung!" the woman screeched. "You're just like that worthless sister of yours. One fine day a few months ago she filled this whole building with such an uproar that we all thought the ceilings would come down on our heads! Weeping, wailing, shrieking like a wild beast, and over what? A letter. Who'd want to send a letter to *her* in the first place, I ask you. What sort of troubles could a little nobody like *that* have? Nothing important enough to turn my peaceful home into a lunatic asylum, believe me! At first I thought the letter came from that '*suitor*' of hers, giving her her walking papers, but *he* showed up while she was still yowling like a scalded cat. He hustled her out the door and no one's seen or heard from her since. He probably did what he wanted with her and now she's on the streets where she belongs!"

"Take that back!" Raisa clattered down the stairs and stood toe-to-toe with the vindictive woman. "Take back what you said about Henda!"

"Why should I?" Her thin lips curled. "My mother raised me to tell the truth and be a respectable person. Perhaps if *your* mother had taught your sister the same—"

Raisa slapped her hard. The impact reverberated up and down the stairwell, and before the echoes died away, the woman threw herself at Raisa, pulling off her kerchief, trying and failing to yank her shorn hair, clawing at her face. Raisa fought back, defending herself vigorously in an escalating battle that brought half the tenement house residents out into the hall and made the other half slam and lock their doors. Someone from one of the first-floor apartments ran into the street, calling for the policeman on the beat. The sound of his heavily shod feet was loud enough to be heard well before he entered the building, while he was still climbing the stone steps outside.

The sharp-tongued witch who had provoked the fight heard the policeman's approaching footsteps, took one last swing at Raisa, and escaped into her apartment, bolting the door behind her. Raisa stood frozen on the landing, her face stinging where she'd been scratched, her heart beating like a hummingbird's wings. One flight above her, Brina sobbed. The cry snapped Raisa out of her temporary daze. She rushed up the steps to embrace the child.

"Here, miss! Up here!" A young woman leaned over the fourth-floor railing, signaling madly. She hurried down to the third floor and grabbed both of the traveling bags. "If you don't want to wind up in jail tonight, follow me *now*," she said, and headed back upstairs before Raisa could get a word out.

Raisa didn't need to be told twice. The policeman's voice boomed in the foyer. Lifting Brina off her feet, Raisa ran where the young woman led her, up three flights of steps to the fifth floor and into one of the apartments.

The clatter of a sewing machine stopped cold when Raisa and Brina came scrambling in. They'd taken refuge in a three-room flat at the front of the tenement. She set Brina back on her own feet in a room mostly occupied by a big black stove. A balding man was just hoisting a weighty iron off the top of it when they came in. His face was young, but his back had the curvature of a much older person, and the arm holding the iron was deformed by twice the muscle of his other one. There was a window set into the wall between the room with the stove and the front room, allowing daylight to reach deep into the otherwise dark kitchen. Raisa saw two more men seated at sewing machines near the street windows. A third man, with a mouthful of straight pins, was busy making alterations to the fancy gown on a dressmaker's dummy in the packed front room. A little boy came out of the completely dark third room with a towering pile of cut cloth in his hands. Two more children, a boy and a girl, peeked out from behind him.

One of the sewing machine workers left his place and came into the kitchen where the presser worked. "Bayleh, what's going on?" he asked the woman who'd brought Raisa and Brina into her home.

She laid a finger to her lips. "Shhh. There's a policeman downstairs."

"A what?" The man's red-rimmed eyes opened wide. "Oy, Bayleh, what are you doing to us?"

"Mottel, *shhh*!" the woman said more emphatically. "Did I marry a fool? Do they *look* like criminals? This girl came here looking for her sister, Henda." She began to say more, but the sound of stumbling footsteps on the stairway outside made everyone in the apartment go suddenly still. A meaty fist pounded on the door and a deep voice boomed unintelligible words. Raisa cast an anxious glance down at Brina, but the child was just as petrified as the rest of the people in the apartment. She reminded Raisa of a baby rabbit when a fox was near, her only hope of survival to stay perfectly motionless, perfectly quiet.

After a short time, Raisa heard the footsteps clomp away, fading as the policeman lumbered down the stairs. Everyone let out a happy sigh.

"So, Henda's sister, you say?" Mottel scratched his closely trimmed beard. "I didn't know she had more than the one who—forgive me, but there was a letter and when that poor girl read it—"

"I'm the only sister she ever had." Tears slipped from Raisa's eyes. She tried to speak, to explain the misunderstanding about her "death," but Henda's image rose up before her. She saw her sister opening the letter, saw how the false news would have been a spear through her heart. The miserable woman from downstairs hadn't lied about everything: Henda's wild sorrow and despair must have filled the tenement.

"There, there, child, don't try to talk." Bayleh put her arm around Raisa's shoulders and steered her to a chair in the front room. Raisa walked carefully, picking her way through a maze of twine-tied cloth bundles. The young housewife gave her and Brina apples from the milk-white bowl on the mantelpiece. Her husband hovered impatiently nearby, his eyes going from the idle sewing machine to Raisa to the clock on the wall and back again.

"Stop that, Mottel," Bayleh said sternly. "The work will get done. What have we become if we can't spare a little pity for one another?" She stroked Raisa's short hair. "I'll have one of the children go find your kerchief, dear. Your poor hair! You must have been very sick. Such a nice color, too. It will be beautiful when it grows back. Your sister's hair was also lovely, and she always kept herself looking like a fine lady. No wonder that no-good lazybones downstairs was eaten up alive with envy! She keeps her hair the way she keeps her house. What would it cost her to pick up a broom or use a little soap? Mrs. Levi never stopped praising how neat Henda was with her things, and how she helped with the housework. All the *decent* people in this building had nothing but good things to say about her."

"Not like that *filthy* liar." The words flew past Raisa's lips before she could think. When she realized what she'd said, she clapped one hand over her mouth, horrified and embarrassed.

To her relief, Bayleh laughed. "What a little tiger we've got in our home! But a tiger who won't use such words again, yes? The children are listening, and they only seem to remember what we'd rather have them forget."

"I'm sorry," Raisa mumbled, nervously twisting the stem of her half-eaten apple. "She made me so mad with all of her lies, especially about the man."

"What man is this?" the housewife asked.

"She said my sister had a—someone who came here to see her. He was dressed fancy, like a rich man, and when she got that letter, he—he took her away."

"Oh." Bayleh sucked in her breath. "I'm afraid *that* is all true."

"No!" Raisa's hands clenched, crushing what was left of the apple to pulp and juice. "It *can't* be. My sister—"

"Please, dear, I'm not spreading evil gossip. I'd sooner cut out my own tongue than suggest there was ever anything shameful in your sister's relationship with that young man. I was here when she got that letter. I was one of the women who tried to help her, to comfort her, to get her to stop screaming and raking her face with her fingernails and tearing her beautiful hair. We were all terrified that if she went on like that, someone would call for the police and she'd be taken away to the crazy house. I'm telling you, it was God Almighty who sent that man just then. We never knew when he'd show up, but there he was, right when she needed him the most! He came bounding up the stairs, took her into his arms like a child, and spoke to her so gently, so softly that none of us could hear a word. Whatever he said, it worked a miracle. She stopped thrashing around, trying to hurt herself. She crumpled against his chest, tears streaming down her face, and let him wrap his own coat around her. He told us he was going to take her for a walk around the block, so she could calm down." Bayleh sighed. "That was the last we saw of them." She got a cloth from the sink in the other room and began wiping the smashed apple from Raisa's hands as if she were a baby.

"Who was he?" Raisa demanded. "How did Henda know him? Surely you wouldn't have let her go off with a total stranger?" A hundred fearful thoughts spun through her mind. She began to shake uncontrollably; Bayleh brought a quilt and swept it around her.

"You poor girl, this is too much for you, I can see that. You're exhausted! I want you to lie down on my bed and rest, sleep a little."

"I can't sleep," Raisa said. "I *can't*. I need to know what happened to Henda. You've got to tell me—"

"I will, I will, I promise." Bayleh did her best to soothe Raisa's unsettled mind. "Only sleep first."

Still protesting that sleep was impossible, Raisa followed Bayleh into the windowless inner room, sat on the edge of the bed, and took off her shoes. Oh, how good that felt! Brina's breath, sweet with apple, warmed her neck when she lay down. The child's hand clasped her own, and she fell headlong into dreamless slumber.

Chapter Six

UNDER THE EYES
OF GOD

Raisa woke up in pitchy darkness, sandwiched between two warm, breathing bodies on an unusually comfortable mattress. She had no idea where she was or how she'd gotten there. Panic closed her throat until Brina's familiar scent calmed her a bit and she realized the child was huddled against her. Turning as much as she could in those cramped conditions, she touched the soft cloth of a woman's nightgown. Bayleh? Her sleep-muddled thoughts made that name seem both familiar and strange at the same time. Then she heard a deep, strident snore from the far side of the bed. *A man?* The happenings of the previous day came flooding back, everything from waking up on board the steamship to learning of her sister's disappearance. Toward the end of her recollections, she glimpsed the face of Bayleh's husband, Mottel, and made a good guess as to the source of that loud snoring.

"Raisa?" Brina's fingers groped over her face in the dark. "Raisa, I need to go."

Groggy and aching, Raisa slipped out of the bed and guided Brina out of the bedroom. The first hint of daylight was stealing through the net lace curtains in the front room. The presser, the tailor, and the other sewing machine worker lay sleeping head to heels on three battered gray mattresses laid out next to the dressmaker's dummy. In the kitchen, the children snuggled together like puppies on a fat comforter leaking goose feathers at the seams.

Raisa and Brina slipped out of the apartment as quietly as they could. The floorboards of the landing creaked under Raisa's stockinged feet. As she crept toward the stairs, a pungent, unmistakable smell brought her up short. It was coming from one of the two doors on the landing, each with a pebbly green glass panel set into the wood. Raisa turned the knob and was overjoyed to discover that the tenement had toilets on more than one floor and she wouldn't need to go downstairs near that horrible woman's apartment.

Wait until I tell Glukel about this! she thought, while waiting for Brina to finish. She recalled the outhouse and chamber pots they'd had to use in the shtetl and tried to imagine how everyone back home would react when she told them of all she'd seen since her arrival.

Wait until I tell . . . Raisa's momentary happiness was gone. "Oh, merciful one," Raisa breathed. "I have to tell Glukel about Henda. How can I do that? What can I say?" She buried her face in her hands.

She heard the toilet door open and felt a now-familiar touch on her arm. "You're sad again?" Brina, too, looked ready to cry.

Raisa knelt before her. "No, sweetness, I'm only tired. We did a lot yesterday, and I'm afraid we have to do more today. But it's nothing for you to worry about. I'll take care of you."

Brina lifted her chin and looked determined. "And *I'll* take care of *you*," she declared.

"Then we're going to be all right," Raisa said, laughing in spite of herself.

By the time they returned to the apartment, Bayleh was up and had a coffeepot steaming on the stove. The children and the three boarders were also awake and ready for the day's labors, their bedding out of sight. One of the sewing machines in the front room was already rattling away; Mottel wasn't waiting for his breakfast to be ready before he got back to work.

As she and Brina drank strong coffee and ate bread spread with salty chicken fat, Raisa watched Mottel run the sewing machine. It was fascinating. The cloth flew under the rapidly bobbing needle; long seams were stitched in next to no time. Almost without meaning to, Raisa drifted nearer and nearer until she was hanging so close to Mottel that he became aware of her presence.

"What *is* it?" he said testily. "Haven't you ever seen a sewing machine this old before? It's a piece of junk, but I'm just starting out in the business. These machines were the best I could afford."

"I think it's wonderful," Raisa said with sincerity. "The woman who raised me is a seamstress, but all we had to work with were needles and thread. I'd love to learn how to use something like this!"

"Oh." Mottel looked sheepish. "Well, like I said, it's not much. I have to run it by pumping the treadle." He pushed his chair back and showed her the seesawing foot plate underneath that powered the machine. "In the big shops—the real garment factories—the machines run on electricity."

"Your sister worked in one of those shops," Bayleh put in. "The American Pride Ladies' Garment Company, I think. But then came the big strike about a year ago. Henda walked off the job with all the others, and I don't blame any of them. The bosses treated them worse than dogs, paid them miserable wages, but that wasn't all. Believe me, there wasn't a single dirty, underhanded trick those *momzers* didn't use to try to cheat the girls out of their pay!"

"Bayleh, for heaven's sake, watch your tongue!" Mottel said, clearly scandalized to hear his wife use a word like *momzers*, even if the people in question did deserve to be called bastards.

"Then tell me I'm wrong!" she challenged. "My darling Mottel, your problem is you're too good-hearted, and God be thanked for that! I couldn't live under your roof another minute if you were one of those slave drivers who finds a way to bleed his workers out of a penny here, a penny there."

"That's the truth!" The presser with the deformed arm

spoke up. "Before I came to work for you, I was stuck in a real sweatshop. I never once collected a full week's wages. The boss was always charging us for this and for that—for the fuel to heat the irons, for breaking a button that was never broken, for the coal in winter and the open windows in summer. And *then* there were the fines if we were too late, too early, too slow, too fast, too alive, too dead, you name it! Always making our pay sweat off a little here, a little there, until a man couldn't live on what he took home. Not like here." He grinned at Mottel.

"American Pride Ladies' Garment . . ." Raisa repeated the foreign name of her sister's company slowly, wanting to be certain she'd remember it. "Is it near here? Maybe someone who worked with Henda knows where she is now. And if they don't, they might know the name of the man who took her away, or—"

"Going there won't help you," Bayleh said, shaking her head sadly. "After the big strike ended, your sister couldn't get her old job back, and after all she'd gone through on the picket lines! Almost four months that strike lasted, and through the worst of winter, from November until February, no less! Hard times, such hard times for those poor girls, and it was sinful the way the bosses tried to force them back to work. They hired strong-arm men to bully and beat up the men, and for the girls they hired prostitu—" A warning glance from her husband made Bayleh bite back the word and instead say, "—vulgar, foulmouthed women to attack them. And the police were all bribed to look the other way. They were so deep in the factory owners' pockets, they could count their change for them."

"My brother says you can find the Messiah sooner than an honest cop in this city," the other sewing machine operator cut in.

Bayleh went on. "Mrs. Levi told how one day your sister came home with a black eye, but she was smiling. She said she grabbed the woman who gave it to her and paid her back double! Then she ran all the way home, because the police were always on the lookout for an excuse to arrest the strikers for 'disorderly conduct.' The next morning she was right back on the picket line."

"*My* sister punched another woman in the eye?" Raisa was flabbergasted.

"Both eyes." Bayleh corrected her with as much satisfaction as if she, not Henda, had been the warrior. "She showed them that they couldn't push her around."

Incredible, Raisa thought. *That's not the same Henda who ran away from home because she couldn't stand up to Nathan.* She was still deeply worried about her sister's fate, but she also felt a surge of pride for the fighter Henda had become.

"But they *could* push her out of a job," Mottel said. "When everyone went back to work, her bosses at American came up with an excuse for getting rid of the girls who'd made the most trouble before and during the strike. No one made a big stink about that, not even the union, because it wasn't worth saving a few jobs when so many people had just gone four months without pay."

"But she *did* get another job," Raisa said. "She must have."

"You're right, she did," Bayleh said. "But where . . . we don't know."

"Go ask the Levis," Mottel suggested. "She was their boarder. They ought to know."

"I'll do that," Raisa said. "And I can't thank you enough for all you've done for Brina and me. I promise that as soon as I've talked to the Levis, we'll pick up our bags and be out of your way."

"Just like that?" Bayleh planted her hands on her hips and looked stern.

"Uh . . . yes?" Raisa was completely confused.

The housewife shook her head decisively. "Then you'll be a wrung-out dishrag by tomorrow night. You listen to me, young woman. You came here expecting to find your sister. You were depending on moving in with her. Since she's no longer here, do you have even the *faintest* idea of where you'll live now, you and that infant?" She made a sweeping gesture at Brina. "If we had the room, you could board with us, but at least we can let you leave your bags here while you look for another place to stay. It won't take you long, believe me. There are more than enough families in this area who would be ecstatic to have such nice, respectful girls for boarders. Why, you might as well start by asking the Levis if they have room! Go, go! The little one can stay here and help me with cleaning up." She smiled down at Brina. "You can do that, can't you, sweetheart?"

"Yes, ma'am," Brina said, nodding. "I can wash dishes. I don't break them. And I can sweep the floor."

"What a treasure, and with such an old head on her shoulders!" Impulsively, Bayleh picked up the little girl and swung her around while her own children watched and giggled. The youngest sidled up to Raisa and tapped her arm before holding out a piece of cloth.

"My kerchief!" Raisa exclaimed gladly, tying it over her hair.

"I told you my little birds would get it back for you," Bayleh said, setting Brina down again. "Now, come with me."

The Levis' apartment was on the same floor as Bayleh's, but at the back of the building. The young housewife knocked loudly on the door until a frail, silver-haired woman opened it. "Mrs. Levi, this is Henda's sister, Raisa, just off the boat. She has to talk to you." That was all the introduction Bayleh provided before striding purposefully back into her own apartment.

"Henda?" Old Mrs. Levi stared at Raisa through thick, chipped eyeglasses. "About time. You owe me rent money. You're lucky my son didn't let me sell your things. Come in, come in." She shuffled into the dim apartment.

Raisa followed her uneasily. The place seemed smaller than Bayleh's home, and was definitely darker and more cluttered. A little daylight seeped in through a lone window facing the back of another tenement, and by its light a man in shirtsleeves bent over an open book, the pen in his hand scribbling swiftly on the pages. He didn't look pleased to see Mrs. Levi come in with Raisa.

"*Now* what, Mother?" he snarled. "Let me guess, you think *this* one's Sadie, too. When are you going to stop dragging one girl after another into my home, claiming you found her? Sadie is *dead,* Mother. She died from polio the year we got here. I take you to visit her grave all the time." He shot a venomous look at Raisa. "I don't know who you are or where she found you, but if you're hoping to leech anything off of my family, you can save yourself the trouble and get out now."

Raisa stood tall. "The only thing I want from you is the name of the factory where my sister Henda was working before she left this place."

"Your sister?" The man stood up from the table and came closer. He studied her face with as much concentration as if he expected to find a treasure map in her eyes. "*You're* her sister? But she was beautiful!"

Raisa swallowed a sharp retort.

"We're sisters all the same," she replied mildly. "She was always sending money home so that I could join her over here. I just arrived yesterday, except they tell me she's been gone for weeks."

"More like months," the man said. "She ran off with some slick-looking—"

"I know all about that, thank you," Raisa interrupted, not

wanting to risk hearing anything that would make her lose her temper again. "What I *need* to know is the name of the place she was working just before she . . . ran off."

"That? The American Pride Ladies' Garment Company."

"No, I mean the place she got a job *after* the big strike," Raisa said.

The man looked amused. "You know about the strike, little greenhorn? Are you sure you just got off the boat yesterday?" He rubbed his chin thoughtfully. "I should know this, but . . . well, to tell you the truth, when your sister got a new job, I was so relieved to have her start paying the rent again that I didn't care where the money came from. It happened right about the same time that I got married, and then I had some aggravation down at my dry-goods store, and *then* my cousin Yichel died the week before his wife and kids were due to show up in this country. Little girl, you shouldn't know from such troubles!"

"So you don't know where Henda was working?"

He threw up his hands. "You can ask Mother if she remembers, but don't get your hopes up. On the other hand, who knows? She loved your sister even when she wasn't positive Henda was actually poor Sadie, come back from the dead. You might catch her in a lucky hour. Mother! Mother, come in here!"

Raisa tried asking Mrs. Levi about Henda's last job, but the woman's son was right: it was a fruitless endeavor. The old woman was cheerful as a happy child, her mind wandering freely. Henda was Sadie, Sadie was Raisa, Raisa was Mrs. Levi's sister, cousin, aunt, and finally Henda again.

"Where have you been, dear?" she asked, squinting through her thick lenses. "We've been very worried about you. Have you come back for your things? I kept them under my bed, so they're safe, but I'm afraid you'll have to take them and go. Now we have my new daughter-in-law living with us, along with poor Yichel's family, and that's not counting the boy who helps at the dry-goods store. Thank God all of Yichel's children are old enough to work, or I don't know how we'd manage! And you, Henda? Where are you working now?"

Raisa reassured Mrs. Levi that she had a decent job and a new place to live, then accepted Henda's abandoned belongings, all of which fit into a single leather traveling bag. Raisa carried it back to Bayleh's place, so deeply discouraged that she felt as if someone had put iron shoes on her feet. Inside the apartment, Mottel and the other men were working diligently. The presser shared the kitchen with Bayleh, who was making dough in a huge wooden bowl, being careful not to let any of the flour reach the garments. Brina wielded a broom twice her size, sweeping up dust, thread, and scraps of cloth. The three children were nowhere to be seen.

"So, anything?" Bayleh asked when she caught sight of Raisa.

Raisa shrugged and dropped Henda's bag. "Only this. But maybe there's something in here that might help me."

"Like what?"

"I don't know. A picture, a letter, *something*." She knelt, opened the bag, and searched the contents. It didn't take long. "Nothing," she said sadly, raising her eyes to Bayleh. "Only her clothes and some letters from home."

"Tsk." Bayleh made a *what can you do?* gesture. "Well then, did you at least ask the Levis if you could have your sister's old place as a boarder?"

"I didn't have to ask; I heard. The Levis don't have room for us, either. I'd better start looking for somewhere else we can stay."

"Try in this building first," Bayleh suggested.

"I don't think that's the best idea," Raisa said. "If we live here, we're going to run into you-know-who again, and then . . ." She rolled her eyes.

"I see what you mean. All right, put your things in the bedroom and start looking. Mark my words, it won't take you long to find a nice place to live."

Raisa did the best she could to pile the three bags out of the way in the windowless inner room, then headed for the door. Her hand had scarcely touched the knob before Brina dropped the broom and flung herself into Raisa's skirt, hanging on to the cloth as if her life depended on it. "Dearest, are you sure you wouldn't be happier staying here?" Raisa coaxed. "I don't know how far I'm going to have to walk. You'll get tired."

"I can walk!" Brina declared forcefully. "I can go as far as you. You'll see."

"But, sweetheart, don't you want to help Bayleh to—"

"I want to be with *you!*" Brina was plainly on the point of tears, and just as plainly struggling to hold them back.

"Take her, take her," Bayleh said gently. "If she stays, she'll cry for you the whole time. Besides, there's nothing for her to do here except sit in a corner. We've all got work to do, and the children will be in school until the afternoon."

"Longer!" Mottel put in proudly. "Today after classes is a special assembly to honor pupils who wrote the best essays about American history. There's one prize for a pupil in each grade, and *my* children are bringing home one apiece!"

"*Your* children?" Bayleh sniffed. "As if *you* gave birth to them? Just listen to yourself, taking all the credit and jabbering away about our precious babies in a way that's practically guaranteed to attract the evil eye, God forbid!" She spat three times to ward off the dreadful possibility. Wife and husband were still bickering over who loved their children more when Raisa and Brina slipped out the door.

A beautiful early-summer day filled the streets of the neighborhood. The weather was warm enough for Raisa to have left her coat behind, but not yet hot enough to double the impact of any foul smells.

Which way should I go? she thought. *Bayleh said it'll be easy to find a place, but I should've asked her how to do it. Well, if it's that easy, any direction will do. Let's see what we can find.*

At first, Raisa walked slowly, concentrating on at least one thing that would make each street and intersection memorable. *I can't get lost,* she thought. *I have to be able to find my way back.* She fixed her mind on a brightly painted yellow sign, a striking display of secondhand furniture covered in red velvet, the smell wafting from a fish market, the unnaturally colorful array of sugary treats behind the window of a candy shop. Once in a while she was able to read the name of a store she and Brina passed, but she didn't trust her ability to remember words as much as her ability to remember sights, sounds, and smells.

One street turned into another. Sometimes Raisa and Brina became part of a wave of people hurrying toward a mysterious destination or away from an unknown disaster. At other times, the two of them hugged the corner of a building at a busy intersection and watched the traffic lumber past. In all of her years of life, Raisa had never seen a tenth as many people as she saw in that single morning. Infants and grandfathers, happy souls and faces nursing a grudge against the whole world, hair of every length and color, eyes bright as new stars or milky white and sightless, clothing that was one step away from the rag pile and fresh, finely tailored garments; Raisa saw it all.

It's too much! she thought desperately. *So many people, so much noise, such confusion!* Her stomach grumbled. *At least I know where to go to take care of* your *wants,* she told it. "Hungry, Brina?"

"Are you?" the little girl asked suspiciously, as if the question were a test.

"Starving." Raisa crouched down and worked a few coins out of the hem of her dress.

Finding food was child's play. Every other shop seemed to

sell a tempting variety of good things to eat, from fruits still carrying the perfume of distant orchards to plump, shining salamis hanging in a row from the top of a window frame. Then there were the pushcarts, and even individual women selling sandwiches and baked goods out of the big baskets on their arms. How to choose where to buy?

Raisa looked at the coins in her hand. *I don't know what these are worth. Any brat on the street could cheat me. How can I prevent that?* She walked from one store to the next, peering in from the doorway, trying to get a good look at the faces of the people behind the counters. She also watched the faces of the customers as they left the shop. Under a wide, red-striped awning she found a bakery where the woman selling the luscious-smelling cakes and pies had an open, friendly face.

She looks *like an honest person. . . . I think. She reminds me of Glukel, and Glukel never cheated a soul.* Raisa lingered just outside the shop until several buyers came and went. Each one left the bakery looking satisfied with their purchase. *Well, that looks hopeful.* Raisa puffed out a breath. *Enough doubt. I've got to start making my own way sometime. It might as well be now.*

Raisa's instinct was sound. The bakeshop woman welcomed the girls by offering Brina a sugar cookie twice the size of her hand. When Raisa tried to explain that they didn't want to buy sweets, the woman said, "But I want to give her one. Such a pretty child! I don't remember seeing either of you around here before. Are you new in the neighborhood?"

"We landed yesterday." Raisa gave Brina an approving nod and got real pleasure out of seeing how avidly the little one demolished the cookie. "Are those onion bialys?" She pointed at a row of round, flat rolls in the bakery showcase.

"Only the best you'll ever taste." The woman showed dimples when she smiled. "How many do you want?"

Raisa slid one of her coins across the counter. "Is this—is this enough for two?"

The woman's brows rose halfway to her hairline. "You *are* new. My brother the rabbi says it's a good thing that the Almighty watches out for greenhorns, or this city would devour you all. Do you have any more money?"

"Why?" Raisa took a step back.

"Do I look like a goniff, girl? I want to teach you what you've got so you won't be easy pickings for the first fast-talking swindler who crosses your path. You don't have to take me up on it, you know. I can't force you to learn. If you just want to buy something and leave, that's up to you."

Raisa ducked to the bakeshop floor. When she straightened up again, her hands clutched the coins and paper bills she'd received on Ellis Island. She spread them out on top of the showcase. "Teach me," she said. "Please."

Raisa discovered that mastering the different values of American money came easily to her. She'd always had a natural talent for arithmetic, helping Glukel keep track of her accounts whenever she could. How Nathan had scoffed at his aunt for allowing Raisa to make entries in the ledger! "Keeping track of money is man's work," he'd said. "All girls understand is how to spend it!"

The baker was impressed by how quickly Raisa learned.

"What a clever girl! You ought to get a job in a bank."

"I don't think I could," Raisa said with a half smile. "Not until I learn English."

"Maybe you can take classes someday. They offer them at the Educational Alliance. If you tell me where you're living I can tell you how to get there."

Raisa scarcely heard the bakeshop woman's mention of English classes. She needed a place to live more than she needed a new language; she jumped at the chance to get help finding one. "Actually, we're *not* living anywhere," she said as she put her money into her handkerchief and tied the corners together. "I thought we had a place, but . . ." She crammed the small bundle deep into one of the pockets of her dress and shrugged, not wanting to bother yet another stranger, even such a kindhearted one, with her story. "Would you know of anyone who's looking to take in boarders?"

"Better you should ask who *can't* use a boarder or two to help pay the rent!" the woman replied. She rattled off the names of about a dozen families who had a little extra space in their tenement apartments, then tore off a scrap of brown wrapping paper from the roll behind the counter and drew a crude map while telling Raisa how to find them. Raisa paid close attention to every stroke of the bakeshop woman's pencil, trying to memorize her every word. She could read the house numbers, but the street names were in English. If she forgot the directions, she might never find her way.

Raisa and Brina left the bakery with the map, a couple of

onion bialys, and a small paper sack containing some stale apple strudel and a fistful of broken cookies that the woman had thrown in for free. "Welcome to the Golden Land," she'd said when she handed the bag to Raisa. The onion bialy really was the best Raisa had ever tasted. Everything looked better now that she had a little something in her stomach.

First I'll find us a place to stay, then I'll start asking about where I can get work, she thought. *Next, I'll find someone to help me write a letter to Glukel. Oh, and another one to Reb Avner! Thank God I have the address Reb Laski sent me for our shtetl's Protective and Benevolent Association here. I don't know what they can do for me, but maybe once we're settled I can go there and they might be able to help me find out where Henda was working after the strike. Maybe they even have ways of learning where she is now!* Raisa tore another huge bite out of the bialy and relished the rich taste of golden baked onions.

Raisa's optimism carried her through until noon. In that time, she and Brina walked to every tenement on the bakeshop woman's map, spoke to one housewife after another, and always got the same answer: "If you don't have a job yet, how can I be sure you'll be able to pay the rent? And how do you expect to get a job with that child to look after?"

It didn't matter that Raisa had enough money to pay for two weeks' rent at some of the apartments she visited. The housewives had all dealt with boarders before. "Pay for one week, pay for two, and then it's nothing but excuses for three weeks after that! I didn't just fall out from under a horse's tail, girly. No one's going to pull that one on me a second time!"

Sometime between the sixth unsuccessful attempt to find lodgings and the noon hour, Brina ate all the broken cookies and half of the stale strudel. Raisa didn't notice until the little girl began to cry from a self-inflicted bellyache. "Oh, Brina, what am I going to do with you?" Raisa wiped the telltale crumbs off Brina's face, but couldn't think of what else to do for the child. At last she picked her up and continued walking through the streets, hoping that the next apartment would be the one to welcome them in.

It was no use. Meeting after meeting ended in rejection. Some were harsh and cold, some sympathetic, but a softened blow was still a blow. One housewife took pity on them and went into the room where her husband was cutting out pattern pieces for ladies' dresses. Raisa glimpsed him working over a thick pile of material, slashing through the layers with the long, hooked fabric-cutting knife. He paused just long enough to berate his wife for bothering him with such stupidity. "No job, no good, end of story."

The woman murmured something inaudible and gestured at Brina, who was curled up miserably in Raisa's lap. A fleeting look of compassion touched her husband's face.

"Hey, you! Girly!" he called out to Raisa. "I'll tell you what; if you can guarantee that kid of yours doesn't get in the way here while you're at work, I'll put in a good word for you with a friend of mine who works at Triangle Waist Company. It's a good shop, very modern. I'd go there myself if they were hiring cutters. Just how good are you with a sewing machine?"

Raisa hugged Brina close. "Good," she said. Her desperation gave strength to the lie. *I will be good running that machine. How hard could it be? I'll get someone to teach me. It couldn't take that long to learn.* "Very good."

"Glad to hear it." He spoke a few words to his wife, who beckoned Raisa. She set Brina down and followed the woman into the front room of the apartment, where a weedy young man, barely out of boyhood, bent over a sewing machine. The cutter ordered him away from his workstation and invited Raisa to show off her skill. She sat down in front of the machine, set her feet on the treadle, rested her hands on the cloth waiting to pass under the needle, and silently began to cry.

The shame of her useless lie weighed her down more heavily than Brina's slight body as she walked on through the streets. Still, she marched on. What choice did she have? The same anxiety that ate away at her hopefulness was a spur that drove her in spite of weariness, sore feet, thirst, and fresh hunger. One part of her mind argued, *Why are you so worried? If you don't find a place to move, do you really think Bayleh will force you out of her apartment and onto the streets tonight?* Another countered with, *Do you want to find out the hard way?*

Whether or not she makes us leave tonight, we'll have to leave sometime, Raisa told herself. *Even if I give her some of my money, I'll only be delaying the inevitable. Henda came here with less than I've got, and she didn't know how to run a sewing machine, either! She was able to take care of herself. So can I.*

But Henda didn't have someone else to take care of, too, came the furtive afterthought. *Someone helpless and alone.*

Not alone! A flash of unexpected strength sparked in Raisa's spirit. *As long as she's got me, Brina will never be alone.*

Sweat trickled down Raisa's spine. When she reached the last of the addresses the bakeshop woman had given her, she began going into other shops, asking if the people there knew of anyone in the neighborhood who was looking for boarders. The names she gathered in this way turned out to be more dead ends, but before she left each failed interview, she asked the women if *they* knew someone else who might be willing to give a jobless girl a chance.

At one point, it seemed she had success at her fingertips. She carried Brina into a shop whose walls were stacked with crates of heavy glass bottles topped with silvery triggers and spouts. Two brawny men pushed past her in the doorway, each shouldering a pair of loudly clinking boxes, but the grandfatherly type inside took one look at Brina's hot, tear-streaked face and insisted they sit down on a couple of empty crates.

"Ever had seltzer, sweethearts?" he asked, picking up one of the bulky green bottles and handing Raisa a ceramic mug still stained with old coffee. He pushed the trigger on the bottle and a hissing stream of carbonated water foamed over the top of the mug. Brina squealed with surprise and glee at the sight, her bellyache forgotten. She drank greedily, then let loose a thunderous burp.

"Good health!" the old man exclaimed, laughing and refilling the mug for Raisa. She drank it in a single gulp, gave him her heartfelt thanks, then asked the question that hadn't been far from her lips all day.

At first he said that he didn't know anyone who wanted boarders, but Raisa persisted. "No one? Not even one person you know? I haven't got a job yet, but I can pay a week—*two* weeks' rent. That is, I think so. I can show you my money—"

"No need for that, *mamaleh.*" The old man stroked his beard. "Last week one of the fellows who works here said his aunt might be looking. He went out with a delivery a while ago, so he should be back soon. We'll ask."

Raisa closed her eyes and murmured a short prayer that this time—*this* time, please, God!—she and Brina would hear the answer they'd been seeking all day. As if by magic, shortly after she'd whispered "amen," the delivery man returned and the old man asked him about his aunt. "See what a clean, respectable girl she is?" he said, gesturing at Raisa. "Honest, as well. She promises to pay in advance. She has no work yet, but if your aunt is willing to put faith in her—"

"Like you put faith in me when you hired me," the delivery man said, grinning. "I'm sure Tante Bluma will be happy to—" Raisa's heart lifted, but then the man frowned and tapped his temple. "Ach! What am I saying? It wasn't three days ago that Mama told me Tante Bluma already found a boarder. Two, in fact! She has no room for more. I'm very sorry, miss."

"Thank you anyway," Raisa said, doing her best to hide her deep disappointment. "We'll keep looking."

"May God watch over you," the old man called after them as they left. "No one ever said life's easy."

His words were prophetic. The two girls trudged on from store to store and person to person with no luck, until little Brina's cheeks looked like ripe apples. Raisa was overheated, as well, so she took off her head kerchief and used it to dab sweat from Brina's face, then her own. She saw how other people on the street stared at her close-cropped hair, but she was too worn-out to care what they thought.

"Come, Brina, let's go ask in this shop if they know someone who's got space to rent to—"

Brina's thin legs folded under her, and she sat down in the middle of the sidewalk. "No more," she said, her eyes pleading. "I can't."

"What are you saying, darling?" Raisa put on a heartening expression she didn't feel. "Didn't you tell me this morning that you could walk as far as I could?"

Brina bowed her head. "Yes." It was the faintest of forlorn whispers. Raisa saw drops of moisture fall into the child's lap, making dark spots on her dusty blue skirt.

"We have to keep going," she said. "We can't quit until we've got a place to stay. I know you're tired and hungry. Listen, would you feel better if I took you back to Bayleh's and I kept hunting on my own?"

"Noooooooo!" Brina leaped like a trout, launching herself at Raisa with staggering force. "Don't leave me, Raisa! Please don't leave me! I'll walk! I'll be good! I'm sorry, I'm sorry, I'm sorry!" She was too panic-stricken to cry anymore.

Raisa prattled all sorts of calming, comforting words to chase the terror of abandonment out of Brina's eyes. The little girl gulped air and fell silent, sucking on her fist like an infant. Someone watching the scene from a nearby storefront laughed and made a mocking comment. A pushcart man gave his unasked-for opinion about ill-behaved children. Two women carrying marketing baskets loudly remarked that *some* people thought they owned the sidewalk. Raisa scowled at them all, then gave Brina her hand and led the child away.

They walked in silence. *I need to rest,* she thought. *Both of us do. Brina looks ready to collapse, except she's scared that if she says anything, I'll leave her. All I want is someplace peaceful to sit for a little while, someplace I can catch my breath, start over. I need to think up a good answer for when they ask me about having a job and who's going to watch Brina while I'm working. I don't want to lie again, God help me, but . . . I don't know what else to do!*

She reached the street corner and tried to decide whether to turn and stay on the same block or cross and see what she could find on the other side. Such a simple choice, yet it made her head spin. In the end, she turned the corner. She was so weary and disoriented that she didn't trust herself to take Brina across the busy thoroughfare in safety.

Halfway down the block, Raisa saw a building that stood out from the rest. Flanked by redbrick tenements, its golden stone face was an island of simple beauty. Where the tenement windows were partly blocked by iron fire escapes, this building's windows were framed with sculpted grapevines, their panes a pattern of colored glass picked out by slender strips of lead. Raisa gazed up to the roof, where a six-pointed star gleamed in the summer sunlight. She tried to read the letters carved above the dark brown double doors, but the words they formed were Hebrew, not Yiddish. She could only sound them out; she didn't know their meaning.

She didn't need to read in order to guess what sort of place she'd happened to find; the glittering Star of David was enough of a sign. "A synagogue, Brina," she said. "I don't think it's the hour for prayers. If it's open, we can go in and rest, but we'll have to be very quiet." She picked up the little girl and climbed the granite steps.

The doors were unlocked and swung back gracefully. Raisa set Brina down, and together they stepped into the cool shadows of an anteroom that smelled of old books and fresh beeswax candles. Another set of doors stood before them, leading into the sanctuary. Raisa pushed one open by less than an inch and peeked into the dark room. She'd never before seen the inside of such a large house of prayer. The shtetl synagogue could have fit inside this building at least four times, perhaps five. A few gas lamps were burning low along the sanctuary walls. The softer glow from the *Ne'er Tamid,* the Eternal Light, shone steadily above the curtained ark holding the congregation's Torah scrolls. Their combined light revealed the rows of rich black walnut pews leading up to the bimah, the raised platform where the Torah would be read. Towering candlesticks and a burnished brass menorah reflected the flames.

"What are you doing in here?" A hoarse voice at her back

made Raisa jump and Brina squeak. A middle-aged man who looked very much like a shriveled monkey shook a broom at them with as much belligerence as if it were a bloodstained battle spear. "If you're looking to steal, you'd better start running or I'll thrash you within an inch of your life!"

"Sir, we're not trying to steal anything," Raisa said, pressing Brina close to her side. She was sure he must be the shammes, the one responsible for taking care of the synagogue building, though the one she'd known back home had never spoken to her so fiercely. "We're good Jewish girls, and all we want is—"

"Greenhorns, from the look of you," the man interrupted.

"Yes. We've been looking for a place to stay. We came in here because—"

"You can't stay here!" he cut in a second time. "Are you crazy? This isn't a poorhouse or an orphanage."

"We know, but we've been walking all morning and—"

"Don't waste your breath." The man held up one hand. He was one of those people who seemed to thrive on not letting others finish their sentences. "I know what you're going to say. I've heard the same sad story from dozens—no, *hundreds* of girls like you since I became the shammes here. You're just off the boat, you don't have anywhere to stay, you haven't got a job, you're poor, you're alone, blah, blah, blah, and you expect to get everything you want by coming into my synagogue just because you were born a Jew. Well, forget it! The Lower East Side is crawling with poor Jewish girls like maggots on a dead ox. Do you think the people here are made of money? Some of us can hardly take care of our own families, and yet you expect us to do something for every one of you who comes scratching at the synagogue door. We'd have a better chance of emptying the sea with a thimble!"

Raisa made one last try to tell the fuming man that all she wanted was a seat and a few moments of peace. "Sir, will you *please* listen? Brina and I didn't come in here looking for your charity. We only need—"

"Out!" the man shouted, pounding his broom on the floor. "Out, out, out *now*!" He spun the broom around like a drum major's baton and shooed them from the sanctuary toward the front doors as if they were wayward chickens. Brina backed away, hypnotized by the sight of his wrathful face. She made a misstep and fell hard on the black-and-white tiles in the anteroom. Her mouth opened in a woeful yowl that flooded the entire building.

"*Shame* on you!" Raisa shouted at the shammes. She dropped to her knees next to Brina. "Frightening a child like that! What kind of a man are you?"

"Don't lecture me, you little beggar. I'm doing my job, taking care of this synagogue, keeping it clean and making sure that the trash goes out and *stays* out." He stared at the two girls meaningfully. Brina took one look at his livid, wrinkled face and howled even louder.

"Mr. Fischel, Mr. Fischel, what's going on here?" A door at one of the narrow ends of the anteroom opened, and a young man wrapped in a prayer shawl burst in on the three of them. "I've been trying to do my studies, but for the last fifteen minutes, all I hear is this. It's like trying to read Talmud in the middle of an alley-cat fight!"

The shammes gave him a dirty look. "And *I'm* trying to do my job! Go back to your books, Gavrel. I'm taking care of things here."

"Yes, and I see how." The young man hunkered down in front of Brina. "Hello, little one. Why are you crying so loud? Did you break the floor when you fell on it? If you did, then I'm afraid you're going to have to pay to have it replaced." His grin made the corners of his green eyes crinkle.

Brina was taking a deep breath, getting ready to let out a fresh barrage of sobbing, when the joking question took her off guard. "I didn't break anything." She sniffled mightily and patted the tiles with both hands. "See? And I can't pay. I don't have money."

"My mistake. I didn't intend to insult you. Allow me to make amends for my false accusation with a modest offer of compensation. How about a piece of cake?"

Brina wiped her nose on the back of one hand and cocked her head, looking at him sideways. "You talk funny."

"So I've been told. Many people say it, but they can't seem to agree on why I'm such a funny talker. Is it what I say or how I say it? What's your considered scholarly opinion, princess?"

Brina thought this over while Raisa looked on, fascinated,

and the shammes grumbled under his breath about time-wasting fools. At last the child declared, "Both. You use pretend words you made up, and when you use real words you don't say them the same way we do."

"Well said, princess! Yes, my Yiddish does sound different from yours. You and your friend here sound like you're Galitzianers, living among Polish people. My parents are Litvaks, from Russia. And on top of that, I was born here, so I grew up hearing a lot of English, especially after I started school." He grinned again. "And once you start going to school, you'll find out that I'm not making up any words. They're all real, as real as *this*." He grabbed a tress of her hair between thumb and forefinger and gave it a playful, painless tug. Brina giggled, snatched the curl from his grip, and stuck the end in her mouth.

"Brina, what are you doing?" Raisa exclaimed. "Don't chew on your pretty hair." She knelt beside the young man and gently pulled the strand out of Brina's mouth.

"Isn't that strange? I offer this little one a piece of cake, but she'd rather nibble *that*?" He put on an expression of exaggerated mournfulness. "Don't you *like* cake, princess?"

"Yes! I want it!" Brina scrambled off the floor, all her tears forgotten.

"Then you'll have it." The young man remained squatting to stay on the child's level. "My name is Gavrel Kamensky, at your service." He offered his hand.

Raisa flinched to see Brina shake it with the same tiny paw

she'd used to wipe her nose, but Gavrel didn't seem to mind. He stood up and turned to her. "At your service, as well, miss, but I think we should wait to shake hands until I've washed mine. And the princess's. Mr. Fischel?" The grouchy shammes looked up when Gavrel hailed him. "Mr. Fischel, the ladies and I have to go now. Would you mind going into the study, putting away my books, and turning off the light? It looks like I'm done for the day."

"'Ladies,' my behind," the shammes muttered, leaning on his broom. "Fine 'ladies' he makes out of thin air, the smart one. Better he should want to be a poet than a rabbi. He's already crazy, so he's halfway there."

"What did you say?" Raisa overheard the old man's grumbling and whirled back to confront him. "Reb Kamensky is good to us, so that makes him crazy? And when Father Abraham welcomed the angels to his tent, not knowing who they were, I suppose you'd have called him crazy, too? Well, you can just—"

"Shhh, enough, let it go." Gavrel took Raisa by the elbow and steered her back toward the doors. "You can't nail sand to a tree. And the princess wants her cake."

Chapter Seven

THE LAND OF OPPORTUNITIES

O nce outside the synagogue, Gavrel paused at the top of the granite steps while he took off his prayer shawl and yarmulke and folded them reverently. Without the shadowy cover of the prayer shawl, he looked much younger, less like a grown man and more like a lad newly out of boyhood, not much older than Raisa. He produced an embroidered storage bag from the pocket of his trousers and tucked his things inside.

"All set!" he announced cheerfully. "And now, I hope you won't mind, but the only place I can afford to offer you ladies some cake is in my home. Don't worry, it's all perfectly respectable; my mother will be there, I promise. We'll have to walk about four blocks to get there. Will that be too far for you, princess? I can carry you if you're tired."

"I'm not a baby. I can walk," Brina replied with regal dignity. "Carry *her*." She made a grand gesture in Raisa's direction.

"Maybe another time," Gavrel said. Raisa thought she saw him blush.

The four blocks to Gavrel's home passed with Raisa introducing herself and Brina, then telling him how they'd happened to come into the synagogue and under the caretaker's sharp tongue. He listened attentively and then, to her surprise, he laughed.

"*What's* so funny?" She was tired, hungry, thirsty, and in no mood to have her recent troubles turned into a joke.

"Nothing. Nothing's funny," Gavrel said hastily. "I have a bad habit. When I'm faced with a mystery or a puzzle or a problem of any kind—one that I've really been cracking my brains over for a long time—and then, without warning, the answer hits me like a thunderbolt . . . I laugh! The rabbi's had to scold me about it repeatedly. It flusters him and disturbs our studies."

"So what's the great mystery you've solved this time?"

"You."

"What's so mysterious about me?"

"What a Deborah you are, what a Judith. I'm still shaking, imagining what you might have done to Mr. Fischel if you'd had a sword in your hands."

"I don't understand what you're talking about," Raisa said sullenly. "If you're making fun of me, it won't work as well if I can't tell how I'm being insulted."

Gavrel stopped and looked at her without a trace of mirth in his face. "I'm sorry, Raisa. It's my fault if you think I'm mocking you. Papa always warns me that I can be too smart for my own good. Deborah and Judith were great fighters among the daughters of Israel. Deborah was a prophetess and a general, commanding whole armies. Judith was a woman alone who used her wits to trick and slay the leader of the Assyrian invaders. From what you've told me about all the encounters you've had since coming to America, I can see why you lashed out at Mr. Fischel. Being a fighter has saved you time after time, but now it's hard for you to know when you can stop fighting."

"You make me sound like a fishwife," Raisa said. "Always quarreling."

Gavrel shook his head. "What I *mean* is that I think you're very brave."

A half smile touched the corner of her mouth. "Why didn't you just say that in the first place?"

Gavrel's family lived in a tenement very much like Bayleh's, except the cellar level and the first floor housed two businesses apiece. Two first-floor shops sold secondhand clothing for men and women, respectively. The tiny stores below street level sold tobacco and candy. The different aromas blended into a rich, sweet, strong perfume that followed Raisa all the way up to the Kamenskys' apartment on the fourth floor.

A stocky, bespectacled woman with gray-streaked black hair was stirring a big pot on the stove when they came in.

"What's this, Gavrel?" she cried when she saw Raisa and Brina. "I thought you were spending the day at the synagogue."

"Just the morning, Mama. I was going to go straight to the store and give Papa a hand, but the Almighty had other plans. It was the most extraordinary thing. I was studying the Book of Proverbs, when who comes walking right into the synagogue but the Woman of Valor herself!" He waved at Raisa. "And who is with her? Royalty! A genuine princess." He picked up Brina and swung her at the ceiling. She shrieked with pleasure.

Mrs. Kamensky sighed, put aside her wooden spoon, and came toward Raisa, wiping her hands on her apron. "Welcome, girl. I'm sure that my son will get around to telling me who you really are when he's ready to stop acting like a goose. Why someone so smart would ever act so silly! You'd think he was only six instead of sixteen."

"Now, Mama, you know you love me," Gavrel said, dipping his head to give her a kiss on the cheek. "Don't give Raisa the wrong idea. She's only been in this country for a day, so she's likely to believe anything."

"Raisa?" The older woman adjusted the thick steel-rimmed spectacles perched on her slender nose and examined her guest closely. Her gaze lingered dubiously on Raisa's shorn head. "You poor thing, did they do that to you on Ellis Island?"

Raisa hugged herself, painfully aware of the *real* question Mrs. Kamensky was asking. "Several months ago, I was sick with typhus. I don't have head lice."

"Who said you did?" Gavrel's mother raised her hands,

claiming innocence. "Well, don't worry, it will grow back. What a shame—such a nice color, like embers. When I was a girl, my mother cut off all my hair because I had the measles. Sit down, sit down, you must be starved!" She herded the girls out of the kitchen toward an oilcloth-covered table near the front window. "We can talk while you're eating. Would you look at this face?" She pinched Brina's cheek, making the child yip like a puppy. "So sweet, I could eat her all up in two bites! Gavrel, don't you dare leave this house until you help me put food on the table for our guests. Your father will forgive you for being late. And if he doesn't, too bad about him! He shouldn't be depending on your help in the shop at all after today."

"After today . . ." Gavrel looked wistful. "Back to the salt mines."

"Don't talk like that," his mother reproached him. "You're lucky to have such a good job waiting for you, and at your age. A cutter brings home a nice salary!"

"I know, I know." Gavrel took pale blue plates and cups out of a glass-front cupboard and laid them out in front of the girls. "I'll thank Uncle Hersch for putting in a good word for me."

"You could also thank your own sister," Mrs. Kamensky said, huffing indignantly as she produced a loaf of bread and a plate with butter and cheese from the kitchen. "Fruma spoke up for you! She told them that you might be young, but that you can do the cutting work of three grown men."

"I don't think they listen to the girls much when it comes

146

to hiring," Gavrel said. He sat down beside Brina. "Especially not for hiring cutters. That's strictly a man's job. But I appreciate her support."

"They listened to the girls plenty during the big strike!" Gavrel's mother looked smug as a well-fed cat. "I went with Fruma to the meeting at Cooper Union, where they called for all the garment workers to walk off the job. There was a little bit of a girl, Clara Lemlich, who got onto the platform with all the men and made the motion that started it all. And about time! Some of those men were so in love with the sound of their own fine speeches, they'd still be talking today, but that Clara got right to the point. After, Fruma told me how just a few months before, the bosses paid to have that girl beaten to within an inch of her life for leading a strike at Leiserson's factory. One hoodlum wasn't going to be enough to face all five feet nothing of her, so they sent a gang. They knocked her down, broke her ribs, left her bleeding on the street, but did that stop her?"

"Mama, please, calm down," Gavrel said, chuckling. "You sound like you're ready to throw down your apron and go get work in a shirtwaist shop just so you can start your own strike!"

"And don't think I couldn't!" his mother said tartly. "If my eyes were better—and God be thanked they're not worse!—I'd get a shop job and show all you young ones how to do things *right*." She stamped back to the stove, where they heard her adding coal to the fire.

Brina looked at the bread, butter, and cheese on the table.

"You said *cake,*" she said with an accusing look at Gavrel.

"I did, didn't I? Let me fix that before I leave." He rose from his seat and went into the kitchen. Raisa heard him speaking with his mother but couldn't make out the words. The longer the two of them talked, the more perplexed she became. *How long does it take to ask for a piece of cake for the child?* she wondered. At last the muffled conversation ended, there was the sound of retreating footsteps, the front door opened and closed, and finally Mrs. Kamensky came back into the front room carrying a tray of food with three tall glasses of tea.

"No cake?" Brina asked plaintively.

"Brina! Be grateful," Raisa chided. "This is more than plenty for us." She put a morsel of cheese on Brina's plate, followed by a thinly buttered slice of bread. "She's had enough sweets for the day," she told her hostess. "Cookies, strudel . . . She gave herself a bellyache. She doesn't need cake."

"*My* cake gives no one a bellyache," Mrs. Kamensky declared, distributing the glasses of tea. She swept a domed porcelain dish from among the framed photographs, candlesticks, and knickknacks on the mantel and removed the cover with a triumphant flourish. "A nice sponge cake filled with raspberry jam. Fruit is very good for children." She plopped a huge serving onto Brina's plate before Raisa could say another word.

Mrs. Kamensky sat down and sipped her tea, smiling her approval as she watched Brina enjoy the cake. "If she gets another bellyache, let the blame be on my head," she said calmly. "I'll make her a hot water bottle, have her chew a nugget of ginger root, whatever is necessary. You won't lose a single wink of sleep even if she's awake all tonight."

"Tonight?" Raisa felt like an idiot, repeating the older woman's final word, but it was all she could do. Her mind couldn't accept what she thought she was hearing.

"You'll have to share a mattress. We've only had one boarder at a time, although heaven knows we could use more! But my husband, he's too proud to admit that. He sees some of these families taking in two, three, four lodgers at a time, with nowhere decent to put them, stacking them up anywhere they can, like firewood. He says that if we ever have to sink that low, it's time to pack up and move back to Russia. As if he ever would!"

"We can stay here?" Raisa asked. Impulsively she reached across the table and clasped Mrs. Kamensky's hand.

"Why not? My Gavrel told me everything. You look like a clean girl, and like I said, we need a boarder. It's the only way I can bring in a little extra money for the house, with my eyes the way they are. You're welcome here."

"That's wonderful! I can pay you our first week's rent right now, if you like."

"Wait until you bring your things over here and meet my husband. I always let him collect the lodgers' rent, even though he hands it back to me at once."

Raisa jumped up from her place. "I can go get our bags right now! Oh, Mrs. Kamensky, I'm so happy! Everywhere else we went, they said they couldn't take us because—"

"I know, I know. Didn't you hear me say that Gavrel told me everything? Sit down, please." Mrs. Kamensky waved Raisa back into her seat. "Drink your tea like a civilized person. Your bags aren't going to run away before sundown. Why the hurry to move in? You haven't even asked how much it will cost you to live here."

"Oh! I—I'm sure you'll ask a fair price."

Gavrel's mother arched one brow. "You are a very trusting girl."

"No, I'm not," Raisa replied. "Not always. But trusting you feels right."

"I could say the same about you." Mrs. Kamensky laced her fingers around her empty tea glass. "Let's hope neither one of us is making a mistake. Listen, Raisa, we have a thing or two to discuss. You have no job. That has to change as soon as possible or it won't matter how much I trust you, you'll have to go. We can't keep you here if you can't pay. I'm sorry, that's just the way it is."

"I understand." Raisa bowed her head. "I swear, I'll find work tomorrow! I'm a good seamstress, except—except not with a machine. But if I can't get a job sewing, I'll look for something else, anything! I saw a couple of clothing stores downstairs. Do you think they'd want to hire me to make alterations? I'm good with numbers, too. I could sell candy, or tobacco, or—"

"Or the moon." Mrs. Kamensky's laugh was a lot like her

son's. "I hope you'll look for a job *beyond* the shops in this building. I have no doubt you'll find one, if not tomorrow, then the next day. It's good for a boss to see you're hungry for honest work, but never let him guess you're starving." She reached for the cake plate and gave Raisa a big slice. "And once you have your job, don't worry about Brina. We will keep each other company. Isn't that right, sweetness?" she asked the child.

Brina's lower lip stuck out. "My tummy hurts."

That night, Raisa and Brina sat down to their first dinner in their new home. A dose of ginger tea and a nap had settled the child's stomach. Mrs. Kamensky beamed to see what a good appetite she had.

The girls met Fruma just before dinner was served. Gavrel's sister came home from work so tired that she nearly tripped over the new boarders' bags by the front door. She stubbed her foot against Henda's battered leather satchel and staggered, her brown straw hat flying off.

"Oh! Let me get that for you!" Raisa rushed to retrieve the fallen hat. "I'm sorry," she said as she handed it back to its owner. "I just brought those over here late this afternoon. I haven't been told where to store them yet."

"You're our new boarder?" Fruma's curly brown hair framed a round face as white and delicately beautiful as a china doll's. "A pleasure to meet you, miss."

"'Miss'?" Gavrel echoed. "My dear Fruma, perhaps you're

not aware that the proper way to address a royal princess's lady-in-waiting is . . . is . . ." He scratched his head. "Well, I suppose it's 'Lady.'"

"What princess?" Fruma asked.

"The one I dosed with ginger tea this afternoon, my darling," Mrs. Kamensky said. "You'll be sitting next to her at dinner. Her name is Brina, that's Raisa, and your brother had better stop all his princess-and-lady nonsense before somebody mistakes him for a lunatic. Now, let's eat."

It was a very enjoyable dinner. Mrs. Kamensky's cooking was simple but delicious. Most of the conversation centered around how Raisa, Brina, and Gavrel had happened to meet.

"That's what I call luck," Gavrel said. "They needed a new place to live, we needed a new boarder, and old Mr. Fischel turned out to be the matchmaker!"

"Don't tell him that, or he'll want a fee," Fruma said. She used her own knife and fork to cut up Brina's carrots.

"Why luck?" their mother asked. "Gavrel, all we've ever heard out of your mouth since you were nine years old was how you want to grow up to study Torah and Talmud, to teach, to become a rabbi someday! And when something like this happens, you call it luck and not the hand of the Almighty? Luck is for gamblers, not rabbis!"

"I'd say we could all benefit from a little luck now and then, Mama," Gavrel replied. "Gamblers *and* rabbis. Papa, tell her I'm right!"

Gavrel's father grunted. It was the only sound he'd made

at the table since reciting the blessing before the meal. As soon as he'd said "amen," he'd buried himself and his dinner plate behind a copy of the *Jewish Daily Forward.* If he was eating back there with a fork or with the fingers not holding up the paper, no one could tell.

Raisa had never seen a Yiddish newspaper before. In the shtetl, Reb Avner sometimes got his hands on a Polish paper, though Raisa had had to take his word for it since the printed letters had no meaning for her. Now, gazing at the newspaper screen Mr. Kamensky had set up between himself and his family, Raisa was happily surprised by how much of the stories she could read. She became captivated, letting her dinner go cold while she strained to solve the puzzle of newsprint.

"Well, Mama, it looks like we've lost another one to the *Forward*," Gavrel remarked with an exaggerated sigh. "That's not a newspaper, it's a swamp. It swallowed Papa long ago, and now it's gulping down Raisa, too!"

His teasing words startled Raisa out of her absorption in the newspaper and left her feeling deeply embarrassed. "I'm sorry, I didn't know I was doing anything wrong."

"Reading isn't wrong," Gavrel said. "Reading while your food just sits there, that's wrong *and* dangerous. Isn't that true, Mama?"

"Why ask me?" Mrs. Kamensky assumed a wounded look. "Putting a good meal on the table night after night isn't important. I *expect* it to be taken for granted."

Gavrel winked at Raisa. "See?" Fruma burst into laughter,

Raisa caught the urge to giggle in spite of her best efforts not to, Gavrel joined in, and Brina decided that if most of the grown-ups were having so much fun, she should go along with it, too, at the top of her healthy young lungs. An irate Mrs. Kamensky loudly berated them all for the sin of disrespect.

"*Excuse* me?" Mr. Kamensky lowered the newspaper. "Has something happened? Has the President of the United States of America made a new law saying it's no longer permitted for a hardworking man to read in peace in his own home?"

"The president doesn't make the laws, Papa," Gavrel said. "Congress does. He only signs them into effect."

"So smart." Mr. Kamensky eyed his son coldly. "Such a genius. So tell me, Mr. Genius, who was the one who let those punk Irish kids steal three whole bolts of cloth from the store this afternoon?"

Gavrel squirmed. "I'm sorry, Papa. I wasn't paying attention."

"Well, you'd better pay attention to the cloth starting tomorrow on the new job or you'll slice your hand off with the cutting knife, God forbid! Now, apologize to your mother."

"Why are you telling him to apologize?" Fruma spoke up. "Do you even know what he did wrong? You weren't listening to us; you were reading!"

"Another county heard from." Mr. Kamensky turned his stony stare on his other child. "This is not how a good girl talks to her father. Mark my words, this country is ruining our daughters. Back talk, defiance . . . What next, Fruma? Are you going to chop off your hair and parade around looking like a man in skirts?"

As soon as the words left his mouth, he took his first really good look at Raisa. "Ah! I beg your pardon, miss. I didn't mean to offend. Short hair . . . it's very attractive on you. So!" He folded the *Forward* and laid it down next to his dinner plate. "What brings you to our table?"

Once again, Raisa recounted the events that had brought her from the shtetl to the Kamenskys' home. She didn't burden her new landlord with the details of her journey, only letting him know that the one thing in her new life of even more importance than finding a job was finding her sister. All this was news to Fruma, as well, but whereas her father listened to Raisa's story in sympathetic silence, she was soon moist eyed and sniffling audibly.

"Frumaleh, this isn't the matinee for the *Jewish Queen Lear*!" her mother exclaimed. "Raisa feels bad enough about her sister without you carrying on as if the poor girl was already dead and buried. Don't be so quick to turn a mystery into a tragedy before it's over."

"I can't help it," Fruma said, dabbing at her eyes with an embroidered handkerchief. "I don't know what I'd do if Gavrel simply . . . disappeared. I'd die!"

"I'll remind you of that the next time you're screaming at me over something I didn't do," Gavrel said, giving his sister's hand a squeeze. "Better yet, I'll disappear and make a fortune selling tickets to your big death scene!"

"*God forbid!*" Mr. Kamensky boomed. "Will you stop being

so *smart* for a change, boychik? To say such things about your own sister, just inviting the evil eye!" He spit three times to avert the curse, although Raisa noticed that he only went through the motions. She didn't want to see what Mrs. Kamensky would do to anyone who actually dared spit on her immaculate floors.

"Your mother is right, Fruma," Raisa said, hoping to restore the family harmony. "You shouldn't get so upset. I'm not." The lie fell out of her mouth like a stone. "I haven't even begun to look for her, not with any *real* effort. But now that my worries about where Brina and I can live are gone, I can take up the search with everything I've got!" She caught sight of the piercing look Mrs. Kamensky leveled at her and was quick to add, "When I'm not working, that is."

Fruma put away her handkerchief and blinked back the last of her tears. "You must let me help you, Raisa," she said. "It would do my heart good if I were the one to reunite you with your sister."

"Would you listen to Mrs. Astor over there?" Fruma's mother made an expansive gesture at her daughter. "A society lady with all the free time in the world to look for needles in haystacks!"

"I'll do *what* I can *when* I can, Mama," Fruma replied firmly. She looked at Raisa. "You can depend on me."

That night, Fruma insisted that Raisa and Brina spread their mattress next to her bed in the tiny room she occupied just off the kitchen. It had the look of an oversize pantry that had been stripped of its shelves and stuffed with far too much furniture for comfort. When the girls added the three traveling bags and the mattress to Fruma's bed, wooden chest, and the pegs where she hung her coat and dresses, there was no room to move unless they stood on the bags, the mattress, or the chest.

Brina fell asleep as soon as she lay down on the mattress. Raisa covered her with a thin blanket Mrs. Kamensky had given them, then sat cross-legged in her nightgown watching Fruma brush her long curls.

"I wonder how soon it will be before I can do that?" she mused aloud.

"Oh, you'll probably have hair down to your shoulders by your next birthday," Fruma replied lightly.

"You're trying to cheer me up," Raisa said, smiling.

"Yes, and if I were as clever as Gavrel, I'd do a better job of it. First I should have asked when your birthday comes. If it's next week, you'll know right away I was lying about your hair."

"You could have gotten away with it. I turned fourteen on the voyage over here. It was the day"—she glanced at Brina, who was deep in tranquil slumber—"the day after her mother died. I couldn't think about anything else that day." *I didn't even mention it to Zusa,* she thought wistfully, missing her friend.

"I'm not surprised." Fruma finished her work with the

brush and began weaving her hair into a braid, to keep it from tangling while she slept. "In that case, your hair *will* be down to your shoulders by the time you're fifteen. Or at least down to your chin. It's better to be happy with little victories than none at all."

"I'd be happy if it grew back enough to cover my ears again. I hate the way they stick out. I look like a man's shaving mug!"

Fruma chuckled. "I used to hate the way I looked when I was fourteen, too. Now that I'm twenty—"

"Oh! You're Henda's age!" Raisa gave a little gasp. Her hands clenched, and she leaned forward sharply.

Fruma was startled. "Raisa, what's wrong? Why are you *staring* at me like that?"

"Fruma . . . Fruma, when you were sixteen, did you look different than you do now?"

"Um, I guess I did." Fruma's fingers froze in the middle of tying a baby blue ribbon around the end of her braid.

"*How* different? A lot? A little?" A note of urgency had crept into Raisa's voice.

"I—I'm not sure. Not *too* much, I suppose." All at once, Fruma's bewildered expression became a look of understanding. "Raisa, come up here." She patted the end of her bed. When Raisa was seated beside her, Fruma said, "You're afraid you won't know her when you see her, is that it? You're scared that you'll go looking for the sixteen-year-old girl who left the shtetl and you won't recognize her now that she's twenty.

You're staring at me and trying to imagine what Henda must look like now, yes?"

Raisa nodded, then bowed her head. Fruma put both arms around her shoulders and hugged her. "Oh, Raisa, don't think such things! She's your sister; even if she's changed, you'll know her! And she's got eyes of her own; she'll know you, too, no matter how many years have passed. Believe it."

"I want to," Raisa murmured. "But I—I miss her so much, Fruma. I've waited four years to see her again, and just when I thought the waiting was over, she's *gone*. It makes me feel so empty, so alone, so . . . afraid." She looked at Fruma. "You must think I'm acting like a child."

"You aren't a child, Raisa." Fruma sat back, hands folded in her lap. "Could a child take such good care of another child?" She indicated Brina's sleeping form. "I think you have every right to feel afraid. You love your sister, you're worried about her, and you're exhausted from everything you've gone through to get here and be with her again. That makes it all worse. Doubts and fears feast on weariness, but once you've had a good night's sleep, you'll rule them instead of the other way around."

"Thank you, Fruma." Raisa gave the older girl a light kiss on the cheek. "I hope you're right." She slid off the bed, and got under the blanket next to Brina.

Just before she closed her eyes, she heard Fruma say, "I meant what I said at dinner. I *will* help you, you'll see. It's a promise."

A promise, Raisa thought sleepily. She stayed awake just long enough to whisper a prayer of thanksgiving for this new shelter and the good people whose roof she and Brina now shared, then gave herself up to dreams.

The next morning, Raisa awoke to the smell of strong coffee and hot bread. Brina still slept, her little fist pillowing her rosy cheek, but Fruma was up and dressed. She sat on the edge of the bed, the *Forward* in her lap.

"You should read this, Raisa," she said. "There are advertisements for jobs you might want. And you should really read this." She turned the paper so Raisa could see the feature she meant.

"'*A . . . Bintel Brief*'?" Raisa read unsteadily. True to its name, the column was a bundle of letters, all of them sent to the *Forward* by readers trying to cope with the great puzzle of their new lives. She looked narrowly at the first few lines of a letter from someone who signed herself A Grieving Mother. Piecing together a word here, a phrase there, and sometimes entire sentences, Raisa read the melancholy tale of how Grieving Mother's only child—a daughter she described as "my priceless pearl"—had fallen in love with one of the young men who worked in the same factory, except . . .

"An *Italian*?" Raisa was shocked to the core. "The girl wants to marry an Italian boy? But they're all Catholics, and she's Jewish!" The memory of Renzo's charming smile and manner made her quickly add, "They could be friends, yes, but married? That doesn't happen!"

Fruma didn't look at all scandalized by Grieving Mother's plight. "It happens a lot more than you'd think. Look, I didn't tell you to read '*A Bintel Brief*' for that kind of letter. People like you, newcomers, write to the editor with questions about all sorts of American things they don't understand. If you read, you learn, and the more you learn, the sooner you'll feel at home here. It will help you find Henda."

"How?" Raisa asked.

"If you lose something precious in a stranger's house, it takes a long time to find it again because you don't really know where to start looking. But if you lose it in your own home, where you know every place it might be hidden—well, there it is! This is a big city, Raisa, but as soon as you learn enough to make it *your* city, you'll see how small it can become."

Chapter Eight

THE SLOW SEASON

For two weeks, Raisa left the Kamenskys' home every morning with her spirits high and her keenness to work practically radiating from every inch of her body. And every evening, she returned with nothing to show for her endeavors but sore feet, rapidly thinning shoe leather, the memory of closed doors, and every so often the apologetic explanation, "It's the slow season."

The first time she heard those words, she repeated them at the dinner table. The four Kamenskys exchanged knowing looks.

"The garment industry is its own little world," Gavrel said. "And like the world, it's got its seasons: designing the new fashions, making the samples, sending out the salesmen to show this year's models to the big department stores, waiting for the orders to come in. They don't have people *making* clothing until they know someone's going to *buy* the clothing they make."

"*That's* when the shops go crazy," Fruma said. "When the orders are in and they've got to fill them in a hurry. It's all right for the owners to make their people wait for weeks to have work, but God forbid their buyers wait for a minute to get their shirtwaists!"

"What's a shirtwaist?" Raisa asked. She'd heard Fruma use the term frequently when she spoke about her work, the English word standing out like a beacon in the middle of Yiddish conversations. She hadn't asked for an explanation before, fearing she'd look like an ignorant greenhorn, but curiosity finally got the better of her.

"This is a shirtwaist," Fruma replied, running her fingertips over the pretty white blouse she wore.

Raisa felt a little embarrassed at not knowing the name of a garment she'd seen thousands of women wearing since she'd first set foot on the streets of New York. "Did you make that, Fruma?"

Fruma laughed. "We don't seem to make anything else in the shop!" She brushed an imaginary speck of dust off the crisp cuffs. "We should get you one as soon as possible, and a nice skirt to go with it. Then you'll look like a real American girl!"

But Raisa's shirtwaist had to wait. The slow season reduced jobs to a trickle. Some factories closed their doors altogether, waiting for the orders to come in and the next busy season to arrive. Any jobs that were available went to experienced people. When the Kamenskys said the blessing before meals, Gavrel's mother always followed it up with her own prayer. Night after night she thanked God for having made her children so skilled with the sewing machine and the pattern-cutting knife that they kept their jobs in spite of the accursed slow season.

At the end of her second luckless week, Raisa sat across the table from Mrs. Kamensky, counted out the rent into her land-lady's hand, then gazed mournfully at what remained. She didn't need to add up the coins to know that there was not enough to pay for a third week's lodging.

She looked up and saw pity in Mrs. Kamensky's eyes. *She won't say it, but we both know what's on her mind: if I don't find work soon, Brina and I will have to leave.*

Mrs. Kamensky put the rent money into the pocket of her apron. "You know, Raisaleh, we do like having you and the little one living here," she said slowly. "You've both been a lot of help to me around the house. That Brina! Such an old soul, God bless her. Such a serious little housewife! If she were tall enough to reach the top of the stove and do the cooking, too, I wouldn't have to lift a finger! I don't think I could get along without her, and so . . ."

Is she saying what I think she is? Raisa's heart beat faster. *If I can't find a job this week, she's going to let me owe her the rent, for Brina's sake! Oh, thank God, this is more than I hoped—*

"And so if you're ever living somewhere they don't want

to look after the child for you, you just bring her to me." She patted Raisa's hand. "I'm sorry, my dear. The trouble is, at this time of year, no one's got a lot of money. Business is down at my husband's store. The children are bringing home salaries, but they've both had to take deep cuts in their pay. There's nothing they can do about it. Choices are for the rich."

"It's all right, Mrs. Kamensky," Raisa replied. "I understand. I appreciate your offer to take care of Brina."

"I wish I could do more for you both. Listen, if you promise not to tell my husband, I think I can let you have *one* more week without—"

"Maybe you won't have to," Raisa said, feeling a great surge of gratitude and affection for the older woman. "Today I'll go back to the Protective and Benevolent Association for my shtetl. They're always kind to me, and as helpful as possible, since the first time I went there to ask about Henda. Someone there might have news about where they're hiring. There was nothing the first few times I asked, but things can change."

"Of course they can," Mrs. Kamensky said in a voice that added, *But they never do.*

"And if that doesn't work, maybe I should go looking for my friend Luciana. Heaven knows, I have the time to do it."

"Luciana?" Mrs. Kamensky adjusted her glasses to peer at Raisa. "The Italian girl from the ship?"

Raisa bobbed her head. "Her people have a grocery store on Mulberry Street, Delvecchio's. They said that if I needed help, to come see them there. One of her brother's friends works in the garment business, and so does his sister. Maybe they've heard of a job I could—"

"Pfff! The slow season treats Italians the same as Jews. They're good people, but proud! As if every one of them were still Julius Caesar, King of Rome! If you go to them for help and they can't give you any, how will that make them feel? The best they might do for you is a job in their grocery store, a job where you'll never earn enough to pay me—" She paused and cleared her throat, red faced over her accidental indiscretion. "Well, a job that you can't *live* on, that's what."

"I wish I knew where else to ask," Raisa said.

Gavrel's mother tapped her lower lip pensively with one work-worn forefinger. "What about the Pig Market?"

The Pig Market was a raucous, swarming, frantic part of Hester Street, where people selling all sorts of goods competed noisily for customers. It was also the place where those who were desperate for jobs waited to be found by people eager to take advantage of their desperation. Raisa saw how the men and women who shared her situation went about attracting potential employers. They stood in the midst of the crowds and shouted their skills to the world, or else they hung back against the side of a building and plucked at the sleeves of passersby, urgently reciting a list of all the abilities they could bring to a job.

Raisa decided to shout rather than to beg. It wasn't in her

nature to make a spectacle of herself, but she was afraid that if she tried the quieter style of seeking work—reaching out to grab total strangers by the sleeve—she might be mistaken for a prostitute. She'd already seen plenty of those unlucky women on the streets, and she knew how they solicited customers. Better to shout like a peasant at a cattle fair!

She bellowed her qualifications and experience as a seamstress for what seemed like hours. A few people gave her curious looks as they walked past, and a handful stopped to speak with her but continued on their way as soon as they learned that she didn't know how to run a sewing machine. Her voice was almost gone by the time a thickset woman stopped and asked her a question in an unintelligible language. Raisa replied hopefully in Yiddish, but only got a puzzled look in return.

A busybody peddler manning a nearby pushcart overheard and called out to Raisa, "That's Ukrainian! She said you look like a good worker and she asked what jobs you can do, but she don't speak Yiddish. You know Polish, maybe?" Raisa nodded. "So let's see if she understands that. Hey, you! Lady!" He tossed a few words of Polish at the woman. Her doughy face broke into a big smile, and she began jabbering back.

Her name was Orynko, and she was looking to hire someone to work in her dress shop. She didn't seem concerned that Raisa wasn't a sewing machine girl. "I'll teach you how to use the machine," she said. "Until then, you will sew for me by hand."

Orynko ran a tiny dressmaker's shop in the basement of a building on Delancey Street, a neighborhood very much like the one where the Kamenskys lived, though just a bit shabbier here and there. Even though the big woman didn't speak Yiddish, the sign in the shop window advertised MADAME ODILE'S FINE TAILORING FOR LADIES in that language as well as in English. As soon as Raisa crossed that dank threshold, her new employer made it clear that Orynko no longer existed and that she was to be addressed exclusively as Madame in the shop. She then put Raisa to work sewing linings into women's jackets, skirts, dresses, and coats.

As Raisa expected, it was piecework. Madame told her she would get a certain amount of money for each finished garment. Two more girls worked in the badly lit basement—one running the rickety sewing machine, the other draping and pinning the articles of clothing. Once a day, a spindly little boy arrived at the shop hauling a bundle of cut pattern pieces. Madame handled the customers, who came to order new clothes, to have old clothes remade, and to collect their finished orders. In addition to Polish and Ukrainian she seemed able to do business in English, but neither she nor the girls in the shop knew a word of Yiddish.

Once or twice, Raisa tried to chat in Polish with her coworkers. She didn't know whether or not the sewing machine girl would understand her, but she'd heard the draper speaking that language with a woman who'd come in for a final fitting. Her attempts at striking up a friendly conversation hit two brick walls. The sewing machine girl gave her a blank look, paused just long enough to cup one hand over the silver crucifix she wore around her neck, and went back to work. The draper shook her head, as if Raisa had spoken to her in Chinese, but before she turned her back, she made the face of a girl who had encountered an open cesspit and in perfect Polish muttered, "She had to hire a filthy Jewess."

Raisa felt the tips of her ears go hot with humiliation, but she said nothing. What good would it do? If she spoke up, Madame might take the draper's side and then—

I'd lose my job. I can't afford that risk. Raisa's frustration settled into a hot lump in her stomach. She remembered times in the shtetl when peasants had come to town to trade but stayed to get drunk. They'd swaggered through the streets, shouting horrible insults at any Jew they met, pulling the beards of respected old men as a "joke," sometimes starting fistfights. But unless their antics turned murderous, no one did anything to stop them. The specter of pogroms was always there, along with the knowledge that the Jews were few in number compared with their neighbors. Glukel herself had taught the girls that it was better to endure insults than to retaliate and bring down something worse on their heads.

"It's just the way things are," Glukel had said sadly. Raisa understood, and complied when she had no other choice, but she didn't like it at all.

After that, Raisa worked in silence and as far from the other two girls as the narrow shop allowed. She focused all her thoughts on doing a good job, the way Glukel had taught her. Every day, Madame counted the garments Raisa finished and wrote the number down twice, once in her own notebook and once on a piece of pasteboard for Raisa to keep.

"Ah, that's good!" Mrs. Kamensky said when Raisa reported this at home. "It means she's going to keep an honest tally of your work so that there'll be no question of cheating you on payday. Frankly, I'm surprised."

"Why, Mama?" Gavrel teased. "Because there's an honest employer out there who's not Jewish?"

"Don't be silly," his mother said with an indignant sniff. "There are plenty of Jewish bosses out there who are worse thieves than any of the goyim!"

At the end of Raisa's first week of work, Madame called the girls up to her desk one by one, asked to see their tally cards, made a big show out of comparing the numbers on the cards with the numbers in her notebook, and handed over their pay. Raisa's turn came last, after the other two left the shop. It had not been an easy week. Aside from the hateful incident with the draper, she had been the object of Madame's almost daily screaming fits over mistakes she'd supposedly made. What made the attacks worse was that, try as she might, Raisa could not see what Madame was complaining about. The stitches that were "too loose, too sloppy!" were identical to other stitches that Madame very grudgingly conceded were "well done, much better."

Madame took coins from a tin box and slid them across the

table to Raisa. "Your pay. Tomorrow is Sunday, so the shop will be closed. Come in an hour early on Monday, sweep and mop the floors." She closed the tin box, clipped a small padlock through the hasp, and rose to go.

Raisa counted her pay, then counted it a second time, perplexed. "Excuse me, Madame," she said. "There's been a mistake. This isn't enough. See?" She pointed to the amount written on her tally card, then at the pile of coins.

Madame spread her hands. "No understand," she said with a false smile.

"But you were supposed to give me *this* much," Raisa insisted, tapping the card. "Look, you wrote these numbers yourself!"

"No understand," Madame repeated. "Closing time. You go." It was amazing how conveniently her command of Polish had deserted her.

Raisa stood her ground. Her eyes smarted from day after day of sewing tiny stitches in bad light. Her shoulders ached from working long hours in a cramped space. She wasn't going to go home with less than her fair pay.

"Madame, if you'll only look at the notebook and my card one more time, you'll see that you owe me—"

"*Nothing!*" The woman's eyes flashed fire. Her fluent Polish came back as magically as it had slipped away before. A flood of vicious abuse rolled from her tongue. "I should have known better than to hire one of *you*. Always grubbing, grubbing, grubbing for the last penny! Stinking Jew, you wouldn't know the meaning of gratitude unless someone beat it into your bones! How dare you suggest that I don't pay my workers *exactly* what I owe them? I have lived in this country for twenty years, I have run this shop for ten, and *you* want to correct *me*? I paid you every cent you earned *after* I deducted everything you owed me."

"What could I possibly owe you?" Raisa felt as if she had tumbled into a madman's dream.

"Are you sly or stupid? First there were all the needles you broke." Madame started counting off Raisa's "expenses" on her fingers. "Then there was all the thread you used, including all the bits you snipped off and wasted. And what about the cost of having your scissors sharpened? And the sewing lessons—"

"What lessons?" Raisa cried. Her head spun. *All those times she screamed at me, criticizing my work for faults that weren't there—merciful God, is* that *what she means by "sewing lessons"?* "You hired me because I know how to sew!"

"I hired you because I am good-hearted," the woman said stiffly. "But I am not a fool. If you don't like it here, there's the door. Go."

Raisa closed her eyes. *I can't go,* she thought. *I can't, and she knows it.* Mrs. Kamensky's words made a melancholy echo in her mind: *Choices are for the rich.*

"I'm sorry, Madame," she said, bowing her head in surrender. "I—I was wrong. I'm just a stupid greenhorn. I don't know any better. You're very—very kind to be so patient with me." When she raised her eyes, she saw the cruelly gloating grin on the Ukrainian woman's face. Madame was relishing her triumph.

"Perhaps you are not so stupid as all that, girl," she said. "Be here *two* hours early on Monday. I think that next week, I will start to give you lessons about how to run the sewing machine."

Four weeks after her arrival in America, Raisa trudged home through the steaming summer streets, her eyelids like lead. Every bone in her body cried out for rest. Her work in Madame's shop was eating her up alive. At night she ate her dinner in a trance and went to bed even before Brina did.

At least I know Brina's happy, Raisa thought as she threaded her way between the people sitting on the stone steps outside the tenement. The hot summer weather sent everyone outdoors, famished for a breath of fresh air. *Fruma and Mrs. Kamensky take such good care of her, and they love doing it!* She sighed. *Brina is fine, but what's happened to the rest of my life? I can't learn like I promised Glukel, and what about searching for my sister? Where's the time for that?* A pang of guilt struck hard. She could almost hear Henda calling out to her, *Raisa! Raisa, where are you?*

She dragged her feet up the four flights of stairs to the Kamenskys' apartment. Everyone was already sitting down to dinner. Brina gave a happy shout when she saw Raisa and ran to hug her. "Guess what?" she demanded, pulling Raisa to the table. "Today I read a *whole letter* from the newspaper! I did it all by myself and I only made one mistake, didn't I, Tante Lipke?" She looked to Mrs. Kamensky for confirmation.

"Brina, you speak with respect to Mrs. Kamensky," Raisa corrected the child automatically.

"Please, she speaks with enough respect," Mrs. Kamensky said. "I told her she should call me her *tante*. I have no sisters or brothers, so how else can I be an auntie?"

Brina chattered on about her accomplishment. Raisa only half heard her. The heat inside the tenement was oppressive, even with the two windows wide open. Mrs. Kamensky had served her family a cold dinner of pot cheese, bread and butter, chilled borscht, and pickled cucumber salad to cheat the humidity, but there was nothing she could do to thwart the smells of rotting garbage and horse manure wafting up from the street. Fruma took five pages of an old copy of the *Forward*, pleated them tightly, and made fans for the grown-ups. Raisa was too drained to do more than flutter hers limply six or seven times before letting it drop into her lap.

"Allow me, miss." With a gallant bow, Gavrel used his own fan to send a faint breeze in Raisa's direction.

"You don't have to do that." Her protest sounded as weak as she felt, but his kindness made her feel human again.

"Doesn't it make you feel better? I don't mind, you know." He waved the fan harder. "And tonight, Papa and I are going to move a couple of mattresses out onto the fire escape so that we can enjoy the evening breezes."

"We can't sleep out there!" Raisa cried. "Brina could fall."

"How? Through the bars?" Gavrel winked at the little girl. "Are you *that* skinny, Brina? Let me see." He turned the paper fan on her and waved it even more vigorously. "Aha! Just as I suspected: she *is* too skinny. She's blowing away!"

"I am not!" Brina snatched the pleated newspaper from Gavrel and flapped it at him. "You're the skinny one! You're the one who's blowing away!"

Mr. Kamensky turned to his wife. "Lipke, do you know how we'll be able to tell when the Messiah's about to come? When I get to sit down and eat one dinner in peace and quiet at this table, *that's* how we'll know." He picked up that day's edition of the *Forward* and retreated to his paper fortress.

"When I get to sit down and eat one dinner without you whining about nothing," his wife replied. "Come, Brina, darling. Help me clear the table for dessert."

Brina was delighted to carry the dinner dishes to the sink. Fruma, too, pitched in, but when Raisa tried to rise and help, Gavrel said, "Not tonight, Raisa. Not unless you want to break every dish you touch, and you know how much Mama would like *that*."

"What are you talking about? I won't break anything."

"Not on purpose. The plates will simply slip through your fingers."

"That's ridiculous!" Raisa reached for the bowl holding the leftover pot cheese.

"I agree." Fruma snatched the bowl away before Raisa

could touch it. "Gavrel *is* being ridiculous. You wouldn't drop a thing, but Mama's already got enough helping hands here. Listen, maybe you could do *me* a favor? Brina might be all right spending the night on the fire escape, but I've never liked it. I'd rather sleep on the roof. The only problem is, a lot of other people in this building get the same idea and then it's so crowded up there, you might as well try sleeping in the middle of Orchard Street. So before I put anyone to the trouble of moving my mattress up two flights of stairs, would you mind going up there and seeing if there's room for it?"

"I'd be happy to," Raisa said. "And if it's nice, Brina and I will join you." She started for the front door.

"Not so fast!" Gavrel spoke up. "I'm the one who'll be hauling the mattresses. I'm coming with you."

It actually took climbing three flights to reach the tenement roof from the Kamenskys' apartment. A narrow set of iron steps behind a door on the sixth floor brought Raisa and Gavrel out under the stars. The rooftop was covered with long planks of wood haunted by the smoky smell of tar. A few families had laid out bedding on the boards already, but there was still plenty of space. A refreshing breeze wafted over Raisa's cheeks, carrying a hint of the sea. She sighed happily.

"I'm going to like sleeping up here. I hope you'll let me help you and your father move the mattresses. The one Brina and I use weighs next to nothing. I think I could carry it myself. Shall we go back downstairs and tell . . . ?"

The words faded from her lips. She became aware that

Gavrel was looking at her intently. The full moon above the New York rooftops provided more than enough light for her to see the expression on his face. For the first time since they'd met, she couldn't see a single glimmer of mirth in his eyes. The Gavrel she knew was always joking, always trying to make others laugh. It was unnerving to see him looking so serious.

"What's the matter?" she asked.

"You're tired, Raisa, that's what's the matter."

"Of course I'm tired," she said. "I just finished a week's work."

"Your boss crams two weeks' work into one, dumps it into your lap, and pays you for half. We have to get you out of that sweatshop."

"Out of there and into where? Gavrel, I have to have a job, and they're not exactly dropping out of the trees. If I don't get paid, Brina and I can't stay, and she's so happy here! If I lose this job, I might never get another, and then—"

"Raisa, *look* at me." He grabbed her shoulders. Someone from one of the family groups already camped out on the rooftop snickered. Raisa felt her face redden with the embarrassment of being a public spectacle, but if Gavrel heard, too, he ignored it or didn't care. "You can't let this job—any job—smother you. The longer you let it grind you into dust, the harder it's going to be to stand up and say, 'No! Enough! I don't deserve to be treated this way. I'm worth *more.*'"

A bitter smile twisted Raisa's mouth. "I don't think Madame is going to give me a raise so fast."

Gavrel's face turned grim. "What you're worth has nothing to do with what you're paid by that slave driver *Madame* or anyone else. Why are you the only one who can't see that?"

"Because it doesn't *matter*." Raisa slapped Gavrel's hands away. "What counts is being able to pay the rent and scrape together enough money to provide for Brina. I'm all she has! If I lose my job at the dress shop, how will what I'm *worth* help support her? Will it give her a bed to sleep in and a roof over her head? Will it put food in her mouth and shoes on her feet?"

"Will it find your sister?" Gavrel asked the question in a barely audible murmur, but it exploded in Raisa's ears with the force of a thunderclap. She stared at him, stunned and heartsick. His stern expression melted into a look of compassion. "I'm sorry. I didn't mean to cause you pain. Papa's right; I'm only smart with books, not people. I only wanted to say that—well, that this job of yours is draining you so dry that you've got no strength left for anything else in your life. Didn't you tell Fruma that you wanted to learn English, to help you ask more people about where Henda might be? I know you told *me* you wanted to keep going back to the Protective and Benevolent Association, just in case someone there has news for you. And what about your plan to find some of the girls from her old job at American Pride and ask them if—"

"*Stop* it, Gavrel." Raisa's hands were fists at her sides. "I don't need to be reminded of all the things I *haven't* done to find Henda. I'm surprised you don't write all of my shortcomings into the letters I send home. While you're at it, you could tell Glukel and Reb Avner and everyone else that I'm still so ignorant that I need someone to write letters for me, and sometimes to read the ones they send back!"

Gavrel's face fell. "I'm not your enemy, Raisa. I *want* you to learn to read, to write, to speak English, to run a sewing machine like an expert so you can get a good job when the slow season's over. I think you could learn anything you wanted to, if you weren't so exhausted all the time. I watched you help Mama with the household budget. You can make numbers dance. You're a very smart girl, Raisa."

"Don't you mean I'm smart *for* a girl?" she retorted.

The old grin came back. "Well, it sounds like you're not too exhausted to be a bigger wisenheimer than me. Where did all your tiredness vanish to? I should argue with you more often; it livens you up."

"If I felt any livelier, I'd be dead," Raisa said. But she returned his smile. "We should go back downstairs. Your parents will think one of us fell off the roof."

"Or was pushed." Gavrel started back for the rooftop door. "Promise me you'll think about what I said, Raisa. I know we need to have a paying boarder in the house, but I'll bet Mama would let you go one week on trust, maybe two, if it meant you could better your situation. And Fruma and I have been keeping our ears open at work, ready to jump the minute we hear about a job for you."

"No big garment factory's going to hire someone who can't use a sewing machine," Raisa said.

"What, you can't use one at all?" Gavrel was astonished at

the news. "I thought you had some practice. Didn't you tell us that Madame promised to teach you?"

"She promised to pay me a fair wage, too." Raisa gave a short, humorless laugh. It was do that or burst into frustrated tears.

"That does it!" Gavrel slammed his fist into his other palm. "That is the last straw. Hear me, Raisa: this Sunday you are going to come with me to my friend Rachel's house and we are going to teach you everything you need to know about running a sewing machine so that when the time comes, you can thumb your nose in *Madame*'s ugly face and walk away to a good job!"

"Your friend, she's got a sewing machine she'll let me use?"

"Her father had a little dressmaking business when he first came over, but last April he died of tuberculosis. Luckily all five kids already had factory jobs to keep the family going. Some of the girls still use their father's machine to do a little piecework on the side, so it's in perfect condition. If I ask Rachel to let us use it, I'm sure she won't tell me no."

"I'm sure she won't tell you no, either," Raisa muttered as they headed back to the apartment and dessert.

Chapter Nine

NEW PATHS AND OLD

Rachel and her family lived in the cleanest tenement Raisa had seen. The Kamenskys' apartment was spotless, and so were the homes of most of the other tenants in their building, but the building itself had its seedy corners and neglected areas. The six-story brick structure where Rachel lived was spick-and-span, from the well-swept sidewalk out front all the way up to the door of Rachel's apartment.

A tall, willowy girl with golden brown hair and amazing blue eyes opened the door at Gavrel's knock. "Rachel, good morning!" he exclaimed. "Forgive me, I should have brought you some flowers. After all, a man shouldn't come empty-handed when he wants to ask a beautiful woman for a favor."

"Gavrel, you know you can ask me anything," she replied, her smile setting off the dimples in her cheeks. "Where have you been hiding? Ever since you got that new job at Triangle, I don't see you anymore."

"Ah." He rubbed the back of his head, tilting his derby hat forward at an awkward angle. "Well, everyone keeps telling me how lucky I was to *get* a job in the slow season, so it must be true. That means I'd better stay busy where the boss can see, or else . . ." He slashed a finger across his throat. "You know how it is."

"I believe I do." Rachel's eyes rested on Raisa. "And who is this?"

"This," Gavrel said, "is the favor."

What did he call me?! Raisa bit her lips to contain the resentment rising in her throat. When Rachel invited them into the apartment, Raisa trailed after Gavrel like a little storm cloud and mumbled her way through the introductions. She responded to Rachel's small talk with one-word answers until she overheard the girl whisper to Gavrel, "If she doesn't even speak Yiddish, how *do* you manage to talk to her?"

"I'm sorry," Raisa said. "I'm being rude. It's just that I'm a little nervous. I haven't seen such a lovely home since I came to this country." Rachel gracefully accepted both the apology and the compliment, and the conversation between the two girls became more natural.

She's going to help me, Raisa thought. *Gavrel's the one who called me a "favor," not her.*

Rachel served her guests tea in pretty china cups with worn gold rims. There were also fancy almond cookies, but Raisa was so eager to start learning how to use a sewing machine that she couldn't think about food or anything else. When it was finally time to begin her lessons, everything went as Gavrel had predicted. She learned the basics quickly and was sewing real pattern pieces together in less than three hours.

"Are you sure you've never done this before?" Rachel asked, holding up the body of a shirtwaist that Raisa had just stitched together. "Look at this! She even set in the sleeves perfectly!"

"I'm not so sure." Gavrel stroked his chin. "The left one looks a little off-kilter."

Rachel rolled her eyes at Raisa. "I forgot what a joker he is. Does he *ever* say a single serious word to you?"

"Once." Raisa smiled inside.

Two weeks later, as the sun was beginning to set, Raisa ran along one of the paths through Washington Square Park, her heart racing faster than her feet. She didn't give a second glance at the monumental marble arch that dominated the north side of the park. Even though her time in the city often left her starved for the sight of the green fields and forests of home, she was too distracted to appreciate the grand trees that loomed over the paved pathways.

Earlier that day, as Raisa was leaving the Kamenskys' building to trudge her way to Madame's shop, she was startled to find Rachel waiting for her. The pretty girl linked arms with Raisa and swept her down the street. "I have the most wonderful news for you, Raisa," she said. "But if this turns out the way I hope it will, I don't want Gavrel grabbing the credit for it."

"Gavrel wouldn't do something like that," Raisa protested.

"Oh, I'm only teasing. And why are you his big defender, hmm?" Rachel gave her an arch look. "Forget Gavrel—listen. My cousin Marjorie's going to have a baby!"

"Mazel tov." Raisa congratulated Rachel's family even though she felt entirely bewildered. "But how does this—"

"Affect you?" Rachel finished for her. She gave a delighted laugh. "Because Marjorie's a sewing machine girl, but now that a baby's on the way, her husband *insists* she quit her job, and where do you think she works?" She didn't wait for Raisa to make a guess. "Triangle Waists! Just like Gavrel and Fruma and—God willing—you, soon. We just heard the news from Marjorie and her husband last night. She's telling her foreman *today*. If you show up right away to fill the vacancy, he'll hire you at once; I *know* it. You're an excellent seamstress, and you learn quickly. This is your chance!"

"Thank you," Raisa whispered back. "I can't tell you how much I appreciate this, but—"

"But what?"

"I can't miss a day of work. Madame will fire me, and I need the money."

"So don't miss a day! Just miss an hour. All you need to do is get to Triangle before Marjorie's foreman goes home. You could tell your boss you're sick, or you're needed at home, or—or—"

"I'll find a way to get away from Madame," Raisa said decisively. "You tell me how to find your cousin's foreman."

Rachel gave Raisa the information she needed and left her on the next corner, hurrying off to her own job. Raisa went to the basement shop on Delancey Street and worked hard all day, her fingers doing the dull, thankless piecework, her mind spinning with possibilities and plans.

The hardest part was calculating the hour. Madame kept no clock in her shop. Quitting time was when she decided it should be, and that was usually later than factories such as Triangle. Raisa couldn't know what time it was, but she had a rough idea of how long it took her to finish each piece of sewing, and so she did her best to estimate the passing hours by the number of items she completed. When she figured the moment was right, she got up and approached her employer with downcast eyes.

"Madame, I need to use the toilet." There was none in the basement shop. Raisa and the other girls had to use the facilities in the building above.

"No, you don't," Madame snapped. "Go use toilet at home when work is done."

"Madame, *please*," Raisa insisted. "It is . . . *that* time for me, but it came early. I was not expecting . . ."

"Oh." Madame's hard eyes narrowed, but Raisa's excuse was inarguable. "Fine. Go upstairs. Here." She picked up a piece of scrap material and shoved it at Raisa. "You can use this. It comes out of your pay. Hurry back."

"Yes, Madame," Raisa said meekly. "Thank you, Madame." She scurried out of the basement and onto the bustling street, with a very convincing look of distress and embarrassment on her face. The instant she was out of sight of the dressmaker's shop, a miracle occurred: her bowed shoulders straightened, her miserable expression became a wide grin, and her feet became wings that carried her like the wind from Madame's shop to a chance at a better future.

Now Raisa dashed out of Washington Square Park on the east side and looked around frantically for the landmarks Rachel had told her to seek if she was going to find the Tri-angle Waist Company. "Asch, Asch, Asch," she muttered to herself, repeating the name of the building that housed the garment factory as if it were a magic charm. Since she couldn't read the signs, she counted the streets, the way Rachel had suggested, until she reached the spot where Washington Place met Greene Street.

Then she saw it. There was no mistaking it. Rachel's words echoed through her mind: *The Asch Building's one of the tallest in that neighborhood, though there are a couple next to it that are even taller. Still, ten stories is nothing to sneeze at! Don't worry, you won't have to count the floors. The sign will tell you you've found it.*

But won't the sign be in English? Raisa had whispered back.

Rachel smiled. *You'll see.*

And she did. Raisa's gaze traveled up the gray facade with its touches of ornamental stonework. At the top of a column of signs for other clothing makers that hung on the corner of the building, she saw one that displayed the image of a triangle in a circle. Rachel was right; she didn't need to be able to read the English words on that sign to know that she'd found the Triangle Waist factory.

Raisa had seen her share of tall buildings since coming to New York, but the sight of each new one never failed to fill her with awe. *Gavrel and Fruma work all the way up there? They must be able to see the whole city! I wonder if I'll run into them? Oh, I hope not! If I don't get this job, I don't want them to know I failed.*

She noted the door that opened onto Washington Place; she started toward it. Just then, a trio of well-dressed men came ambling out of the building. Their suits, hats, and shoes were far too elegant and costly looking for shop employees.

That's not the door the workers use, Raisa thought, and walked briskly around the corner onto Greene Street. Here she saw another entrance to the building. *This must be it,* she thought. *If it's not . . .* She hesitated.

Somewhere, a church bell rang. A few people began to emerge from the Greene Street door, and in that instant all of Raisa's second thoughts vanished. *Quitting time! I have to find Marjorie's foreman before he leaves!* She ran down Greene Street and through the doorway, outracing every thought except *I have to get this job!*

🔥 🔥 🔥

Mrs. Kamensky was peeling potatoes in the kitchen with Brina when Raisa came bursting into the apartment like a whirlwind of joy. "I did it!" she shouted, sweeping Brina into the air and twirling wildly. "I did it, I did it! I got a new job, and you'll never guess where, and—"

"And the baby is going to throw up all over my clean floor if you don't put her down right now and stop acting like a wild thing." Mrs. Kamensky took Brina out of Raisa's hands firmly and cooed, "Are you all right, sweetheart?"

"Again!" Brina cried, trying to wriggle out of Mrs. Kamensky's arms and back to Raisa.

"So, where is this new job?" Mrs. Kamensky asked while keeping an unbreakable hold on Brina.

"Triangle, that's where!" Raisa collapsed onto one of the kitchen chairs. She thought she would never be able to get the smile off her face as she told Mrs. Kamensky and Brina the whole story. "Madame nearly tore my head off when I got back. She thought I'd slipped away to see a boy. You don't want to know the names she called me!"

"I can guess," Mrs. Kamensky said drily. "And what did you call her?"

The question took Raisa by surprise. "Her? Nothing. I don't start work at Triangle until next week, and I don't get paid where I am until Saturday. The old herring steals enough of my money without my giving her an excuse to take it all!"

Mrs. Kamensky nodded. "Gavrel is right, you *are* a smart girl. Now, can you also be a *good* girl and give an old woman a little pleasure?"

"Anything," Raisa said and meant it. "What do you want me to do?"

"Don't say a word about the new job to anyone else until after dinner, when I bring out the dessert."

That night, after serving a modest meal, Mrs. Kamensky stunned her family by emerging from the kitchen bearing a towering apricot torte for dessert, the rich golden cake crowned with clouds of sweetened whipped cream. The sight of so much extravagance at the dinner table lured Mr. Kamensky out from behind his newspaper to ask if he'd forgotten someone's birthday.

"It's for Raisa," Brina announced. "But it can be my birthday, if you want."

With a go-ahead nod from Mrs. Kamensky, Raisa shared her news. The apartment rang with congratulations.

"Oh, Raisa, this is so lucky! The three of us can all go to work together!" a delighted Fruma cried.

"Maybe not the *three* of you, for too much longer," Mrs. Kamensky said coyly.

"*Mama!*" Fruma sounded mortified.

Raisa was confused by her friend's crimson-cheeked reaction. She turned to Gavrel for some sort of explanation.

"Nothing much to explain," he replied jauntily. "If a girl marries the right young man, it's good-bye and good riddance to shop work, and our Fruma is—"

"Gavrel, don't you dare say another word," Fruma said in darkly threatening tones.

Gavrel raised his hands in surrender. "My lips are sealed. And now"—he lifted a forkful of cake halfway to his mouth— "they're unsealed again." Between bites of the delectable dessert, he turned to Raisa and said, "You should get a new job more often. We'd eat like kings!"

Madame's screeches of outrage still burned in Raisa's ears as she bounced down Essex Street, looking into every store window she passed. The memory of the Ukrainian woman's furious face at the moment that Raisa pocketed her final week's pay and told her now-former employer that she wasn't coming back was like sweet honey on her tongue.

I'm free, she thought. *I'm* free! *I'll never work for such a greedy, grasping, coldhearted creature again.* She turned a corner and ran the rest of the way to the building housing her shtetl's Protective and Benevolent Association. Her job at Triangle didn't start for two days. She knew exactly how she was going to spend them.

The man behind the desk in the association's one-room office recognized Raisa from her previous visits. His watery gray eyes lit up in response to her joyous greeting. "Ah! You've found her? Mazel tov!" he blurted before she could say anything more. "So where was she all this time?"

A little of Raisa's elation left her. "I don't know. I haven't found her yet."

"Oh." The man's big walrus mustache drooped. "I'm sorry, but when you came in here looking so happy, I naturally assumed—"

"I'm happy because I've got a good job now. It starts in two days. Until then—"

"Say no more!" He raised his plump hands. "I wish I had some news to give you, but we've already asked everyone from home if they've seen or heard of Henda. Have you considered putting an advertisement in the *Forward*?"

"I don't think I could afford it."

"You know, this association shares resources with three others, representing the neighboring villages back home. We've asked all of them to keep an eye out for your sister. We even sweetened the pot with the offer of a reward."

"A reward?" Raisa's eyes widened. "I can't pay a reward."

"Not you, child. Reb Laski contacted us as soon as your first letter reached him, letting him know about Henda. He's a saintly man, openhanded and benevolent. The reward was his idea. If you write and ask him, he would probably send money for the advertisement, too."

Raisa shook her head. "Reb Laski has already done too much for Henda and me. We can never repay him. Once I start my new job, I'll be able to save enough money to pay for the advertisement on my own." *It's what Henda would do,* she thought staunchly. *It's what she'd want* me *to do, too!*

"I know better than to argue with a woman." A strong sigh riffled the walrus mustache.

After leaving the association office, Raisa trekked to the Educational Alliance, on East Broadway. On the way, she paused at Seward Park and watched the children having a grand time on the playground. They raced over the cinder-covered ground as though they were flying through the sweet green grass of a meadow.

What a nice place! she thought. *I'll have to bring Brina here, and soon. I can't wait to see how much she'll enjoy it.* Imagining the fun Brina would have on the playground made Raisa smile.

The Educational Alliance was an imposing brick building the color of a terra-cotta flowerpot. Raisa stood across the street, gazing up at the windows, unable to get herself to walk over and through the doors.

So big! she thought. *How will I find anything in there? If I get lost and start wandering around inside, how will that look? Like I'm a stupid greenhorn, that's how! So stupid I can't even find my way to a classroom.*

She thought back to the previous night at the Kamenskys' dinner table, when Gavrel took a sip of tea and said, "You know what else you should do, since you have a couple of days to yourself? Find someplace you can start learning English."

"Gavrel's right!" Fruma chimed in. "The Educational Alliance gives night classes."

Raisa shook her head. "At night, I'm too tired to do anything but sleep."

"Not anymore. Not once you start the new job. Trust me, once you're free of that Simon Legree you work for, you'll have the energy to go out after work and do something besides collapse like a house of cards."

"Who's Simon Legree?" Raisa asked.

Fruma promptly told everyone at the table the story of *Uncle Tom's Cabin* and the poisonous villain of the book. Her enthusiasm was so catching that her father let the *Forward* drift to one side while he listened. Mrs. Kamensky wept over the death of Little Eva and insisted on hugging Brina to her bosom for the rest of the story. Then Fruma recounted Uncle Tom's death, and Brina buried her face against Mrs. Kamensky's chest, whimpering.

"Now look what you've done," Mr. Kamensky grumbled at his daughter, while Raisa and his wife did their best to comfort the child.

"It's only a book," Fruma protested. "And an old one, at that. We read it when I was in school."

"It's a *wonderful* book," Raisa said. "You almost had me crying, too, Fruma."

"I was only telling the story," Fruma replied. "It's much better the way Mrs. Stowe wrote it."

"I wish I could read it." There was true longing in Raisa's words.

"You can if you learn English," Gavrel cajoled. "And *lots* of others."

"Well . . ." Raisa was deeply tempted. She remembered how much better Zusa's shipboard reading lessons had gone when they studied from *The Wishing-Ring.* For her, some reading was like stumbling through a rocky field, but a good story could lift her from her feet and send her sailing after it like a kite on a string.

Those times seem so far away, she thought. *Zusa and Luciana and me, looking after Brina together, and now . . . just me. They're like Yitta and Avigal, out of my life, left behind. It would be so good to see them again! At least there's no ocean between us, and I do know where to find Luciana; I just need the time to do it. Maybe now that I'm no longer Madame's slave, I can look for Henda and my friends.*

"Couldn't *you* teach her English, Gavrel?" Brina asked, wiping her nose on the back of her hand. Mrs. Kamensky tutted and rubbed the smear away with her own handkerchief while Brina kept on talking. "You know English. If you taught her, she wouldn't have to go somewhere else at night. I want her here!"

"Brina's right," Raisa said. "That would be perfect."

Gavrel shook his head. "Taking night classes would be better for you."

"Why don't you want to teach her?" Brina persisted. "Don't you like being with her? Do you think she can't learn?"

"No and no and where do you get such ideas, little monkey?" Gavrel whisked Brina out of his mother's lap and bounced her on his knee until she giggled. "But I have to learn, too. I'm not going to spend my whole life cutting out pattern pieces at Triangle Waists. I'm going to be a rabbi one day! I go to my own lessons whenever I can. Your sister can't learn English if she doesn't have regular lessons *and* the opportunity to practice speaking it the right way."

"Raisa's not my sister," Brina said. "And I'm not a little monkey."

"I beg your pardon, princess," Gavrel replied with mock solemnity. "But you must acknowledge that she loves you as if you were her sister."

"*Henda* is her sister." Brina spoke to Gavrel with the patience of a teacher helping a struggling student with the most basic lesson in the world. "She has to find her."

"And she will, I promise you. Learning English as quickly as possible will help her do that. It will let her go to many additional places where they might have information about what happened to Henda, but also where they don't speak any Yiddish at all."

"Then *they* should learn Yiddish, and Raisa should stay home with me."

Everyone laughed, making Brina indignant because she didn't see the joke. At last Gavrel stopped chuckling long enough to say, "But alas, princess, they refuse to do that, and we can't make them change their minds."

"Oh." Brina became thoughtful. "Then I think Raisa should go learn English. Then she can talk to the stupid people who don't know Yiddish, and they can tell her where to find Henda, and then we can all be together." A momentary worry troubled her. "If Henda likes me."

Now, standing on the sidewalk across from the Educational Alliance, Raisa remembered how she'd run around the dinner table to reclaim Brina from Gavrel and assure the child that Henda, too, would love her. *Gavrel's right,* she thought. *I need to learn English. But Brina's right, too—I wish he were the one to teach me.* She took a deep breath and crossed the street.

❦ ❦ ❦

Raisa's first day at Triangle Waists was so different from her time in Madame's shop that at first she thought it was a happy dream. After breakfast, she walked with Gavrel and Fruma to the towering Asch Building, just off Washington Square.

"I wonder what Glukel would say if she could see me now, going to work in a place so high that I've got to ride an elevator to get there?" Raisa said happily. "I don't know if she'd be proud or scared."

"Why should she be scared?" Fruma asked.

"The building's so tall, what if I got too close to one of the windows? What if I fell out, God forbid? What if this, what if that"—she shrugged—"you know."

"If Glukel was a second mother to you, like you say, I bet she'd *talk* like she was scared, but in her heart she'd be so proud of you, she could burst," Gavrel replied.

"I can't wait to write to her about this," Raisa said, then paused and corrected herself. "I mean, when you have the chance to write to her for me, Gavrel."

"No you don't," Gavrel said, wagging a finger in her face. "You're going to write your own letters soon. Why else did you sign up for that night course?"

"It's an *English* course," Raisa reminded him. "Glukel can't read English."

"Well, there's still no excuse for you not learning how to write your own letters. What am I, your servant?" he teased. "Lincoln freed the slaves."

"So did Moses," Raisa countered. "So you've got *two* excuses for not helping me: one American, one Jewish."

"Why should there be a difference?" Fruma said.

They entered the building together and joined the crowd waiting to take the small elevators reserved for employees. Raisa got separated from Fruma and Gavrel in the crush of bodies, but wasn't concerned. The three of them didn't work on the same floor anyway, and they'd already made plans for where to meet when the workday was over, before they headed home.

The Triangle factory occupied the eighth, ninth, and tenth floors of the Asch Building. The only thing higher was the roof. When Raisa was hired, she was assigned to a ninth-floor workstation. Though she'd seen her new workplace when she came to apply for the job, she was still impressed by the size of the shop.

Her eyes traveled over the eight wood tables that ran almost the entire length of the factory floor. Each four-foot-wide table actually consisted of two smaller ones, each with fifteen sewing machine operators facing one another over a central gutter to hold finished pieces for pickup. The aisles between the workers in their rows of wooden chairs were narrow and crowded even before all of the girls were at their places for the day.

This is incredible. And to think all this belongs to two men who came here through Ellis Island, just like me! They call Mr. Blanck and Mr. Harris the shirtwaist kings, but I didn't know they had a real kingdom! She looked at the arrangement of tables more closely and a practical thought pushed aside all the rest: *I hope they put me at a machine on the end of the row, or else I'd better start praying I don't have to get up and use the toilet too much.* Then, remembering something Fruma had mentioned about working conditions before the big shirtwaist makers' strike: *If they let us use the toilet as much as we need it, that is.*

Raisa was still standing near the elevator, gawking, when a girl who looked only a bit younger than Fruma came up to her and said, "You're a new face. Can I help you?"

Raisa beamed at the familiar sound of Yiddish words. "Yes, yes, please. I'm new. I start today, but I don't see the man who hired me."

"Oh, don't bother looking for a man. On this floor, we work for a forelady."

"A fore*lady*?" Raisa's eyes widened in surprise.

The young woman grinned and shrugged. "America, right? Come on, I'll take you to her. By the way, my name is Gussie."

"Raisa. Thank you."

Gussie presented Raisa to the ninth-floor forelady, a competent, courteous woman who introduced herself as Miss Gullo. "You'll want to hang up your hat in the cloakroom before you begin work," she said kindly. "I'll show you where that is."

"And I'll get to work!" Gussie said cheerfully. "See you later, Raisa."

On the way to the cloakroom, Raisa and Miss Gullo passed workers seated in front of a row of shuttered windows. Their tables were piled high with finished garments that they were inspecting for mistakes. When Raisa wondered aloud why the shutters weren't open to provide additional light, she was told that it wouldn't make much difference. Those windows only looked out over a nine-story drop into a small, bleak inner courtyard, although Miss Gullo added that they also opened onto the fire escape.

After Raisa hung up her hat, Miss Gullo assigned her to her machine. While it wasn't on the end of a row, as she'd hoped, at least it wasn't all the way down where the tables butted up so close to the Washington Place side of the building that they might as well have grown out of it. Instead, it was halfway to the aisle in a row that was closer to the toilets and cloakroom.

Raisa sat down and examined her new surroundings. She was seated between a serious-faced young brunette who spared her a quick, mechanical smile and a motherly woman whose whispered "Welcome, how are you?" was warm and sincere. Raisa checked her machine and was pleased to see that it was well maintained and properly lubricated for problem-free operation. A small wooden container just under the table kept her skirt safe from any oil that might drip down. A wicker basket filled with cut pattern pieces rested on the floor beside her. Miss Gullo had told her she was going to start out by sewing shirtwaist bodices, and perhaps later move on to more complicated assignments. She hoped the change would come soon. The most repetitive task in the world wasn't quite so boring if it challenged her sewing skills.

The whole table hummed. The motor that provided power

for all 240 sewing machines on the ninth floor sent its power coursing down the whirring axle under the long tables as the workers bent to their tasks. Raisa took the first pieces of light, flimsy material from her wicker basket, pressed her foot down on the treadle, and got to work.

"To Raisa!" Gavrel raised his glass of water over the empty plates still on the dinner table. "May tonight be the first step on the road to greater and greater knowledge!"

"You're making a big fuss over nothing." Raisa looked down at her hands, folded in her lap. There were times she couldn't tell whether Gavrel's elaborate way of speaking was sincere or if he was making fun of her. "It's just a basic English class. It started a week ago, and everyone else is probably so far ahead of me that I don't know if I'll be able to catch up."

"Then why did you sign up for it if you think you're going to fail?" Mrs. Kamensky got right to the point.

"Because—because the woman I spoke to at the Educational Alliance said that they go slowly at the beginning, and if I didn't join this class, I'd have to wait *weeks* for the next one to start."

"And who says she thinks she's going to fail?" Fruma cut in.

"Why look at me? Did *I* say such a thing?" Mrs. Kamensky got up and went into the kitchen. She came back bearing a small, flowered plate with slices of apple drizzled with honey and placed it in front of Raisa. Brina made a grab for the sweet

treat and was dumbfounded when Mrs. Kamensky inter-
cepted her hand. "When *you* start school, I'll give you apples
and honey, maybe even cake. Tonight, this is all for Raisa, so
that she will always remember learning is sweet."

"Then I want to go to school now, too!" Brina said.

"In a year or two, God willing."

"Mama, why can't Brina go now?" Gavrel asked. "You
sent me to the *melamed* on Eldridge Street for Hebrew lessons
before I started elementary school. What was I, three, four
years old?"

"You find me the money for lessons and a *melamed* willing
to teach a little girl Hebrew and you can go ahead and send
her, Mr. Wise Guy," his mother retorted.

Gavrel leaned closer to Brina and said in a stage whisper,
"It's all right, princess. I'll teach you Hebrew, if you like."

"You will?" Brina's eyes widened. She turned to Raisa and
proudly declared, "Gavrel wouldn't teach *you* English, but
he's going to teach *me* Hebrew. That means he likes *me* best!"

"What can I say?" Gavrel raised his hands to show he was
powerless in the face of such perfect logic. "It was a horri-
bly difficult decision to make, a problem worthy of King Solomon, but I stand by my choice."

"And how will you break the news of your decision to
Rachel, O mighty Solomon?" Raisa seized the chance to tease
Gavrel, for a change. "Since you're setting your heart in order,
where does *she* rank?"

"Who's Rachel?" Brina demanded.

"Rachel is a girl from Gavrel's old shop," Raisa answered. "A very *beautiful* girl. Gavrel told her so himself."

Brina stabbed Gavrel with an accusing look. "Are you going to marry her?"

"How did we get from compliments to marriage so fast?" Gavrel appealed to everyone at the table for a little help out of his predicament.

"You're not answering the question," Fruma said, getting into the spirit of things.

"Very well." Gavrel stood up, hooked his thumbs behind his suspenders, and struck a pose worthy of a Tammany Hall politician about to give an electioneering speech. "In that case, allow me to state for the record and before witnesses that it is my sincere and honorable intention to ask Rachel for her hand in marriage—"

Raisa froze where she sat. Not even Mrs. Kamensky's flabbergasted cry of "*What?*" could reach her.

"—just as soon as her fiancé, Mr. Joseph Mayer, asks me to take over for him."

Mrs. Kamensky clapped one hand to her bosom. "Don't you *ever* frighten me like that again!"

Gavrel feigned innocence. "Well, if the idea of my getting married is so hard for you to take, Mama, then I swear I'll never ask any girl to—"

"Enough!" Mrs. Kamensky decreed. "No more foolishness, Gavrel. God knows I want nothing better than to see you happily married, but when that day comes, I want you to *tell* me, not turn the news into a—a—a jack-in-the-box!"

"All right, Mama, I promise." Gavrel went around the table to give his mother a kiss on the cheek. "Now, enough jokes. Raisa has to go to her first English class, and look! She still hasn't tasted a bite of sweetness."

Able to breathe again, Raisa said the proper blessings over the sliced apple and honey. When she took the first bite, the Kamenskys all broke into shouts of "Mazel tov!"

Raisa saved the last slice of honey-drizzled apple for Brina. "If Gavrel is going to give you Hebrew, *I'm* going to do the same with English," she announced.

Brina gobbled the apple, but eyed Raisa doubtfully. "You don't *know* English," she said, mumbling the words around a mouthful.

"But I will," Raisa said. "And when I do, I'll share my lessons with you, so that when it's finally time for you to go to school, you won't have to catch up with the other children. It will be good practice for me, repeating the lessons, and someday you'll be the smartest student in your class!"

Mrs. Kamensky snorted. "A man had no troubles, so he bought a goat," she said, invoking an old proverb about taking on needless complications in life. "Where will you find time for all this?"

"I don't know, but I'll try. And teaching Brina won't be work; it will be a pleasure."

Gavrel gazed at his mother with melodramatically pleading eyes. "Surely you won't deny a hardworking girl and a brand-new English scholar like Raisa one simple pleasure, Mama?"

Mrs. Kamensky appealed to heaven. "This is the thanks I get for trying to help the girl live a sensible life! Everyone turns against me."

Gavrel hugged his mother. "If she's too sensible, she'll never enjoy her life; she'll just endure it. Why don't I get a little more honey from the kitchen so we can all remember that our days should be sweet?"

"Fine, but I'll get it," Mrs. Kamensky said. "You'll only make a mess." She started back for the kitchen.

"Thank you, Mrs. Kamensky, but I can't wait," Raisa said, standing up from her seat. "If I'm going to be on time for my first class, I have to go now."

"I'll get my hat," Gavrel said, making for the hooks by the front door, where his straw boater hung.

"What are you doing?"

"What does it look like? I'm getting ready to walk you to school." He dropped the hat onto his head, where it rode perfectly level atop his dark curls.

"I can go by myself."

"I didn't say you couldn't," Gavrel replied cheerfully.

"I did," Mrs. Kamensky said. "It's your first time, so you've got a lot on your mind. You could get distracted, maybe even lost, God forbid! At least if Gavrel walks you there and home again, after, you'll have one less worry."

"It's only for tonight," Fruma said. "Once you're a part of the class, you'll meet lots of other girls, you'll make new friends, and you'll be able to walk to and from school with them."

"What if they don't live near us?" Raisa asked.

Mrs. Kamensky pooh-poohed the idea. "In this neighborhood, *everyone* lives near us!"

There was no need for Raisa to make conversation as she and Gavrel walked through the nighttime streets. He began talking the moment they stepped onto the sidewalk and didn't give her a chance to get a word in edgewise until the Educational Alliance building was in view. At every corner, at almost every step along the way, he pointed out landmarks and offered advice for remembering them.

"Soon you'll be able to read the street signs," he said. "But for now, maybe you could try memorizing what the letters look like without knowing what they mean."

"You know, I'm not in diapers anymore," Raisa said, exasperated. "I *did* find my own way here earlier today. You didn't need to come along tonight."

"It's no trouble," Gavrel assured her. "And this way, I—the family won't sit up fretting until you're safely home."

"Well, you don't need to hang around waiting for me to finish class. With all the directions you've given me, I can remember the way back."

"But I want to wait for you! I won't be bored, if that's what's on your mind. There's going to be a show at the Rooftop Garden tonight with music, maybe a comedian. The Garden is a wonderful part of the alliance, and the show is free. Why don't you come up there after class and find me? I'll save you a seat."

Raisa smiled at him. "Won't that make us late getting home? Aren't you afraid *that* will make your parents sit up fretting?"

He returned her smile with interest. "Let that be *my* worry."

The show at the Rooftop Garden was still going strong when Raisa got out of her first English class and went looking for Gavrel. She spied him sitting at the end of a row of chairs facing the left side of a platform, where a small orchestra was giving a spirited performance of Rossini's *William Tell* overture. All of the seats in the row except for the one next to Gavrel were filled. With a backward glance and a silencing finger laid quickly to her lips, she crept up on him just as the music ended and the applause began.

"Hello, Gavrel," Raisa said. "Was it a good concert?"

"Wonderful!" he exclaimed, looking up at her. "But it's not over yet. They're going to play Mozart next, something from *The Magic Flute*. Look, there's room; I saved you a seat."

"Thank you," Raisa replied, grinning like a cat stuffed with cream. "But we need two." She stepped to one side and gestured at the girl who had been standing behind her. "Gavrel Kamensky, I'm *very* happy to have you meet my friend Zusa Reshevsky."

Smiling, Zusa stepped forward and offered Gavrel her hand. "A pleasure to meet you," she said in measured English just as the orchestra leader rapped his baton on the music stand before him, calling for the performers to pay attention and the audience to settle down.

"We'd better find seats," Raisa said. "I see some in the back."

"I'll come with you," Gavrel volunteered, rising from his place.

"No, stay where you are." Raisa laid a hand on his shoulder. "It doesn't pay for you to move when they're only going to play one more piece. Meet us when it's over."

As they hurried up the aisle to the empty seats at the rear of the Rooftop Garden, Zusa linked arms with her and whispered, "Your boyfriend's a handsome one, isn't he?"

"Gavrel's just my landlady's son," Raisa said quickly. "He's not my boyfriend."

"Really?" Zusa squeezed her arm. "Good."

"Why 'good'?"

"Oh, no reason." Zusa shrugged and steered Raisa to the back of the Rooftop Garden faster.

Raisa's jaw clenched with annoyance, though if anyone had offered her a hundred dollars to admit *why*, they would have gone home with the money in their pocket.

Chapter Ten

THE GOOD WORKER

Summer waned and autumn brought a welcome coolness to the city. A new year began for the Jewish community with the celebration of Rosh Hashanah in early October of the Christian year. Raisa and Brina sat with Mrs. Kamensky in the women's section in the balcony of the synagogue, watching with pride as Gavrel was called upon to chant from the Torah.

Raisa ran her hands over her lap, contentedly smoothing the front of her new, dark blue skirt. She spent all day handling fabric at Triangle Waist, but she knew that no cloth could ever feel as splendid as this. The skirt was a surprise from Fruma, begun in secret the same evening Raisa had come home to show off the prettily pleated shirtwaist she'd made for herself on one of the sewing machines at the local settlement house. She'd gone to the settlement house at Fruma's suggestion, because it was a popular gathering place for young people.

The more I spread the word about Henda, the greater the chance that someone will recognize her from my description. Back in the shtetl, there was no better way of making sure that news got around than from lips to ears.

Raisa's inquiries at the settlement house didn't turn up any leads about her sister, but she did find a welcome refuge in the activities offered there for working girls like herself. It was a relief to her aching heart to be able to snatch a few moments of distraction from her search. Her handmade shirtwaist was proof that she could still make whole garments skillfully, not merely run up seam after seam after seam. It was a reminder that she was more than just another sewing machine girl among thousands, that she was still Raisa, and that Raisa was somebody who mattered.

Now she sat tall and felt as if she was finally a part of New York. As Gavrel's clear, confident voice filled her ears, she felt her heart beating faster. She was only half-aware that her hand was drifting up to touch her mother's circlet of gold and pearls, pinned to the bosom of her shirtwaist. Her fingertips brushed the spot where the single pearl had fallen out of its setting, but the small, empty space held a memory:

Only four years old, Raisa sat fidgeting between Glukel and Henda in the shtetl synagogue while Reb Avner called upon respected men of the congregation to read from the Torah scroll. Nathan sat with the men, looking very self-important. The day was hot and Raisa was bored, but Glukel and Henda had come prepared to deal with a restless child. First one and then the other slipped her little treats, and when there were no more raisins and bits of broken cookie to distract her, Henda picked her up and carried her out into the autumn sunshine.

Raisa kicked and protested. She didn't want to sit still, but she didn't want to leave the synagogue, either. Her little friends Yitta and Avigal had told her about the moment that Reb Avner would raise the shofar to his lips and blow a series of wonderful loud blasts on the twisted ram's horn. If she'd ever heard the sound before, she didn't remember. Her holiday memories from before the day she and Henda had come to live with Glukel held only visions of Mama kindling the Shabbos lights.

"Hush, Raisaleh, hush. Don't worry, I'll bring you back inside when it's time for the shofar," ten-year-old Henda promised. "Go play with your friends." She indicated the swarm of toddlers and other children too young to last patiently through the long Rosh Hashanah services. They were all romping happily under the watchful eyes of nursing mothers and a few community elders too worn-out with age to attend the services without a respite. "I'll come back out for you, I promise."

Raisa became alarmed. "No!" she cried, digging her thin little fingers into her sister's arm. "Don't go! Don't leave me!" She began to cry at the top of her lungs. Everyone stared, and when the shammes stuck his head outside to demand what was going on, poor Henda was mortified. She scooped up Raisa and ran down the street until they were a good distance away from the synagogue. Only then did she set her little sister down, crouch in front of her, and ask, "What's wrong, sweetheart? What are you so afraid of?"

Little Raisa stared at the ground between her worn but spotless shoes. "Not come back," she mumbled.

Henda's hand lifted her chin. "Is that it?" she asked tenderly. "You think I won't come back? But I said I would. I promised."

"So did she," Raisa said, and tears bathed her face as she whispered, "Mama."

Henda hugged her so fervently and so close that the little child squeaked with alarm. "Sometimes things happen, Raisaleh," Henda murmured. "Big things we can't change. Things like . . . Papa and Mama being gone." She rocked back on her heels, holding Raisa at arm's length. "But that doesn't mean we can't change something. I believe that, Raisaleh. Do you?"

Raisa nodded her head reluctantly. She wasn't old enough to understand everything her sister was trying to tell her, but she did know she loved Henda, and she clung to that love the same way she clung to her sister's arm. "I believe you," she said.

Henda smiled and straightened up. "Good. So when I say I'll bring you back inside in time to hear the shofar, what will you do?"

"Believe you!" Raisa crowed happily, and skipped all the way back to the little synagogue, holding tight to her sister's hand. . . .

Raisa let go of the broken pearl brooch. *We'll be together again, Henda,* she thought. *That's my promise, believe me!*

Gavrel finished his Torah portion and received the congratulations of the rabbi and cantor before going back to his seat among the men.

"It's a shame Fruma wasn't here for this," Raisa whispered to Mrs. Kamensky.

"It wasn't her idea," Mrs. Kamensky hissed back. "It was

that dragon of a future mother-in-law who forced *my* daughter to go to *her* synagogue. If this is how she bullies my precious baby now, heaven help Fruma once she marries into that family!"

"Aren't you *happy* Fruma's getting married?" Brina asked. The five-year-old's notion of a whisper carried well beyond Raisa and Mrs. Kamensky, and the choir of shushing she provoked from nearby seats had no effect on her. "When she told us Morris Zalman asked her to marry him, you yelled 'At last!' and 'I thought this day would never come!' and 'Thank God, little Miss Picky finally realized she's not that young anymore,' and—"

Raisa clapped a hand over the child's mouth and murmured promises of a cookie soon and wedding cake to come.

After morning services, the Kamenskys walked home to a dinner that was a true feast. The mouthwatering smell of a slowly pot-roasted beef brisket filled the apartment. The meat was cooked to such tender perfection that Raisa was able to cut her slice with the edge of a fork instead of a knife.

"I *really* wish Fruma were here for this," she announced.

"I'm putting a plate aside for her, for later," Mrs. Kamensky said. "She'll be lucky if she gets a dog's dinner at *that* woman's table."

"Well, *this* is going to be a jolly wedding," Gavrel muttered.

"What did you say?" his mother demanded.

"Speaking of putting things aside, do you know what Raisa

did this week?" Gavrel talked fast, dodging the question. "For the first time since she came to this country, she had enough money saved to send some home to the woman who raised her!"

"You're a good girl." Mrs. Kamensky plopped another slice of pot roast on Raisa's plate.

"It's only right. I can never repay Glukel for everything she's done for Henda and me. The letters she has Reb Avner write say she's fine, but he writes to me on his own and says that now she's got nobody in the house to help with the sewing, and sometimes she falls behind and the customers get mad. He's afraid she's going to make herself sick trying to keep up. If I keep sending her money, she won't need to work so hard. Today, in synagogue, I made myself a promise to send her something every two weeks."

Mrs. Kamensky raised her eyebrows. "Is this a promise you can afford to keep?"

"I'm going to try." Raisa took a bite of boiled potato. *For Glukel's sake, I have to do more than try. This is the least I can do to comfort her the way she always comforted me.*

At the end of October, the tenement roofs of the Lower East Side sprouted a miniature city of wooden huts, temporary structures where observant families would celebrate the Feast of Tabernacles, Succos. Raisa and Brina were invited to share a meal in the Reshevskys' succah.

As often as she thought about it, Raisa couldn't get over the fact that she and Zusa had been living within two blocks of one another all this time. *Mrs. Kamensky was right*, she thought as she and Brina climbed the steps to the rooftop. *In this neighborhood, everyone* does *live near us!*

Zusa's cousin Selig had built a beautiful succah for the family. According to Jewish law, the sky had to be visible through the wooden slats and leafy branches making the roof. Sturdier structures were forbidden, because in addition to being a harvest festival, the holiday commemorated a time when the Jewish people had lived in temporary dwellings after the departure from slavery in Egypt. An acceptable succah had to be easy to take down when the seven days of Succos were over.

A plump yellow citron, the *etrog*, lay on the table beside the bundle of palm, willow, and myrtle branches that comprised the *lulav*. Selig held the *etrog* in his left hand and the *lulav* in his right, recited the blessing, and waved them to the four points of the compass as well as up toward heaven and down toward the earth. He took great care in putting away the *etrog* in a wooden box lined with velvet, then excused himself to go downstairs and use the toilet.

"Now, girls, can I trust you?" he asked, joking. "I don't want to come back and find that one of you is so desperate to have a baby that you've bitten off the *etrog*'s stem!"

"Get out of here, you rascal!" Zusa's mother exclaimed, giving him a shove toward the stairs. "Why are you teaching them such superstitious nonsense? And why *now*? First let them find husbands, then they can worry about babies!"

"I think the *etrog* stem is safe," Raisa said, joining in the jest. "None of us is thinking about marriage."

"Not the little one, but you two girls are another story. I wasn't much older than Zusa is now when I met her father," Mrs. Reshevsky countered.

"Yes, but the only reason you met him was because your parents arranged it," Zusa said. "That's not how it works over here."

"Listen to the Yankee!" Zusa's mother said sarcastically. "Less than a year in this country and you're an authority on America. Keep it up and someday you'll be an old-maid authority! What, you love that job of yours so much that you want to work there until you die?"

"I didn't say I wasn't going to get married," Zusa replied serenely. "And I know my job's no bargain."

She and Raisa exchanged a quick, conspiratorial glance. Raisa already knew her friend's plans to leave her present job as soon as possible. *"I'm not looking for the Garden of Eden,"* she'd confided in Raisa. *"Just somewhere the foreman's not a snake. And a snake with hands! Pinching, touching, squeezing— I've had enough. I haven't said a word about it at home because cousin Selig would want to go over there and do something about it. My foreman used to make a living doing bare-knuckle boxing down in the Bowery, so I know how that would end! I'm going to have to take care of this myself."*

"So what are you saying, then?" her mother persisted.

"Just that when it's time for me to get married, I'll be the one to say when and where and who." Zusa smiled like someone hiding a sweet secret.

"I know who!" Brina cried out. "She means she wants Gavrel! She always looks at him funny whenever she comes over to our house. She did it last week, when we had a special honey cake for Fruma."

"For what, the engagement?" Of course Mrs. Reshevsky knew all about that, or believed she did. "I thought the Kamenskys made a nice *oneg* Shabbos for that at their synagogue already."

"This was just for Fruma's new job," Raisa said.

"She's leaving Triangle?" Zusa pricked up her ears.

"She got a job that pays a little better at another shop, but nothing long term," Raisa explained. "She doesn't mind. It's going to bring in more money before the wedding, and her fiancé says she won't need to work after they get married."

"Now *that* is a *smart* girl," Mrs. Reshevsky said, pointing the words straight at her daughter.

"Zusa's smart, too," Brina said loyally. "I think it's *very* smart to want a nice man like Gavrel. But she can't have him. He likes Raisa better than he likes her, and he likes *me* best of all!"

Zusa looked at Raisa. "Remind me why we took care of this one on the ship."

"There was nothing else to do," Raisa said, and they both laughed until Brina began to cry and Mrs. Reshevsky ordered them to act their age and stop teasing children.

Raisa sat at her sewing machine at Triangle Waists, listening to the first November rain pour down outside. It would have been nice to see the patterns that the raindrops made, but the garment-factory windows were thick with grime inside and out. The rain could do only so much to wash away the dingy film of smoke and dust.

Just as well, Raisa thought, running the side seam of a shirtwaist under the swiftly bobbing needle. *This is no place for daydreams.*

It hadn't taken long for her initial joy at securing a job in such a big, modern garment factory to wear off. Even though sewing at Triangle was better than slaving for Madame, the work was still monotonous and tiring. She knew that the shirtwaist makers had gained some advances in the wake of the big strike, including a fifty-two hour week and other benefits, but in spite of that, the way that she and the other employees were treated seemed aimed at making them all feel less than human.

We're packed together at these tables like canned sardines swimming in sewing machine oil, she thought. *Then when it's quitting time, we turn into sheep, herded together to wait our turn at the exit while they search us, one by one, to make sure we haven't stolen anything.* She finished another seam and sighed. *Thank God for Zusa! She always cheers me up when we get together. Things are the same at her shop, but she's got the gift for finding something to laugh about, and that makes it easier.*

When the quitting bell sounded, Raisa headed for the cloakroom with the rest of the crowd. As she donned her coat, she heard her friend Gussie calling her name from the crush of bodies in the far corner of the room.

"Raisa! Hey, Raisa, Jennie and I are going to the moving-picture show tonight. Do you want to come with us? My treat!"

"Oooh, you hear that?" one of the other girls butted in. "Get a load of the big shot!"

"Oh, shush, you," Gussie shot back good-humoredly. "Can't a girl save a little money for herself, too? I send plenty back home every month, so once in a while I do something for me." She smiled at Raisa. "And my friends."

"Well, *I* think it's a good idea," a third young woman said. "It's nice to remind ourselves that we're not just a bunch of cogs in a great big sewing machine. Even if that's what the big men upstairs *want* us to be."

"What are you, a troublemaker? Better watch your mouth or you'll be out of a job. If the bosses hear so much as a *whisper* of union talk—" the first girl said.

"Don't be a goose; those days are over. They can't fire us for joining the union," said the other.

"Maybe not, but they can be real good at finding another excuse!"

While the two women argued, Gussie wormed her way to Raisa's side. "Whew! All I wanted was to invite you to the picture show, not start a war."

"Thanks, Gussie, but I can't go. My friend Zusa and I have plans."

"Something fun, I hope. You're always so *serious*, with the night school and all."

"Well, *some* of us weren't lucky enough to be born over here, Gussie," Raisa said, smiling. "We have to learn English the hard way."

"Not *too* hard for you," Gussie replied. "I've heard you trying it out on some of the girls who don't speak Yiddish. You're good!" She linked arms with Raisa as they made their way to the line of workers waiting to have their belongings searched before they were allowed to leave the shop floor and go home. "So, what are you and Zusa doing?"

"We're going to a reunion."

"Oh, Raisa, you found her! You found her! I'm so happy for you!" Gussie's shriek of glee turned heads. Raisa had told her about Henda long ago, as she told everyone else whose path she crossed, always in the hope that once—just once!— Henda's name or description would kindle a spark of recognition in somebody's eyes and at long last Raisa would hear someone say, *You know, I think I know that girl. I've seen her. Let me tell you more. . . .*

"No, Gussie," Raisa said. "Not her; not yet." She pushed down the hard knot of failure that burned in her chest, and forced a smile. "This is a reunion with a friend."

Going to Mulberry Street was like going to a different world. Raisa and Zusa strode arm in arm along the sidewalk, taking in everything with the captivated gaze of brave explorers venturing into virgin territory.

The rain had stopped, which was a mercy. Given the hour, the streets were filled with workers heading home as well as preoccupied housewives rushing to do some last-minute marketing. The stores remained open, their proprietors eager to accommodate customers until no more came by. The smells in the air were not much different from those Raisa encountered in her neighborhood, though when she and Zusa walked past a fishmonger's shop and saw the beady black eyes of silver-gray shrimp and the curling tentacles of little purple-red squid, she couldn't help jumping back just a bit.

And everywhere was the sound of Italian!

Though they knew the name of the grocery store they were seeking, neither Raisa nor Zusa knew how to say "grocery store" in Italian. When Zusa said, "Delvecchio, Delvecchio!" and mimed eating an apple, she got some nervous looks, some mocking laughter, and no help. One old woman grabbed the cross around her neck and made a hand sign that Raisa was willing to bet served to ward off the evil eye.

They finally found the place by trial and error, walking along Mulberry Street with their eyes sharpened. Raisa gave a happy cry when she spotted the sign. "Look, Zusa, I think that's it!" she exclaimed.

Zusa cocked her head and sounded out the letters: "Del-vek-chee-o. Well, that's not how Luciana pronounced it, but it is a grocery. I guess they got a good deal from a sign painter who couldn't spell as well as *you*, Miss Professor."

They entered the little store and breathed deeply, filling

their nostrils with the beautiful aromas of fresh herbs and wholesome greens. Raisa couldn't help picking up a bunch of basil and inhaling its rich scent as if it were a bouquet of flowers. As she was putting it back down, a familiar voice greeted her.

"*Posso aiutarla, signorina?*"

She turned to face Luciana's brother Paolo. The young man stared at her for an instant, then his face transformed with happy recognition. "Ah! I know you! You are the friend of Luciana, yes?" he exclaimed in English. Then, almost shyly, he added, "It has been some time. You understand English?"

"Who does not?" Zusa replied with a nonchalant flourish of one hand.

He strode to a doorway at the back of the shop, calling loudly, "*Luciana! Luciana! Vieni e vedi!*"

There came the sound of light footsteps from above followed by a clatter of shoes on an inner stairway, and then Luciana burst through the doorway into the shop. She threw her arms around her shipboard friends, but instead of a torrent of unintelligible Italian, Raisa and Zusa were joyfully surprised to hear Luciana welcome them in now-familiar English: "Oh, my friends, my friends! You come see me. Too long, yes? But so happy you come now!"

As the three girls hugged and laughed and cried and babbled at one another in the language they now shared, Paolo approached his sister with a question in Italian. Luciana frowned at first, then smiled, nodded, and turned to Raisa and

Zusa. "I ask you upstairs for coffee and cake but—Mama is sick. Not bad, but not good. Paolo says I take you to good place near here for coffee and cake instead. Wait." She disappeared through the rear doorway again, to return wrapped in a thick shawl. "Now, come."

Luciana brought her friends to a little storefront café. Raisa felt strangely exultant to be having a real conversation in English—even if some of it was broken English. It made the language seem like a true part of her life at last instead of something she just practiced in the classroom. *If I can use it like this, to talk to Luciana, I can use it with other people, too. I can go somewhere besides the shtetl Protective and Benevolent Association and ask for help tracing my sister! They won't treat me like just another greenhorn if I can speak to them directly in English.* A new door opened and fresh hope streamed through it, filling Raisa's heart with confidence.

The first reunion of the three shipboard friends had to be a brief one. Luciana needed to go back to take care of her mother; Raisa and Zusa had to go home for dinner.

"I am sorry I eat so much cake," Raisa said. "If I do not eat dinner, Mrs. Kamensky will take my head off." She was very proud of herself for using such a complicated turn of phrase in English.

"Take off head?" Luciana was alarmed.

"A joke, a joke!" Zusa reassured her. "Raisa is . . ." She searched for the right words, finally gave up, turned to Raisa, and asked in Yiddish, "How do you say 'a big show-off' in English, Miss Professor?"

Raisa nudged Zusa with her elbow. "Stop making fun of me," she said in Yiddish. To Luciana she said, "Zusa and I learn English in school. Ed-u-ca-tion-al Al-li-ance. Where do you learn it, Luciana?"

Luciana shrugged. "Here. There. Renzo helps. Paolo, too. But I think I need school."

"You should come to our school," Raisa said.

"Ah?" The Italian girl looked uncertain. "Is it not for—for your people only?"

"I have heard more than one person there speaking your language, after class. And others." It might have been a different story if Luciana still spoke only Italian, but since she obviously knew some English, Raisa couldn't imagine the teachers being unable to communicate with her and turning her away.

Luciana nodded. "Good. I try. In my old shop, better for girls who know English."

"Shop? You make clothes?" Zusa mimed using a sewing machine.

Luciana nodded. "Old shop was bad. Bad boss, bad machines, everything bad." Haltingly, she went on to tell her friends about the day that the air of her old shop had echoed with a sharp, metallic *snap*, then filled with a poor girl's shrieks of agony as she cupped a hand over her right eye, unable to hold back the bright trickle of blood.

It was a freak accident; sewing machine needles broke all the time under the stress of so much intense use. Who had the time to check for wear and tear during the height of the workday rush? And who wanted to ask the foreman for a new needle too quickly, especially when the cost came out of the worker's pay? So they ran the machines until something gave, when the needle splintered off and the shard went spinning. That time, the metal sliver found a target.

"Boss makes two other girls take her away to clinic, then yells at us, blames us for being careless. Later, the two come back, he says they are not paid for time they spend taking blind girl to clinic. He says in English, but someone repeat in Italian. It is too much. Some of us are so angry, we protest." She spread her hands. "We are fired."

"You will find another job, Luciana," Raisa said. "Another job in a better shop."

"I wish I could, too," Zusa said. "This week, again my boss tries to cheat me. I would not let him. Maybe next week I lose my job for that, but I will have what is mine. I work for it, I—I *deserve* it. If I have to find another job, I can. I am a good worker; so are you."

"A good worker," Luciana mused. "Sometimes, my old boss, he pinches my cheek and says I am a good worker."

"Another snake with hands," Zusa muttered in Yiddish for Raisa's ears alone. To Luciana she said, "You do not like that, do you?"

"Who likes that? No one! He does it to other girls, too. Why must he touch me? He can say I am a good worker without the pinch, or sometimes a little slap on my—on the back of—" Luciana let out a small cry of frustration and anger. "No! I do *not* like it. I am such a good worker, I can get another job where the boss does *not* touch me. And I do! My cousin Nicola, she works at a good place, big, modern. She says they hire, so I go and they say yes! I start next week!" She accepted her friends' congratulations.

"If your new job is in such a big shop, maybe they could hire *all* of us," Zusa suggested. "I would be happy to change shops. I am sick of fighting with my boss every payday. We could work together, go out together, go to English class together, like sisters!"

"*Especially* go to English classes!" Raisa put in.

"What is the shop name?" Zusa asked.

"It is Tri—" Luciana wrestled briefly with the pronunciation of the alien word. "Tri-an-gool Waists."

"That's where I work!" Raisa exclaimed.

"Oho!" Zusa raised one eyebrow. "Not just you, Miss Professor. Are you forgetting about Gavrel?"

"Who is Gavrel?" Luciana asked.

"A young man," Zusa said nonchalantly. "A *handsome* one— very smart, very sweet, like this." She dabbed up a cake crumb with the tip of her index finger, popped it into her mouth, and made exaggerated signs of enjoyment.

"Zusa . . ." There was a distinct warning in the way Raisa spoke her friend's name.

"I said nothing bad." Zusa brushed off all responsibility for her words.

No, you didn't, Raisa grudgingly admitted to herself. *But why do I still feel like slapping that cake crumb out of your mouth?*

On Thanksgiving Day, Fruma's in-laws-to-be invited the entire Kamensky family to their home for dinner. Fruma assured Raisa and Brina that they were welcome at the Zalmans' table, too. Raisa could hardly hold back her excitement—her first real American Thanksgiving, just like in the stories they'd been studying in English class! Brina was equally thrilled. Raisa always shared her lessons, and was enormously proud of how quickly the child had learned to read words like *Pilgrims, Indians, turkey*, and even *Thanksgiving*.

"What a good little scholar you are, Brina!" Raisa exclaimed after having the little girl read aloud for the family.

"What a good teacher she's got to thank for that." Gavrel murmured his praise so softly that Raisa wasn't sure she'd heard it. But when she looked at him, he smiled at her as innocently as if he'd said nothing at all.

In spite of Fruma's assurances that Brina and Raisa counted as part of the Kamensky family, once they arrived at the Zalmans' home, the flinty expression on their hostess's face told a different story.

It was a very awkward meal. Everyone was dressed in their best outfits, as if for synagogue. Raisa kept Brina close beside her and watched over her like a hawk, fearful that the child would blurt something that might embarrass Fruma. Gavrel tried to break the ice with his usual good humor, but only Fruma's fiancé seemed to appreciate it. Without his usual copy of the *Forward* to hide behind, Mr. Kamensky looked as naked and gawky as a newly hatched chick. To keep himself distracted, he ate almost nonstop from the moment Morris's father said the blessing before meals until the only thing left in front of him was an empty coffee cup and a scattering of cake crumbs.

Fruma was marrying into a family for whom America really had turned out to be the Golden Land. Although Morris Zalman still worked in a garment factory, his mother made sure to let her guests know that her adored boy was on the point of completing the qualifications for his *true* career, and that when 1911 dawned, he would begin a new life as a druggist.

"*My* son is going to be a rabbi," Mrs. Kamensky announced.

"Isn't that nice," Mrs. Zalman said coolly. "When?"

"Soon."

"Next month? No? In three months, then? Half a year? Nineteen eleven? Nineteen twelve? Nineteen—?"

"Nineteen fifty-two," Gavrel cut in from his place between Raisa and his sister. "Anyone can become a rabbi, but *I* intend to start as the world's oldest!" He gave his hostess a smile so pleasant and unruffled that it was obvious he meant it to rile her.

"Isn't that nice," Mrs. Zalman repeated, and she acted as if Gavrel were invisible for the rest of the evening.

Fruma's intended husband, Morris, was a slim, clean-cut man whose pale blue eyes squinted at the world through thick glasses. He spent most of the meal with his gaze fixed on Raisa, a quizzical look on his face. It was the sort of ongoing stare that made her feel more curious than uncomfortable: *Is there something on my face? Do I have food stuck between my teeth? Maybe it's my short hair. But it's not that short anymore, and I've seen a few of the factory girls who wear theirs like this.*

As Mrs. Zalman rose to make a halfhearted offer of more coffee and Mrs. Kamensky leaped in with a too-eager reply that her family really *had* to be going, Morris finally snapped his fingers and announced, "*That's* who you look like!"

The abrupt declaration startled Raisa like a gunshot, but that was nothing compared with her reaction when Morris added, "My eyes are good for doing close work—any distance and I don't trust them, so it took me a while to be sure, but now I'm *positive*. You remind me of someone I know. Do you have any relatives in this country?"

"Relatives?" Raisa's voice trembled. *Merciful God, can it be? So many places I've gone, so many people I've asked, so many letters to Glukel, trying to keep up her spirits even when I've had to tell her I'm no closer to finding Henda than before, so much waiting, hoping* . . . "Yes, I do. One."

"Aha! A cousin, a sister, maybe even a very young aunt? Because you are the *image* of a good friend of mine from when I worked at American Pride Ladies' Garments. We both lost our jobs after the general strike, but we tried to keep in—"

"Henda!" Raisa cried, jumping to her feet. "You know my sister, Henda!" Her face radiated hope.

"Henda, that's right," Morris said. And with his next breath, he innocently crushed Raisa's heart. "You should have brought her, too. How is she? It's so long since I saw her, it's as if she fell off the face of the earth."

Raisa dropped back into her chair as if she'd been shot. When she clutched her hands together under the table, they were ice cold. *Not again,* she thought. *Every time a door opens for me, it just leads to a brick wall. I can't give up. I mustn't give up but—oh, dear Lord, sometimes I'm so* tired! *So very, very tired.*

She was only distantly aware of the sound of Gavrel's voice as he questioned Morris, whose answers were no more to her than the background noise of crowds and traffic that she heard every day. Someone called her name, but she didn't respond until a gentle hand closed on her shoulder and Fruma's voice roused her, saying, "Raisa. Raisa, Gavrel is talking to you."

"Seven Arrows," Gavrel said with the air of someone who had been repeating the same information for some time. "Morris knows where Henda got a job after she left American Pride. The shop where Henda worked last is called the Seven Arrows Cloak and Suit Company."

Morris nodded. "Yes, that's the name; I remember it well. It's one of the newer companies, farther uptown."

"Do you realize what this means, Raisa?" Gavrel grabbed her hands and brought her to her feet. "Now that we know the last place Henda worked, we can discover if any of her coworkers there have any news about her! One of them might even know the name of that mysterious young man who took her away. And if we can find *him*—"

"We can find her." Raisa dared to smile.

Without warning, Brina flung her arm around Morris's

neck and gave him a big kiss on the cheek. "You made Raisa happy. I'm *glad* you're marrying Fruma."

"I'll tell you a secret," Morris stage-whispered. "So am I."

"Isn't that nice," said his mother.

Mrs. Kamensky had a good deal to say about that Thanksgiving dinner party, and she said it all the way home. Almost every sentence began with "Morris is a good boy, a fine husband-to-be. I've got nothing against him, *but*—" and soon turned into a fresh list of grievances against Mrs. Zalman. Mr. Kamensky and Fruma walked beside her, a captive audience. Her husband had no choice, and her daughter felt honor-bound to put in the occasional good word for her fiancé's family. This only turned Mrs. Kamensky from grumbling about Mrs. Zalman to bemoaning the hell on earth that her poor little girl would endure as That Woman's daughter-in-law.

Raisa, Gavrel, and Brina began the walk home only a few paces behind the others, but the more they heard Mrs. Kamensky's litany of complaints, the greater that distance grew, until there was nearly half a city block between the two trios.

"Are you doing all right, princess?" Gavrel asked, looking down at Brina. "Tired? Want a ride home?"

"You *always* want to give me a ride home," Brina said huffily. "I keep telling you, I'm *not* a baby."

"Brina! That's no way to talk to Gavrel. He only wants to help you."

"I don't *need* help," Brina shot back.

"Then just say, 'No thank you.' Someday you might want

his help, but if you're rude to him now, he won't want to give it to you then."

"Yes he will." Brina was utterly positive. "He likes *me*." She broke away from them and ran ahead to grab Mr. and Mrs. Kamensky by the hands, begging for a game of "one-two-three-*up!*" She whooped with excitement as they swung her high in the air at every fourth step, though the game didn't seem to stop Mrs. Kamensky from continuing to give her opinion of Fruma's future mother-in-law.

Raisa rolled her eyes. "I give up," she said to Gavrel. "I want her to learn manners, but I guess I'm not a very good teacher."

"I wouldn't say that," Gavrel replied. "I've seen you sharing your English lessons with her. She picks up everything you teach her quickly and she remembers it."

"That's because she's smart."

He shook his head. "That's because you know how to make new things simple to understand. You don't just force her to repeat words like a little parrot; you help her see connections, the way one lesson relates to another, and you give her tricks for remembering the rules more easily. And you don't teach her only from books. Remember that Sunday morning I went with you two to the playground? Every game you played with her was a hidden English lesson!" He slipped his arm through hers. "She learns well because you teach well, Raisa."

"Gavrel, what are you doing?" Raisa whispered, beginning to draw her arm away.

"Oh." He looked as if she'd slapped him. "I'm sorry, I didn't mean to upset you; I only—"

"I'm not upset." Suddenly she realized that walking with Gavrel like this, arm in arm, felt like the most natural thing in the world. She settled her hand comfortably on his wrist and looked up at him, smiling. "I was just surprised."

They walked in amiable silence for a few more steps. Then Gavrel said, "When I said you're a good teacher, I wasn't just trying to sweet-talk you, Raisa. I meant it. Do you *like* teaching?"

"I never thought about it before. I know I like going to classes, learning. I feel good whenever my teacher says I'm showing progress. I admire her for being able to help so many of us, who come in speaking all different languages. Last week, one of her former students came into the classroom to thank her. He told us that he used to be like us, a greenhorn, but now he's going to become an accountant! He was going to tell us about some of her other students who'd gone on to better things, but she made him stop because she said it would be"—she spoke her teacher's words as she'd heard them, in English—"'an o-ffence against hu-mil-ity and proper de-co-rum.'"

"Your teacher is a modest woman," Gavrel said, nodding his approval.

"She is a *wonderful* woman." Raisa's hand tightened gently on Gavrel's wrist. "And sometimes—sometimes when I'm helping Brina, I realize that I *do* like teaching and I wish I could be like my teacher, do what she does, make a difference

for other people's lives." She bowed her head. "But all I make
are shirtwaists."

Gavrel stopped walking and made her turn to face him.
"That's what you're doing *now*," he said, gazing intently into
her eyes. "It's not what you have to do for the rest of your life.
Right now I make a living as a cutter at Triangle, but I'm not
going to be a cutter when I die. As sure as I'm going to become
a rabbi, you can become a teacher. You'll have to make time in
your life for more classes, but if you want to teach . . ."

"How can I, Gavrel?" Raisa replied. She kept her voice
low, not wanting the Kamenskys to hear her, but they were
so far ahead and so cheerfully distracted by Brina that there
was small chance of that. "How can I spare time for anything
except looking for my sister?"

"I know, I know. It's why you came to America, it's
why—"

"No," Raisa said suddenly. "That's not true. I was always
supposed to come to this country—*we* were, Henda and I
together. We never believed the fairy tales about gold in the
streets, but we knew there was something better here for us,
and better for Glukel, too, someday. We had dreams. . . ." She
closed her eyes, unable to go on.

"You should always have dreams, Raisaleh."

She felt the soft touch of his fingertips lifting her chin. She
opened her eyes to see Gavrel gazing at her with a strong,
determined expression as he said, "I promise you on my life,
I'm going to do whatever is in my power to give you your
dreams."

Chapter Eleven

SEVEN ARROWS

Raisa sat at attention in her seat as the uptown trolley lurched along its route. She only glanced at the changing street scene, so different from her own neighborhood, and the people who inhabited it. She felt a passing twinge of envy for the obviously wealthy women, their hands warmly snuggled into luxurious fur muffs. Her own hands were cold and a little stiff from clutching the precious piece of paper in her lap.

All the way uptown, Raisa kept looking from that scrap to the street signs rumbling past. Gavrel had written down the address she was after, along with a small sketch map. It wasn't the only thing he'd done to help her follow the clue to Henda's fate that Morris Zalman had given her at Thanksgiving, five days ago.

She remembered what Gavrel told her that evening, when

he'd made her dreams his own and they'd walked along as if they were the only two people in the world: *We have to be practical, Raisa. You need to go to Seven Arrows, to ask the people there if they've got any idea, even a hint about where your sister might be now. But to go so far uptown and ask around like that, you'll need time. So you go. Don't worry about missing work. I'll talk to people. I'll see if I can't work out something for you, maybe me putting in extra hours or something. No offense, but I'm a cutter and cutters make more than sewing machine girls. As soon as I can fix this for you, you go.*

And he did fix it for me! she thought, so very proud of him. All of a sudden, she spied a big sign on the side of a building. A gaily painted bald eagle clutching a bunch of arrows in its left talon and a lightning bolt in its right spread its wings above the name SEVEN ARROWS CLOAK AND SUIT COMPANY.

Raisa leaped to her feet and pulled the cord to request her stop, then hopped off the trolley. She raced from the trolley stop to the tall building housing the Seven Arrows Company. The trip uptown had taken longer than she'd anticipated, even though she hadn't wasted any time trying to locate the factory itself, and now it was almost the start of the workday. If she wanted to ask any of Henda's former coworkers if they'd seen or heard from her sister, she had to hurry.

She began talking to the shopgirls the moment she found herself in their midst at the building entrance. Seven Arrows wasn't the only garment factory in the building, but as soon as she determined which girls did work there, she peppered them with questions. From the front door to the elevator to the shop cloakroom, Raisa grilled one girl after another. Some were new hires; they'd never heard of Henda. Some had worked at Seven Arrows for months, even years, but didn't know her. Some knew her as just another face in the crowd. The ones who did know her were casual acquaintances, not close friends.

"Sure, I remember her. Just to say hello, good-bye, how's the weather, you know."

"Wasn't she the *really* pretty one? I remember how jealous I was every time I looked her way. But looking that good's more trouble than it's worth to girls like us. Some of the salesmen gave her a hard time, always hanging around her machine, pestering her, but she didn't give them the time of day. That's pretty much all I knew about her."

"I knew Henda. We used to go to the picture show together sometimes. So you're the sister? I'm so sorry, I haven't heard a thing about her since she took off, but I can tell you this: she never stopped talking about you. Every payday, the first thing she did was look in her envelope, smile, and say, 'I've almost got enough to send for Raisa!'"

A harried-looking woman rushed out of the cloakroom, her pince-nez glasses crooked and her hair coming out of its tight bun in wisps and strands. She was clearly in a hurry, but when she overheard Raisa questioning one of the other girls about Henda, she stopped short.

"*You* knew Henda?" She peered into Raisa's face. "Oh my God, such a resemblance; you must be her sister! What are you doing here? She hasn't worked at Seven Arrows for—" Raisa's swift explanation made the woman gasp in distress. "You poor girl, I don't know what to say. Believe me, I know how you feel. She was my best friend. We used to talk about how she was going to move into my building as soon as you came over and got a job of your own so the two of you could afford to live somewhere better. She said the Levi family was nice, but it was getting too crowded, the son was getting married, and it broke her heart every time the mama thought she was her dead daughter, Sadie. Look, I'd love to talk more with you, but I've got to get to my machine." She started away.

"Wait!" Raisa called, following her onto the shop floor. "Please, you might be the only one who'd know. Was Henda seeing anyone, a young man who dressed really well?"

"Yes, I think I remember—but please, I'm sorry, I can't talk now!" the woman replied, flying down the narrow aisle between the rows of sewing machines. Other workers were also scrambling into their seats, getting in Raisa's way as she tried to pursue Henda's friend. She bumped into one woman who was carrying a basket full of thread spools for the machines. The impact wasn't hard, but it was awkward enough to send the basket flying. Spools clattered across the floor and the woman gave a loud shriek of distress.

"*What the hell is going on here?*" A bald man exploded out of a dark oak door on the edge of the factory floor while Raisa knelt to help the woman gather up the scattered spools. The workday was young, but his clothing was already so rumpled that the sagging trousers and sweat-stained white shirt looked as if their wearer had just put in eight hours in a boiler factory. "You!" He leveled one finger at Raisa, who was conspicuous as the only person on the floor still wearing an overcoat. "Who the devil are you, and what are you doing in this shop?"

Raisa straightened up to face him as the woman tossed the last spool back into her basket and scurried out of harm's way. "Mister, I am sorry, I only came here because—"

Raisa's attempted explanation was cut off by another torrent of abuse and obscenity. The bald man ordered her into his office, then bawled at the sewing machine girls to get to work. "I'm not paying you to stand around talking! This time's coming right off your pay; you see if it doesn't!" He slammed the office door.

With her hands clasped in front of her, Raisa told the man the reason for her presence at Seven Arrows as succinctly as possible. He heard her out while chewing the end of an unlit cigar he'd taken from the pocket of the jacket hanging on the back of his chair. Though there were two other chairs in the office, he didn't offer her a seat, or anything but a stony, silent stare. When Raisa finished her story, he finally spoke.

"Sure, I remember that girl. Pretty. Too damn pretty, if you ask me. One time the owners had some important businessmen visiting, and one of them asked to see the shop floor because he wanted to talk with the workers. He's one of these goddamn rich Jews, the German ones who act like enough money makes them *real* people!"

Raisa flinched at the man's ugly words, but she held her tongue. Part of it was the old lessons of endurance from the shtetl, yet more than that was the sole reason she'd come to this place: *He remembers Henda, so he might know something that will help me find her. For my sister's sake, I have to hear this venom.* She pressed her lips together and let him rant on.

"That one, his old man owns a bunch of high-class department stores, so they're one of our biggest accounts. That means *I've* got to bend over backward and kiss *his* ass. Who sent for him? He could sit home all day on his backside like a prince, but *he* wants to learn all about the business, like he's a regular clothing buyer, sticking his big nose in where it don't belong. He said the big strike last year made things real bad in his daddy's stores, because they couldn't get stock. Well, boohoo, poor little rich Jew. He said he wanted to talk to my girls to make sure things were better in the shops, so there wouldn't be any more trouble, but I didn't see him going to any of the *ugly* girls for answers.

"Yeah, she knew a good deal when she saw one, a first-class meal ticket," he went on. "Young and a big deal and not half bad-looking. But she was a sly one. When he talked to her, all he got was yes-sir-no-sir-I-gotta-do-my-work-sir. Nothing like playing hard to get when you're fishing for the big one! And it worked, too. When I didn't see him up here with some excuse or other, I caught him waiting around downstairs in the street at quitting time. And now I don't see him *or* her coming around here anymore, so I guess the fish bit hard." His mouth twisted into an ugly, insinuating grin around the fat cigar.

"I see." Raisa wanted nothing more than to knock both the cigar and the leer off the bald man's face, but until she had every bit of information he might possess, all she could do was gulp back her feelings. "Thank you very much, sir. This is . . . a great help to me, knowing more about the young man. Please, can you tell me his name?"

"Why, so you can go pester him and say I sent you? Sure, that's just what I want to do, send some little bunco artist after one of our biggest customers!"

"Bunco artist?" It was an English term Raisa had never heard before.

"Don't play dumb with me, girly. I know a grifter when I see one. That girl must've lived in your neighborhood, and you figured to come up here with a fake sob story so you can get your paws on her back pay. And now you want that rich guy's name so you can go crying after him, too?" He jumped up and hit the desk with his fist, his face turning purple. "Well, you can forget that! Get the hell out of my shop now, damn you! And I swear to God, if I ever see your face around here again, I'll call the cops!"

Raisa fled the office. She didn't wait for the elevator, but headed for the nearest stairwell. She wanted to escape Henda's former boss as fast as she could, but her exit was blocked by another man, who commanded her to stop so that he could search her purse. It was a familiar, if humiliating ritual, one she went through every day at Triangle Waists. In the eyes of the owners and the bosses, every worker was a potential criminal, a thief avid to stuff her pockets with company property. When the man finally handed back Raisa's purse and unlocked the stairway door, she nearly knocked him over in her haste to breathe fresh air.

Once outside, she felt better. *I'll wait for quitting time,* she thought. *That lady upstairs said she was Henda's best friend. I've got to talk to her some more in case she knows anything else about what's become of my sister. I'll walk around the neighborhood until then, and when I see her leave the building, I'll—*

A gust of cigar smoke enveloped her. Puffing like a teakettle, Henda's former boss emerged from the building, caught sight of her, and came strolling up. "What the hell are you still doing here? Move along!"

"Mister, you are not the boss here on the street," Raisa said grimly. Then, remembering something she had learned in English class, she added, "This is a free country!"

"Oh, a smart one, huh?" he sneered. "Well, if you think you're going to wait around and get that guy's name from someone else in the shop, let me save you a lot of grief. I told my girls that if I caught any of 'em talking to you, I'd show them the door. And I mean to make it stick, even if I've got to hang here before and after work, keeping an eye out for you." He took another puff of his cigar. "No skin off my nose. Only place I can have a smoke since the owners said no one can do it upstairs. What do they think, that I'm dumb enough to take a lit cigar out onto the shop floor?" Still muttering, he dropped the glowing butt in the gutter and went back inside.

"Holy cow, what flew up *his* butt?" A ragged newsboy who had been hawking his papers on the corner came up to Raisa and gave her an admiring look. "Good for you, lady, standing up to that plug-ugly. He likes to push people around too much. Sometimes he's down here mornings and if he sees me trying to peddle my papers to the girls, he puts a stop to it, says I'm keeping them from getting to work on time." He stuck out his tongue and blew a raspberry. "So what's his beef with you?"

"I need to find a man who might tell me what became of my sister," Raisa said. "*That* one knows the man's name, but will not say it."

"That's rough, lady. A regular sphinx, huh?"

Raisa looked up at the Seven Arrows sign ruefully. "The most he told me was that the man I want is Jewish and comes from a rich family. They own department stores."

"Yeah, always look for the rich ones, that's the ticket!" The newsboy showed a gap-toothed grin. "Look, if you got nothing else to go on 'cept his folks own department stores, why'n't you try going to a few and asking around? Not on the sales floor—up in the office."

"And what am I to ask? I do not even know the young man's name!"

"So you ask about stuff you know. Ask if the owner's Jewish. Ask if he's even *got* a son. You look like a smart lady; you'll think of something. Say, can you read?"

"A little."

"Tell you what." He pulled a newspaper from the pile under his arm and held it out to her. "This's got lots of ads for the big stores. G'wan and try your luck at a couple, three. Whaddaya got to lose?"

Raisa took the newspaper. "You are right. Thank you."

"Glad to help, lady." He stuck out his hand. "That'll be a penny."

Chapter Twelve

ENDINGS
AND BEGINNINGS

I t was already growing dark when Raisa took the downtown trolley home. It was so jammed with passengers that she had to stand the entire way. She felt beaten. She had tried the newsboy's suggestion, against her better judgment, and regretted it with every fiber of her aching body.

What a waste! she thought. *I should have known. If I worked in an office and some strange girl came in off the streets asking if my boss was Jewish and did he have a son, how would I react? I'm just lucky no one called the police to get rid of me. That was no way to find Henda. I'd have more luck searching for a pin in the sea.*

Raisa came back to the Kamenskys' apartment just in time for dinner. As soon as she opened the door, Brina came flying out into the hallway to greet her.

"You're back! You're back!" she crowed, alternately hugging Raisa and dancing eagerly in place. "There's a big surprise for you!"

"I wouldn't say I'm a *big* surprise." Raisa's head whipped up at the sound of Zusa's voice. Her friend peered around the doorjamb, grinning. "But then again, I wouldn't talk about a surprise before it happens. It spoils things."

"Brina doesn't spoil anything," Raisa said, taking the little girl's hand and leading her back into the apartment. She was feeling too tired to appreciate Zusa's sense of humor. All she wanted to do was take off her shoes and rest her aching feet.

"That's because I didn't tell her everything. What she doesn't know, she can't repeat." Zusa gave Brina a wink to let the child know she was only teasing.

Despite being weary to the bone, Raisa perked up her ears. "What are you talking about? What's happened?"

"Nothing bad, I promise. But I'm not saying another word until we eat. Mrs. Kamensky will twist my ears off if her food gets cold while I'm talking to you. Come on; everyone else is already sitting down."

Raisa hung up her things and joined the family at the table, where they all recited the blessing over the bread. While Mrs. Kamensky began filling their guest's plate, Gavrel turned to Raisa and asked, "How did it go?"

Raisa only shook her head and stared at her plate. "Not well." She had no appetite. She was wrung out from the frustrations of the day. "Excuse me, please." Raisa stood up. "I'm going to go lie down."

"You can lie down later," Mrs. Kamensky said. "Now you eat."

"Mama is right, Raisa," Fruma said. "You don't look like yourself. You should eat; it'll make you feel better."

"I'm all right; I'm just very tired," Raisa said. "And I'm not hungry."

"Why not?" Mrs. Kamensky challenged her. "You want me to worry that maybe you're too sick to eat, God forbid?"

"Mama, Raisa herself said she's *not* sick," Gavrel said. "She didn't have a good day, and that takes a lot out of a person. I'm sure she'll eat something later. Let her go lie down now, if that's what she wants."

Raisa gave him a deeply grateful look, but his mother wasn't listening to anyone but herself. "I am *not* running a café in this house! We eat together, like civilized human beings, at dinnertime." She ladled a huge portion of mashed potatoes onto Raisa's plate. Flecks of pepper and little brown bits of savory fried chicken skin dotted the white mound. It was one of Raisa's favorite dishes and it smelled delicious, but she was still too distressed to eat anything.

If I take one bite, I'll throw up, she thought. *Now I know what Yossel's anvil feels like. Blow after blow after blow, it never stops! Fine, I'll eat, if that's the only thing that will make them leave me alone, and one of them can mop the floor after!* She tried a tiny bit of the potatoes, and when it stayed down, she ventured to eat some more. The heavy food became an anchor, centering and warming her. Soon her plate was empty, and she became aware that everyone else at the table was watching her.

"I told you you'd feel better if you ate," Fruma said.

"Better enough to tell us what happened to you at Seven Arrows?" Gavrel asked.

Raisa reported everything she'd experienced that day, especially the rather one-sided conversation with Henda's former boss. "He called me a—a 'bunco artist'?" She looked to Gavrel for help with the odd English term.

"A *dreykop*, a *goniff*, a *shvindler*," Gavrel offered.

"All that?" Mrs. Kamensky clicked her tongue. "What a language, English!"

"And what luck that you've got such a nice dictionary in the house." Zusa smiled playfully at Gavrel before looking back at Raisa.

Raisa wasn't smiling.

Zusa's whole manner changed. "Raisa, I'm sorry you went all that way uptown and still nothing about your sister—no *real* luck—but at least you learned *something*, right? Can't you smile about that, at least?"

"About what? A wasted day?" Raisa helped herself to some pickled cucumbers with onions. "I'm just lucky I won't get fired for it." She slipped Gavrel a grateful glance.

"Really? Too bad," Zusa said with an airy flip of her wrist. It wasn't in her nature to stay serious for very long. "Because if you got fired, I could get your job at Triangle and—"

Raisa put down her fork and stared at her friend. "*Stop* it, Zusa. I'm too worn out for games tonight."

"Oh, fine, don't play." Zusa pretended to pout. "It'll just be

Gavrel and me, then." She flashed him a smile, ignoring Raisa's sour look. "Go ahead, Gavrel, tell her."

Gavrel fidgeted, a little nervous under Zusa's vivacious attention. "She's here because I invited her," he said. "We ran into one another at Triangle today."

"Triangle?" Now Raisa was intrigued. "Zusa, you mean you lost your old job?"

"Ha!" Zusa snapped her fingers. "More like *they* lost *me*. I knew I deserved better, so I quit. But that's not the whole story. *Tell* her, Gavrel." She nudged him with her fingertips.

"I was at work early, putting in some extra hours," he said.

"Which was where we met," Zusa cut in. "And which is why he was the very first person to hear the news that I, Miss Zusa Reshevsky, will now be sharing my extraordinary garment-making talents with the management of Triangle Waists, starting *tomorrow*!" She concluded her announcement with a dramatic gesture and nearly smacked Gavrel in the nose. "*That's* the big surprise."

"Really?" Raisa was thrilled to hear of her friend's good fortune. At the same time, she couldn't help feeling a little irritated with her. *Why does everything have to be such a big production with Zusa? And why does she keep trying to drag Gavrel in on it?*

"Yes, *really*." Zusa did a perfect imitation of Raisa's intonation. "And it would have been an even bigger surprise if this little bird hadn't come *that* close to blurting out the whole thing the instant you walked in the door." She leaned over to pinch Brina's cheek. "Someone should teach you how to keep secrets, sweetheart. If a girl doesn't know how to hold on to a little air of mystery, the boys lose interest. How would you like to come stay with *my* family for a change, so I could teach you what's worth knowing? We have plenty of room, and I know Mama and cousin Selig would love you." She was teasing again, but Mrs. Kamensky took it seriously.

"Fine lessons you want to teach her! *You* couldn't be troubled to keep track of her once you got off the boat, and we should entrust this precious child to *you*?" Mrs. Kamensky mashed Brina to her bosom, her eyes blazing.

"Please, please, I didn't mean it," Zusa said, laughing. "It was only a joke."

"Not a very funny one," Fruma said under her breath.

The atmosphere at the dinner table had turned distinctly cold. Even happy-go-lucky Zusa noticed, and toned down her bubbly nature. She left as soon as she could, though not without making Raisa and Gavrel promise that the three of them would travel to and from work together from now on.

No sooner had Mrs. Kamensky locked the door behind her guest than she turned to her family and announced, "I don't like that one."

"She's not a bad girl, Mrs. Kamensky," Raisa said. "And she's been a very good friend to me. She helped me a lot on the ship, and with Brina, and—"

"You're *off* the ship now," her landlady said tersely.

"Come on, Mama, Zusa's all right," Gavrel said. "It's just that sometimes her sense of humor runs away with her. I like her."

"You would, always with the jokes," his father spoke up. "Two of a kind."

"But God willing, not a pair," Fruma muttered for Raisa's ears alone.

"I think I should put Brina to bed now," Raisa said hastily.

As she was tucking Brina in, the little girl looked up at her and asked, "Are you mad at Zusa?"

"No, darling. It was a long day and I was angry at other people, but not her." She kissed Brina's forehead, then mischievously added, "Not unless you run away to live with her. You won't do that, will you?"

"I'll stay here." Brina had made up her mind. "Tante Lipke makes good cookies."

When Raisa woke up early the next morning, Mrs. Kamensky greeted her with a rare breakfast treat, a couple of soft-boiled eggs. "To give you back some strength from yesterday," she said.

Fruma came to the table with dark rings under her eyes. "I don't know what's the matter. I tossed and turned all night. I think you got my share of sleep as well as your own, Raisa," she said with a feeble smile. "I can't wait to get married so I won't have to go to work every morning!"

"Yes, marriage is one big holiday," her mother said drily.

"It's not?" Gavrel kept a straight face. "And here I thought I was going to do some poor girl a big favor by asking her to be my wife!"

"A *big* favor," Mr. Kamensky repeated, matching his wife's sarcasm. "She won't be able to thank you enough for making her Mrs. Penniless Pattern Cutter."

"Mrs. Penniless *Rabbi*," Gavrel corrected him. "I'm going to be ordained in less than three years, if I keep up my studies. And if every girl got married for money, there'd be a lot more bachelors in the world. Fruma, tell the truth—did you say yes to Morris because he's going to be a big-deal druggist, or because you just wanted to quit factory work, or because you love him?"

"I thought you knew," his sister replied. "It's because I can't get enough of his mother's company."

"Everyone in this house thinks they're funny," Mrs. Kamensky grumbled.

After breakfast, Gavrel offered Raisa his arm. "May I have the privilege of escorting you to work this morning, madame?"

Raisa looked at Mrs. Kamensky. "Go on, take his arm," the older woman said grudgingly. "He won't go out the door until you do. You know how stubborn he is."

The two of them walked out of the apartment arm in arm. They had to let go of one another in order to get down the narrow stairs, but once out on the street, Gavrel took Raisa's hand and threaded it back through the crook of his elbow. "In case

Mama's watching us from the front window," he explained smoothly, indicating his mother's possible lookout post with an upward roll of his eyes. "I think she *enjoys* disapproving of things, so who are we to deny her a little pleasure?"

Raisa lowered her eyelids. "We're going to be late." She left her hand where it was.

Zusa was waiting for them outside her building. "What's this?" she said, raising her voice theatrically when she saw them come strolling up as a couple. "What a gentleman you are, Gavrel, protecting little Raisa from all the dragons on Hester Street!"

Her sally got only a serene "Good morning, Zusa" from the pair in reply. She accompanied them the rest of the way to the Triangle Waist Company in sullen silence, with her chin tucked into the fake otter-fur collar of her winter coat.

It was impossible to keep Zusa's high spirits down for long. By the time the three of them reached the Asch Building she was once more all smiles and kidding remarks. When Gavrel left them to join the rest of the cutters on the eighth floor, she began teasing Raisa unmercifully. "So, when's the wedding?"

"Don't you think you're making too much of this, Zusa?" Raisa replied. "All we did was walk here together, arm in arm."

"Arm in arm so close you couldn't slip a ray of sunshine between the two of you," Zusa pointed out.

"That's hardly a marriage proposal. He can't even consider getting married until he finishes his studies and becomes ordained as a rabbi, and I need to know for sure, one way or—God forbid—the other, what's become of my sister before I can think about anything else so big in my life."

"Mmm, so much attention to details, so much forethought after just one walk together, but *I'm* the one who's making too much out of this?" Zusa giggled as she saw the effect of her words. "And I thought 'blushing bride' was only a saying!"

As much as she loved her friend, Raisa was secretly relieved when Miss Gullo showed Zusa to a workstation that was far from her own, at a machine that was nearly all the way up against the Washington Place windows.

At the end of the day, Gavrel waited for the girls downstairs, just across the street from the Asch Building. "Well, how did you like it?" he asked Zusa, taking Raisa's arm as naturally as if it were something he'd done for years.

"I'm glad we've got a fore*lady*," Zusa replied. "I've had enough of fore*men* to last me the rest of my life."

"Oh, they're not all bad. I feel sorry for ours. No one's supposed to smoke on the job—you don't want to know how fast some of that fine lawn and linen we cut can burn, once it catches fire, and the paper patterns can go up in flames if you *look* at them the wrong way—but some of the older cutters do it anyhow. They claim that if it weren't for them and how good they are at fitting pattern pieces onto the fabric so there's next to no waste scraps, the company'd be bankrupt, so if they want a smoke on the job, they'll take it. It keeps the foremen jumping, trying to catch them at it and make them put out their cigarettes."

"What kind of fools are they, smoking around all of that cloth and paper?" Raisa asked. "Do they want to burn the whole building down?"

"That can't happen," Gavrel responded. "That's what the owners claim, anyway. With one breath they insist that one tiny fire escape down the air shaft is more than enough, that there's plenty of firefighting gear on hand, that we're making a big deal over nothing. With another they say that any changes would be a waste of money; the Asch Building is guaranteed fireproof."

"Yes, but I'm not!"

"I wouldn't mind smelling cigarette smoke if it covered up some of the other stink on our floor," Zusa said. "I didn't know how much I hated the smell of oil until I got stuck in a room with that many sewing machines burning through the stuff like there's no tomorrow!"

"If that's your biggest complaint, you're lucky," Gavrel said.

Suddenly, Raisa looked back toward the entrance to the Asch Building and began waving, calling out, "Luciana! Luciana!"

"Ah! Raisa! Hello!" The Italian girl ran across the street, holding on to her hat with one hand. Soon all three shipboard friends were embracing and chattering enthusiastically in English.

"Is it not marvelous that this has happened?" Luciana said. "We all work here now, together. It is exactly what we spoke of that evening. When I go home and tell my family, Mama will say it is proof that miracles happen."

"I wish *this* miracle did not smell so much like sewing machine oil," Zusa remarked.

December brought the dreary winter months to Raisa's work at Triangle, and the dreariness wasn't helped by the fact that money was tighter than ever. Gavrel's Uncle Hersch lost his job. The veteran pattern cutter had gotten sick after so many years of breathing in all the little threads and lint in the factory's air. He stayed home coughing so hard he couldn't even get out of bed, so he was fired. The Kamenskys sent his family a little something to help out with the rent, which affected their own household budget, but they refused to do otherwise.

In the mornings, Raisa and Gavrel would go to work with Zusa, and Luciana sometimes joined them along the way. In the Asch Building, Gavrel and Luciana got off the elevator on the eighth floor, while Raisa and Zusa got out on the ninth, not to see one another until the workday ended.

It hadn't taken Zusa long to make lots of friends among the ninth-floor workers. The cloakroom always broke into a storm of welcoming laughter as soon as she came in. As for Raisa, her own group of friends at the shop was much smaller—just two girls, Gussie and Jennie—but she didn't envy Zusa her popularity. The way Raisa's life was, she had scarcely a free moment. Besides her job, nearly every minute was devoted to her schoolwork, Brina's lessons and playtime, writing to Glukel, marking Shabbos and the festivals, and above all, her ongoing search. What good was it to have a multitude of friends if she couldn't do anything more than bid them hello and good-bye at the two ends of the workday? She saw more of Zusa and Luciana because the three of them went to and from work together and shared classes at the Educational Alliance.

Gussie and Jennie didn't need to learn English. Gussie was proud to call herself a born New Yorker, but little, birdlike Jennie could claim even higher status: her mother was American-born, too! Raisa cherished the few instances when she was able to steal a little time with them. Their outings were simple—long walks, window shopping, a free lecture. They couldn't afford much more, but that didn't discourage them. Once, when they were strolling arm in arm along Broadway, Jennie had stood on tiptoe to whisper, "You know, Raisa, your English is getting better and better. You must have a very good ear; when you talk, sometimes you sound like Gussie and me!" Raisa had accepted the compliment modestly, but inside she had danced with happiness.

Raisa's mornings were always brighter when she was able to trade a few friendly words with Gussie in the cloakroom, then wave to Jennie at a machine several tables away from her own, but by December, the brightness had faded fast. As day followed day, the mechanical, mind-numbing repetition dragged her down. She sewed the same pattern pieces in the same way at the same machine, hour after hour. All she could think of as she endured that drudgery was how her sister must have endured it, as well.

I try and I try, Henda, she thought as the needle bobbed up and down and the factory air reeked with sweat and oil and dampness. Every stitch seemed to anchor the winter darkness to her spirit. *I try to discover some new way to find you. Gavrel, God bless him, is there for me. He's doing what he can to learn the names of the big department store owners, to see which of them are German Jews, whether any of them has a son, but when does he have the time to ask such questions? He needs time for his studies, too. He'd give me every free second he had, but I can't let him sacrifice his dreams for mine.*

During the second week in December, Raisa was taken from sewing simple bodice seams to the more intricate work of setting in shirtwaist sleeves. It was the high point of her whole month, until what happened on New Year's Eve.

On December 30, as she, Gavrel, Zusa, and Luciana were walking south through Washington Square Park, Gavrel announced that on the following night they should all go to a restaurant for dinner and then on to Times Square to watch the New Year come in.

"I thought the New Year already came for *us* back in October," Zusa said archly. "And *you* say you are going to be a rabbi!"

"Oh, so now you've learned enough English to be a smart

aleck in two languages?" Gavrel replied, taking Zusa's jibe in stride.

"Four!" she said proudly. "You forget that I also speak Polish and German."

"Then bring all four of your sharp tongues to the party, and we'll welcome nineteen eleven in real American style!"

"What does that mean?" Raisa asked.

"What, they haven't taught you about it in your English class? And they call themselves an *Educational* Alliance?" He chuckled, obviously pleased to have a real surprise in store for them.

Raisa was positive that what Gavrel had planned would never happen. All the way home that day she imagined how his mother would react. Mrs. Kamensky could not forbid her son from going wherever he pleased—he was a wage earner and a Talmudic scholar, and he'd counted as an adult in the Jewish community since becoming a bar mitzvah four years ago—but she *could* make his life very unpleasant, before and after the fact, if she wasn't happy with his choice. He might decide that the price of her disapproval was too steep to pay for one night of fun.

To Raisa's surprise, Mrs. Kamensky not only told them to go and have a good time; she also suggested that Fruma and Morris join the group. She put her foot down only the following night, when Brina saw Raisa, Fruma, and Gavrel getting ready to leave. She begged to come along, as well, and kept up her clamor until Tante Lipke gave her a cookie as a consolation prize.

That night, Raisa stood in Times Square, in the middle of a mass of tens of thousands, huddling close to her friends. Morris kept whispering warnings about pickpockets until Fruma made him stop. Luciana had brought Paolo along for security, and now she held on to his arm like a drowning woman clinging to a life preserver. Zusa sized up the handsome young Italian and took his other arm, announcing that she was afraid to be an unescorted girl in such a mob.

"Are you cold, Raisa?" Gavrel asked.

"A little." She looked around in awe at the boisterous crowd choking the streets. *So many people, pressing so close, and yet when a crowd gets this big, it makes you feel like you're all alone.* Then she felt the warm weight of Gavrel's arm slipping around her shoulders and the sense of isolation vanished. She let him draw her closer. With her head leaning on Gavrel's chest, she couldn't tell if Zusa was watching them, making mocking comments, or if she was too busy bantering with Paolo to bother.

Let her say what she likes, Raisa thought. *I don't care. This feels right.* She closed her eyes with a happy sigh.

"Raisaleh, are you falling asleep on your feet? It's almost time. Look!" Gavrel's gentle voice called for her attention. The noise level of the mob around them was mounting by the second, a slowly growing rumble of anticipation. Raisa watched, starry-eyed, as the mammoth wood-and-iron ball made its descent from the peak of the flagpole atop the Times Tower, its galaxy of electric lightbulbs dazzling in the night. When it reached the bottom of the pole, the crowd's rumble exploded into roars of *"Happy New Year!"* and thousands of wooden rattles, horns, and other noisemakers added their clashing sounds to the din.

"Happy New Year, everyone!" Zusa shouted, throwing her arms wide, as if she wanted to hug all of Times Square.

"Buon anno nuovo!" Paolo and Luciana cried.

"Happy nineteen eleven," Morris said, smiling affectionately at Fruma. "I know one reason why it's going to be the happiest year of my life."

Gavrel turned so that he and Raisa stood with their backs to their friends. "Happy New Year, dear Raisaleh," he whispered, and kissed her. She closed her eyes, swept away by a sweet thrill unlike anything she had ever experienced, and when she opened them again she knew that she'd awakened to a wonderful new world.

They told no one about how things had changed between them, though it seemed impossible that the people they knew best noticed nothing different. Whenever she and Gavrel were together in the house—at dinner, at breakfast, or simply when everyone was home—Raisa often found herself casting secretive glances at his mother, checking for any hint that Mrs. Kamensky was aware that her son and her boarder were in love.

It was Raisa's idea that they say nothing. She mentioned it to him as the two of them walked home on New Year's Day after parting ways with Zusa. Gavrel wanted to tell the world, but she asked him to keep quiet, for her sake. When he asked for a reason, she answered, "If we say one word about it, Brina will start talking about us as if we're getting married tomorrow and you *know* she won't stop."

"Let her talk," Gavrel murmured, hugging her and taking another kiss. The Lower East Side streets were never totally deserted, but at that hour there were no hawkeyed, gossip-starved neighbors to see them. He released her from his embrace and added, "If you're afraid of what Mama and Papa will say, you shouldn't be. They love you, too. I don't need to hear them say so to know that. And they adore Brina as much as I do!"

"*Please*, Gavrel . . ."

"Oh, all right. For you. But you tell me when you're ready to stop this nonsense."

Nonsense . . . Raisa thought as they walked on. *But is it nonsense? I've never felt like this about a boy before. I* do *love him. It makes me happy just to be with him, and when he gives me help and strength to go on, there's not a single doubt in my mind, except . . . it's all happening so fast. I need time to think. All I need is time.* She touched her hair self-consciously. It had grown back to just below her ears.

"A penny for your thoughts, Raisaleh," Gavrel breathed in her ear.

"I was only thinking that I'm very happy." It wasn't a lie, just a half-truth. She was happy; she just didn't know how long she could stay that way. Nothing was certain or permanent. If people knew that she and Gavrel were sweethearts, whatever happened between them would become a spectacle. If Gavrel woke up with a change of heart tomorrow, or in a month, or in a year's time, she wouldn't be able to save herself from the hurt of losing his love, but at least she could save herself from the unbearable awkwardness of continuing to live under the same roof with so many pitying eyes. The Kamenskys had become like family to her and Brina. She didn't want anything to uproot the child, or herself, from their lives.

"That's what I want," he said, squeezing her. "But I warn you, I don't come from a stupid family. They know I like you, and as more than just a friend."

"Then they don't need to know how *much* more," Raisa said. Boldly she stood on tiptoe and kissed him.

"No, but I bet they'll guess."

Chapter Thirteen

SPARKS

The memory of that night stayed with Raisa when she went back to the monotony of her work at Triangle. She and Gavrel stole moments together when they could, but there were very few opportunities for it. Most of their days were eaten up by the factory, and most of his free time had to be devoted to Torah and Talmud studies, just as she still had her night-school classes.

One morning in early February, Raisa came to the ninth floor of Triangle to find another girl at her place on the long table. For an instant she was about to scold the invader and send her packing, or fetch Miss Gullo to make her leave. *Wait a minute, what am I doing? There's no real difference if I sit here or there,* she realized. She asked Miss Gullo to move her to another workstation for setting sleeves, but the small change in her usual way of doing things bothered her the whole day.

"I don't understand it," she said as she, Gavrel, and Zusa waited for Luciana on the corner of Washington Place and Greene Street. "The machines are all the same, the chairs are all the same, so why was I so miserable?"

"Given enough time, a prisoner gets attached to his prison," Zusa said offhandedly.

"My job is not a prison!" Even as she objected to what Zusa had said, Raisa began to wonder. "I'm not saying this place is perfect. They 'fix' the clocks so they can keep us at work longer. They make us take the freight elevators because to them we're equipment, not people. They pack us in at the workstations like pickles in a jar. But do you know what? It's the same everywhere, and some places it's worse."

"Is *that* a reason to leave things the way they are, to put up with bad conditions?" Zusa argued. "If someone drops me into a pot of boiling water, I should accept it and be grateful it's not boiling *oil*? Raisa, if we spend our lives always looking down, only seeing the people with heavier burdens, we'll forget we've got the power to look *up*—look up and then *reach* up, too! And after we've pulled ourselves up to better things, we'll be able to reach back down to help others. When I see a person who's worse off than I am, I'd rather do more for her than mumble 'Thank God that's not *my* life' and walk away!"

"Listen to you, Zusa!" Gavrel said. "You sound like a regular union girl."

"And what if I am? I'm not stupid, Gavrel. I know that I

can't do anything to change the way things are by myself." Zusa thrust her hand into her purse and pulled out a union membership card. "There! What do you say to *that*?"

Gavrel took out his wallet and produced his own card. "I say, welcome, sister." He grinned.

"Gavrel! When did you join the union?" Raisa exclaimed. "Do your bosses know?"

"If they do, they do. You can't be fired just because you're a union member. Some of the longtime cutters here told me that was one of the concessions we got from the owners after the general strike, along with shorter hours and better—a *little* better—pay."

"Even if they could fire us for joining the union, I'd still belong," Zusa maintained. "I want to be *paid* like a person and *treated* like a person, not another machine. But I suppose *you'd* want to play it safe," she said to Raisa.

"You're right, I would," Raisa answered back, not letting Zusa's taunt touch her. "I need my job. I'm the sole wage earner for Brina and me, and I'm sending money home to help Glukel, too. Reb Avner writes that she's got arthritis in her hands now, so she can't work as much or as fast. She needs my help, even if she'd die before she'd say it. So yes, Zusa; yes, I *do* want to play it safe." She took the union membership card from her friend's hand. "Tell me how I can join, too."

Zusa gave Raisa a funny look. "Do you *like* confusing me?"

"I like listening to you, Zusa," Raisa said. "You know how

to use words to make me *think* about things, not just take them as they are."

"She's right, Zusa; you're very eloquent," Gavrel said. "You ought to speak at meetings. The general strike went on a long time and took a lot out of us. The owners wanted to starve us back to work by filling our jobs with scab labor. They tried to break us; they bribed the police to look the other way when they sent gangsters to attack us. We got some concessions in the end, but nowhere near enough. Many people are too worn-out from fighting to understand that we can't stop now. Someone with your gift for words could make them see that!"

"You're not so bad yourself," Zusa replied.

Just then, Luciana came running up to join them. "I am sorry! My foreman is slow today. He takes a long time looking in the girls' purses before he lets us go. You are too cold, waiting?"

"Don't worry, Luciana," Gavrel said with a gallant tip of his hat. "We found a way to keep warm."

Raisa thought that she would be happy to see March come. Fruma had told her that sometimes the month brought warm weather to the city, and always more hours of daylight. She was famished for the sight of new green leaves and tired of coming out of the Asch Building at quitting time into a world of darkness.

Inside the walls of the ninth-floor shop, every day was like the one before. She was bored with doing nothing but setting in sleeves. When she'd worked with Glukel, the work had been hard, but the variety of tasks and dressmaking problems to solve kept it interesting. The same could be said for her time spent with "Madame Odile." Somehow, knowing that more than a hundred other girls were trapped in the same tedious rut made it all worse. At Triangle there was never any opportunity for creativity, just eternal duplication. She wanted to try her hand at some other part of the process for assembling shirtwaists, but she never had the chance to approach the forelady about it before or during the workday, and when quitting time came, she just wanted to escape.

Raisa was unaware of how much the dreariness of her job was seeping into the rest of her life until one Sunday morning in mid-March. While Mrs. Kamensky and Fruma were paying a reluctant visit to Morris's mother and Gavrel was studying with the rabbi, Raisa took Brina for a walk down to Mr. Kamensky's dry-goods store. It was almost Purim, one of the most joyful holidays of the year, a time for feasting, drinking, and celebrating how Queen Esther had saved the Jewish people of ancient Persia from annihilation at the hands of their enemy, Haman. Brina couldn't decide whether her favorite part of Purim was getting to eat hamantaschen— triangular pastries stuffed with jam or poppy seeds—or dressing up in costume.

"You'll have to wait for the hamantaschen," Raisa told her. "But today we can see if Mr. Kamensky has any fabric scraps or remnants to give us for making your Purim costume."

Mr. Kamensky's small store was very close to the tenement where his family lived. Like many of his Jewish neighbors, he kept it closed on Saturday to honor Shabbos, the divinely ordained day of rest. Sunday was neither his Sabbath nor his customers'. KAMENSKY'S DRY GOODS was blazoned boldly in the center of the store window in large letters, with Yiddish words in smaller print at the corners. When Raisa and Brina went in, a little bell over the door jingled merrily.

"Ah, what a wonderful surprise! Come in, my dear children. Come in and tell me to what I owe the pleasure of this visit!" All smiles, Mr. Kamensky rushed from behind the counter to embrace Raisa and twirl Brina off her feet until the child shrieked with laughter. Away from home and his eternal copy of the *Forward*, he was a different man, talkative and jolly.

"We—we're here to find material for Brina's Purim costume," Raisa said.

"And you've come to the right place. Hey, Louis!" Mr. Kamensky hailed the pimply young man who was still behind the counter. "You take this little princess here back to the storeroom and you show her the brightest, prettiest, best leftover fabric we've got in this place." He patted Brina on the head and told her, "Take your time making your choice, sweetheart. You may be our princess, but you only get to be a queen once a year!"

"Isn't Raisa going to come with me?" Brina asked shyly. She didn't know Mr. Kamensky's clerk, and she remembered all the lessons everyone in the Kamensky household had taught her about strangers.

"Listen to the wisdom of it!" Mr. Kamensky laughed with

pleasure. "It's all right, darling, I wouldn't send you off with Louis if I didn't trust him. Besides, the storeroom is right through that door, which will stay wide open. If you really need Raisa with you, so be it, but I thought you might like having the chance to play that you're a grown-up woman shopping on her own."

With a serious face, Brina looked from Mr. Kamensky to Louis and back again. "I *would* like that," she stated.

Louis offered her a kindly smile and his hand. "Anytime you want the young lady to come join us, just holler for her," he said. "She'll be able to hear you real good."

Brina sniffed with disdain. "I know that." She permitted the clerk to lead her away.

"It's true, you can trust Louis completely with the child," Mr. Kamensky said. "I would sooner cut off my right hand than place her in jeopardy. Now, Raisa, while Brina is busy, I'd like to talk with you."

Raisa felt her body tense up. *So that's why he sent Brina into the back room! He knows that Gavrel and I are more than friends and he's mad about it. He doesn't think I'm good enough for his son. What's he going to do?*

"My dear," Mr. Kamensky began, "I'm very glad that you happened to come into my store today. If you hadn't, I'd have needed to make the opportunity to tell you what I must. I have seen how things are between you and my son."

"Mr. Kamensky . . ." Raisa's stomach lurched. *Is he going to tell me to leave Gavrel alone? Is he going to say that Brina and I have to move out?*

"A blind man could see it," Mr. Kamensky went on. Then he smiled. "Luckily for us all, my wife is neither blind nor a man. If she's noticed anything, she hasn't said a word about it, which leads me to conclude that she hasn't seen a thing." He chuckled, but then he caught sight of Raisa's expression. "Child, why such a face? You look as if you're waiting for a death sentence! Believe me, if my Lipke *did* know about you and Gavrel, her only objection would be that you are both still very young and that he has not yet finished his studies." He took her hand in both of his. "You're a good, honest girl and I know you'll take proper care of our son. I'd have to be a fool to object to him marrying you."

Raisa could hardly believe what she was hearing. "Mr. Kamensky, I promise you, Gavrel and I haven't even mentioned marriage. If we had, I know he'd tell you and his mother first."

"I hope not! What is he, our son or our puppet? If he talks about marriage to *anyone* before you, then the first word out of your mouth should be 'No!'"

Raisa laughed so loudly with relief that Brina peeked out of the back room to see if she was missing anything good.

"It's nothing, *mamaleh*," Mr. Kamensky told her. "I was just telling Raisa about the time I stuffed chickpeas up my nose when I was a little boy. I know *you* would never do anything so silly."

"I don't *like* chickpeas," Brina said firmly, and went back to her search for the perfect costume fabric.

Once she was gone, Mr. Kamensky said, "So, is that why you've been so sad lately, Raisa? Because you were afraid that Lipke and I would find out that you and Gavrel were sweethearts and that we might be angry at you?"

"What?" The question startled her. "I haven't been sad."

"And a fish doesn't notice the water. My dear, you used to light up our home, but lately it's like having a poor little ghost who drifts in and out of the place."

Raisa pressed her lips together. "I wish they'd give me a different job at the shop, that's all."

Mr. Kamensky gently touched her chin and made her meet his eyes. "I was right to call you an honest girl, Raisa. You're not a very good liar. I don't think your job is the only thing that's been troubling you, though I believe it does bear the guilt for a lot of your problems. How much time have you had to search for your sister since you began working at Triangle?"

"Why bother?" Raisa replied dully. "I've run out of places to look. I've been trying to find her for months, and I hardly know more now than when I first arrived. Suppose I did have all the time in the world to go to every department store in this city—what am I supposed to ask? If the owner has a son who's run off with a poor girl? Even if I knew his name, what good would it do? It's useless. It's over."

"This is what's devouring your spirit, this hopelessness. Listen to me, my dear. I know what it is to believe that everything is lost. I came to this country because back in Russia, I saw my whole life go up in flames and blood—my parents, my brothers and sisters, all slaughtered in a pogrom. The priests would not stop spewing hate, preaching to the peasants that we killed their god, turning them into bloodthirsty wild beasts and setting them loose to murder us. My baby brother, Gavrel, was yanked out of his cradle and smashed against the wall, and for what? For killing *God*? He couldn't even feed himself!

"My father was cut down trying to protect him. My mother grabbed me by the neck and shoved me out the back door along with the rest of the children. When I looked back, I saw the drunken peasant who killed her. I saw others catch my little sisters, Fruma and Pesha, and my brother Velvel and drag them back into our house before they burned it to the ground. I hid in a ditch all night until dawn, when, God have mercy, my uncle found me. I came to America with him and what was left of his family. What reason did I have to hope I could ever know joy again? And yet"—he spread his hands—"here I am, a husband, a father, a man who is able to feed his family, a *person*!"

He dropped his hands onto Raisa's shoulders and spoke softly. "Why stop hoping? The world spins and things change, good to bad, bad to good. If you give up, it spins you away. Maybe someday you will have the time to go looking for that young man. You might come across some person in one of the department stores who has reason to sympathize with you and who *will* tell you something to bring you closer to what you seek. But if you give up, you could be walking right past that same person on the street and never know how close you were to finding your sister."

"What's the use?" Raisa said. "I don't even know if she's dead or alive."

"That is true," Mr. Kamensky said. "But only because you don't want to know."

His words wounded her to the heart. "How can you say that?"

"I'm sorry; I spoke badly. I know how brave you are, how strong, but I also understand that even the bravest soul sometimes hides from the truth, if that truth is cruel. I understand why you haven't sought information about your sister everywhere possible."

"And how can you say *that*? I've gone to every synagogue, I've asked at the settlement house, I've spoken to as many people as I can, I've gone back to the Protective and Benevolent Association so many times!"

"But when you were there, you never asked to see the records of the *chevra kidusha*, the burial society. And you never went to the city morgue, or the hospitals. I think you would have told us if you had. I can't blame you for it. How can you go to such places to ask a question when you fear that the answer will break your heart? You couldn't." Mr. Kamensky took a deep breath. "I did."

"No." Raisa was aghast. "Oh, no. *No*. Henda is—?"

"Shhh, shhh!" Mr. Kamensky took her hands, speaking as

quickly as he could to drive the look of horror out of her eyes. "That's what I'm trying to tell you. She is *not* dead. She is *not*. When the members of your *chevra kidusha* said they hadn't buried any young woman who fit your sister's description, I went to others, all the others I could find. She wasn't one of their people, but they might have buried a stranger out of charity. I had to know, one way or the other. I even went to the city morgue. But I found nothing, thank God! I didn't tell you any of this until now because it wasn't as if I'd learned where Henda was, only where she wasn't. Also, I didn't want you mad at me for minding your business."

Raisa threw her arms around Mr. Kamensky's neck. "How could I be mad at you for giving me such a precious gift?"

"So you don't think I'm an old busybody, a yenta in trousers?" he asked. Raisa shook her head. "Good, because that makes it easier to tell you this: I also wrote a letter or two to the *Forward* on your behalf. I put in as much about your sister as I knew. Who can say? If they publish one of my letters, she might read it and come running."

"Henda doesn't know how to read," Raisa said.

"Neither did I, when I first came here. Neither did you, yes? Ah, but *now* . . ." He made an expansive gesture. "This is a wonderful country for making changes."

"In that case, I'll start hoping she reads the *Forward*," Raisa said, giving Gavrel's father a fond smile.

"Who *doesn't* read the *Forward*?" he responded. "And even supposing she can't or doesn't read the *Forward,* maybe someone who knows her *will* read it, and will tell her about it. Now, Raisaleh, isn't it better to be worrying about whether or not your sister reads the *Forward* than whether or not she's still alive?" He pinched her cheek.

Raisa hugged him harder and kissed him on the forehead. "How can I ever pay you back for so much of your time?"

Mr. Kamensky shrugged. "As long as I can rely on Louis to mind the store on his own—a *little*—my time is my own. You'll pay me back by getting your head out of the shadows. Here." He reached into his pocket and pressed some coins into her hand. "Go to the moving-picture show. Laugh. Cry about things that aren't real tragedies. Enjoy yourself. You're too young to act so old and broken."

"Mr. Kamensky, I can't." Raisa tried to give back the money, but he pulled away, hands held high.

"Don't insult me! I'm not doing this out of pity. I'm looking out for my own happiness. As glad as I'd be to see you and Gavrel together, I don't want you thinking that marriage and children are the only possible escape from your sorrows. My son deserves better than that and so do you. So you see, I am a very selfish man." He gave her a quick peck on the forehead. "Take Brina and go see a nice show."

Purim came and went with all the festivities and rejoicing anyone could desire. Brina surprised everyone by *not* eating herself sick on hamantaschen, though Raisa suspected it was because Mrs. Kamensky had promised her additional treats if she behaved well. At services, Gavrel was given the honor of reading from the Scroll of Esther. Whenever he mentioned Haman's name, all the children twirled their *groggers* energetically, using the rattling noisemakers to blot out the name of their ancient enemy. Between the joy of the holiday and her sense of renewed hope thanks to Mr. Kamensky, Raisa was in a good mood as she joined Zusa and Luciana for their English class the following evening.

Sometime during the first half of class, Raisa looked up from her book just as her teacher, Miss Bryant, was hearing one of the other students, a girl who worked in her parents' fish market, recite a grammar exercise. Raisa found herself making the same corrections under her breath that Miss Bryant was making aloud. When the girl became confused and lost her place in the recitation, Raisa knew exactly how Miss Bryant would help her find her way back.

It's not that different from when I teach Brina, she thought. *Or when I help Luciana.* She returned her eyes to the open book in front of her, but her ears held the ghostly echoes of the conversation she'd shared with Gavrel when they'd walked home arm in arm on Thanksgiving.

"You should always have dreams, Raisaleh."

That was when she made her decision.

When Miss Bryant announced it was time for the class break, Zusa and Luciana joined the rest of their classmates in the mass race out the door to the water fountain, but Raisa stayed behind. Squaring her shoulders, she walked up to the teacher's desk and said in her best English, "Miss Bryant, may I speak with you, please?"

Miss Bryant was a tall, slender woman whose tight chignon of raven hair was never out of place and who always dressed modestly in simple, unstylish dresses. A red-gold wedding ring gleamed on her left hand, but she still insisted that the class call her Miss. Raisa, Zusa, and Luciana often speculated over the possible reasons for this. Her name and accent clearly marked her as Irish, which led the three girls to wonder what had brought such a woman to teach English in an institution created by and primarily for Jews.

"You may, Raisa," Miss Bryant said. "Please sit down. However, do remember that the interval is short. You would do well to speak with all dispatch."

"Yes, Miss Bryant." Raisa often didn't recognize the fancy words her beloved teacher used when speaking to her, but she liked the challenge of trying to understand them. She was disappointed if a class went by without the need for her to hunt down new vocabulary in the fat dictionary on the teacher's desk. "Thank you very much. I have a question of . . ." She searched her mind for the phrase she'd heard her teacher use more than once in class. "Of pressing importance."

"*Very* good, Raisa." Miss Bryant was obviously pleased to hear her stretching her use of English. "Please feel free to ask it."

"Miss Bryant . . ." Raisa pressed her lips together for a moment, then let her dream fly. "Miss Bryant, do you think that someday *I* can be a teacher, too?"

Yes! She said yes! Miss Bryant's approval and support sent Raisa's heart dancing all the way through the second half of the class. The teacher's words surrounded her like clouds of purest gold: *"You have made remarkable progress in this class. You seem to have a natural aptitude for learning, and I have overheard you taking an interest in your classmates' progress. If you are willing to accept the fact that achieving your ambition will take time, I will do whatever lies within my power to assist you. In short, it is my belief that someday you will become not only a teacher, but a good teacher, and I promise you that when that day comes, I will rejoice."*

I wish I knew all of the words she used, thought Raisa, *but, oh, I know what she meant! She meant yes! Yes! Yes!*

Raisa could hardly wait to tell Gavrel. She wanted him to be the first to know, because he was the only one who'd shared her dream, the one who'd encouraged her to follow it. And so she had to endure a thousand prying, nagging questions from Zusa and Luciana all the way home that night. Both of them were ferociously curious to learn why Raisa had stayed in the classroom for most of the break. Raisa tried to put them off the scent by saying she'd only wanted to ask Miss Bryant to suggest some additional English readings from beyond the classroom texts that a student of her level might enjoy—stories, poems, even novels. (And it *was* true, in a way; she *had* gone on to ask the teacher for more demanding work, as eager to speed her education as she was hungry to read more interesting English than "The boy has nine apples" or "The girl will buy a new broom.")

Luciana was willing to accept this, but Zusa had an instinct for knowing when her friend was not telling *quite* the whole story. She refused to let the matter drop. When her questions didn't turn up answers that satisfied her, she turned to sarcastic remarks about "Miss Professor" all the way home, until Raisa was ready to slap her.

Zusa relented and begged Raisa's pardon just before they parted, but her apology sounded thin. Raisa was still steaming when she returned to the apartment. Gavrel and his mother were the only two family members still awake, drinking hot tea and sharing a plate of apple slices. Mrs. Kamensky took one look at her boarder's frowning face and remarked, "What's wrong? You didn't study enough? You answered wrong too much? Your teacher scolded you?"

"My teacher says *I* could be a teacher someday!" The words burst from Raisa's mouth as if they were a curse.

"She did? Mazel tov!" Gavrel exclaimed. "But why is that making you so mad?"

"It isn't. I'm not. It's only . . ." Raisa took off her hat and coat, then sat down at the table. "I wanted to keep it a secret until I got home, but Zusa kept picking and *picking* at me every step of the way until—"

"Tsk. That girl." Mrs. Kamensky poured a glass of tea for Raisa. "So smart, so pretty, but she can't stand for anyone else to be smart and pretty, too. She should stop hungering after what's on your plate and enjoy what's on her own."

The next morning as Raisa and Gavrel were walking toward Zusa's house, he took advantage of their small measure of time alone together to give her a big kiss on the cheek. A gang of boys loitering near the gutter saw the gesture and began hooting and making rude suggestions. Men and women from the neighborhood took notice. Raisa recognized some of them from other apartments in the Kamenskys' tenement and feared they also recognized her.

"Gavrel, what are you *doing*?" she hissed, turning bright red. "Someone's going to tell your mother about this, I know it!"

"Let them tell," he declared blithely. "Can't a man kiss his bride-to-be?"

"What are you talking about? You're crazy! I'm not your bride-to-be."

"Mmmm, you're right. I've neglected one very important thing." He stopped on the spot and raised her hand to his lips. "My dear, beautiful Raisa, I love you with all my heart. If you feel the same for me, then please, make me happy. Say that you'll be my wife."

Raisa could hardly breathe. There was a fluttering in her throat. The countless different sounds of people, animals, and traffic that made up the hubbub of the crowded streets faded into nothingness. "Oh, Gavrel . . ." She spoke his name as softly as a sigh. "I—how can I say yes? How can we even think about getting married? *I'm* too young, *you're* too young—"

"You're too serious, that's your problem," he said. "You spend so much time looking at the details that you don't see the big picture. Of course we're too young to get married *now,* but now isn't forever. *Now* is dull work and long hours and bad pay. Every morning when I say my prayers I thank God for having given me a door out of *now.* And don't you see? He's given you one, too! Raisa, we can have a different future—me as a rabbi, you as a teacher—and we can have it sooner than you think, if we work for it hard enough. Well? What do you say? Yes or no?"

She squeezed his hand tight. "I love you, Gavrel. I love you very much."

He smiled. "Not a yes or a no, but I can live with it." He kissed her again, this time on the lips. A group of middle-aged women flounced past, clicking their tongues loudly in disapproval. "That's right, ladies, keep on clucking!" Gavrel called after them. "We can use the eggs!"

On the way home that evening, after they'd bid good night to Zusa and Luciana, Gavrel asked Raisa, "Shall we tell my family tonight?"

"Not yet." She rested her hand on his arm and leaned close. "You know what they'll say."

"Too young, too poor, too far from my ordination, too soon

to think of you as a teacher and not a pupil? Yes, I *do* know, but I don't care. I want to tell them, Raisa."

"Can we at least wait until we've got some kind of solid proof to give them?" she begged.

"Proof of what?"

"Proof that we're *serious* about wanting to make our own life. Gavrel, I'm going to start working more hours at Triangle. I put in my fifty-two a week, but at this time of year there's plenty of extra work. My forelady likes me; she'll give me the chance to earn more. I want to be able to pay my rent and send something to Glukel *and* still put aside a little extra every week. I'm going to save my money so that when we do tell your parents about our plans, I can slap it all down on the table and tell them, 'See? We've *planned* for this. We're responsible people. We're not just going to live on air and dreams.'"

"No, we're not," Gavrel agreed, tugging at a wisp of her hair. "But I still want to share your dreams and make them all come true."

Chapter Fourteen

FLAMES

Zusa was just coming out of the ninth-floor cloakroom when she bumped into Raisa. "Well, look who's here!" she exclaimed. "And on Shabbos, too. Don't tell Rabbi Gavrel." She giggled.

"Oh, Zusa, stop teasing." Raisa smiled as she sidled past her friend to get into the cloakroom. As she hung up her hat and coat she added, "Anyway, I've worked on Saturdays before."

"Not *every* Saturday, like Luciana and me."

"Yes, but now"—Raisa plucked one of Brina's stray hairs off the shoulder of her coat—"Miss Gullo knows I'll be coming in on Saturdays from now on, besides my weekdays. She was happy to approve the change."

"Forget Miss Gullo; why didn't you let us know? We could have walked up here together, the way we usually do."

"I should've thought of that. I guess that since this is something different for me, I didn't connect it with any of the other things I do on an ordinary workday."

"Oh, so now your friends are only a part of what's *ordinary*, huh?" Zusa laughed. "Gavrel's *really* not going to like hearing that! If you ask me, that boy's got plans for you that are anything *but* ordinary."

"Which is why nobody asked you," Raisa replied, joking back. "Now, stop making everything into a big romance and let's get to work. I'd just like to earn a little more money, that's all."

"You're not the only one." Zusa's eyes swept the long shop tables as the two girls headed for their workstations. "This place is just as packed on Shabbos as during the week. If our old rabbi from back home could see how many Jews are spending the day sewing and cutting instead of resting and praying, he'd have a fit! I'd feel worse about it if I didn't know that plenty of the Christians work on Sundays, too."

"Wouldn't it be nice if we got paid enough so that none of us had to make these kinds of choices?" Raisa said with a sigh. "Someday . . ."

"I'll be *old* someday. Forget about it; I've got a good idea for *today*. Let's spoil ourselves a little, after work. We could go to Mrs. Goldman's restaurant for a bite and then to the movies."

Raisa remembered the fuss Mrs. Kamensky had made the last time she'd missed dinner at home without telling anyone.

"I'd like to do that, but I'll have to send word home. Could you help me find one of the other girls to take a note to my place when it's quitting time?"

"Sure, but why do you have to go through all that?"

Raisa shrugged. "My landlady worries."

"Hmph. That sounds less like a landlady and more like a mother." Zusa nudged Raisa. "Or a mother-in-law."

"If you don't stop teasing me, I'm not going to sit next to you." It was a friendly joke, not a real threat.

"Ha! As if we sit next to each other anyway! Maybe if you were attaching cuffs today, like me—never mind, I'll find someone to carry that mother-may-I note for you. Say, if Luciana can't join us, I'll bet she'll do it. Meet you at the usual place!" She started to make her way through the obstacle course of chairs and employees to her workstation at the end of one of the already crowded aisles, where the tables butted up against the grimy windows.

All that day, Raisa worked diligently at her station, setting in sleeves, snipping threads, and watching the river of shirt-waist fabric flow under her fingers. The drone of the belt powering her machine and the eternal up-down-up-down rattle of the needle were no longer reminders of a life doomed to one place, one task. Every seam she sewed was one more step on the path she and Gavrel would take out of the factory. Every bobbing stroke of the needle brought her closer to the door. Once she reached it, they could be together. They could be free. She bent to her work with renewed energy.

As it got closer to four forty-five—quitting time—Raisa looked up from her machine to see Miss Gullo handing her the pay for the week. The amount was disappointing, as always, but there was nothing she could do about it except work more hours. *Next week will be better,* she told herself. *Working Saturdays will make a big difference.*

Miss Gullo finished distributing the workers' pay and started for the freight elevators to ring the quitting bell. Some of the workers had already gotten their hats and coats and were following her toward the exit that led to the freight elevators and Greene Street. Raisa put her last completed garment into the trough in front of her and debated whether or not to squeeze in work on one more shirtwaist.

In the end, she decided against it. *I'm tired, and I can always work longer this coming week. After all, Zusa and Luciana and I don't go out together every day, and I'll bet Mr. Kamensky will be pleased to hear I'm treating myself. Maybe there's a Mary Pickford movie! Gavrel loves Mary Pickford, too. I should let him know what we're doing tonight. He wouldn't be able to meet us in time for dinner, but he could catch up to us for the movie. I'll put that in the note I'm sending to his mother! Perfect.*

Now that she had her mind made up, she tidied her work space as quickly as she could. She wanted time to write her note and find the right messenger to deliver it. *I can't depend on Luciana going home,* she thought. *Maybe Gussie or Jennie could do it, but I don't remember seeing either one of them here today. I should've paid more attention.*

The bell rang, and the power running the sewing machines was cut off. The few early quitters waiting to have their purses searched at the narrow doorway leading to the freight elevators would soon be engulfed by the mass of departing workers. Raisa was among the first in the crowd of girls jostling to get their hats and coats from the cloakroom. They laughed and chattered around her. Everyone was happy that another week of back-bending, eye-straining work was over and it was finally time to go home. Raisa craned her neck, vainly hoping to catch sight of a friend who could carry her note. *Either they didn't come in today or they slipped out early,* she thought. *Now what am I going to do?*

"What a pretty pin!" A blonde girl who looked close to Raisa's age nodded at the gold-and-seed-pearl brooch Raisa always wore.

"Thank you. It belonged to my mother," Raisa replied. "And *I* love your hat, especially that blue-ribbon trim. Where did you get it?"

"My brother works at Adler's tailor shop, down on—"

"I know Adler's! It's just across the street from Kamensky's Dry Goods. Do you live in the neighborhood?" The blonde girl nodded. "Please, would you mind doing me a *great* favor on your way home?" She explained what she wanted, and the girl said she'd be happy to do it. Raisa almost clapped her hands, overjoyed at her good luck.

As she dug pencil and paper out of her purse and scrawled the note, she heard one of the other girls in the cloakroom begin to sing a popular tune. The girl's high spirits were contagious; others soon joined her, and even Raisa found herself humming along as she handed the blonde girl the note. "I can't thank you enough for doing this," she said. "You know, I usually walk to and from work with friends. Would you like to join us?"

The girl smiled. "I'd like that. I haven't been here very long and I—" Suddenly she wrinkled her nose. "Do you smell something funny?" Before Raisa could answer, she heard the first scream:

"Fire!"

Raisa and the other girls in the cloakroom rushed out into a scene of chaos. Flames were leaping up from below, their bright tongues licking at the wooden frames of the windows behind the garment inspection tables. Workers swarmed for the Greene Street door, no longer an orderly line but a panic-stricken mob. Smoke seeped in and rose in ghostly shapes, stinging the eyes, choking the throat. Shrieks, screams, and sobs of terror echoed beneath the high ceilings as distraught men and women called out the names of coworkers who were also friends and kin. Outside in the enclosed courtyard, a draft whirled through the flames, sending them scaling the inner walls and feeding them until the sheer power of so much heat smashed the loft windows inward as if with a sledgehammer. Fire fell on the piles of garments laid out on the inspection tables and began to advance across the shop floor.

The blonde girl whimpered and ran blindly back into the

cloakroom. Others followed her. Raisa stood frozen, watching people shoving one another aside, running for the narrow stairwell and freight elevators of the Greene Street exit. The crowd surged back and forth and some would-be escapees came staggering back, distraught. "The eighth floor's in flames! It's reached the stairs! We can't get down!"

Someone shouted that if the way down was blocked by fire, they should go up to the tenth floor and the roof beyond, instead. "And from there, what? Grow wings?" someone else retorted. More people plunged through the doorway and didn't return. Through the mounting smoke, Raisa saw a few girls climbing onto their workstations. The cluttered aisles between the long sewing machine tables were clogged with chairs, wicker baskets filled with flammable bits of flimsy shirtwaist material, and people desperate to reach a doorway. If they couldn't get through, the younger, nimbler ones were determined to get over by leaping from table to table.

The air was filled with scraps of burning fabric. Raisa saw a second mob rush past the cloakroom door, heading for the second exit, the Washington Place stairs and elevators. These were the elevators reserved for carrying the owners, the salesmen, and the all-important customers to the tenth-floor offices and showrooms. With her eyes still fixed on the flames, she backed into the cloakroom to avoid being carried away in the stampede. Something caught her heel and she stumbled backward, falling on her rump. She had tripped over the blonde girl's body, sprawled full-length across the cloakroom floor in a dead faint. The pretty hat with its bright blue ribbon lay crushed in the middle of the group of people who had taken refuge in the cloakroom.

We can't stay here, Raisa thought, strangely calm. *We have to get out. Even if the fire cuts us off, we have to try to get away.* Raisa knelt beside the blonde girl and worked hard to revive her, rubbing her wrists, slapping her face lightly, until at last she saw the girl's eyelids flutter.

"Water . . ." The girl's lips mangled the word.

"Later. Get up. Get *up*, I said!" She stood and hauled the girl to her feet. Then, in a voice loud enough to fill the cloakroom, she shouted, "We've got to get out of here!" Without waiting to see whether anyone heeded her or not, she plunged back to the burning factory workroom, dragging the blonde girl behind her.

They took one step forward and were swept into the roiling crowd. They had no choice but to run with them or fall, and if they fell, they'd be trampled. The stink of burning oil and burning fabric filled Raisa's nose, along with other smells, infinitely more horrible: burning hair, burning human beings.

She was tossed from side to side worse than in any storm she'd ever endured while at sea on her voyage to America. Dozens of voices battered her ears. The wave of people broke against the closed elevator doors. One woman cried out, begging the elevator operators to hear them and bring the cars up to save them. Another threw back the bitter words that if the building was going up in smoke, the elevator operators must be long gone, abandoning their cars and saving their own skins. A third protested that no, that wasn't so, they were good young men, decent, God-fearing! They must know a fire had broken out. How could they leave so many innocent people to die? How could they live with that burden on their souls? The cars would come.

And it was true, they came. The wild-eyed mass of girls rammed themselves into the tiny elevator cars, packing them to the point that the doors couldn't close. There was a frantic burst of more pushing, shoving, pulling people back so the doors closed and the cars began their descent. "Hurry back," Raisa whispered, clinging to the blonde girl with one hand, to the shoulder of a girl in front of her with the other. "For God's sake, hurry back!"

She turned her head and looked back at the shop floor. The fire poured in through the windows, rolling across the floor, in some places reaching the oil-soaked sewing machine stations. Some of the operators who had not been able to escape from the overcrowded aisles were being herded back and cornered by the flames. Raisa saw men and women beating at their smoldering clothes in a frenzy and heard a sound out of a nightmare as the fire reached out and turned a girl's hair into a torch.

She tore her eyes away from the hypnotizing horror of it all. The people close to her weren't just waiting patiently for the elevators to finish their slow descent and return, nine floors each way; they were fighting for other ways to save themselves. There was a stairway next to the Washington Place passenger elevators, a stairway that might well be their last hope now that the Greene Street stairs were blocked by the fire on the eighth floor—their best chance, since the elevators were supposed to take only fifteen passengers at a time when hundreds were begging for their lives.

"The door is locked! The door is locked!"

Hands pounded on the door to the Washington Place stairs. They beat against the glass inset with its web of reinforcing wire, they pushed against the heavy wood door, forgetting that it only opened inward because the stairway behind it was too narrow to let it swing out. Raisa saw the hands of young girls who had kissed their mothers and fathers good-bye just that morning, of women who worked to support children waiting at home, of men young and old with sweethearts, wives, children, all in a world that lay on the other side of one locked door.

Locked because they were afraid we'd steal. Her thoughts seemed to come to her from far away. The smoke, heavy with burning oil from the machines, was making her head spin. *What are we to them, to the owners, the bosses—what? Tools? Thieves? Were we ever* people?

The futile hands attacking the door wavered as though she were seeing them through the ripples of the cool, rushing brook that flowed sweet and clean through the woods back home. Glukel's image flickered before her stinging eyes, the older woman's face contorted with sorrow. *Why? Why wouldn't you listen to me, Raisa, Raisaleh?* the phantom haunting her mind keened. *Was keeping your name more important than keeping your life? The Angel of Death is sleepless and he has a long memory. You stepped out of one fire thinking you had escaped him, but here you are, burning, burning, and he still knows your name!*

Raisa's knees began to give way. There was hardly any air left fit to breathe. More screams were coming from the shop floor. Groggily, she turned her head to see, in spite of what she dreaded seeing. The shapes of men and women wove a hideous dance through the oncoming flames. She heard the sounds of breaking glass, wailing, prayers, and names— always people crying out into the fire, calling the names of the ones they loved. In her oxygen-starved trance, the names became garlands of burning roses that wound themselves around her arms and dragged her down.

"Hey! Wake up! Move!" The blonde girl slapped her face hard, reviving her with the pain. Raisa gasped as the girl she'd dragged out of the cloakroom started pummeling her shoulder before giving her a second slap. "Your coat was on fire, stupid!" she snapped. Her face held no fear, only fight. "I'm not going to die here because I tripped over *you!*"

The elevators came up for another load of passengers and Raisa was rammed forward, into the car. The operator was a young man who begged the fear-maddened crowd not to overload the machine. He swore he would come back as long as the elevator could run, but if they mobbed the car, keeping the doors from closing, no one was going anywhere.

Packed into the very center of the slowly descending car, Raisa still had to struggle to breathe. For an awful stretch of time, she imagined that the elevator would never reach the ground floor and that she would be trapped forever in the press of weeping, shuddering, shrieking, terrified bodies. When the car finally came to a stop, it was like pulling the cork from a full rain barrel. The people streamed out across the lobby. They were laughing, crying, often both at once, and so very many of them were still calling out names, names, names!

Raisa staggered along with them. Her vision was blurred, her head throbbing, her throat raw. She'd lost her grip on the blonde girl's hand the instant the elevator doors had opened. Ahead, she saw the door leading out onto Washington Place. Her smoke-addled mind could think only of how good it would be to race out of that dark street and into the glorious, living greenery of the park beyond. All she wanted to do was breathe fresh, sweet air. She sobbed as she ran toward the door.

A big policeman loomed up abruptly before her, barring her way. He was trying to hold back everyone in the crowd who had just gotten off the elevator. "It's okay, you're safe now, stay where you are. You *don't* want to go out there!" he said. "Stay inside! For the love of God, stay inside!"

Stay inside? Raisa thought incredulously. *Stay here? Does he think we're crazy? I can still smell the burning. I can hardly breathe. I have to get out!* Her brain reeled, alternating between stark fear and bizarre, depthless serenity, and she was powerless to control it. *I certainly do want to go out into the street,* she thought calmly. *I need to find Zusa and Luciana. They'll be worried if I don't meet them. It's not polite to keep your friends waiting.* She walked toward the door, ducking under the outstretched arms of the policeman who was trying to keep her inside. When he yelled after her to come back, she smiled and in her best English said, "I am sorry, but I cannot. We are going to the movies."

Raisa stepped over the threshold and into the street. The air outside was laced with smoke, but after the inferno of the ninth floor it was pure as springwater to her. She stopped in her tracks, closed her eyes, and took a deep, blissful breath. *I didn't know you could taste air!* she thought. *And I never dreamed it could taste so good!*

"Miss! Miss! My God, what are you doing?"

A rough-looking man grabbed her around the waist and lifted her clear off her feet, dodging his way around men, horses, and fire engines, jumping over snaking fire hoses and splashing through the gutter until he set her down on the corner diagonally across from the Asch Building. Raisa was too shocked to protest at first, but when he set her down and she drew breath to demand an explanation, the words died unsaid.

A body plunged through the smoke-laden air, clothes and hair ablaze. It struck the pavement on Washington Place with a dull thud that would haunt Raisa's dreams and memories forever. Another fell after it, a woman's body, the force of its descent lifting her skirts like the petals of a windblown flower. It crashed to the street only steps from where Raisa had been standing.

Smoke climbed the March sky, smearing away the failing daylight. Fire leaped behind the high windows of the Asch Building, wrapping burning tendrils around the bodies of those people now cut off from any hope of escape. Raisa could see their faces, openmouthed, twisted, crying out for help that never came.

She grabbed the man who had carried her across the street and clung to his jacket like a burr. "Why are they not *doing* something?" she demanded. "Why do they not save them, the girls?"

"Don't you think they're *trying*?" the man replied, his voice hoarse as more and more figures appeared on the window ledges eight and nine stories above the street. Neither he nor Raisa could look at one another while they spoke, for as long as their ears were forced to listen to the *thud, thud, thud* of so many impacts, their eyes refused to turn away from the plummeting shapes. "The ladders won't reach, you understand? They don't go that high! Wait, look, they're trying something else, see? They've got nets, blankets—"

"Oh, thank—"

A girl leaped from the ninth-floor ledge. She fell so fast from so far up that when her body hit the net that the firemen had spread to catch her, it was torn from their hands. Elsewhere on the two besieged streets other young women and men made the same choice, to jump instead of stand and burn. They crawled out of the windows with the fire reaching as if to pull them back inside. They clung to the ornate, frivolous decorations between the windows. They did not slip or stumble or miss their footing—they jumped. By ones and twos and threes, they chose the fall and not the fire and took one final step into forever.

The fire department nets, the tarpaulins stretched out by heartsick workmen with the bad luck to witness such ghastly sights, the horse blankets spread and held ready by ordinary people who would never think of themselves as heroes, all failed. Bodies shot down at such speed that they either broke straight through the sturdy cloth or yanked it out of the strongest grip before smashing on the pavement.

"Jesus, have mercy!" The man broke Raisa's hold on his coat and fled, making sounds like a wounded animal. Raisa stood where she was. She couldn't look away. The bodies fell, and she watched them drop. Some spun through the air like falling flower petals. Some trailed fire from their clothes and hair, young girls as delicate as newly opened roses, now flowers dying in flame.

Some did not jump. Raisa saw a young man stand in one of the windows looking down on Washington Place, a hat on his head as if he were going out to meet his sweetheart. He held out his hand and with an awful gallantry helped a girl up onto the sill, then lifted her to the other side and let her go. Two more girls followed without any sign of a struggle, consenting to the quicker, kinder death. The fourth was different. She paused in his arms and kissed him tenderly before she, too, allowed him to hold her out over the street and let her go. He followed.

Raisa's legs were cold. Without realizing it, she had sunk to her knees on the street corner, the chill of the pavement seeping through her skirt. Her eyes never left the Asch Building. She saw the fire hoses pumping endless streams of water up to flood the blaze, but it came too late for too many. On the uppermost floors of the fireproof building, the trapped girls were crammed against the windows by the flames until there was a great crash as the weight of so many bodies broke the window. They fell with fire and smoke streaming from their clothes and their hair. In the gutters, the water from the fire hoses ran red.

"Yisgadal veyiskadash sh'mei raba . . ." Raisa heard a woman whispering the Mourner's Kaddish, the Jewish prayer for the dead. It was one of the first prayers Henda had taught her, after Mama died, though her sister had been so intent on making sure Raisa memorized the words that she had never bothered teaching her their meaning. She remembered how surprised she had been when she'd finally asked Gavrel about it and he had told her that the prayer never once mentioned death or loss, but only praised God and acknowledged the wisdom and righteousness of all His judgments, acts, and decrees.

Another body fell from the heights, a girl whose clothing

flamed and smoked. The material caught on a steel hook protruding from a sign on the front of the building. The body dangled there until the fire nibbling away at her dress freed her for the final drop to the street.

"O'seh shalom bim'romav, hu ya'aseh shalom aleinu, ve'al kol Yisra'el." The prayer ended by asking for peace from the eternal source of peace, but Raisa heard the mourner's voice stumble, break, and fail before the final amen. She looked around and saw that the only people standing near her were men, their eyes still lifted to the burning crown of the Asch Building. The prayer she'd heard had been her own.

Peace . . .

She got to her feet slowly, turned her back on the last of the fire, and began the long, numb walk home.

They were waiting for her on the stoop in front of the tenement. It looked as if the whole street was out in the cold March night, waiting. While Raisa had been walking home, the news of the Triangle fire had raced ahead of her, spreading through the neighborhood as fast as the fire itself had gutted the top floors of the Asch Building. It was strange to be the only person walking when everyone else was either running uptown toward Washington Square or standing so tensely that anxiety and fear seemed to crackle over their skin like a web of lightning.

"I see her! I see her! Raisa! Raisa! Raisa! Raisa!" Brina's feet flew as she threw herself at Raisa so hard that the two of them nearly tumbled over. The child's face was slick with tears, her nose running, her body nothing but sobs. "I knew! I knew you were all right!" Brina kissed her countless times, her lips turning black from the soot smearing Raisa's face. When Mr. and Mrs. Kamensky caught up to the little girl and tried to make her let go of Raisa, she flailed at them with fists and feet until they gave up and stood back.

"Thank God," Mr. Kamensky murmured over and over. "Thank God."

"You came home alone?" Mrs. Kamensky asked.

"Of course she did!" her husband snapped. His eyes were rimmed with red. "What, you think two people could find each other in the middle of that Gehenna?"

"I'm sure Zusa and Luciana are fine," Raisa replied dully. "It was bad on nine, but Zusa is smart. If I could get out, she could, too, and Luciana worked on eight where—"

"With the cutters," Mrs. Kamensky said. "With Gavrel. Maybe she's home by now, your Italian friend. Maybe she saw him."

Raisa blinked. She was hearing every word her landlady spoke, but she couldn't understand a single one. They made no sense. "It's Shabbos, Mrs. Kamensky," she said as if explaining simple matters to a baby. "Gavrel never works on Shabbos. He goes to synagogue, he prays, he studies with the rabbi, but he never works on—"

Mr. Kamensky's stony voice cut off her words. "He left the house this morning after you were gone. We thought he was going to synagogue early, but he wasn't there. We got worried until Fruma told us what he'd told her, that he wanted to start working Saturdays for a while, that there was something very important he wanted to do, but he needed to earn extra money to do it."

Raisa felt the blood leave her face. Still holding Brina, she began to sink to the sidewalk. Mrs. Kamensky took Brina away. Mr. Kamensky got his arm around her. She never knew how he managed to steer her up flight after flight of stairs, only that somehow she was in the apartment, in Fruma's tearful embrace as the two girls sat side by side on the bed in their room.

Outside, the street began to fill with howls and cries and keening. Sometimes the sound of a joyful reunion broke through the cries of loss. In the Kamenskys' apartment there was only silence. Even Brina sat quietly, sucking her fingers like an infant, her other hand knotted in Raisa's skirt. They waited and waited.

Gavrel did not come home.

Chapter Fifteen

CINDERS

"Raisa, put on your coat. It's cold." Mrs. Kamensky stood with her husband by the front door, waiting.

Raisa wrapped her shawl more tightly around her shoulders. "I can't wear it," she said. "I can't."

"All right. I'm not going to argue with you." There was a strange, brittle note in Mrs. Kamensky's voice, like a thin sheet of ice over a bottomless pool. One wrong step would shatter it and she would plunge from sight, lost forever.

"Lipke, my dearest, don't you think Raisa should rest? After what she's been through." Mr. Kamensky spoke softly as he held fast to his wife's shoulders. All that sleepless night and all that bleak morning he had hardly let go of her once. It was impossible to say whether he was comforting her or whether he was afraid that if he let her go, he would no longer be able to stand.

"I'm all right, Mr. Kamensky," Raisa replied, her fingers fumbling to secure her shawl with her mother's gold brooch. "I need to go."

"I don't understand why you won't let me come with you, too," he persisted.

His wife slammed her fist into the apartment door so abruptly that everyone jumped. "Do you *want* to take my last drop of strength?" she shouted. "I *told* you, it's Sunday. You will take care of the store, as always. Haven't we got enough troubles without letting the business go, too?"

"But, my dear, don't you think the customers will understand?"

"Understand what? That you want to sit shivah before we know for sure he's dead, God forbid? Do we have such riches to our names that we can *afford* to do that? Fruma will take care of Brina; Raisa and I will take care of—" Her voice caught on something in her throat and tore into a dry sob, but she recovered quickly. Pulling herself tall, she concluded, "It's settled."

"Yes, Lipke." He bowed his head. "I'll go soon."

"We can come with you, Papa," Fruma offered. She was still seated at the table in the front room. Brina sat in her lap, her face pressed hard against Fruma's shirtwaist. "In case Louis isn't there."

"Where else would he be?" Mrs. Kamensky's words shrilled through the apartment. "You and the child stay *here*. If someone comes with news and no one is home, what then?" She whirled on her husband. "*Tell* her!"

Mr. Kamensky sighed. "Listen to your mother, Fruma," he said. "Please."

"Be a good girl for Fruma, Brina," Raisa called out. "We'll be back as soon as we can, I promise." She got no answer.

Just as she and Mrs. Kamensky were about to walk out the door, Fruma called, "Raisa! Raisa, wait just a moment. I have something for you. It's on top of my bureau. I'd get it for you, but . . ." She nodded at Brina, cradled in her lap.

Raisa went into the bedroom and returned holding an unsealed envelope. "This is all I found on the bureau, Fruma."

"That's what I meant. It's a letter. I wrote it this morning when I couldn't sleep. It's for you."

Raisa was confused. "Why would you write me a letter?"

"I didn't write it *to* you, Raisaleh; I wrote it *for* you, for you to send to the woman who raised you, Glukel."

"Since when does she need someone else to write her letters for her?" Mrs. Kamensky chafed at the delay. "In Yiddish, in English, she knows how!"

"I know that, Mama," Fruma said softly. "I did it to help her. Who knows how far or how fast the news about the fire can spread? Across a country, across an ocean—who knows? She's told Glukel the name of the shop where she works— used to work. Better for a letter that says 'There was a fire, but I'm safe and well' to reach that good woman before she hears about what happened from somewhere that talks only about the dead."

Raisa took the letter out of the envelope and read what Fruma had written. She could have wept with gratitude. Without concealing the truth, Fruma's every sentence would set Glukel's heart and mind at ease.

When Raisa lowered the paper at last, Fruma looked up at her friend. "You're carrying so much, Raisa. I wanted to share the burden. If you don't like what I've done, tear it up. I won't be offended."

"God bless you for this, Fruma." Raisa bent to kiss her friend's cheek. "How could I be offended by this? I'll sign it and—"

"Fruma wrote it; let Fruma sign your name to it and see that it's mailed," Mrs. Kamensky snapped. "I can't wait any longer. We must *go.*" She strode out of the apartment and Raisa had to scramble after her.

Mrs. Kamensky walked down the street like a queen, her eyes set on some far-off goal that only she could see. Every sentence was a royal command. "First we will go to look after your friends. Then we will hear what they know about my son. Then we will see."

They came to Zusa's home first. Raisa led the way up the dark and narrow stairs to the Reshevsky apartment. Cousin Selig answered the door before Raisa was able to rap more than twice. He looked like a man hoping for a miracle, but when he saw who the visitors were and that they weren't smiling, his face fell.

"Anything?" he asked. Raisa shook her head.

"We are going to look for my son," Mrs. Kamensky said calmly. There was no need to ask if anyone under this roof had news of Gavrel; the air echoed with emptiness.

"I was just about to go, too," Selig said. "But I didn't want to leave Dvorah alone." He nodded back into the eerily still apartment, where somewhere, out of sight, Zusa's mother waited. "One of our neighbors said she would stay with her. I thought you were her. I can't leave until she gets here."

"We're sorry, we can't wait." Mrs. Kamensky was firm. "There will be many other people."

Selig nodded. "Like last night and this morning. We only came home a few hours ago. Were you there, too?"

"What are you talking about?" Mrs. Kamensky spoke so sharply to Zusa's cousin that Raisa jumped back, shocked.

"The shop," Selig said. "The building where . . . The moment we heard the news, Dvorah and I went uptown. God, so many people filling that park across the street! We must have numbered thousands, tens of thousands! The police were struggling to hold us back. I heard one man say that the whole fire was over in less than half an hour. Half an hour! Can you imagine that? So little time, and yet—"

"We didn't go uptown last night," Mrs. Kamensky interrupted. "We're going today, *now*." She spoke urgently, raising her voice as if to keep Selig from saying any more. "We have to be on our way."

Selig leaned against the doorjamb. Slowly he slid to the floor, the expression on his face unchanging, his eyes still filled with the horrors of the night. "As soon as they could, the firemen began bringing down the bodies that were still in the building," he said. "They lowered them from above in nets. Someone in the crowd said that the elevators collapsed during the fire, before everyone could get out. The rails they ran on buckled from the heat and the weight of so many people trying to get into the cars. Some of the girls left behind threw themselves down the shafts. Better to break than to burn. We heard that the fire escape over the back courtyard also gave way, twisted into nothing but a tangle of metal. The girls who were still on it fell, they fell. . . ."

Raisa knelt beside Selig. "Let me help you up," she said, slinging the man's arm over her shoulders. It was a struggle, but she got him back on his feet. "You should go inside and sit down. Lean on me and we can—"

"No!" Standing on his own once more, Selig jerked away from her as if her touch had burned him. "Don't you see? If I sit down, I don't know when I'll be able to move again, and I have to! It's all in my hands now. I have to find her, our dear one, our little Zusa." His face was suddenly awash with tears.

"I—I can look for you, if you want." It cost Raisa a lot to make that offer. "Not just—not just at the—where we're going now. There are hospitals to visit, too. I promise you, I'll look for—"

"She is *our* Zusa," Selig declared. "After all we witnessed, trying to find her last night, I can't just let this pass into someone else's hands. You don't know what it was like. We saw everything from the crowd. They set up electric searchlights. The firemen and the police were gathering the bodies and—and stacking them. They covered the stacks with tarpaulins. In the old country, that was how I stacked *wood* for the winter fire! Wood for the burning . . . wood . . ." He bent his head and covered his face with one hand.

"You're right, we *weren't* there," Mrs. Kamensky said. After her small outburst, she was again cold as stone. "We waited at home. Now we've waited long enough."

"Wait!" Selig uttered a stuttering, crazy laugh. "That was what they told us last night, to wait. As if we were back on the lines at Ellis Island, waiting for someone to open the gates to the Golden Land! But how could we wait? The sidewalk was littered with their things, their torn, burned, ruined, pitiful possessions. A trampled hat. A broken hair comb. A single shoe with the heel torn away. No, no, we couldn't wait. We rushed the police lines. Some of us broke through, but not for long enough. They thrust us back. They used their clubs against us. They kept us away from our dead."

"You don't *know* that she's dead!" Mrs. Kamensky grabbed Selig's arms and shook him. "Don't say such things when you don't know. Listen, we're leaving now for—for the morgue. God willing, from there all of us will be able to go to the hospitals."

"The morgue?" Selig echoed bitterly. "The city morgue is too small for this. It didn't even have enough coffins. In the crowd, we heard that they had to send to the hospital on Blackwell's Island for more. We stood watch in the cold when the ambulances came, and the dead were coffined and taken away. They aren't in the morgue; they've been taken to the covered pier on Twenty-sixth Street, by the East River. We would have followed them, but by then, she"—he gestured weakly back into the apartment a second time—"could take no more. So I brought her home."

"You should stay home yourself," Mrs. Kamensky said. "We will look for your Zusa, too. We will look for her when we look . . ." The hardness left her voice and seemed to take her strength with it. Her body crumpled, but Raisa was there to catch her and hold her up. "When we look for my Gavrel, my baby, my son!"

Mrs. Kamensky's collapse had a galvanizing effect on Selig. He put his arms around her and, with Raisa, brought her into the apartment. Zusa's mother was nowhere in sight; the door to the bedroom was closed. Selig got a bottle of cherry schnapps from the sideboard and poured glasses of the strong fruit-flavored liquor for everyone. It made Raisa's throat burn, but she drank it down. Before they were done, a neighbor came to the door to sit with Zusa's mother, so Selig was able to travel to the Twenty-sixth Street pier with them after all.

They saw the line of people long before they saw the pier. It stretched for blocks and moved with deliberate slowness. Raisa pulled her shawl up over her head. She could hardly stand the sight of all the grief-stricken faces in the crowd, the despairing eyes of mothers, daughters, husbands, wives, sons, sisters and brothers, even aged grandparents who had come seeking their cherished dead. The sound of weeping and moaning ran softly through the line, but there were worse sounds, as well.

There was laughing. At first Raisa couldn't believe what she was hearing, but when she turned her head to look behind her, she saw the group of flashily dressed young men and women huddling together, the girls giggling with nervous anticipation, their escorts puffing out their chests, proud of themselves for having come up with such a clever way to find entertainment on a Sunday morning.

"Yes, Misery Lane, that's what they called the pier after the *Slocum* disaster," one of the young men was explaining to his fascinated girlfriend. "This is where they brought the dead from that fire, too."

"The *Slocum*?" the girl repeated, wide-eyed.

"You wouldn't know about that one, sweetheart," he said, chucking her under the chin. "It happened some seven years back, when you were still in pigtails. The *General Slocum* was one of those big paddle-wheel steamers, and a bunch of dutchies from Little Germany rented it for a picnic excursion out to Long Island. They didn't get far, I'll say! The boat burned down to the waterline and over a thousand of 'em died—almost all women and kids, too. I remember my dad taking me down here then to watch the show. Man, that was something to see!"

"Is this going to be *very* dreadful, Johnny?" the girl asked in a false-sounding babyish voice.

"Don't you worry, sweetheart, I'll take good care of you," her boyfriend replied, putting his arms around her waist.

An unshaven man in a raggedy coat sidled up to the cooing couple. "Buy the lady a souvenir, mister?" he offered. He held out a small, covered cardboard box. "A little something special to remember the day? I got a real nice choice of rings here, gathered up myself, with my own two hands last night off the sidewalks by Triangle. Rings right off the hands of the jumpers, and more besides. Bracelets, watches, combs, even a couple of handkerchiefs. My little miracles, I call 'em. Not even a singe on 'em, but you can't say the same for the girls who owned 'em. Here, how about this? A pretty rose you can pin on your hat. Go on, pick it up, give it a sniff. That's a smell you're not going to run across every day, if you're lucky. If that don't guarantee this is the genuine article, I don't know what—"

Three men seemed to come out of nowhere and close in on the seedy little peddler. One of them knocked the box out of his hands, sending the contents flying. The other two dragged him away while he squealed in protest. There were many policemen on duty all up and down the line, but not one of them even blinked in his direction.

"You, too." The man who had knocked away the box of trinkets positioned himself between the sensation-seeking couples and Raisa. "You have no business here. Get out or I'll make you get out, you . . ." He said something in Italian. The meaning was clear even for someone who didn't speak a word of that language.

"Now, look here, this is a free country and we've got a right to be here!" one of the male gawkers blustered.

"And I will have the right to break your miserable face," the young man countered.

Raisa recognized the voice. "Paolo?" She touched his back gently. Luciana's brother turned to look at her. It was an ill-timed move. Still eager to impress his girlfriend, the young man who'd been gleefully recounting the *Slocum* disaster took advantage of Paolo's momentary distraction to take a swing at him.

"Paolo, look out!" Raisa shoved him to one side just as the young man's fist swung through empty air. Paolo sprang forward, catching the young dandy in the belly with his shoulder, lifting him high before throwing him clear of the line. He rolled over the cobbles like a beer barrel, landing flat on his back. His friends ran after him to help him to his feet. All his cheap finery was torn and soiled.

"Get out of here, or I will give you something more!" Paolo shouted.

"I'd like to see you try it! I'll sic the cops on you, just you wait and see!" the young man yelled back, but he didn't fight it when his companions hustled him away.

"Raisa, it is—it is good to see you," Paolo said as his friends rejoined him. His happiness was deeply shaded with personal sorrow, but there was nothing halfhearted in the way he scooped her off her feet and hugged her. Mrs. Kamensky and Selig looked on, not knowing what to make of this strange display.

"This is Paolo," Raisa said as soon as he set her down again. "He's my friend Luciana's brother."

"Your sister . . . ?" Mrs. Kamensky didn't need to finish her question.

"That is what we have come to learn," Paolo replied. "My mamma, she could not bear this, and Papa is sick. I am the only one who must be strong enough to look for our Luciana." He glanced back to the end of the line. "We had better go or it will be night before we are allowed inside."

Mrs. Kamensky grabbed his wrist and pulled him into line with them. "You stay here." She glowered at the people just behind them in line, defying them to say a word. They were too broken and wrapped in their own misery to make any objection.

Raisa didn't know one of Paolo's friends, but she recognized Renzo. "It's good—it's *truly* good to see you again," he said. "If you wouldn't mind, I'll say a prayer of thanksgiving for you to the Blessed Virgin."

"Thank you," Raisa said.

The line worked its way to the iron gates of Misery Lane. Raisa saw more than a few people in the crowd who were as well dressed as the thrill-seeking group that Paolo and his friends had sent packing. Sometimes they were ordered out of the line by the police; sometimes they made it all the way to the entrance to the ugly yellow building before being turned away, under loud protest. Too often they were able to sneak in, either by attaching themselves to a group of the truly bereaved or by finding an official who didn't see the harm in pocketing a little extra money for looking the other way. At last, Raisa and the others were allowed to go in.

The coffins lay in a double row under the harsh glare of electric lights. Each box was numbered, the pitiful contents partially draped to spare the searchers the added pain of seeing what fire or a bone-shattering fall had done to their dear ones. The victims' heads were propped up so that their faces could be more easily recognized, at least for those who still had faces. The air was filled with sobs and sighs, with shrieks and howls and wailing.

They made three circuits of the rows, searching, searching, first for an undamaged face, then for some small resemblance, then for any clue at all to reveal the identity of the remains. Mrs. Kamensky walked with her backbone turned to steel, glancing quickly left and right, only lingering when the remains in a coffin looked to be male. In some cases, it was hard to tell. Raisa walked in her shadow, looking hard into every coffin they passed. She was seeking more than Gavrel. Though her stomach lurched every time she saw one of the fire's more terribly burned victims, she forced herself to look closely, in case there might be some small sign on the blackened body to tell her that here lay Zusa, here was Luciana, here was cheerful, generous Gussie or tiny, birdlike Jennie, or the girl who'd run the sewing machine to her right side or to her left or across the finished-garments bin in the center of the long wooden tables.

All I can do to help them now is to find them, she thought. *If I can do anything to cut short poor Selig's search, or Paolo's, I must. How can they stand it, looking into one coffin after another, especially the ones where the body is—where the body's hardly there anymore? I have to help them—*

A heartrending cry tore through the air of Misery Lane. Selig stood transfixed at the foot of a coffin. In some cases, the city officials had ordered the personal possessions of the dead kept separate from the bodies, to prevent theft by the pickpockets who had infiltrated the pier along with the ghouls and gawkers. But in those cases where the fire had made the bodies nearly unrecognizable, the dead were permitted to keep their few small treasures.

Now Selig pointed at the charred thing in the coffin and said, "I gave her that locket. Look, there's a little bunch of forget-me-nots etched on the cover. I told her—I told her that someday she could keep her sweetheart's picture in it and she said . . . she said that she was never going to get married because all of the good men were already in love with other girls. Joking! Always joking, always making us laugh, even when things were bad. Oh, Zusa, dearest child, no more, no more laughter! No more ever again, my darling little girl!" He burst into storms of tears.

Mrs. Kamensky and Paolo had their arms around him

before Raisa could get near. A weary official approached the distraught man, ready to take down the information that would be needed before Zusa's coffin could be mercifully closed, then marked as identified and claimed. Raisa heard a weird, animal-like noise echoing loudly in her ears and realized she was listening to the sound of her own grief. She called out her friend's name with so much force that she felt her throat go raw, but even so, her cry was only one small note of anguish in the chorus of despair around her.

"*Now* aren't you glad I gave that stupid mick cop a tenner?" The self-satisfied voice snapped Raisa's attention to the dapper, milk-faced man strolling past the coffins with two of his equally well-tailored friends. "It's better than anything running in the theaters, believe me, and won't the boys at the club be envious when we tell them where *we've* been today!"

A pair of high-society ladies stood within earshot, cheeks aflame. "How dare you speak that way?" the older of the two exclaimed. "Have some respect for the dead."

The man snorted. "Go play your charity games somewhere else and mind your own business."

"Mind *yours*." Renzo grabbed the man's shoulder, spun him around, and punched him in the jaw. His companions raised their walking sticks, shouting threats, and closed in on Renzo, but their attempt to take him on, two against one, was stopped cold when Paolo and his other friend came running.

It was a short brawl, truly little more than a scuffle. The five men stumbled back and forth just long enough to collide with the two society women. The older one let out an indignant squawk, but kept her footing. The younger, however, turned pale and went soft in the knees. The whites of her eyes showed as the horrors of Misery Lane caught up with her and she stumbled, fainting against the edge of the nearest coffin.

Raisa ran forward to catch her before she could sprawl across the ghastly contents of the long wooden box. Gently she lowered the young woman to the ground and supported her body with one arm, her own pain temporarily banished by concern for another. The young woman's expensively plumed hat rolled away across the morgue floor. Raisa raised her free hand to pat the unconscious woman's cheeks, the only remedy she knew of for a faint.

Her hand froze. Her heart beat faster. For a moment that became its own eternity, Raisa could not draw another breath. And when at last she could speak, she was only able to whisper a name: "Henda?"

Even as the word left her lips, her mind rejected the possibility. *No. How could it be? Look at her, how expensively she's dressed, the jewelry she's wearing! Impossible. It's been years, but still . . .*

She stared into the young woman's face, drawn along a trail of memories. The last image of her sister was a glimpse of Henda's desperate face the night she'd fled Glukel's home. Raisa remembered her sister's features, how pretty she was, but also how pale and badly fed she'd been, nothing at all like this stylish, rosy-cheeked beauty. *No*, she thought again.

There's only a resemblance, but I want it to be more than that so much it hurts! I've lost Gavrel, so I'm grasping at dreams. She patted the young woman's cheeks and saw her eyelids begin to flutter open once more.

"Hey! What are you trying to pull there, girly?" Strong hands hooked themselves under Raisa's arms and pulled her to her feet while a handsome, elegantly dressed young man threw himself forward to cradle the waking woman in his arms. The woman's eyes suddenly went wide. She raised her hands and grabbed at Raisa's shawl, but whoever was behind Raisa, dragging her away, was too strong. The woman's grip on the shawl broke after the shortest of struggles.

The heels of Raisa's shoes scraped over the floor as a gruff voice in her ear muttered about the plague of thieves and pickpockets infesting the pier. "Like this wasn't hell enough. Damn buzzards! I'd like to skin all of you down to your crooked bones."

Raisa squirmed around until she saw that she was in the grip of an exasperated policeman. "Let me go!" she exclaimed. "I wasn't doing anything wrong."

"No, I guess trying to rob a helpless woman's just hunky-dory where *you* come from," the policeman sneered.

"Officer, what are you doing to that poor child?" The older society lady rushed up to plant herself in front of Raisa and the policeman. "Hasn't she suffered enough? I give you my word as a witness that she was only trying to help Mrs. Taylor. Let her go at once!"

"If you say so, ma'am." The policeman released Raisa, touched the brim of his cap, and walked away without a word of apology.

"Are you all right, my dear?" the older woman asked. Her concern was sincere.

"Yes, I—who did you say I helped?" Raisa's glance darted back toward the spot where she'd been jerked away from the fainting victim. There was no sign of the fashionable young woman or her escort.

"My friend, Mrs. Harrison Taylor. Poor dear, the strain of being in this awful place was too much for her. If you hadn't caught her when she fainted, she might have done herself an injury."

"She shouldn't have come here, then," Raisa said harshly. She felt as if a great weight was crushing her chest. Mrs. Harrison Taylor! Such a name came from another universe, far removed from the shtetl, even beyond the world of a German Jewish family, no matter how wealthy. *I'm a fool*, Raisa thought. *A fool*. She lashed out to relieve her anger and bitter frustration. "Don't you have something better to do than stare at *this*?" Her gesture embraced the nightmare of the pier.

The older woman's eyes filled with sympathy. "You mistake our purpose, miss. We've come to see if there is any way we might be able to help provide—"

"Raisa!" Mrs. Kamensky strode up the aisle between the coffins and took her hand. "We're going. I've looked and looked. He's not here. He's *not* here!" Her voice was a tangle of fear, triumph, joy, and uncertainty. Raisa had to scramble in order to match her pace as they fled from Misery Lane into the blessedly fresh air outside.

They walked home like dreamers trapped in a city of smoke. Mrs. Kamensky linked her arm through Raisa's, but it was impossible to know whether she did it more to give support or take it. When they were within a few blocks of the Kamenskys' apartment, Raisa dared to break the silence. "I'll go to the hospitals tomorrow. I'm sure I'll find him."

"Yes. You are a good girl, Raisa. I will come with you. We'll look for him together, the way we looked for him today, in that place, in that dreadful place. . . ."

There was a fragile, distant sound to Mrs. Kamensky's voice that made Raisa uneasy. "Mrs. Kamensky, he wasn't *there*. He wasn't at the pier. We're going to find him *alive*."

"Yes, of course, alive. Did I say otherwise?" Her words were like glass shattering on a stone. Her face was set in a stiff smile, but tears poured from her eyes, a flood so blinding that she missed her footing and stumbled over a curb.

Raisa grabbed her arm with both hands and saved her from a bad fall, then pulled a clean handkerchief from the cuff of her blouse and forced it into the older woman's hand. "Mrs. Kamensky, do you want to stop? Do you want me to find you someplace to sit down?"

"I want to go home, Raisa. I want to go home. I want to close my eyes and not think about what I saw today, about what I might see." She paused and touched Raisa's cheek.

"You don't cry. You're strong. Good. You can take me home."

Mrs. Kamensky's words took Raisa by surprise. *She's right,* she thought. *I'm not crying, but it's not because I'm strong, it's because I* can't. *Why can't I? Zusa is dead. Oh, God, my friend is dead and I can't weep for her? Selig's anguish, the thought of how her mother will have to hear the news, the anguish I saw every- where I turned in that dreadful place—it's all too much! It's as if all the horrors I've seen in these past two days have scraped me hollow inside. And worse than knowing Zusa is dead is* not *knowing what's become of Luciana, or Gussie, or Jennie. And Gavrel. My Gavrel. If I lose you the way I've lost Henda, I'm scared to death I won't be able to laugh or cry or ever feel human again.*

It wasn't until they reached home that Raisa realized she had lost her mother's brooch. *It must have happened when that policeman hauled me halfway down the pier,* she thought. She touched the empty place where it had been. It was such a tri- fling loss compared to the chasm that had opened in the heart of the city, but for Raisa, it was like touching a fresh wound.

She sank to her knees and, to her heartfelt relief, she wept.

Chapter Sixteen

ASHES

The next morning, as Mrs. Kamensky was getting ready to begin the visits to the city hospitals in search of Gavrel, she caught sight of the mirror that hung above the mantelpiece in the front room and pointed at it with a shaking hand.

"Who did this?" she cried in an unearthly voice. "Who covered the mirror? May God strike you dead for such cruelty! I tell you, I swear to you on my own life, my Gavrel was not among the dead!"

Mr. Kamensky, Fruma, Raisa, and Brina all exchanged confused looks. The mirror hung as it had always hung, catching the weak spring daylight, reflecting the front room. By tradition it would be covered, along with every other mirror in the home, if the family was in mourning.

"Lipke, darling, what are you saying?" Mr. Kamensky spoke soothingly to his wife. "Look, there's nothing hiding the mirror. Maybe your eyeglasses are smeared. Here, let me clean them for you." He reached out to her, but she slapped his hand away.

"Liar! Liar! I know what I see! It's covered with a white cloth, white as an angel's wing, white as ice and snow!" She grabbed for the imaginary veil, her fingernails skidding down the naked glass. "Oh, God, why won't it move? Why can't I tear it away? *Why?*" One second she was standing in front of the mirror; the next she was unconscious on the floor.

They put her to bed, where she lay with her eyes open but unseeing. Raisa and Fruma took turns sitting with her for the first three days, while a distraught Mr. Kamensky continued to look after the store. There was no question of sparing anyone to go to the hospitals looking for Gavrel, and the situation turned Raisa's insides into a blazing knot of frustration.

"It's not necessary that we go," Mr. Kamensky said. "Wouldn't he tell them himself to send word to us if, God willing, he's well enough to speak? And if not, God forbid, then we will know that soon enough." He closed his eyes. "Soon enough."

Raisa wanted to object, to forcibly turn his mind from such despairing thoughts. She wanted to fall to her knees and beg him to let her go to the hospitals alone, but then she looked into his exhausted eyes, and Fruma's, and knew what she had to do. *What will happen if I go now, and find him, but find that he's—? God forbid! God forbid! To bring such news into this house now, when all of us are stretched out thin as threads that a breath could snap? How could I destroy the people who have been so good to me and Brina? I will wait.*

When Mrs. Kamensky's condition remained unchanged on the fourth day, her husband sent for a doctor to come. He seemed almost regretful that the doctor could find nothing wrong with her body.

"All that can help her is rest and time," the doctor told them.

There were some small mercies. She would drink and eat, but only if one of the girls set the cup or the spoon to her lips. It was like feeding a wax doll. From time to time she would rise from the bed and walk to the toilet on her own, though she seemed baffled by the door. She would stand staring at the wooden panel until Fruma or Raisa held it open, and she would not come out of the toilet until one of them fetched her back to the apartment. Brina watched Mrs. Kamensky's mindless comings and goings with dumbstruck terror. From the day of the landlady's collapse, the little girl never spoke above a whisper in the apartment.

On the fifth day, Fruma went back to work. She had no other choice; the month of March was coming to an end, and the rent would be due. For the next three days, Raisa became the woman of the Kamensky household, busying her hands in order to distract her mind. But it was no use. Wherever her eyes roamed in the small apartment, she saw things that reminded her of Gavrel. When she looked out the window, all she could think was, *Somewhere in the city, he's waiting. He's alive; he has to be alive! Somewhere he's lying helpless in a hospital bed, nameless, unknown, with no one to claim him. Oh, Gavrel, I* will *come for you; I haven't abandoned you! But for now, I can't abandon your family, either. May God forgive me, I must stay here.*

One by one the other women in the tenement came by with gifts of food and offers to sit with Mrs. Kamensky so that Raisa and Brina could go out to do the shopping. Raisa gratefully seized each and every chance to flee, though not for her own sake. She couldn't stand to see how small and scared Brina was while they remained in the apartment. As soon as she set foot on the sidewalk, she transformed into a normal, happy, high-spirited little girl, but once she crossed the threshold going the other way it was like seeing a leathery black wing cast an evil shadow over the child.

During one of those blessed escapes, Raisa and Brina ran into Zusa's cousin Selig at a butcher shop on Orchard Street. He looked haggard, his face haphazardly shaved, his clothing hanging on him like rags on a scarecrow. Raisa was a little nervous that his appearance would frighten Brina, but she needn't have worried; the butcher's little daughter was one of Brina's best friends. As soon as they laid eyes on one another, the two children skipped outside to play hopscotch on the sidewalk.

"Ah! Raisa, how are things going for you?" Selig asked, trying to smile. Without waiting for her reply, he added, "You'll have to forgive me. I should have sent you word. You were her dearest friend. You deserved to know."

"To know what?"

"When we buried her. But I—I couldn't do that to her poor mother, having her see you standing there, alive, while our Zusa is—was . . ." He lifted his eyes to heaven. "Raisa, don't misunderstand. We don't begrudge you your life. Never, never once in all her grief has my cousin Dvorah said one word to wish that you had died instead of Zusa when the Triangle shop burned, or even that you had died at all!"

"I wish—I wish I could say the same thing," Raisa murmured.

Behind the counter, the butcher slammed down his cleaver and made the sign against the evil eye. "Do I hear right?" he bellowed. "You lived through that Gehenna and now you say something like that?"

"Yes, I was there," Raisa said, meeting the butcher's scowl without flinching. "I was there, in the fire. I saw the people I'd worked with fall and burn and die, but I was left alive and unharmed; I could walk away. Why *me*? I'm nobody. If I'd died, the only family I'd leave behind is Brina, and we're not even kin. I'm nothing—just a girl, a silly greenhorn like hundreds, *thousands* of others. And so many of them are prettier, smarter, more talented than I can ever hope to be! Why did I survive when they didn't? For what? For *what*?"

Selig shook his head. "How should I know? How should anyone?"

The butcher made an impatient noise. "And what does that matter, in the end, all this *knowing*? What will it change? Maybe there *is* no reason you are still among the living, or maybe it's right in front of you. Just because you can't understand it doesn't mean it's not there. And maybe it's still waiting for you to find! Who knows? What I *do* know, what I see, is that you are here, alive and strong. You hold a priceless gift. Share it or keep it, but *open* it, girl. Open it." He picked up his cleaver again and added, "Now, did you come in here to aggravate me or to buy some meat? Because if it's for the aggravation, I'm already married."

His words struck Raisa to the heart. She could feel the tears rising. She turned on her heel and ran out of the butcher's shop with Selig behind her. She grabbed Brina away from her game with the butcher's daughter, in spite of the child's surprised protests, and didn't slow down until the middle of the next block. She didn't want Selig to see her crying. His life was already more than half drowned in tears.

By the time Selig caught up to her, she was in control of herself once more. He patted her back. "The butcher's a simple man, Raisa. That's why he's so . . . plainspoken."

"I know," she said. "He meant well." *But it still hurts. Blunt words cut.*

"Listen, come home with me," Selig said. "Talk to Dvorah. Now that we've buried our girl, I think it would do her some good to talk to someone who really knew Zusa, someone who could share good memories."

"But I have to go home," Raisa said. "The neighbor's been sitting with Mrs. Kamensky for a long time already, and I still need to buy meat, and—"

"*Please*, Raisa." Selig's entreaty was piteous. "Tell me what you need to buy and I'll bring it to your apartment myself. I'll sit with Mrs. Kamensky until you come home. You don't have to stay long. Dvorah might even send you away at once, but I beg you, *try* to talk to her about Zusa."

"All right." Raisa gave him the money she'd brought to pay the butcher. "I'll try."

On a Tuesday morning, eight days after she had seen the phantom veil across the mantel mirror, Mrs. Kamensky woke up, got out of her bed, and began to cook breakfast. Raisa, Brina, and Fruma came out of their room to see the miracle. They stared so long and hard that at last Mrs. Kamensky snapped, "What, did I grow another head? Sit down at the table. Try to behave like people."

An uneasy stillness hung over the breakfast table. Mr. Kamensky sat with his copy of the *Forward* in his lap, unread. He ate with one hand and with the other kept folding the paper into a series of tiny pleats, like a lady's fan. Brina refused to look at her tante Lipke at all. She stirred her bowl of oatmeal into elaborate landscapes but never raised a single spoonful to her mouth. Fruma and Raisa ate their breakfast as quickly as they could. Only when Fruma was done and timidly announced that she was going to work was the silence broken.

"You go nowhere until someone tells me what's going on." Mrs. Kamensky stood up at her place between Raisa and her daughter and pointed a steady finger at her family. "You're all acting strange, like there's something you don't want to tell me. Did someone come here with news last night while I slept?"

"My dearest," Mr. Kamensky ventured. "My precious wife, my sweet bride, you have been . . . asleep for longer than you know." As gently as he could, he told her how she had spent the previous eight days.

"Ah." Mrs. Kamensky blew out a short breath. "I see. And since then—any news?"

"If you mean bad news about Gavrel—" Mr. Kamensky began.

"Bite your tongue! Don't tempt the wrong thing!" Mrs. Kamensky's old vigor surged back as she leaped to protect those she loved from the evil eye. "I *know* there's no *bad* news come about my boy. If he were gone, God forbid, do you think I wouldn't see it in your faces? Especially *yours*?" She whirled on Raisa.

"Mrs. Kamensky, I—"

Her landlady silenced her with a curt wave of her hand. "Just because I chose to say nothing doesn't mean I couldn't see how it was between you two. You don't need to deny or defend what you've done, Raisa. I'm not accusing you of any crime."

Raisa bowed her head. "But I am. Gavrel . . . He went to work that day because—because—"

"To earn more money," Mrs. Kamensky said without emotion. "Just as any responsible young man would do who wanted to take a bride. Did you *tell* him to do it?" Raisa shook her head. "Could you have *stopped* him?"

"I didn't even know he was going until . . . after." Tears dropped into Raisa's lap.

"Then enough. If you blame yourself for something that's not your fault, you'll eat yourself up alive. You can't afford to do that. You have no job and now, with Gavrel—*missing*—we need your rent money more than ever. Besides, do you believe Brina can live on air?"

"Tomorrow," Raisa said. "I'll look for work tomorrow."

"Not tomorrow," Mr. Kamensky said in a voice as hushed as if he stood beside a deathbed. "Nothing tomorrow."

"And why not?" his wife wanted to know.

"Tomorrow is the day they give burial to the last ones," he replied. "The ones nobody could identify or claim."

Fruma fetched her purse and took out a leaflet printed in Yiddish, English, and Italian calling for all the workers of the city to join together to mourn the seven unknown souls from among the ranks of the 146 dead. "I won't be going to work tomorrow," she declared. "I know we need my pay, but—forgive me, Mama—I'm going to march with them."

Mrs. Kamensky embraced her daughter. "I would never forgive you if you made any other choice."

"I'm going, too," Raisa said. "That is, if you don't need me here."

"Go with my blessing," Mrs. Kamensky replied, sitting down again. "I'll take care of Brina."

"But I want to go, too!" Brina exclaimed.

Fruma stroked the child's curls. "You can't, dearest. There'll be too many people. It won't be safe."

"Wouldn't you rather stay home with me, my pretty one? You can help me bake something good to eat." Mrs. Kamensky reached for the child, but Brina shrank away from her, huddling against Raisa.

"I'm sorry," Raisa said softly, wanting the power to remove the look of pained surprise from Mrs. Kamensky's face. "She was—she was scared to see you so sick for so many days."

"Ah." Mrs. Kamensky nodded. "So she is still afraid of me. I understand. Take her with you, then, if you must."

Raisa shook her head. "No, Fruma's right; it won't be safe. The crowds will be enormous."

Mr. Kamensky rose to take Fruma's unoccupied seat and put his arm around his wife. "You were ill, so you couldn't know how it's been. The whole city's torn apart. Everywhere there is a great uproar, a shout for justice loud enough to reach the gates of heaven. The papers are filled with accounts of what happened that day, with accusations and denials. The fire chief, Mr. Croker, is saying that the disaster was inevitable, the way the building-code laws stand. God help us, sometimes the voices that are raised to reject the blame for this disaster are louder than the ones that weep for the dead."

"Money." Fruma spat out the word. "Mr. Croker himself said it. He was supposed to speak at one of the memorial meetings last Sunday, but when he couldn't be there, he sent his words. I will never forget them! 'It all comes right down to dollars and cents against life.' Buildings without enough stairways because it costs too much to install them, without fire towers to hold water on the roof! Shops with locked doors because it's more important to save the owners from petty thievery than it is to save the workers from death!

"Mama, did you know, both of the owners were in the Asch Building when the fire broke out? Blanck and Harris, the ones the newspapers call the shirtwaist kings. Oh, wonderful kings! Blanck was there with his two little daughters. They all escaped by running up to the roof. Some of the students from NYU made a bridge from their classroom and saved them, but what do we hear from the owners now? Even a *whisper* of responsibility?"

"Why should there be?" Mrs. Kamensky said. "It wasn't their children who burned." She looked at Raisa. "Take good care of our Brina tomorrow."

"I can't bring her to the march," Raisa said.

Brina lifted her head. "Can I go see Tante Dvorah?" she asked. "I like her."

"Tante Dvorah?" Mrs. Kamensky echoed. "Your friend Zusa's mama?"

Raisa nodded. "A few days ago, Selig asked us to go see his cousin, to talk to her about Zusa. She was sitting by the window when we came in. She looked as fragile as a fallen leaf, and when she spoke, it was like hearing a ghost. But then, almost as soon as we stepped into their apartment, Brina ran right up to her, hugged her, kissed her, began to cry. Selig told me later that Mrs. Reshevsky hadn't shed a single tear from the time he came home from finding Zusa's body."

"So she cried, too, with the child?" Mrs. Kamensky asked. Raisa nodded once more. "To be able to cry when there is so much pain—that can be a blessing."

"Brina's been asking to go back for another visit. She really does like Mrs. Reshevsky. I was hoping to let her do it so that I could finally start searching the hospitals for—" She caught herself and looked at Mrs. Kamensky cautiously, afraid her words might rekindle the older woman's illness.

"For Gavrel." Mrs. Kamensky's voice didn't waver. She was her old, strong self once more. "God bless you, Raisaleh; you've done more than enough for this family. It was a lucky day when my son found you. God willing, we'll live to see an even luckier one, *all* of us!" She reached out and clasped Raisa's hand. "I will go to the hospitals. He will be found."

"And Brina?" Raisa asked softly. "I'd like to take her to the Reshevskys' tomorrow. I hope—I hope that's all right with you."

"What, is Brina *my* child? Let her go where she wants to, where she's happy, where she brings that poor woman's soul a little peace." Mrs. Kamensky flicked a drop of moisture from the corner of her eye. "Where she's not afraid."

There were three funeral processions on the afternoon of the fifth of April, all of them for the nameless dead. One began near Seward Park, another farther uptown, around Twenty-second Street and Fourth Avenue, both converging at Washington Square Park, in full view of the Asch Building. Rain fell from an iron sky and fog haunted the upper floors of the lofts and skyscrapers along the route. The streets filled with water and mud.

Raisa and Fruma were with the Seward Park group when all three met at the ferry to Brooklyn. It was their first sight of the third procession, the one that actually carried the remains of the seven bodies that had been left unclaimed by any living friend or relative. The city officials had removed them from Misery Lane to the morgue, and it was from the morgue that eight horse-drawn hearses had made their slow progress, two by two, through the dismal streets while mourners and sorrowing spectators lined the way. The two girls were part of the crowd that now saw the black horses, the black wagons with their white draperies, the black boxes under their wreaths of roses and orchids.

As Raisa stood in the drizzling rain, she heard a girl beside her ask her companion, "Why are there eight coffins? I thought there were only seven bodies."

"When the police and firemen searched the Triangle shop floors after the fire, sometimes all they found were . . . pieces. Burned scraps."

The first girl gasped, appalled. "My God, are you talking about our people as if they were leftover bits of *cloth*?"

"If they had been cloth, maybe the owners would have thought they were worth saving."

It was dark by the time Raisa and Fruma came home. They had watched the hearses cross the East River on the Twenty-third Street ferry, but there was no room for them on board. By elevated train and streetcar and on foot they made their way to Brooklyn, part of a wave of mourners all headed for the Evergreens Cemetery. They arrived after the final coffin was lowered into the long pit dug to receive the last victims of the fire, and they stood hatless in the rain while four men sang "Nearer, My God, to Thee." Then they returned to Manhattan.

Fruma rushed back to her parents, so that they might comfort one another on this dreadful day, but Raisa had to stop at the Reshevskys' apartment to pick up Brina before she could go home. Selig answered her knock at the door, and his face went white when he saw her. "Raisa, you're soaked! Are you trying to catch pneumonia? Come in, let me give you something to throw off the chill."

"I'll be fine. Where's Brina?"

He made a motion for Raisa to be silent, then led her to the front room. Mrs. Reshevsky sat in a well-padded armchair at the window overlooking the street, with Brina asleep in her lap. At Raisa's approach, the woman looked up from the child cradled in her arms and smiled, her eyes shining with tranquility. When Raisa bent down and took the sleeping child from her, Zusa's mother kissed them both on the cheek and murmured, "God bless you, dear ones. God bless you."

Raisa found work before the week was out; or rather, Fruma found work for her. "They're hiring in my shop," she announced at the Shabbos dinner table almost as soon as her father finished saying the blessings over the bread and wine. "I told the foreman I knew a good worker. They just got a big order for uniforms, and they need girls who can run heavy material through the machines without breaking too many needles."

"What kind of uniforms?" Mr. Kamensky asked.

"Soldiers, sailors, doormen, Sousa's whole marching band—what's the difference?" his wife cut in. "What matters is that they'll be happy to have our Raisa."

"Well, do you want the job?" Fruma asked.

"Anything," Raisa replied. *Anything but shirtwaists,* she thought. *Oh, thank God it's not shirtwaists!*

By the time the following week brought the feast of Passover, Raisa was once again part of a daily routine. The difference was that now it didn't feel like a prison so much as a shell she'd closed around herself to keep out the pain. She and Fruma left the house together. Brina had gotten over her timidity toward Mrs. Kamensky and usually was happily helping Tante Lipke make breakfast for the two working girls. Some mornings, though, she would clamor to visit "Tante Dvorah." On those days, Raisa and Fruma would take her with them and drop her off at the Reshevskys' apartment. Sometimes Mrs. Kamensky came to get her, and to spend some time with Zusa's mother, but the little girl was more than capable of finding her own way home whenever she liked.

From there, they went to work. The world outside their factory ached and flared with the pain of loss, echoed loudly with protests and demands for justice. At her new job, no one knew that Raisa had survived the Triangle fire. She had begged Fruma to keep it a secret, and she prayed that none of the other survivors would find their next job under the same roof as she.

"You should think about going back to the Educational Alliance," Fruma remarked as the two of them walked home together. "You always loved your English classes. Why don't I join you? I'd like to read faster."

"Fruma, I know what you're trying to do," Raisa replied. "Don't worry, you won't have to come with me. I'm not afraid to go there on my own."

"You don't have to go alone," Fruma insisted. "There'll be other girls from the neighborhood, you know. You'll meet new people, make new friends."

"Of course I will," Raisa said, but they were empty words that echoed inside her shell.

Day after day, the shell held tight, and yet there were times when hairline cracks snaked across its surface. A fresh one shivered open every time she heard Mrs. Kamensky talking about her latest attempt to find any news of Gavrel in the hospitals that had sheltered the Triangle casualties. It was worse when she made her own hospital visits, certain that her eyes would find him where his mother's had failed. She stole scraps of time and haunted the same places she'd once visited in hopes of finding her sister. Now she carried two wandering souls on her shoulders, and the weight turned her feet to lead.

Worse than her burden of frustration and grief was having to hide it from the family. She learned how to cry in her bed at night so that no one would hear her, but she refused to learn how to give up.

On the eve of Passover, Raisa, Brina, and the Kamenskys walked through the streets in their best clothes to join Zusa's mother and cousin Selig for the first seder. The letter Selig had sent them was more of an entreaty than an invitation: *Your presence would be a blessing for us, especially for Dvorah, who loves you with all her heart and often speaks of you as if we were part of a single family. Be with us, please, so that we may have something left to celebrate.* How could they say no?

The apartment door was flung wide the moment Mr. Kamensky knocked on it. Selig stood before them looking healthier and happier than he had since the tragedy. "Did you hear the news?" he blurted. "They've been indicted! Blanck and Harris were indicted on manslaughter charges yesterday. I only just read about it. They're going to stand trial for their crimes. The murderers have been brought to justice!"

"It's the first step, God willing," Mr. Kamensky muttered as Selig led them all to the beautifully set seder table with its embroidered eggshell white cloth and the gleaming dishes that were used only during the eight days and nights of the holiday. Zusa's mother was too busy at the stove to realize that her guests had arrived. Their words were lost to her over the bubbling and sizzling of the pots.

"God?" Selig echoed. "If there were a God, the charge would be murder! 'God willing'? I'd rather put my faith in the law. Raisa, if they come to you to testify, speak for us all! Tell about everything you witnessed. Make every word an iron bar to build a prison around the ones who killed your friend."

"Be *quiet*," Mrs. Kamensky hissed. "Do you want your cousin to hear you saying such things?"

Selig cast a nervous glance toward the stove. "Sorry," he mumbled, looking embarrassed. He didn't say another word about the indictment and upcoming trial of the shirtwaist kings. But that night, when they all sang about how the hand of God had avenged the slavery and deaths of His chosen people, Raisa only had to glance at Selig to know that he was not thinking of the Egyptians.

Chapter Seventeen

DUST

Spring passed and summer came. Raisa worked long hours in the factory with Fruma, letting her thoughts glide away along the seams of every garment she sewed. *You hold a priceless gift, a gift, a gift . . .* Why did the butcher's words rattle through her head each day, dancing to the rhythm of the clattering needle? She worked harder, was praised by her foreman, received a small raise in pay, and went home to sleep every night wondering if her dreams would be filled with fire.

She went back to her English classes, just as she'd promised Fruma. Miss Bryant greeted her return with a strange combination of warmth and formality. The tall, elegant teacher asked her to stay after class just long enough to present her with a book of poetry.

"Welcome back, Raisa," was all she said when she handed

her the book, a beautifully bound volume with gold letters on a rich brown leather cover. When Raisa protested that she couldn't accept such a gift, that she was still too ignorant to appreciate it, Miss Bryant replied, "This not a gift, Raisa. I consider it to be my pledge to the future, to *your* future. Accept it for my sake." She made no mention of the fire or the absence of Zusa and Luciana, but as Raisa walked out of the classroom, she thought she heard a sob behind her. When she turned back, the door swung closed.

One day at work, she overheard one of the girls tell another that a friend of hers had been approached by the assistant district attorney to give testimony before the grand jury that had indicted Blanck and Harris. "There were some men hanging around the court who tried to get her to change her words, but they were thrown out. As if she would have listened to them! They could try to beat her or buy her, and she'd still give the same evidence."

"That's nothing," her friend replied. "You want to talk about buying? I heard that those murderers have been pouring money into the newspapers, trying to excuse their crimes by taking out ads week after week."

"That was nice of them," the first girl said. "My family always needs toilet paper." She laughed.

Raisa found herself laughing, too, laughing so loudly that the two girls looked her way. "I'm sorry," she said. "I didn't mean to eavesdrop."

The first girl peered at her from behind her sewing machine

while she continued to feed the fabric under the needle. "You look familiar," she said at last. "I see you every morning. You're sometimes walking with a little girl. You take her into a building in the middle of my block."

"That's Brina. I've taken care of her since she was orphaned."

"You do? She's a relative?"

"She is now, the only one I know I've got. I have a sister, too, but I don't know where she is."

"You poor kid." The girl's machine stuttered to a stop. "Was she *there*?"

"You know, at the Triangle," the second girl put in, trying to be helpful. Her friend elbowed her sharply.

"Do you think we have to say the name? What else is everybody in this city *still* talking about?"

"We'll see how long *that* lasts." The second girl was openly skeptical. "The slack season is coming. People will be scrambling to make a living. Nobody cares about justice on an empty stomach."

"It will last as long as we make it last," Raisa said, drawing the girls' attention back to her. She had no idea what moved her to speak up like that, only that she *had* to do it. "It will last as long as someone in this city can't go to sleep without seeing flames. You"—she addressed the first girl—"You remind me very much of my friend Zusa. She always knew how to make me laugh. That was her gift. Mine—mine is to remember her."

"God in heaven." The first girl laid one hand to her throat. "*You* were there."

She would have said more, but just then the foreman came over to scold them all for sitting idle at their machines. When the workday ended, the two girls sought out Raisa and walked home with her and Fruma. They introduced themselves as Sophie—the one who was so much like Zusa—and Lena. Nothing more was said about the fire. By the time they reached the stoop outside the Reshevskys' building, the foursome were joking and gossiping like old friends.

They parted ways, promising to share the journey to and from work every day for as long as they all stayed in the same shop. Before she went on to her own home, Sophie kissed Raisa's cheek and said, "You're right, you know; this *will* last. We'll make it last until we've won."

Early summer days warmed the city. Raisa, Fruma, and their new friends rejoiced when their shop's contracts for uniforms carried them through the slack season in a way that orders for more fashionable garments never could. One fine morning, Raisa took some of the money that she didn't need for rent, or for clothes and shoes for herself and Brina, or to send back to the shtetl to help Glukel, and used it to pay her first dues in the International Ladies' Garment Workers' Union. Fruma, Sophie, and Lena accompanied her and treated her to an ice cream sundae afterward, to celebrate.

As they sat in the ice cream parlor, Raisa heard a piping voice call her name. She set down the spoon that was halfway to her lips and turned to see little Jennie come rushing toward her.

"Oh, Raisa! Raisa! I never thought I'd see you again!" she exclaimed as the two girls hugged. "Gussie said you were on the ninth floor when . . ." She couldn't go on.

"Gussie? Gussie's all right?" Raisa asked.

Jennie nodded. "She was up on the tenth floor that day. Nearly everyone up there survived and I—I wasn't in the building at all. My cousin Joseph was becoming a bar mitzvah that Saturday and his family lives in Queens. I put in extra hours before that and made an arrangement with Miss Gullo so I could take the time off. My family and I were gone all day."

"Thank God," Raisa said. Holding Jennie's hand, she introduced her to the other girls at the table. The conversation soon turned from Raisa's new union membership to the matter that was never far from any of the young garment workers' minds.

"So, Raisa, do you think you'll be asked to testify?" Sophie asked. "You know, when the trial happens."

"*If* it ever happens," said the ever-cynical Lena.

"If I'm called, I'll go," Raisa replied.

But the call never came, and the trial still did not happen.

One hot evening in late June, Mrs. Kamensky folded her hands on the dinner table and said, "I'm done."

"Done?" her husband repeated, at a loss. "Done with what?"

"Looking for him. May God witness, I have gone to every hospital in this city, looking for my boy. If he ever was in any of them, they have no record of his name. If I hadn't fallen ill, if I'd begun to look for him sooner, maybe it would have been different." She took a deep breath and let it out so slowly that Raisa thought she'd never speak again. But then: "And maybe not."

"Lipke, my dear, don't talk like that. You burdened yourself too much. You know we would have helped you, if you'd let us," her husband said.

"It's true, Mama," Fruma chimed in. "We would have helped you look. The four of us could have searched the hospitals faster."

"For what? So we'd know even sooner that there's no hope?" Mrs. Kamensky closed her eyes and pinched the bridge of her nose. "I'm too tired even to cry."

Raisa looked down at her plate and said nothing. What good would it do to say that *two* pairs of eyes had been looking for Gavrel all this time and still had failed to find him?

That night, Raisa had Brina help her drag their mattress to the roof. They had the vast, flat space all to themselves. The really steamy summer weather hadn't arrived yet, but ever since the fire, Raisa couldn't sleep at all if she was cooped up in a room when the temperature began to climb. Brina cuddled up next to her contentedly.

"I like it up here," she declared. "Can we live on the roof?"

"Ask me again when it rains," Raisa teased her.

Brina fell silent. For a while, Raisa thought the little girl had fallen asleep. She began to drift off herself, but then she heard Brina ask, "*Is* Gavrel gone?"

Half asleep, vulnerable, Raisa hadn't been prepared to hear that name. It pierced her like a spear. All she could do at first was echo, "Gone . . ."

Brina mistook the word for Raisa's answer. "But gone *how*?" she demanded. "Like my mother? Like Luciana? Like Zusa? Like your sister?"

"No, Brina," Raisa spoke firmly. "My sister is *not* gone. Not like that. You know I haven't been able to look for Henda for a long time, but that doesn't mean she's gone."

"Good," Brina said, satisfied. "Then Gavrel isn't gone, either. Tante Lipke got so tired that she had to stop looking, but that's all right. Now it's my turn."

Raisa had to smile at the child's determination. "And will you let me help you look, too?"

Brina gave the question lengthy thought, then said, "Yes, but only if you promise that you won't get tired of looking for him, not *ever*."

"I promise."

That fall, when Rosh Hashanah and Yom Kippur came, there were empty places in Raisa's synagogue.

Not only here, she thought. *In the other synagogues, in the churches . . . I don't think there's a single house of worship in this neighborhood that's been untouched.*

The divine Book of Life, which the faithful believed was

opened on Rosh Hashanah, was sealed on Yom Kippur. The name and fate of every mortal creature was inscribed there by God's own hand. In the year just past, too many of those names had been written in letters of fire.

Mrs. Kamensky herself refused to attend services. She and Zusa's mother had become friends, and she claimed that Dvorah needed another woman's understanding at such a time. She took Brina with her, since the child was still too young to sit calmly through the long ceremony.

Before she and Brina left the apartment, Mrs. Kamensky said, "God knows, this is how it must be. If Dvorah has to hear prayers of praise all around her when the only prayer she can utter is 'Why? Why? Why?' then her heart will never be whole again and her soul will drown in bitterness. Better that she takes the time she needs to heal. God will forgive her, and— may it be so—someday she will forgive God."

The evening of Rosh Hashanah, Mrs. Kamensky brought the Reshevskys over to share the festive New Year's meal she had prepared. It did Raisa's heart good to see how Zusa's mother took quiet pleasure in giving Brina slices of apple laden with honey. Though Dvorah still looked a long way from being able to smile freely, having the little girl near her seemed to bring her comfort.

Frigid weather came into the city long before the calendars declared that winter had arrived. Raisa continued to wear nothing but a shawl over her street clothes, even though the weather called for a heavy coat. Her own coat hung untouched and shunned, even though Mrs. Kamensky had performed the miracle of banishing every whiff of smoke from the fabric and repairing the mark of the fire. One day, Raisa saw that the peg where her coat had once hung was empty. By the time she came home that evening, a new coat had taken its place, a coat of dark green wool with black wooden buttons.

When she cast a questioning look at Fruma, her friend shrugged and said, "What did you expect? It was easy enough for them to sell the old one. They don't want you to say anything about it, all right?"

Raisa nodded, but that night she kissed Mr. and Mrs. Kamensky before sitting down to dinner.

The coat was not the only change in Raisa's life. After class one evening, Miss Bryant told her that her level of skill in reading and writing English made it a waste of time for her to stay on in the elementary class.

"I hope that your schedule will accommodate the change in class time, Raisa," she said. "I will still be your teacher, of course. It pains me to confess that if that were not the case, I might have held you back, for purely selfish reasons."

"I cannot believe that," Raisa replied.

"The class begins on the sixth of December. I look forward to seeing you there."

Two days before Raisa had to face her new course, the manslaughter trial of Isaac Harris and Max Blanck began with the selection of jurors. In the time since their indictment, Raisa had become as much of a newspaper hound as Mr. Kamensky. Unlike him, she didn't read the Yiddish press exclusively. Instead, she practiced her new language by reading every scrap of English newsprint she could find about the case.

She didn't know why she hadn't been called to testify or even to give a statement, but she reasoned that perhaps it was all for the best. *If it took them this long to begin the trial, who knows when it will end? I will never forget what I saw, and I will never be silent, but if the prosecutors already have enough people to bear witness, I can stay at work with a clear conscience. We need the money. Fruma's put off her marriage until spring, but she can't delay it forever. Her mother won't stand for that. Once Fruma leaves, and until they take in an additional boarder, I'll be all they have to rely on, besides the store. I will always stand witness, but, may God forgive me, I'm glad I don't have to do it now.*

On the day after Harris and Blanck made their first appearance in the criminal courts building, to be met by a mob of black-clad women screaming for retribution, Raisa went to work as usual. That evening, she found her new classroom at the Educational Alliance building, held her breath for a moment, and went in.

A grand surprise was waiting for her.

"Raisa! Is it you?" Renzo rose from his seat and ran to welcome her. "This is wonderful!" He babbled on in Yiddish, to the puzzled stares of the other students, until Raisa begged him to stop.

"You know how strict Miss Bryant is about only speaking English in the classroom," she said.

"That is true." His smile was blinding. "Ah, it is so much better to see you here than where we last met."

"Renzo . . ." Raisa lowered her voice. "Renzo, will you do me a great favor? Please tell Paolo that I understand why I was not invited to Luciana's funeral. It must have been the same reason why I was not told when they buried Zusa. I would like to come and visit him and the family, to share memories of Luciana with them, but . . ." She hesitated. "But only if that would bring them comfort, not more pain."

"That would be wonderful, Raisa," Renzo said. "I am certain Paolo and his family would be happy to see you. But there is something you must know: there was no funeral for Luciana. That day, that awful day at the pier, we found nothing. She was not among the dead."

Raisa stared. "Like Gavrel," she whispered. "Renzo, what did Paolo do when he could not find her? Did he go to the hospitals?"

"As soon as he could, as many as he could," Renzo replied. "But there are so many, and none of them had anything useful to tell him! He went to the Red Cross, too. They said they would help, but they were very busy. So many people sent them contributions to help the families of the dead! Such kindness! There are times that I don't know what to think of human beings. How can I believe that the ghouls and thieves who came to gawk and prey on the dead and the living come from the same blood as the good souls who suffer with us?"

That night, after class, Renzo walked her home. At every corner where the weather had turned the street to slop, he took her arm to help her over the worst of the mess. Before they reached her building, he was holding her arm with every step. The attention made her uneasy, but she didn't know what to say about it.

When they arrived at the stoop leading up to the Kamenskys' tenement, he said, "There's no class tomorrow night, but if you like, I can come by to bring you to the Delvecchios' for that visit. I'm sure you will be welcome."

"Thank you, yes, I would like that," she said, and was surprised by how much her answer made him smile.

When the next evening came, Renzo appeared at the Kamenskys' door after dinner. Gavrel's family looked on doubtfully as he helped Raisa into her coat. Renzo's attention made Raisa feel uncomfortable enough without the Kamenskys' critical stares.

"I'm only going to spend a little time with Luciana's family," she said. "I won't be out too late."

"Who said anything?" Mrs. Kamensky replied with a shrug. "You are a young woman, and you know how to take care of yourself. Go wherever you want."

As Renzo had predicted, Raisa's visit was warmly received. The Delvecchio apartment was filled with people and the smells of cooking and baking. Raisa spoke to Mrs. Delvecchio mostly through Renzo as they shared coffee, cake, and stories about Luciana. The walls of the little apartment were covered with many sketches Luciana had done of the family, and even one of Brina on the ship to America. Raisa took bittersweet pleasure in telling Luciana's mother about the way her daughter had helped comfort and care for the child during those strange days aboard the steamship.

They did not talk only about Luciana. Mrs. Delvecchio insisted on hearing everything Raisa had to tell about the fire, too. Raisa tried to hold back her words to protect herself from revisiting the horror, but she soon found the story spilling from her lips, with Renzo scrambling to interpret, until she broke down sobbing. Luciana's mother embraced her. Someone else—Raisa was too lost in tears to see who it was—pressed a strong drink into her hand. It smelled of lemons and burned her throat, but it helped her calm down.

"I am sorry," she said, looking into Mrs. Delvecchio's sympathetic eyes. "I did not want to say so much. I did not want to upset you." She looked to Renzo to translate her English into Italian, but there was no need. Mrs. Delvecchio gathered her back into her arms and let her know that everything was all right.

It was later than she expected by the time Renzo walked her home. The Kamensky apartment was quiet and dark. She had a hard time getting ready for bed with no light to guide her in the windowless room, but she didn't want to disturb anyone. She lay down on her mattress, expecting to find Brina already asleep with the whole blanket wrapped around her, and gave an involuntary cry of surprise when she found she had both the blanket and the mattress all to herself.

"Brina's not here." Fruma's drowsy voice came through the darkness. "She's spending the night with her best friend, Ruthie from upstairs."

"Oh, Fruma, I'm sorry. I didn't mean to wake you. I'll be quiet." She closed her eyes and, as she always did, began to recite in the softest of whispers her prayers before sleep.

Tonight the whisper was not soft enough; Fruma overheard.

"I didn't know you still pray." She sounded surprised. "Just like Papa. He gives thanks to God for Mama's recovery every day."

"So do I," Raisa said very softly.

"You still believe in God?"

"Yes."

"That's incredible."

"I don't think so." Raisa's hands clenched the blanket. *Why, Fruma?* she thought angrily. *Why are you making me feel that I'm confessing a sin instead of simply telling you that I still pray, that I still have faith? You sat next to me at services during the Days of Awe. Why did you think I was there?*

"You mean that after what happened to you, to your friends, to Gavrel, you can still . . . ?" She clicked her tongue. "Well, I suppose it's because *you* came through it all right."

"You believe that?" Raisa's voice broke with pain.

Fruma gasped as if she'd been slapped. "Oh my God, Raisa, I'm sorry! How could I have said anything so cruel to you?" Her hand fumbled for Raisa's in the darkness. "Forgive me. It's just that—this all hurts so much, I don't know what to do. There are times when I want to curl up and cry for hours, but then I see you, so strong, going ahead with your life, helping us when Mama was sick. I know how much you loved my brother. I can't imagine how you must be feeling, not knowing where he is, if he's alive or, God forbid . . ." She couldn't say the final word. "Every time I look at you, I know I haven't got the right to give in to grief, to be weak. I wasn't there!"

"Yes, you were." Raisa squeezed Fruma's hand. "Even if Gavrel and Zusa and Luciana had come home safe that day, even if you didn't know a single soul who died in the fire, you were there with us. Did you see how many people walked behind the hearses on the day they buried the nameless ones? Hundreds of thousands, the newspaper said. I believe that all of them were there, too—not just at the funeral, but at the fire, in the flames. It isn't weakness and you don't need my permission; you have every right to cry."

She felt Fruma pull her hand away, and she expected to hear the sound of tears follow. But there was only a long silence, broken at last by a weird little laugh. "Oh, Raisa, isn't it strange?" Fruma said. "I don't think I *can* cry now."

On December 27, in the early wintry twilight outside the criminal courts building in the heart of a throng shouting, "Murder! Murder!" Fruma cried at last.

She fell sobbing into her friend's arms while Raisa's head still reeled with echoes of the impossible verdict that had been pronounced on the owners of the Triangle Waist Company. *Not guilty. . . . Not guilty?* There had to be a mistake. *Not guilty.* Someone must have gotten the information wrong. *Not guilty.* It made no sense. *Not guilty.* Any minute now, someone else would come through the doors or open a window and shout out the real verdict, the only one that could be true: *Guilty!*

But that verdict never came.

Some of the people stood as stunned as Raisa, some wept like Fruma, some raised their voices, crying out in pain and indignation for justice. An elderly man pressed his neatly laundered and folded handkerchief into Fruma's fingers and muttered, "Justice? Whose justice? The dead can't hire lawyers. Let their mothers take comfort; the locked door that killed their children saved the owners enough money to buy the best defense they could find!"

"We will have our justice the moment they show their faces!" a woman shouted. A roar of agreement went up from the crowd, but soon word spread that Blanck and Harris had been smuggled out of the criminal courts through the infamous Tombs prison, which shared the building.

"Follow me!" a young man called out. "I saw where those bastards left their limousine. We'll get them there!" Raisa and Fruma became caught up in that part of the mob that chose to run after the young man, but when they reached the waiting car, Raisa saw that there was already another swarm of enraged mourners surrounding it and no sign at all of the shirtwaist kings.

"Fruma, let's get out of here," Raisa said. "They're not coming, and even if they did, even if I were to come face-to-face with both of them, I don't know what I'd do."

"Spit in their faces," Fruma said through gritted teeth. "Make them bleed for what they've done. Are they allowed to go home to a fine house and a hot dinner and a family that hasn't been destroyed? Why? Because the law couldn't *prove* they were guilty? Why do we have to prove what everyone *knows*? If the law won't do justice to them, I will!"

"My God, Fruma, and what will you do the next time a mob decides that *we're* to blame for something that nobody can prove? Please, let's go home."

Fruma permitted Raisa to steer her out of the horde around the limousine. As they walked away, Raisa overheard someone say that Blanck and Harris had abandoned the besieged car and chauffeur to their fates and had sneaked away into the subway at Lafayette Street. They were long gone.

They walked home, in spite of the cold. Neither one of them said a word, but somehow both understood that the crowds and noise of any kind of public transportation would be too much for their nerves to take. There was also the very real chance that they would have to share the subway or the trolley with some of the other people who had been present at the court when the verdict came down. They couldn't endure the thought of being trapped in a small space with so much powerless rage and resentment.

As they came closer to home, Raisa turned to Fruma and said, "Will you please tell your mother that I'll be a little late? I told the Reshevskys and the Delvecchios that I was going to attend the verdict. I think it might be kinder if they heard it from me, not the newspapers."

"There's no way this news can be kind," Fruma said. "Look, let me help you. I'll go to the Reshevskys' for you; you see the Delvecchios."

"I wish we could do it the other way around," Raisa said.

"Why? You know Luciana's people and I don't."

"I know, but—" She bit her lower lip. "I just hope Renzo's not there."

"Isn't he your friend?"

"Yes, and he's a good friend, too, but lately I feel on edge when I'm in his company. Look." She stopped under a street-lamp and pulled something out of her purse. The lamplight brought out the rich amber and deep brown of a small tor-toiseshell comb. "He said that since my hair is so much longer and . . . *prettier* now, I should have something pretty to adorn it. I tried to give it back, but he swore I'd insult him if I didn't keep it. I think . . . I'm afraid he wants to be more to me than just a friend, and that's impossible."

"Because he's not a Jew?"

"Because he's not Gavrel."

"All right, Raisa," Fruma said. "I'll tell the Delvecchios; you tell the Reshevskys."

She shook her head. "No, I'm being silly. You're right, I

know the Delvecchios and you don't. Besides, I'm a coward. I don't think I could stand to see how the Reshevskys take the news that Zusa's murderers are free men tonight."

Raisa threw open the door of the Kamensky apartment with such force that it hit the wall with a bang like a cannon shot. Her face was blazing from the cold and from all the blocks she'd run. She held on to the doorjamb, afraid that if she let go, her knees would buckle and she'd go sprawling. She heard the sound of chairs in the front room being pushed back, of running feet as her landlords and Fruma hurried to see who had come bursting into their home. They gaped when they saw her, framed in the doorway, gasping for breath, her face stretched to the limit by a smile so wide it made her eyes ache.

And yet she would have smiled even wider if she could have.

"Raisa, child, what is it?" Mr. Kamensky raised one hand, but stopped short of touching her.

Raisa caught fast, shallow breaths, struggling to speak. The sound of footsteps climbing the stairs and crossing the landing behind her broke the spell. She took a few steps into the Kamenskys' apartment and turned back to hold out her hands toward the door.

"Tell them," she said, her words tangled up in laughter. "*Tell* them!"

Framed in the doorway, Luciana Delvecchio leaned on her brother's arm and in slow, musical English softly said, "Your son is alive."

Chapter Eighteen

BY THE GLOW OF
EMBERS

All the way up into Westchester County on the New York and Harlem Line, Raisa found it impossible to stay in her seat for more than five minutes at a time. None of the people with whom she traveled said a word to stop her, though once the conductor tried scolding her for bothering the other passengers. That was a mistake.

"Young man, if you want to throw your weight around, find a better target," Mrs. Kamensky declared, rising like a thundercloud to stand with Raisa. "This girl is bothering no one. *We* know her." She indicated the seat where Mr. Kamensky sat with a dozing Brina in his lap, her own empty place beside him, then in quick succession Fruma, Paolo, and Luciana. "As for the rest"—she made an imperious gesture that included the only three passengers in the car who were not part of their traveling group—"do any of these people *look* like they are being disturbed?"

"Well, she oughta sit down anyhow," the conductor blustered through his thick mustache. "If the train takes a curve or stops short, she could get hurt bad, standing up like that."

"And how many times do your passengers go tumbling down the aisles? Can't your engineer drive this train better than that?" Mrs. Kamensky lifted her chin and buried the man in scorn. "If you had any idea of what this girl has survived, you would not babble at her about a little bump or bruise or scratch she *might* get. If you had seen half the sights she has, and lived to walk away—"

"What'd *she* do, huh?" The conductor had a good supply of his own sarcasm to fire back at Mrs. Kamensky. "Jump off the *Maine* and swim back here from Havana?"

Gavrel's mother gave him a withering look, but all she said in reply was, "*That* is her friend." She pointed at Luciana.

The conductor was not a stupid man. One look at the Italian girl's face and he understood. The marks of fire were there, plain to see. Even though she wore a shawl pulled up over her head, it was impossible not to notice the patches of skin where the hair had been burned away. More than nine months had passed since the Triangle burned, but the newspapers were filled with reports on the verdict, refreshing all the horror of that March day. "God bless you, girls," he muttered before striding quickly out of the car.

"Raisa, will you sit with me?" Luciana reached for her friend's hand, drawing her down beside her. Raisa couldn't understand the Italian words Luciana spoke to Paolo, but she could guess their meaning when he moved to another part of the car. "We are almost there," Luciana said as soon as the two of them were alone. "Soon you will see him. Before that . . . I need to tell you something."

"What?" Raisa felt a chill that had little to do with the late-December weather. "Is he very badly burned? Has he lost a leg, an arm, an eye to the fire? I do not care about that. I love him, Luciana."

"I know. Raisa, I have scars, but where I was burned there was no deep damage done to my body. Your Gavrel, it is the same, even better. So little of the fire touched him that you would call it a miracle, if only—if only . . ." Luciana looked down at her hands, still lightly wrapped in bandages. "The fire does not only burn the body."

For a little while, the only sound was the passage of the railway car over the tracks, speeding north. Raisa waited for her friend to speak again. She had seen strange ghosts hiding in Luciana's eyes and she didn't dare say anything, for fear of calling them out into the daylight.

At last, Luciana went on. "Gavrel and I, we were very lucky. We worked on the eighth floor, where the fire began, so we had the most time to escape. The cutters like Gavrel hang the paper patterns from wires. They stuff the scraps that are left over into bins under the tables. The owners keep the scraps to sell, but the man who comes to collect all of those rags does not come every day. That was where the fire began, in the rags. We saw it happen. Gavrel and some of the other men tried to put it out with the fire buckets, but there were not enough. So we sent word to the other floors and then we ran. But Gavrel—your Gavrel did not run down the stairs into the street. He tried to run up the stairs to you."

Luciana looked into Raisa's eyes. "He would have died. I could not let that happen. I ran after him, but the fire grew worse. The hanging patterns were burning, sheets of flame flying through the air. One fell on me and I screamed. Gavrel heard, and turned back to help me. I think he must have beat out the flames on me with his bare hands, then he got both of us out of the shop and down into the street. He had just left me in the care of an ambulance driver—" She began to shudder.

"You don't have to tell me, Luciana," Raisa said. "Don't talk about what happened that day. *Today* he's alive. That's all that matters."

"But I *must* talk, Raisa!" Luciana insisted. "And you must know. Once I was safe, Gavrel turned to go back into the building. He wanted to find you! The firemen in the street stopped him. They thought he was crazy. He fought with them so fiercely that I was afraid he would win and rush back to his death! I could not let that happen; he saved my life. I ran from the ambulance, I grabbed his arm, one of the firemen and I began to pull him away from the building." She shook even harder, her whole body trembling so violently that Raisa stripped off her own coat and settled it carefully over her friend's shoulders just as Luciana said, "That was when the body fell beside us.

"Oh, Raisa, the sound of her striking the street! It will never leave me. And the sight of what was left on the pavement! The fireman, big and strong, I thought he would faint. Gavrel and I stood like ice, like stone. All we could do was stare at the poor, burned, broken thing. That—that was how we still stood when another body fell and struck us down."

"Luciana!" Gently and carefully, Raisa hugged her friend. For all the dreadful things she had witnessed herself that day, she couldn't imagine how it must have been for Gavrel and Luciana, engulfed by horror.

"For a long time after that, I did not know where I was or what had happened to me after—after the second body . . ." Luciana turned her face away from Raisa to gaze out the window at the peaceful landscape slipping past. "When I was myself again, the women told me that months had passed."

"The women," Raisa repeated. "The hospital nurses?"

"I was not in a hospital then, Raisa. At first, yes, to treat my injuries. But when I—when I came back, I was in the place where we are going now. It is not a hospital, but a place . . . a place of rest, created years ago as an act of charity by a society lady whose husband is a great doctor, very wealthy. She runs it, even works there—though she is not a nurse—with other ladies like her who don't turn their backs on the poor. Thank God it exists, such a shelter for people like Gavrel and me, whose worst hurts were in our minds! Those in charge of the place did not want us sent to the city shelters for—for the . . ." She lowered her voice, shamed by the word. "Insane."

Insane! Raisa, too, cringed at the word. Most people she knew—even the kindest—regarded mental illness with the same childish ignorance and fear Brina had shown when Mrs. Kamensky was ailing. They were still too ready to drop the weight of blame for it squarely on the backs of its helpless victims.

"The women were very good to us, very kind," Luciana went on. "They tried and tried to help me speak again, to come back to the world. They wanted to let my family know I was alive, but how could they, when they had no idea who I was? They had no clue, and I stayed silent. I had seen and heard too many horrors, so I—I . . ." She struggled to explain. "I suppose I *chose* to forget for a while, until I became strong enough again to remember. It was the same for all of us in that place—for me, for Gavrel—"

"Tell me, Luciana," Raisa said, her voice low. "How is he? Tell me the truth."

"I came back," Luciana said. "He did not."

From the train station, they traveled in a hired wagon through tranquil country roads. Raisa sat up front beside the driver, Brina in her lap. The child was delighted by everything she saw, but for Raisa, each hedge and fence and house they passed only made her skin prickle with tension because it was not the house where Gavrel waited. At last the wagon turned up a tree-lined path to a house set well back from the road. Luciana told everyone that it was the summer cottage of a wealthy family, but in name only, the same way that the great mansions of Newport, Rhode Island, were "cottages." Judging from the number of windowpanes flashing in the sunlight, it must have boasted at least twenty rooms. Even in winter the wide lawn and ample garden surrounding the house were impressive.

As soon as the carriage came to a stop in front of the cottage, Raisa spun around and swung Brina over the back of the driver's bench into Mrs. Kamensky's arms. Then she leaped down and ran to the front door, her hat blowing off her head and tumbling down the gravel walkway behind her. She banged the shining brass knocker against the door so furiously that it was a miracle the wood didn't split. She hardly glanced at the gray-haired woman who answered the door. She was across the threshold and flying through the house, his name on her lips, his face before her eyes.

She found him in an airy room on the second floor. He was propped up in a high-backed wicker wheelchair with his back to the window. She stood in the doorway, gazing at him with an unearthly combination of happiness, disbelief, and fear that if she took a single step forward, he would vanish. *It is him,* she thought, her pulse thrumming. *Luciana told us the truth and my eyes aren't lying. It's him, he's here, he's alive. He's alive!*

"Gavrel! Gavrel!" She called his name as she rushed forward, arms outstretched. She grabbed his hands, raised them to her lips and covered them with kisses. She knelt beside him and sincerely believed that if the world were to end in that moment, she would go into eternity without regret.

But the seconds passed, and she realized that he was not responding. The room might as well have been empty. His eyes were open, but if they saw her, there was no sign. The hands she held so tightly were limp and cold in hers.

"Oh, please, don't you know me?" she implored. "Can't you see that I'm *real*? I'm here, your family is here, too—your parents, your sister, even little Brina! Luciana told me what happened to you, but that's over. Look, I'm just as alive as you are. I didn't fall, I didn't die, I'm here, we're both here, and I—I love you, Gavrel. I love you so much. Say something. Say *anything*. Come back to me, Gavrel! Please, *please* come back!"

His eyelids flickered at the sound of his name, but that was all.

Raisa covered her face with her hands. *"Gavrel!"* His name was a long, desolate, animal cry, a pain that burned its way out of her soul.

Strong hands seized her shoulders from behind and gently brought her to her feet. "Dear God, you poor girl. Let me help you." A sweet voice spoke to her in lightly accented English. Raisa turned, lowering her hands, eyes half blinded by tears.

Before she saw the woman's face, before she was fully aware of the sparkle of gold and pearls pinned to the woman's crisp white collar, she saw the empty space in the circle, the tiny hollow where a single pearl no bigger than a sesame seed had once been. She looked a little higher and recognized the woman who had fainted among the open coffins on Misery Lane, the woman whose fine clothes, healthy looks, and grand name made it impossible, unthinkable for her to be—

"Henda?"

They stared at one another for a heartbeat, for two, and then—

"Raisa? Is it really you?" The Yiddish words barely left the woman's lips before she crushed Raisa to her chest. "It is! It can't be, but thank God, it is! It is!"

Raisa couldn't speak. She was drowning where she stood, new tears of amazed thanksgiving flowing into the tears she'd shed for Gavrel. All she could do was sob and press her face so close to Henda that she could feel their mother's brooch marking her cheek with its broken circle of pearls.

"Don't cry!" Henda exclaimed. "I'm scared that you'll make *me* cry, and then how ungrateful would we look for such a miracle? To find you alive when I thought you were gone forever—Raisa, *please* stop crying!"

"I—I want to." Raisa choked out the words. She heard the sound of approaching footsteps from the hall. "I don't—I don't want Gavrel's parents to find me like this. They'll think the worst, even though—oh, Henda, I'm so happy, but I don't know *how* to stop crying like a fool!"

"To stop crying, my Raisa . . . laugh." A hoarse, familiar voice made her catch her breath sharply. A warm hand curved around her own in a perfect fit. His face was pale and too thin, but when she looked into Gavrel's eyes, Raisa rejoiced to see that they were alive again, and lit by the smile she knew so well.

Before she could respond, the Kamenskys came in. Gavrel's

room became a storm of hugs, kisses, more tears, and soon enough, arguments. Brina tried to swarm onto Gavrel's lap, only to have Mr. Kamensky hold her back, warning her that she might hurt him. That made Brina yowl, which in turn made Mrs. Kamensky scold her husband only a breath before she ordered Fruma not to touch her brother until she had taken off her overcoat.

"It's carrying cold air from outside. Do you want him to catch pneumonia, God forbid?"

"Mama, you can't catch pneumonia from a cold coat!"

"Since when are you a doctor?" Mrs. Kamensky turned to Henda, whose plain blue dress worn under a spotless white bib apron gave her an official look. "Young woman, you're a nurse; *you* tell her I'm right."

"I'm sure you are, ma'am," Henda replied. "But not about me. I'm not a nurse." She put her arm around Raisa's shoulders. "I'm only her sister."

While Raisa pushed Gavrel's wheelchair, Henda led everyone into an improvised parlor down the hall. She explained that it had once been the cottage library, until the owner of the property had turned the house into a refuge for those people whose minds and spirits had been scarred. As everyone settled down into the comfortably upholstered sofa and chairs, Henda tugged at the bell pull hanging on the wall beside the unlit fireplace. When a young girl in a dusting cap and apron answered her summons, Henda said, "Molly, will you please ask Mrs.

Voss to send up tea and a luncheon for eight—" Her eyes fell on Brina. "I mean, for nine guests. Have Joshua help you, and let him bring in some of the small tables from downstairs."

"Yes, Mrs. Taylor." The girl dropped a curtsy before hurrying away.

Henda turned to her guests. "There will be food and drink for you shortly. Meanwhile, would you all mind if I took a short walk with my sister?"

"Short, long, whatever you like!" Mr. Kamensky exclaimed, grinning. "We won't be lonely." He and his wife had moved their chairs to either side of Gavrel, with Fruma hovering behind him. It looked as though they were afraid he would grow wings and take flight if they didn't hem him in.

Henda got a coat and led Raisa out of the cottage, into the sleeping garden. They walked the winding path in silence, until Henda paused beside an empty birdbath caught in a tangle of dead ivy. Here she removed the brooch pinned to her collar and held it out to her sister. "When I woke from my faint, that day at the pier, I thought I'd lost my mind . . . again."

"Again?" Raisa echoed as the circlet of gold and pearls was placed in the palm of her hand.

Henda's face distorted with painful memories. "The letter—that letter—it shattered me, Raisaleh. It tore away the world." She closed Raisa's fingers over their mother's pin and cupped her sister's hand with both of her own. "It was a dark time for me. Even after I was well, sometimes I still doubted myself, wondering if I could tell reality from dreams. That awful day, in the midst of so much horror, how could I be seeing *your* face leaning over me, when that cursed letter said that you were—?" She shivered. "God forbid. But I *wanted* to believe my eyes, and when I grabbed your shawl just as you were being dragged away, and I found Mama's brooch left behind in my hand, I knew you were real. It gave me hope. From that moment on I was certain I would find you again."

"Henda . . ." Raisa ran the fingertips of her free hand over the rough stone rim of the abandoned birdbath. "How hard did you look?"

"I know what you're saying," Henda said sadly. "If *I* had looked for you myself, it wouldn't have taken nine months and a miracle for us to be standing here." She squeezed Raisa's hand that held the brooch. "As soon as my husband brought me out of the pier, into the fresh air, I told him that I'd seen you and I had to go back inside at once. He refused, insisting that I needed to go home and rest. I can't blame him for that—I was frantic, almost hysterical, clinging to his coat like a mad-woman. I promised to go home at once if he'd stay behind and try to catch you when you came out—I described you to him exactly—but again he refused."

"Why?" Raisa's fingers tightened on the cold stone.

"You sound ready to condemn him," Henda said softly. "But hear me out, please. He knew what I'd suffered when I received that accursed letter. He had no reason to believe you were alive and every reason to think that what I'd seen at the pier had overwhelmed me. When I calmed myself enough to show him the brooch and tell him what it meant, he went back immediately. But by that time it was too late.

"He hired a private detective at once. Poor man, he felt so guilty for not having believed me earlier! He was afraid to let me risk my health by undertaking the search, and persuaded me that a professional would find you faster." Her mouth twisted. "He didn't know that the man was a bumbler, a cheat, and a drunkard, eating up our time and money, filling our ears with false hopes, and doing nothing to find you. My husband finally fired him last week, after hiring a second detective to observe and report on his 'work.'" She sighed. "All that time, wasted. How could we have been such fools for so long?"

"I was foolish, too," Raisa said. "When your friend told me that I'd just helped Mrs. Harrison Taylor, that name was enough to convince me that you *couldn't* be my sister. I heard that your young man was a German Jew, not some Yankee."

"I always call my husband by the name he was born with: Hillel Schneider," Henda said. "A few years ago, his father decided that the family would have a better chance of min-gling with the *right* people—whatever that means—if they had *American* names."

"Whatever *that* means," Raisa muttered.

"And on my wedding day, Hillel's father tried persuading me to change *my* name to Johanna," Henda said. "I almost said yes."

"Why would you even *think* of agreeing to such a thing?"

"Because I was so grateful to that man," Henda replied. "I loved his son almost from the day he first spoke to me. Hillel was so kind, so caring. He treated me, a poor sewing machine girl, with as much courtesy and respect as if I were a princess. If he hadn't been a rich man's son, I would never have kept him at arm's length for as long as I did, but I was afraid that if we became sweethearts, it would make trouble between him and his parents. Why would they want a penniless nobody for a daughter-in-law?"

"But if he loved you—" Raisa began.

"He loved his parents, too. And I loved him enough so that I never wanted him to have to choose between us. All of that changed on the day I got Reb Laski's letter. Oh, Raisa, even now I can't remember anything that happened from the time that I read those awful words until the moment I found myself in a strange room, a strange bed, with a beautifully dressed lady keeping watch over me. That was how I first met my Hillel's mother. Hillel saved me, Raisa, he and his parents together. When I was insane with grief, he brought me into their home and they took me in, healed me, comforted me, found doctors who brought me back among the living. The healing took a long, long time. When I was stronger, they took me upstate for a rest cure near Saratoga Springs. While we were there, my Hillel would take me for walks in the countryside, and one day that was where he told me he wanted to marry me."

"What did you tell him?" Raisa asked.

"The truth. That I loved him, too, but that I would sooner

vanish back into the streets than repay his parents' kindness by stealing their son."

"Yet here you are, Mrs. Harrison Taylor!" Raisa smiled at her sister.

"Yes, I am, because that night, his father came to me and said that he and his wife knew how Hillel and I felt about one another, and that they would be happy to welcome me into their hearts just as they'd welcomed me into their home." A sudden wind came up, biting cold. Henda dug her chin into her coat collar in just the way Raisa remembered her doing in the winter months back in the shtetl. "We should go back."

As they returned to the house, Raisa asked, "Henda, have you written to Glukel since—?"

"No. Not to her, not to Reb Laski, to no one. At first it was because I couldn't. I was too ill. And when I was better, even though we had only a small, private wedding, the preparations left me too exhausted to do more than live from day to day. After that . . ." She took a deep breath. "After that, I was afraid to write."

"Afraid?"

"Afraid that if I did send word after such a long silence, I'd be blamed for not having done so sooner. How stupid, I know. Because the longer I hesitated, the more silence grew between me and Glukel. If I broke it, what would she say? That I was a selfish, ungrateful girl to leave her? That I was worse than that for pretending she didn't exist for so long? And the worst thing is, she'd be right." She looked down sharply. "I'm so ashamed."

"You couldn't help it, Henda."

"I should have *tried*," Henda said fiercely. "I did write to her, Raisa—to her through Reb Laski—but I never could make myself finish the letters. I should have been stronger! I should have done—"

Raisa held her close. "You did what you could when you could. You were as strong as you were able to be. We'll write to Glukel together, today, and to Reb Laski, too. I promise you, when they read what we have to tell them, they'll understand and they'll rejoice."

Henda smiled. "Thank you, Raisaleh."

The sisters walked on, their arms around each other's waists. They were almost to the door of the house when Raisa murmured, "You were so sick for so long, under so much strain, and yet—why were you at the pier that day, Henda?"

"I had to be there," Henda answered quietly. "The people I was with—new friends I've made through my husband—felt the same way. They knew they had to witness the full, ugly truth of what had happened. We had to see the faces of the tragedy, even when the faces themselves were gone. And for me, those faces were a part of my life. I worked with girls like those who lay in coffined rows on that pier. I walked with the dread that my next step might bring me to the foot of a wooden box holding someone I'd once known, a friend.

"You know, Raisa, when you have enough money to live a life of ease, it can warp your sight. It lulls you into looking at disasters as if they were only stories, stage shows, moving pictures. You close the book, you put down the newspaper, you leave the theater, and you're free of it. You can go back to your comfortable life and pretend nothing happened because it didn't happen to you. My friends and I don't want that to happen to us. We felt that we had to remember that each of the one hundred and forty-six who died, even the nameless ones, was a *person*, not a number. Numbers burn too easily, and they're too easily forgotten. What happened once can happen again if all that we remember are the numbers."

She gestured at the cottage. "This house was the gift my friend Dorothea received on her wedding day from her husband."

"Luciana mentioned him," Raisa said. "I didn't know that a doctor could be so wealthy."

"He was born to wealth, to a prominent New York society family," Henda said. "But he refused to settle for a life of empty pleasures. He wanted to make a difference in the lives of those who needed help, to heal them so that someday they might help others. Dorothea felt the same way, and used her own money to transform, maintain, and run this place as a rest home. After the fire, she opened its doors even wider, to make it a refuge for anyone whose mind was affected by the fire—anyone, not just Triangle workers but their friends, their families, even the people who stood as witnesses when the bodies fell.

"As soon as my friends and I heard about the fire, we began raising funds to help bring relief to the survivors and to the families of those who—who were not so fortunate. Still, I felt it was not enough. The moment Dorothea told me of her plans, I knew what else I could do, *had* to do, and so I volunteered at once to work here. That day at the pier, I saw the dead, but I also saw the despair of the living. I knew what it was like to have your sanity shattered when someone you love is torn away from you without warning. I knew what it was to be whole in body, but still . . . broken. I knew that they would need peace, rest, time, and that I could help bring that to them."

"It's a wonderful gift you've given them, Henda," Raisa said.

Her sister smiled at her. "I've received a better one."

Ten days later, the Kamenskys' neighborhood buzzed with excitement as a fine carriage pulled up in front of their building and an elegantly dressed young couple stepped out. Their arrival caused almost as great a thrill as the one that had stirred the whole block five days earlier, when Gavrel had come home.

When Henda and her husband entered the Kamensky apartment, it was already a hubbub of Yiddish, English, and Italian. Luciana was there along with her mother, Paolo, and Renzo. Only the horror of losing a day's much-needed income had prevented her father from joining them for the grand luncheon that Mrs. Kamensky had cooked to celebrate her son's return.

Raisa took an immediate liking to Hillel. The handsome, dapper young man she'd seen so briefly on the pier was also friendly, sincere, and modest, with a sense of humor to rival Gavrel's. Even if she hadn't been aware of all he'd done for her sister, she would have welcomed him into the family.

The food was excellent, as always, and vanished swiftly from the plates. Although many of the dishes were alien to them, even Luciana's family were tucking into their lunch with gusto. Henda leaned across the table, plainly delighted to see how heartily Luciana and Gavrel ate.

"There were days when we couldn't get either one of you to eat more than a sip of milk and a crumb of bread. Now look at you! Especially you, Gavrel. You know it's all right to *chew* your food, yes?" she teased.

"Don't blame me for how I'm eating, Mrs. Taylor," Gavrel responded. "Blame your sister."

"*Me?*" Raisa's voice rose in surprise.

"Now, let's be honest, dearest," Gavrel said to her. "I know I love you, but I've got no idea if you can cook. That's why I'm eating all the *good* food I can get now, so that after we're married, at least I'll have my memories."

Everyone laughed but Raisa. "And who said I'd marry you? Maybe you can also get along with only memories of *me*," she retorted.

Gavrel became suddenly serious. "Where do you think I was for so long, Raisa? Living with memories. Waking or sleeping, all I could see was the fire and the . . . and the ones who fell. All I could think about was how I'd failed to go back into the flames and save you."

"But you didn't have to save me, Gavrel," Raisa said, taking his hand.

"I didn't know that. Who knows how the mind works?

Mine locked me away in a place where the only good memories I had were of you. That was why I didn't react when you first came into my room that day. I was sure you were just another dream. But when I heard your sister call your name"—he cradled Raisa's cheek with one hand—"it called me back, too."

He kissed her as if there were no one else but the two of them in the room, in the city, in the world.

A FIRE IS ALSO A LIGHT

Raisa and Gavrel walked together along the wide streets of the Upper East Side, enjoying the beauty of an early June night. They had taken a taxicab north from the Educational Alliance building, but once the driver crossed Fifty-seventh Street, Gavrel had asked him to stop.

"Why did you do that?" Raisa asked after he had paid the fare. "We've still a long, long way to go before we get to Henda's house."

Gavrel sighed as if he were the most put-upon man in the world. "And I can walk every step of that long, long way. Raisa, my dear heart, it's been almost three years since I came home. I've gone back to work. I've gone back to my studies. I'll be ordained as a rabbi before Rosh Hashanah, God willing. I've even been blessed with two years of marriage to the sweetest little greenhorn who ever stepped off the ferry from

Ellis Island." He kissed her soundly. "I'm well enough for all of that, so when am I going to be well enough for *you*?"

Raisa stepped out of his embrace, smiling. "So many arguments! I'm surprised you're becoming a rabbi and not a lawyer."

He matched her smile with one of his own. "Then as a rabbi-to-be, I decree that we have to walk the rest of the way, because it's Shabbos, after all."

"If your mother could hear you making jokes like that—"

"She'd agree with me that God must have a sense of humor or He would have gotten rid of all of us long ago." He linked his arm through hers. "Shall we?"

With every block that brought them nearer to Henda's home, Raisa became more and more excited, until she was almost bouncing as she clung to Gavrel's arm. He looked down at her fondly. "Did I make a mistake and bring Brina with me after the ceremony?"

"I'm sorry, I can't help it," Raisa said. "I'm too happy! Oh, Gavrel, will I ever be able to thank Miss Bryant enough for what she's done? All those extra lessons, the tutoring through the high school curriculum, and now she says she's going to find a way to have my independent studies certified as good enough to get me into a teachers' college. Gavrel, do you know what this means to me?"

"That you want a divorce so you can get a job?"

"Stop that. It's been *years* since it was illegal for female teachers to be married."

"I apologize for my ignorance," Gavrel said with a comic bow. "Allow me to make it up to you. I'll treat you and Miss Bryant to dinner next week. It can be my way of thanking her for organizing a ceremony in the Alliance theater to honor her advanced students. Did you see the Delvecchios' faces when Luciana crossed the stage to accept that certificate? And Renzo was applauding his little bride-to-be so loudly, the noise cracked the ceiling. I swear I felt flakes of plaster snowing down on us!"

His good-humored expression faded. "But that was nothing next to how Mama and Papa looked when you got up and started talking about the fire. So much pride, even when they were weeping along with everyone else in the theater! You have a gift, Raisa. You made us all relive that day, but not the despair. You reminded us that all the deaths and suffering weren't for nothing. That there are new laws now, changes—not enough, but more will come, and they'll have to come from us. My God, from the way the crowd was listening to you, a person would think that *you* founded the Factory Investigating Commission yourself!"

"I wish I did have that power. But if all I can do is speak and teach and bear witness, I will. This isn't over."

That was too true, and they both knew it. The Triangle company had been brought back into court several times in the previous year because they were still locking doors with the workers inside. Raisa took some comfort from the fact that at least now there were officials willing to bring such things to light and fight them, instead of shrugging them off.

But for Raisa, that knowledge did little to take the sting out of another memory. She recalled Mr. Kamensky's face that March, when he read the news that Triangle had finally paid reparations to the families of the fire victims, but only for twenty-three cases. The company had the time and money to outlast most of the people who had brought suit against them, dragging matters out until the plaintiffs lost heart and let the matter drop. And what did those twenty-three families receive for their anguish? Seventy-five dollars. Seventy-five dollars each, no more.

"It's not over," Raisa repeated. "Gavrel, somewhere in this city there's another Zusa—smart, strong, brave, and beautiful. I want her to work where she'll be safe, and paid a fair wage, and where her life will be worth more than seventy-five dollars."

Gavrel smiled and hugged her. "Maybe *you* ought to become the lawyer."

"Maybe I will," Raisa replied. "God willing, law school will give me the gift of persuasion."

"Who needs persuading?" Gavrel asked. "Unless you mean Mama, always dropping those *subtle* hints about grandchildren."

"I mean Glukel," Raisa said. "For *years* we've had the money to bring her here, but still she refuses to leave the shtetl. First she said she had to help Yossel and Sarah with their new baby, then Reb Avner got sick and she wouldn't leave until he recovered, God be thanked, and then one excuse after another, so many we lost track."

"Well, you know my theory," Gavrel said casually. "Once she found out Henda had married a rich man, Glukel was afraid she wouldn't be good enough to mingle with his family. And once she learned you'd married a poor one, she was afraid we wouldn't be good enough to mingle with her."

Raisa frowned. "This is *not* a joking matter for me, Gavrel."

"I know, Raisaleh." He changed his tone at once. "And I know how much you want to have her here with you again. But who knows how another person's heart rules them? The love that Glukel feels for you and Henda, the uncertainty of leaping into a completely different world, the desire to see your faces again, after all these years—and the new little face, too—the fear that she might be a burden to you here, even though you tell her a thousand times that she'd be a blessing! All of that and more is pulling her back and forth every day."

"You're right, Gavrel." Raisa sighed. "I suppose that all I can do is keep reassuring her that the door is open, and that we'll wait as long as it takes until she's ready to come home."

When they reached Henda's house, they were surprised to be greeted at the door by her husband and not by the family butler. "Is anything the matter, Hillel?" Raisa asked anxiously. "Henda, the baby, they're all right?"

He reassured her with a smile. "Don't worry, I'm only answering my own door because the butler's sick, poor man, not because anyone else is. Mother and son are just fine, I promise you. They've had a very long day, but both of them took it in stride. They're stronger than I thought, those two. I'm sorry I made such a fuss that Henda couldn't attend your ceremony tonight. She should have overruled me and gone anyway, baby and all, but she's fallen into the bad habit of spoiling me too much."

"And that's *another* reason I like your sister," Gavrel whispered. Raisa ignored him, following Hillel from the foyer into the hallway between the dining room and the family parlor. The heavy doors to both of these rooms were closed.

"Here they are at last!" Hillel declared, sending the parlor doors sliding into their wall pockets.

A streak of golden curls darted out of the parlor. Tall and seeming to grow taller every day, Brina carried an armful of roses in all the colors of sunrise. She pushed the bouquet into Raisa's hands and gleefully asked, "Did I surprise you?"

"You certainly did!" Raisa drank in the fragrance of the flowers. "I thought that after the ceremony you were going home with everyone else."

"Oh, they're here, too," Brina said. She waved casually at the gathering in the parlor. Aside from Henda, who occupied the sofa, her infant son asleep in her arms, Raisa beheld everyone she'd last seen in the Educational Alliance theater— Fruma and her husband Morris, the Kamenskys, the Delvecchios, Selig and Mrs. Reshevsky, even her beloved teacher, Miss Bryant.

"You told me you were going home!" Raisa exclaimed. "How did you get here?"

"By invitation." Fruma's sense of humor could be almost as provoking as her brother's. "And by taxicab. I suppose we could have walked." She winked at Gavrel.

"I'm sorry that I couldn't be there for your speech, or to give you something to mark your achievements," Henda said. "I hope you'll let me fix that now."

Raisa hurried to sit beside her sister. Still cradling the roses, she carefully leaned over the sleeping baby and kissed Henda on the cheek. "Thank you, dear. This gathering is a wonderful gift."

"*This* isn't your gift, Raisa."

Henda stood up and gave the baby to his father, then took Raisa by the hand. She led her out of the parlor, across the hall to the closed doors of the formal dining room. Henda motioned for Raisa to open them. They slid smoothly back into the walls at her touch.

The dining room was mostly shadow. No one had turned on the electric chandelier or the wall sconces, but when Raisa reached for the wall switch, Henda blocked her way. Even so, she was able to see the room by the light seeping in from the hall behind her. The long table was covered with blindingly white linen and laden end to end with a feast of hot and cold dishes, all beautifully displayed on porcelain platters and silver trays. Ripe fruit spilled over the edge of a tiered serving tower. Droplets of moisture twinkled on the curve of a crystal punch bowl and the sides of ice buckets filled with chilling bottles of champagne.

There was only one small space on the groaning table that was not covered with food or drink. It held the only light in the room. The Shabbos candles burned low, but their glow was bright enough for Raisa to recognize the silver candlesticks that held them.

In the far corner of the dining room, the door to the kitchen passage opened. Glukel stepped through it and held out her hands. By the leaping light of the welcoming flames, with her long hair coming loose and tumbling down, Raisa rushed into Glukel's arms, filling them with roses.

AFTERWORD

I first heard about the Triangle fire by chance. While channel-surfing one day, many years ago, I happened to catch a story on a New York City news station that showed a gathering of people marking the anniversary of the tragedy. I was fascinated and deeply affected by the brief account of the fire, then horrified as I watched a fire engine extending its tallest ladder to demonstrate that even with modern equipment, the victims trapped on the upper floors of the Asch Building could not have been reached.

Who knows why certain stories claim us? All I can say is that somehow, after having seen that news item, I felt that I both wanted and *needed* to learn more. I bought Leon Stein's book *The Triangle Fire* and read it. The more I learned, the more I felt that I *had* to write a book of my own. It would not be a history book—as much as I love reading about history, I'm no historian—but a novel whose characters and story would make my readers know and remember the horrors of that day, its aftermath, and the social conditions that let such a devastating event happen.

Why remember? There are always people who are ready to argue that remembering the past is unimportant, irrelevant, over and done with, that the Triangle fire belongs to the last century. There might even be some cold-souled enough to say, "Why care about it? We've got our own troubles. It's over. By now, everyone involved is dead."

True, in part, but . . . not exactly. It's *not* over; not even though the Triangle fire ignited, burned, and was extinguished on a single spring day a hundred years ago. Everyone involved is not dead. The Asch Building still stands—it is a fireproof structure and survived the blaze, even if the people trapped inside did not. It is now a part of New York University and no longer houses a clothing factory where workers labor under dangerous conditions. However, though a hundred years have passed since the fire, and the Triangle Waist Company is gone, sweatshops are not. They still exist, and not just in third world nations, but in the heart of Manhattan.

While such things exist, the core of the Triangle fire—human life demeaned, exploited, and lost—is still with us.

I wrote *Threads and Flames* because I think we should remember not just the Triangle fire, but what it really meant to the people who were there; the *people*. When you read about it in history books and see how many men and women died, it's only a number. Numbers have no faces, no families, no lives before the fire, no one to mourn them after the last ember has been extinguished. Through Raisa's story—and the stories of Brina, Zusa, Luciana, Gavrel, and all the rest—I want to help my readers remember that more than just a list of numbers vanished that day.

Threads and Flames is a novel, not a history book. There are moments in the course of recounting Raisa's adventures—such as certain points concerning her experiences coming to America—where the immigration procedures of the time would have shackled the plot. I do not regret the choices I made, since I took only minor liberties with bureaucratic procedures that were not important to the main focus of Raisa's story. I took no such liberties when recounting the events of the Triangle fire and its aftermath (based on the best information I could find).

I wanted to tell a story about an event that is still important to me, in the hope of making it important to you. I hope that I've succeeded.